B

# AIR
# SIDE

## Also by James Swallow

### The Marc Dane Series:

*Nomad*
*Exile*
*Ghost*
*Rough Air*
*Shadow*
*Rogue*
*Outlaw*

# AIR SIDE

## JAMES SWALLOW

WELBECK

Published in 2022 by Welbeck Fiction Limited, an imprint of Welbeck Publishing Group
Based in London and Sydney.

www.welbeckpublishing.com

A CIP catalogue record for this book is available from the British Library

ISBN (HB): 978–1–80279–034–4
ISBN (XTPB): 978–1–80279–038–2
ISBN (E): 978-1-80279-035-1

Printed and bound by CPI Group (UK) Ltd., Croydon, CR0 4YY

FSC
www.fsc.org
MIX
Paper from
responsible sources
FSC® C171272

10 9 8 7 6 5 4 3 2 1

*For Robert – the best crew chief*
*I could ever ask for.*

*Noun:* **airside**

*"The area of an airport terminal beyond passport and customs control."*

# ONE

The storm's first traces came in thin lines that ran along the windows of the shabby Opel taxi, the invading rain's advance guard ticking off the glass. The sun had set, but dregs of watery light lingered over the German countryside, the slow approach of the heavy clouds chasing it down.

Slumping untidily in the back seat, Kevin stared out at the flat scenery beyond. In his mid-forties and average in almost every aspect, his features were fixed in the too-serious expression that had become his default in recent months. The grass and the trees and the occasional house passing along the roadside were ghostly impressions, barely connecting with him.

Kevin drifted inside the warm bubble of the taxi's interior, rocking with the gentle motion of the vehicle. He willed his mind to stay blank, to stay rooted in this empty moment and as far from harsh reality as possible.

*Hollow.* That was what he wanted to be. Nothing in his mind, nothing in his heart . . . Nothing at all. Just to be free of everything for a while, before the hammer came down and his life continued to fall apart around him.

His gaze dropped to his lap and he felt the giddy trickle of panic building behind his eyes. It came and went as a wave, washing in and out.

Kevin's hands contracted into fists around the strap of his shoulder bag, the black bulk of it lying next to him, the edges of the nylon band biting into his palms as he gripped it, his knuckles whitening.

His eyes flicked up to the windscreen, briefly catching sight of his dejected reflection in the rear-view mirror, then down to the dashboard. The taxi cruised at a steady seventy kilometres per hour, and Kevin had a mad moment when he entertained the idea of jerking open the door and rolling out onto the hard shoulder zipping by outside. He imagined himself tumbling into the muddy ditch at the side of the road, vanishing into the undergrowth, the taxi receding into the distance as if nothing had happened.

The driver misinterpreted Kevin's turn of the head and glanced up to make eye contact via the rear-view. 'Do not worry,' he said, exposing a broad smile. 'You are my last fare of the day, but you will make your flight.'

Wedged into the driving seat, the man was Afro-German and round like a barrel, and he radiated a good-natured joviality that rebounded completely off his passenger's morose mood.

Despite the proudly displayed Ghanaian flag dangling from the mirror, the taxi driver spoke English with the characteristic pronunciation Kevin had come to associate with *Plattdeutsch*, the 'low' dialect used throughout the local area of Rendsburg-Eckernförde and the greater Schleswig-Holstein region.

He'd quickly learned not to bother with his limited grasp of German after his first few trips to the country. Almost every local he met spoke English with classroom precision, and gave him the same tight smile that said *stop mangling our language, we'll do this in yours.*

'Was this your first visit to Germany, my friend?'

'More like my last.' Kevin automatically pitched down his accent a few notches, unconsciously smoothing off the edges of his native Londoner intonation.

The driver's floodlight smile dimmed. 'You don't find it to your taste?'

He gave a grunt of bleak amusement. 'No, it's the other way around, I reckon. I'm the one who's not wanted here.'

'Ah.' The driver gave a sage nod, as if Kevin had imparted some nugget of wisdom to him, then turned his eyes back to the road as they changed lanes.

The taxi shifted on to the airport approach, the ring road around the complex framing two runways connected at their northernmost points. A commuter jet lofted upward from the airstrip, running lights blinking as it rose into the hazy embrace of the heavy clouds.

From the air, Flughafen Barsbeker looked toy-like, with the black lines of the runways and the clumps of buildings sitting on a level disc of grassland. It rested on a rump of coastline south of the nearest town and several hours of autobahn driving east of Hamburg. One side of the airport ran down to low trees, a rocky shore and the cold waters of the Baltic Sea, over which approaching jets would make their final turn before landing. It didn't serve anything bigger than short-haul airliners and private planes, taking in meagre traffic from Scandinavia, neighbouring Poland, Latvia, Lithuania and Estonia, even the odd Russian arrival. Only one airline ran flights into Barsbeker from the UK, and over the past six months Kevin had become more familiar than he ever wanted to be with them. He had been in and out of the small municipal airport so many times that he could practically navigate its passenger-facing spaces blindfolded.

Having killed the conversation, Kevin spent the last few minutes of the trip trying to recover the comforting blankness he had felt before. A tension headache gathered at the base of his skull and he tried to will it away, without success.

As he looked up again, the taxi rolled to a halt at a drop-off outside of the main terminal. Long and low, the building was an uninspired box of glass and metal with the charm of an industrial greenhouse.

Kevin put his hand on the door handle and hesitated, as a sense of finality settled on him.

*Last time.*

Once he stepped out of the car and entered the terminal, he would never come back. The final flight home to England and the grim truth past it was all that awaited him.

Then the driver was at the taxi's boot, recovering Kevin's other piece of luggage. That done, he opened the passenger door for him. 'Sometimes the lock gets sticky.'

'Right.' Kevin climbed out, dragging his shoulder bag like it was one of those black iron balls on a length of manacle chain. He registered a dot of rain on his cheek as he dug out his wallet, found a fold of euro notes and overpaid.

The taxi driver thanked him and his expression changed, becoming almost fatherly. He took Kevin's hand and shook it. Kevin reciprocated without thinking.

'You will be all right, my friend,' said the driver, and his warm smile showed again. 'Never forget, it could always be worse!' He patted Kevin on the shoulder as an afterthought, and clambered back into the taxi with a cheery wave.

Kevin watched the Opel depart and the man's words triggered a brief, searing flash of anger, the force of it so strong it surprised him.

*It could be worse?* Kevin's jaw hardened, suddenly seething with resentment at the other man's glib platitude. *Everything is going wrong with my life and* that *is the facile bit of genius advice you want to leave me with?*

'What the fuck do *you* know about it?' The hissed words escaped him as he glared at the road, giving voice to the rest of his thought. His resentment vented loudly enough that he drew the attention of an elderly couple walking in from the nearby parking complex.

The old folks tutted, and Kevin's jolt of fury was immediately doused by the impulse to apologise. He gave a weak smile they pointedly ignored and, sheepishly, he followed them into the building. He pretended he couldn't understand them talking about how rude and boorish the British had become these days.

Kevin crossed the threshold of the automatic doors, releasing a sigh as heavy as the weight of the world.

His case was a boxy 'Pullman' with roller wheels and a long handle that let him drag it across the terminal's polished floor. Matching his shoulder bag, it was made of dark ballistic nylon and styled to look like something a covert agent would use in a high-octane espionage thriller. *Tactical, military-specification luggage for the business-warrior at large*, said the label.

Kevin remembered buying the bags at a high-end luggage store in London because he thought they looked cool, much to the amusement of Sadie, whose tastes ran to gaudy brands with lots of flashy gold detail. She'd mocked him about the purchase, he remembered, and not with gentle humour.

*Honestly, put the word 'tactical' in front of anything and a man will buy it*, she'd said. *You're Kevin Tyler from Hackney, you're not Jason bloody Bourne.*

In retrospect, comments like that – a million of them over the course of their marriage, if he was honest – had marked the path to their divorce.

Two years after the separation, going home to an empty house and an empty life still weighed more as a curse than a blessing. But marrying had been a mistake, for both of them. Neither Kevin nor Sadie had been what the other really wanted or needed in their life, and it had taken too many years of decaying feelings between them for that truth to become inescapable. The whole thing had been a waste of time.

*Well. Not completely.* There was Madeline. Their daughter, bright and beautiful, somehow the synthesis of the best bits of her mother and her father with the worst of their traits left behind. *We did that part right, at least.*

Thinking about Maddie always lifted Kevin, and it briefly pushed back the gloom from his thoughts. He wandered the concourse, his path taking him past the landside branch of Relay near the arrivals board. The open-fronted store was racked with newspapers and magazines, jostling for position with tourist knick-knacks and colourful displays of sweets. He didn't see what he wanted there and carried on without stopping.

Predictably, Kevin's brief peak of better mood faded as he approached the check-in desks. Dwelling on his daughter brought a different kind of dejection to bear – guilt this time – and he pulled the shiny black tile of his smartphone from an inner pocket of his jacket, thumbing the power switch to wake it. As he expected, there were more text messages, joining the list of those he still hadn't replied to. He read the most recent one.

*Just checking in again*, it began. *Late class this eve. Screening of* Yojimbo *at the Film Forum for study, so phone will be on silent. Text me, Pop, plz?* Maddie ended the message with *XOXOX* and a smiling emoji.

Kevin raised an eyebrow at the idea of her voluntarily sitting through a ponderous samurai epic, but then chided himself for the ungenerous thought. She never took things too seriously, except when it came to her studies, and then the needle swung the other way.

Madeline Tyler wanted to direct movies one day, and her dedication to that goal had netted her a scholarship to the New York Film Academy. She was the first member of Kevin's family to do something like that, the first Tyler in living memory to break away from their dirt-under-the-fingernails, working-class roots and go out into the world as an *artist*.

He was immensely proud of her, even if he felt awkward trying to articulate it. But that was overshadowed by how much it worried him. Kevin had no idea how the film business worked beyond pushing the right button to watch loud, kinetic blockbusters on Netflix.

It was alien to him, as a man brought up in a work ethic where only hard graft, cunning and the occasional bent rule made you money. He didn't know how to counsel her, let alone how to keep her safe in that sort of world.

At the start, in a rare moment of post-divorce unity, he and his ex-wife had tried to talk their daughter out of going to America. Both of them were quietly fretting about their only child living in New York City, with its larger-than-life, hair-raising reputation, both afraid that she might fail out there and be chewed up by an unforgiving system. Kevin imagined Maddie coming home bitter and tearful, his brilliant girl's vital spark of creativity snuffed out by cruel reality.

But she won her father around to her point of view. She convinced him with her relentless enthusiasm. Sadie didn't see it, of course, but then Maddie's mother rarely changed her mind once it was set.

He remembered another airport, another bland terminal building, when they came to see Maddie off at Heathrow. Kevin gave her a silly going-away present – a keychain of a tiny clapperboard – as Sadie cried theatrically into the shoulder of the bloke she was currently shacked up with.

*If anything ever happens to her over there, I'll blame you.* After Maddie boarded her plane, Kevin's ex had jabbed him in the chest to underline her point. *It'll be your fault and I'll never forgive you.*

And something *had* happened to Maddie over there, just not the kind of thing that either of them had expected.

The stab of guilt returned. Considering that Kevin was approaching the end of a day that had practically been assembled out of fuck-ups, the one that lingered, the one that tormented him the most was assuredly *his* fault and his alone.

# TWO

'*Der nächste bitte*, next please.' The desk agent had the enthusiasm of someone whose shift was minutes from ending, for whom the ticks of the clock could not come quickly enough.

'Good evening,' offered Kevin, with an equal lack of intensity, advancing towards the check-in.

'Welcome to KnightSky Air.' The woman – German, middle-aged, and businesslike with it – displayed a plastic smile that didn't reach her eyes. 'Any hold luggage, sir?'

'No, just these carry-ons.'

Kevin had made an art of austerity in his packing over the past few months, stripping it down to the absolute minimum that would fit in an overhead locker, all so he could get on and get off the plane as swiftly as possible. Anything that could pare off even a few seconds from the tedium of air travel was worth the effort. Standing beside a baggage carousel was the dullest part of the ordeal, staring blankly at other people's cases drifting by while you waited vainly for yours to emerge.

He handed over his passport and ticket. The agent eyed the paper dismissively. 'You do know that you can use your smartphone rather than print a boarding pass?'

'I'm aware,' he replied. 'I just prefer . . . You know. *A real thing*. Something in my hand.' As much by trade as by personality, Kevin was an engineer, and that mindset brought an attachment to physical objects and a healthy scepticism about the reliability of technology. The one time he hadn't brought a paper copy, he'd been stuck at Gatwick for hours when KnightSky's buggy smartphone app had decided to eat his flight reservation.

'It is more efficient,' the desk agent said pointedly. 'Better for the environment.' She inclined her head towards a sign extolling the virtues of the airline's green policy, complete with a guilt-inducing photo of a polar bear clinging to an ice floe.

Kevin had gone through this conversation on each flight in and out of Barsbeker. Normally, he would have let it go, but today his tolerance had worn to nothing. He resisted the opportunity to suggest that the airline actually *do* something about their awful environmental record instead of dumping responsibility on their passengers, and settled for some light sarcasm.

'I'll offset my carbon footprint by not getting out of bed for a week, OK? Can we . . . ?' He made a vague *move-this-along* gesture.

'Of course, sir.' Her fingers racing over her keyboard, the desk agent switched off the smile, and replied in the tone of voice one would use to say *whatever, idiot*.

Kevin's gaze slipped to the neighbouring desks, to the Elite Class counter for LuftFluger's flights to Southern Europe and the Mediterranean. They even had a length of red carpet to walk down. He wondered what it would be like to board an airliner and turn *left* for a change.

*No money for indulgences, Kev-oh.* Kevin heard the words of Colin Fish echoing in his head. *Got to watch the pennies, eh?*

Colin was Kevin's business partner and the co-owner of Luna Designs, the money guy to Tyler's engineering savvy. He prided himself on squeezing every pound until it screamed, and while that was a useful asset for a small-scale enterprise like theirs, there were times when Kevin wished he could afford to dine on steak instead of quarter-pounders.

Everything he had earned, every asset Kevin owned had been poured into keeping Luna afloat, and now he wondered if it had all been tossed into a black hole. The wave of his bleak mood started to build again, and the desk agent picked up on it, seeing the shadow pass over his face.

Her expression softened and her tone grew sympathetic. 'Sir, I'm sorry, but there is a problem with your boarding pass.'

Kevin sighed. 'Of *course* there is.' The day had not quite finished the business of repeatedly kicking him in the balls.

She told him the laser scanner wasn't registering the barcode. 'It happens a lot. If you had the app on your phone . . .'

He leaned forward. 'Can I have that back?'

The desk agent returned the pass and Kevin pointed at the forest of black bars on the sheet. 'The printing impinges on the space around the lines. Should be clear all the way around, otherwise the scanner glitches when it tries to read it.' He smoothed out the paper and scraped away some of the offending ink.

'How do you know that?' said the woman. She rescanned the pass and her computer gave an agreeable chime.

'We use the same kind of thing at my company,' he explained. 'Automated handlers scan the product, send it where it is supposed to go. If the code's smudged, it doesn't work.' Kevin reached into his shoulder bag for a sample – he always carried a few to hand – and passed an empty, tan-coloured water bottle to her. It too had a barcode embossed on the side. 'Here, keep it.'

'Thank you.' The desk agent exchanged the bottle for his now-stickered pass, and weighed the container in her hand. 'Very light.'

'But strong. Made out of recycled paper. Lasts for months, but it's also biodegradable. Much better for the planet than those.' He jutted his chin at a plastic water bottle sitting next to her keyboard.

'Oh, *toll*,' she replied, turning it over. '*Luna*,' she said, reading out the logo on the bottom.

'We make them,' said Kevin, and then sighed again. 'We try to. It's not easy convincing the pop makers to switch from plastic and cans, you know?'

'Pop?'

'*Limonade*.'

'Pick up the pace, please?' A terse, plummy voice issued out from behind him, and Kevin turned to see a man with an expensive suit and an impatient, purse-lipped expression. Like Kevin, he held a British passport, but unlike him, he also clutched one of KnightSky's frequent-flyer cards, clearly expecting it to smooth the path for him.

Kevin returned a sour look and made a show of stepping aside. 'Be my guest.' Mr Gold Card didn't hesitate and barged past to the check-in. Kevin gave the desk agent an apologetic look and walked off, heading to the arch that delineated the landside and airside sectors of the airport.

The departures gateway was a sunny yellow, to hint at the idea of warmer climes and holiday fun awaiting those who passed through it.

Kevin had nothing like that to look forward to, and he glanced at his wristwatch as he joined a short queue for the nearest security lane. The bulky Promaster told him he was on schedule, with plenty of time to make his flight, provided nothing else went wrong.

*What are the odds of that?* Kevin asked himself. He fiddled absently with the strap of the titanium watch; made for divers, it was one of the few extravagances he allowed himself, and while the closest Kevin had ever come to scuba was swimming-pool snorkelling, he held on the fantasy that one day he might actually be able to do the real thing.

His boarding pass was rechecked, rejected, and rechecked again, earning him stern looks from the unsmiling customs officers manning the automated barriers. Kevin couldn't hide his tension, which made him wonder if he looked shifty, and that in turn made him even more self-conscious.

He went through the motions of the next stage of security, where a scanner arch and x-ray conveyor belt were waiting. *Belt off, jacket off, coins and phone and watch and wallet in the pockets, bags in the tray, trays on the conveyor.* Kevin completed each action with the robotic precision of a veteran traveller, aware that every move he made was being scrutinised.

Ahead, a group of noisy Englishmen in football shirts clowned around, generally making life difficult for the customs officers, and Kevin kept his distance, not wanting to be associated with their disruptive behaviour.

He watched his trays roll away as he stepped through the metal detector, and heard a strident ping. *Problem.*

'What now?' he muttered.

Another security officer used a sensor wand to give him a close inspection, and the offending issue turned out to be foil from a half-tube of boiled sweets in a trouser pocket. Satisfied, the officer waved him on.

When Kevin reached the other end of the conveyor, his trays had vanished.

His heart jumped in his chest. Everything he needed was in them, money and credit cards, passport and ticket. If they were stolen, he literally would have only what he was stood up in: not even a belt to stop his trousers slumping at his waist.

'Herr ... Tyler?' A laconic voice with a thick slice of the local burr drew his attention. Kevin pivoted on the spot, finding not a security guard, but a uniformed police officer at a counter off to one side. Kevin's trays were arranged in front him, including his passport open at the photo page. The policeman beckoned. 'Come, please?'

'Here, mate,' said the last of the football fans, as he elbowed by to join his friends. 'Don't let him take you out back and grab your nuts, right? Reckon he fancies you!' The comment drew a torrent of mocking laughter that did nothing for Kevin's anxiety, which flipped through a roller coaster rise and fall as he approached the policeman.

He felt relief that his stuff hadn't taken a walk, then trepidation over whatever had caused the German cop to pull him out of the line.

*Could it have something to do with the deal?* He shook his head before the panicked thought could take root. *Unlikely.* His anxiety saw connections that didn't exist. Or so he hoped.

Kevin took a deep breath, forced himself to adopt a neutral expression, and uttered the mantra of every innocent man. 'Is there a problem, officer?'

The policeman frowned at the question, deep lines building across his oval face. He had searching brown eyes set behind a pair of black-rimmed spectacles, and the kind of bulldog quality Kevin always associated with coppers. He was a few years Kevin's senior, wearing a stab vest emblazoned with the word **POLIZEI** over a light blue shirt. He made a show of taking off his peaked cap and putting it aside.

'Herr Tyler,' he repeated, cocking his head, 'what kind of explosives do you have in your bag?'

'*What?*' Kevin felt his colour rise and he froze on the spot. His unease jumped through the roof.

17

'We have detected traces of volatile materials.' The man had an identity pass hanging off his vest, and Kevin saw the name Alfons, B. written on it. He gestured with a chemical swab, giving the Englishman a measuring look. 'Perhaps you have been on a military base recently? Are you *in* the military?' He said the last in a tone that suggested he thought it unlikely.

Kevin had the sudden impulse to say *I could tell you, but then I'd have to kill you*, and he let out a nervous laugh. 'Uh, no,' he managed. 'Wh-what kind of material? Did you detect, I mean?'

Officer Alfons glowered at the readout of a device in front of him. 'Cellulose residue.'

'Oh. *Oh!*' Kevin snapped his fingers, as his brain caught up with what was happening. 'I have production samples in my carry-on. Cardboard bottles. They have a cellulose component in them, they might have tripped your, uh . . .' He trailed off.

'May I?' Alfons asked for permission to open his bags, but didn't wait to get it. The policeman rooted through the contents, deliberately taking his time.

When he didn't find anything that looked bomb-like, he ran a second swab around the bag and through the chemical sensor, then relented, apparently satisfied at the benign nature of Kevin's shirts and underwear.

'Very well,' he intoned gravely. 'Now comes the difficult part.'

Kevin blinked. 'Pardon me?' He had a sudden premonition of a strip-search and rubber glove session, the football fan's warning ringing in his ears.

'Now you must put it all back,' Alfons explained, smirking slightly as he spread his hands, indicating the mess of unpacked clothes.

Kevin bit down on his annoyance, realising that the policeman was amusing himself at his expense. Typical cop behaviour, he reflected, like the man's blunt question about the explosives. Designed to deliberately wrong-foot you, in the hope you might say something incriminating.

Alfons stood back, arms folded, and under his watchful glare Kevin did his best to restore order to the messed-up contents of his baggage. It was awkward in the cramped area alongside the security arch, and it took longer than he would have liked. At one point, the Gold Card guy strolled past along the express pre-check lane, grinning at Kevin's predicament. Kevin resisted the urge to give him the finger as he carefully rolled his socks into tight cylinders and repacked them.

'Sorry to inconvenience you,' said the policeman, more to fill the silence then out of any actual regret. 'But with the way the world is, we all have to do our part to watch out for the terrorists, yes?'

Kevin wondered how likely it was that gun-toting fanatics would target some unremarkable airstrip in the back-end of the German countryside. He zipped up the bag. He just wanted to be gone.

'We are so busy looking for them, ordinary felons do as they please.' Alfons continued, scowling at his own observation. Then he leaned forward menacingly, extending one hand to point at a poster on the wall. 'Keep your eyes open, *ja?*'

Kevin glanced at the sign. It showed a woman frowning seriously in the direction of an abandoned bag, beside a telephone number for the airport's security hotline.

*Wenn du etwas siehst*, read the message beneath, *sag etwas.* 'If you see something, say something,' Alfons translated, then waved him away.

Kevin put his watch back on and checked it again. The buffer of time in his schedule was quickly dissolving, which meant he needed to get moving if he wanted to make it to the gate. The better places among KnightSky's cheap seats tended to go quickly once economy class boarding began, and Kevin had learned from experience that if he wasn't near the front of the line, getting the prized exit aisle row would be impossible.

He threaded through the duty-free area, following a trail snaking past ostentatious displays of perfume, gin and cigarettes, and emerged into the plastic reality of the terminal proper.

The rectangular building extended away to the north and the south. Exiting security, low-numbered boarding gates were on the left, high-numbered on the right. Two levels were open to the public, the upper for the incoming arrivals and the lower for departures. Broken up by thick pillars of white-painted concrete every few metres, the main concourse of Barsbeker airport was divided into sections for a few shops and a cluster of fast-food concessions on one side, with passenger waiting areas along the other. The latter were optimistically described as 'lounges' but in reality they were just rows of chairs clustered around TV screens suspended from the roof, forced up against the glass looking out across the runways. *A fish tank has more style*, Kevin reflected.

The change in atmosphere after passing through security was palpable. Landside, where taxi drivers milled around with handwritten signs, or expectant families waited for their loved ones, there was a kind of weary flatness to everything – as if the building itself said *you're here now, you have no reason to stick around*. Landside didn't want you to dwell.

In contrast, airside was an aimless no man's land, the null space where you weren't quite actually on the ground, but you weren't exactly on the wing either. Airside was anticipation, anxiety and boredom captured in a big glass box.

Kevin always felt disconnected in airports, as if part of him was rendered rootless, searching for somewhere to put down, to be grounded once again. Like theme parks, shopping malls and casinos, airports were more machines than they were buildings, pumping mechanisms made to flow humans from one end to the other as smoothly as possible. Airside was cut off from the real world, in a little pocket reality of its own.

The tiny wheels of Kevin's Pullman case ticked across the floor as he steered it around other passengers who clearly were not in anything approaching the same hurry as him. He knew the best path to take in the shortest possible time, but that didn't account for the people who strolled, dithered and vacillated as if to a plan of their own. A plan to make Kevin Tyler's schedule fail miserably.

On a day when whatever *could* go wrong *had* gone wrong – catastrophically, ruinously so – every tiny delay or impediment that followed, no matter how minor, innocent or circumstantial, was one more jab directed specifically at him.

Kevin's attention was on that thought and not where he was going, so when the big man in the green jacket slammed into him, the hit was so hard he literally spun about with the force of the collision.

Shocked more than annoyed, Kevin looked up into the broken face of a streetfighter, all deep-set eyes and crumpled nose. He tried not to recoil from the aura of casual menace radiating from him.

'*Entschuldigung*,' said the man in the jacket, grinding out the word as if he were chewing on a chip of granite. The expression meant 'excuse me', but his tone made it sound like a dire profanity.

Kevin tried to dredge up a feeble complaint, but the other man had already turned his back and walked away. Cheeks burning, Kevin snatched irritably at the handle of his carry-on and continued towards the departure gates.

# THREE

Dieter Boch straightened his jacket and walked away from the gawping foreigner without waiting to see if he would offer a retort.

He didn't expect one. In Boch's experience, most people who had the misfortune to get in his way tended to back down quickly when confronted. Those who didn't learned the full stupidity of the wrong choice swiftly enough.

Boch surmised the man was British. There was something in the way they carried themselves that made it obvious. There were only two kinds, thugs and snobs. One would bark like a dog and have to be put down with a nose-breaking punch, and the other could be cowed by the threat of the same.

For a brief instant, Boch had the sense that he actually recognised the foreigner. Something about him did seem vaguely familiar, but he couldn't place from where. After a moment of searching his recollection, he came up empty and dismissed the distraction, his mind snapping back to more immediate considerations.

He scanned the terminal for any sign of the courier, finding nothing. His lip curled in irritation. *He should be here by now.*

Boch didn't like this place. The confines of the building, the scrum of idiot civilians, crying children and chattering women eroded his patience. Everywhere he looked, Boch's sight picture was crowded with the undisciplined and the thoughtless, stumbling through their day without care or attention. Any one of them could suddenly present a problem if the wind blew the wrong way, and it was the nature of his profession that he had to be ready to deal with that – quickly, and with the heavy application of force – whenever the moment might arrive.

He automatically measured everyone he passed in terms of what damage would have to be done to incapacitate them. A punch here, a kick there. It was habitual, the trigger for his violence waiting below the surface. Waiting for an excuse.

*Dieter Boch does not have an off switch.* That was how the counsellor had put it, before they discharged him from the Bundeswehr. His time in the German army had brought it to the fore. He was unable to go through life without perceiving it down the barrel of a metaphorical gun. For Boch, everywhere was a danger zone, every street a potential ambush site, every person he encountered either a target or an obstacle. They told him to seek therapy, to find a way to flip back that switch in head. To get some peace.

They didn't understand. Boch didn't *want* to turn it off.

Peace bored him. He liked living like this, like a shark cruising through an ocean of minnows. It gave him clarity of purpose, and what more could a man ask for?

Of course, there had been problems at first. Out of the military, he struggled to find employment where his attitude could be a benefit instead of a hindrance. Nightwatchman, club bouncer, truck driver – those jobs hadn't been a good fit, each falling short of accommodating his talents. But when Boch had become a *bodyguard*, he finally fell into his ideal profession. He could be a one-man army in that role, protecting his principal and intercepting any threats.

And if he was sometimes called upon to perform other, riskier duties, ones that exposed him to greater danger and skated over the edge of legality ... That was where he could be his best, most capable self.

Dieter Boch considered himself both blessed and cursed in equal measure. Blessed, because few men could say they were truly at home in their work. Cursed, because of the sorry circumstances that tied him to his current employer. But he had learned long ago that life was a trade-off between what a man could tolerate, and what drove a man to violence.

Up ahead, Boch saw a heavy-set figure in a dark suit and red tie enter the airside zone, casting around with a questioning expression. Their gazes locked for a fraction of a second and the man gave an imperceptible nod. His name was Ansel Fuchs, but whatever passport he carried would have said something different.

Boch feigned interest in the view out of the terminal's window, watching a twin-engine Dash-8 turboprop accelerate down the runway and claw its way into the heavy sky. Fine rain lined the glass, but Boch's focus was more on the reflection in it than what lay outside.

He observed Fuchs finding a seat in one of the waiting areas, in front of a departure gate that had long since closed, near an automated vending machine.

Boch approved. He could approach and make it look like he was buying a drink without arousing suspicion. His old comrade had not lost any of his skills.

Employing Fuchs for this task had been a pragmatic decision on Boch's part, accommodating his boss's demands as best he could in the short amount of time provided. He knew he could rely on his ex-army colleague to be discreet and thorough. Plus, Fuchs was always looking for extra work to pay off his debts, so he jumped at the chance to earn some additional euros. Ansel's weakness was poker, and Boch remembered games in the barracks where Fuchs had lost so much, he made it seem like an Olympic sport.

Boch had his own weakness, of course. His would have brought him to ruin, had other parties not intervened.

He licked his lips and pushed that thought aside, walking to the vending machine. He made a show of selecting and purchasing a bottle of Schwip Schwap, before settling into a chair to sip at the gassy, orange-infused cola. Neither man looked in the other's direction.

'Dieter,' Fuchs said quietly, by way of a greeting.

'Ansel,' he replied. 'You look well. How is the wife?'

'Left me.' Fuchs shrugged. 'Surprised it took her this long.'

Boch made a noncommittal sound. He wasn't really interested in the other man's private life. He glanced at the black gym bag sitting on the floor between them, tucked slightly under an empty seat. A red tag on the handle showed the bag had been cleared through security. 'You got it here with no problems?'

'Obviously,' said Fuchs, shifting in his seat. 'No one flagged it. Baffles in the lining make it look like books in there.' He produced an airline boarding pass from his pocket and studied it. 'So, are we done? I don't have long . . .'

'Your money will be waiting when you land in Berlin.' Boch anticipated the next question.

'Good.' Fuchs pushed the bag in Boch's direction with his foot as he stood up. 'Are you still working for that rich prick from Hamburg? Is this for him?'

Boch shut him down with a shake of the head. 'Don't spoil your good work by getting nosy.'

'I'm just looking out for a fellow veteran.'

Boch glanced up at Fuchs for the first time, his eyes narrowing. 'Did you open it?'

'Don't insult me.' Fuchs was affronted by the suggestion. 'I'm not an idiot. I know how this works.'

'I'm sorry.' Boch relented. 'Of course you do.' *I would never have employed you otherwise.*

Fuchs sighed. 'Will you take some advice, Dieter?'

'I'm sure you'll give it to me even if I say no.'

'That idiot paying you. Everyone dislikes him. There must be better people who can bring you work.'

'He's brought you work too,' Boch shot back.

'No, *you* brought me the work, he's only funding it. Seriously, from one *stoppelhopser* to another ... ' Fuchs used the old military slang for a soldier, calling on their shared history to bolster his argument. 'Cut your ties with Von Kassel before he drags you down.'

'It's not that simple.'

'Isn't it? What's stopping you from walking away? I could get you a new job by tomorrow morning.'

Boch didn't respond to the question, unwilling to entertain the answer. As for the latter part of the statement, he had no doubt that was true.

Fuchs worked for a criminal gang, operating as muscle and breaking the occasional leg. The other man had been company boxing champion back in the army, so he was good at it. But that wasn't the life Boch wanted. He knew himself well enough to understand that if he was only paid to hurt people, there would come a day when he wouldn't be able to stop doing it.

'No disrespect intended,' he said, 'but roughing up late payers who owe money to the Turks? I will pass.'

'At least it's honest thuggery. You work for a politician.' Fuchs said sourly. He straightened his jacket and glanced at a nearby departures screen. 'My flight's boarding, I have to go. *Mach's Gut.*'

'*Mach's besser.*' Boch sipped his soda as the other man set off towards one of the gates. Fuchs had barely been on the ground at Barsbeker for an hour, just long enough to deliver the bag.

When he was sure that no one was paying attention to him, Boch put aside his drink and drew the gym bag around, turning it to examine the zip fastener holding it closed and the tiny padlock that secured it. He had the only key, and used it to remove the lock.

Checking one more time to be certain he wasn't being observed, Boch drew back the zipper a little way and put his fingers through the gap, tracing over the shape of the contents within. He could tell from his cursory examination that everything was present and correct.

Pocketing the padlock, he gathered up the bag and walked back across the terminal, in the direction of the shopping concessions and the food court.

He replayed his old friend's comments as he carried out the next step. Fuchs was right. Hardly anyone beyond a core of loyal supporters had a good word to say about Lars Von Kassel – the moneyed, controversial, always self-indulgent minister of the Federal Cabinet. Yet Boch's employer continued to rise upward, buoyed by society connections, base cunning and a kind of crass charisma that appealed to his more common constituents. Boch would never have voted for such a venial man himself, but that was a moot point. For better or worse, he remained tethered to the politician's fortunes.

In an ideal world, the bodyguard would have made sure that his principal stayed as far from tonight's business as possible, but Von Kassel never took advice from anybody, especially from someone as lowly as a member of his staff.

*I can make this work,* Boch told himself. He shot a look in the direction of Barsbeker's first-class lounges, where he had installed his employer at an open bar with instructions to remain there for the duration. All he needed was for Von Kassel to *stay in his lane,* as the Americans said, and the hand-off would pass without a hitch.

Boch could pretend the odds of that were good, but that would be pointless self-delusion. It would be best if he got this done before Von Kassel's typical recalcitrance became an issue.

*In a couple of hours, we will be back on the autobahn,* he thought, *and this will be in the rear-view mirror.*

Kevin's expression soured when he saw a thick clump of passengers already filling the waiting area in front of the gate for the London-bound KnightSky flight. Any chance of getting a better seat allocation evaporated. He'd been in this situation before, the last time on a plane packed with a school party heading home after an international field trip. Kevin endured that flight crammed into the corner of a back-row window seat, and the only way he could have been farther from the front of the plane was if he had stayed on the tarmac.

This departure was always busy, the last of the day from Barsbeker to the UK, but on this rainy evening it seemed worse than usual. Bored, grumpy passengers milled around in front of the gate and none of the KnightSky staff was remotely interested in dispersing them.

The group wasn't anything approaching a *queue* – it was at best a *mass*, lacking the orderly manners that came naturally to the British. Working extensively in Europe, especially here in Germany, Kevin had quickly learned that the locals on the continent didn't go in for that sort of thing. You pushed your way to the front, and if other people's feet were run over by your case, that was on them.

He tried to see if the aircraft that would take them home was already at the gate. By now it should have been disgorging its cargo of arrivals, while the on-board crew gave the cabin a cursory clean-up before packing in the next load of human freight.

But he couldn't see anything, and that didn't bode well. Giving a resigned sigh, Kevin didn't bother to join the back of the waiting group, and he wandered to the wide alcove across the way, where the Kaffee Tek franchise was located.

The man working the noisy coffee machine looked up as he approached, and for a second he showed a blank face; then his expression caught up and he smiled widely.

'All right, mate?' He had chirpy East End London drawl completely out of place in a German municipal airport, and a cheerful manner that Kevin found endearing, if slightly irritating. 'How's it hanging?'

'Low,' Kevin admitted, letting his shoulder bag drop as he leaned on the counter.

'Let me get you the usual. Latte, right? Extra shot?' Off an affirmative nod, the barista set to making the drink, working the machine with deft, swift movements.

Richie – or Coffee Rich, as Kevin had come to think of him – was in his early thirties, and he had one of those odd faces that was boyish and rugged all at once. His eyes were a watery blue and his straw-coloured hair was scruffy, but his most defining features were large ears that gave him the air of a gangly, overgrown child. Richie's talkative manner had turned him into something of a fixture in Kevin's life over the past months. Travelling in and out of Barsbeker so frequently, Kevin had made a ritual out of getting Richie to make him an eye-opener, either to wake him up on arrival or keep him alert on departure.

In the first instance, Kevin had decided that finding another London lad over here was a good omen. Something about having that connection on each journey made him feel a little less outside his comfort zone.

Over the course of dozens of coffees, he learned that the younger man had come up in a neighbouring borough to the Tyler family, that they followed the fortunes of the same football teams, even frequented the same pubs, albeit years apart.

Like him, Richie was the product of lacklustre comprehensive schools and dead-end council estates. Both of them had got into trouble in their youth, but where Kevin had broken away from that to make a career in engineering, the younger man told the story of how his ejector seat had been a trip around the Low Countries. For Richie, when the time came to go home, he didn't bother. He'd bounced around Europe, finally coming to rest working the Kaffee Tek franchise at Barsbeker. He lived what seemed – at least to Kevin's eyes – a relatively carefree existence.

'Get that down you.' Richie placed the drink in front of him and the smell of the fresh-ground coffee perked Kevin up a little. He handed over a ten-euro note and the other man automatically scanned it under a counterfeit checker black-light by the till before ringing up the purchase.

'Thanks.' Kevin dumped too many sachets of sugar into the drink, but in his current mood it felt pointless to hold back on the small indulgence. 'Seriously, man, thanks for the coffees.'

Richie opened his hands. 'It's my job.'

'No, I mean . . . I won't be buying any more.'

The other man nodded. 'On a detox? We sell them wheatgrass juices, you know?' He pointed at a rack of bottles of bile-green liquid.

Kevin shook his head. 'No,' he repeated. 'I won't be coming through here any more. My job is . . . ' He trailed off, unable to find the words.

'Done?' Richie offered helpfully.

He held in a sigh. 'Yeah. *Done.*'

'Mate,' Richie continued, 'you do *not* look like a happy bunny right now.'

Kevin accepted his change and took a sip of the hot drink. He waited for the caffeine hit to invigorate him, but it didn't come. 'I'm all right,' he lied, the impulse to cover up his failure automatic and instinctive. 'Just knackered.'

For a moment, Richie's cheery demeanour faded, and Kevin got the sense that the barista could tell he wasn't being truthful. But he didn't press Kevin on it, offering him a way out via a pat explanation. 'Tough day?'

'You have no idea.'

Richie sucked his teeth. 'Not done yet.'

The tone of the other man's words sounded like a warning. 'What do you mean?'

The barista nodded solemnly at the crowded waiting area. 'Your flight's been delayed. They haven't announced it yet, but they're gonna, any minute.'

Kevin turned to look back at the gate staff. They didn't appear any more animated than they had a few minutes earlier. 'How do you know?'

Richie gestured at the Kaffee Tek booth. 'Mate, I'm here every day, I see them working. I know the signs. Trust me, you ain't going nowhere.'

It was the last thing Kevin wanted to hear.

After this day – *this fucking shitstorm of a bastard day* – every fibre of his being wanted to get as far away as possible from this country. He didn't want to remain here, being reminded of the fiasco, for one second longer than he had to.

'Tell you what,' Richie said from behind him, 'have this, on the house. Farewell gift for a good customer.' He dropped one of the unpleasant-looking detox drinks into Kevin's hand. 'And next time I'm back in the Smoke, I'll look you up. We'll go for a pint down The Queens, yeah?'

'Yeah,' echoed Kevin, but his voice faded as he saw one of the KnightSky staff pick up the public address microphone at the desk and clear her throat.

'*Meine damen und herren, ladies and gentlemen,*' she began, her monotone switching back and forth between German and English, '*entshuldigung, KnightSky Air regrets to inform you that flight four-zero-four to London Gatwick has been delayed.*'

'Told you,' said Richie.

'*Bollocks!*' The swear word left Kevin's mouth at exactly the moment when a lacuna of perfect silence fell across the lounge, and everyone within earshot looked his way.

# FOUR

With a catlike shrug, Sasha shook off the rain on her leather jacket and strode into the hangar. She paused inside the tall, wide doors, casting a look in the direction of the terminal building on the far side of the runways.

Nothing struck her as troublesome, but that didn't ease her tense disposition. Scowling, she carried on, running a hand through her shock of spiky, cut-short brown hair.

Of average height with a Slavic hint to her features, Sasha cultivated a deliberately masculine look with her biker boots and matching jacket, heavy jeans and dark shirt. Complex tattoos of thorny roses grew up around her throat and emerged along the backs of her hands, the images a warning for anyone who might have dismissed the slight young woman at first glance.

*Look, but don't touch* was the ink's message, one that Sasha would willingly underline with the slide-knife she kept in her back pocket. The tattoos didn't cover up the stark white comma of scarring that marred the flesh of her jawline, but that was another deliberate choice on her part.

The only aircraft in the hangar was her employer's Gulfstream G550, half-covered in tarps where the maintenance crew had been working on it. Oleg Gorod's private jet didn't see much use other than the occasional trip down to the Emirates, and Sasha imagined that the real reason it was parked here was as an escape option.

Oleg was old school in his training and his thinking, a product of the worst of the Cold War. He'd once told her that he never entered a room without knowing two details – *how to escape it, and who he would need to kill to do so.*

Sasha understood the value of having a way out, even if you had to cut it from blood and bone. That kind of thinking had kept her alive, and it gave her a kinship with Oleg.

She looked at the clock on the far wall, near the doors that led through to the adjoining buildings. He would be here soon, which meant she didn't have long. She picked up the pace.

The men were gathered around a half-dozen steel containers, each one just under three metres long, secured with heavy latches and orange nylon straps. As she approached, Sasha met Vincent's gaze and the skinny, ochre-skinned Frenchman gave her a respectful, knowing nod. Tall and seemingly made out of nothing but sharp angles, Vincent stood to one side watching the other men playing a spirited game of cards, listening as they laughed and swore at their luck.

Sasha noted Roberto's presence, and it appeared that he was in possession of the worst hand. The burly, pig-eyed man slammed down his cards and banged a thick forefinger on one of the containers, the sound echoing as he demanded to win back his losses. His bad cards would soon be the least of his problems.

The containers were dented and scuffed with use, the company name spray-painted on their flanks in faded Day-Glo yellow: *Memoria Tranzyt*, with the simple logo of a dove of peace. Sasha thought that was a grisly touch of black humour, given the true nature of Oleg's business.

'Repatriation' was the word they used, a fancy way of describing a shipping company whose cargo was corpses. Death was a steady trade, and it had the added bonus of being something most people wanted to keep at arm's reach. Those two elements made the perfect legal front of Oleg's criminal enterprise.

Dying was not a predictable thing. People perished when they were far from home, on working trips or holidays, killed by illness, violence or misadventure. And that meant leaving distant loved ones with the sombre task of transporting their deceased relative back, to be interred in their native country. For a generous fee, Memoria Tranzyt managed the shipping and handling of bodies throughout Europe and Scandinavia, moving them through their hub at Barsbeker, storing the remains in the refrigerated lockers adjoining the hangar.

Most passengers flying on commercial airliners had no idea they were sharing their journey with a few of the recently dead in the cargo bay. Pilots would declare the number of 'souls on board' their flights before take-off, counting up the passengers and crew. *Souls*, but not *bodies*. Then, if an aircraft crashed and remains were recovered, there would be an accurate count of who had been alive on departure, and not dead all along.

Sasha looked away from the ranks of metal coffins and saw Roberto staring at her. 'What's she doing here?' He asked the question to the room, as if Sasha wasn't capable of answering herself.

'Come to make sure you are working,' she told him. 'Don't stop. I can see you are busy.'

'What?' Roberto feigned ignorance, as if he didn't know what Sasha was saying. A favourite ploy of his, he would pretend he couldn't understand her. He blamed it on her native accent, going on about how Poles like Sasha couldn't speak German without sullying it.

She didn't repeat herself, refusing to play along. One of Roberto's friends muttered something *sotto voce* that Sasha didn't pick up, but the leer on both men's faces made the content clear.

Roberto patted his cheek in the place where Sasha had her scar. 'Why don't you cover that up? And smile sometimes?' He chuckled and shuffled the cards. 'You'd be pretty if you smiled.'

Sasha poured silk into her voice, making it breathy and seductive. 'You know what would make me smile?' She leaned close. 'Your balls, in my mouth.'

Roberto gaped like a landed fish, caught between shock and arousal at Sasha's reply. Suddenly, he could understand her perfectly.

'Your tiny little balls,' Sasha continued, revealing the slide-knife with an oiled click of spring-loaded metal. 'After I cut them off and boil them like *kochklopse*.' She aimed the point of the blade at Roberto's crotch as Vincent and the other men burst into laughter. Roberto joined in half-heartedly. He shot an angry glare in her direction, seething at being made to look foolish.

Sasha walked past Vincent, and Frenchman spoke so that only she would hear what he said. 'He doesn't learn,' he noted. 'You're not to be fucked with.'

'He'll learn a lesson tonight,' said Sasha, catching sight of movement beyond the hangar. 'They all will.'

A BMW M3 saloon in metallic green livery rolled to a halt by the hangar doors, headlights catching sparkles of rainfall in their powerful beams.

Everyone stopped laughing at once, as if a button had been pushed. They knew who the car belonged to, and what it signified, that Oleg Gorod was making an unexpected visit.

Roberto and the others scrambled to gather up their winnings, hiding the cards and the ashtrays full of cigarette butts. It was one thing to slacken off when no one saw it, but they would never dare do so in front of their employer. Oleg's fearsome reputation was richly deserved, and nobody wanted to earn his displeasure. He rarely came to the hangar for reasons other than travel, and with his private jet out of action, they could only guess at the purpose of this visit.

Sasha walked to the car as Oleg's driver came around to the passenger door. Miros was tall, in his forties but old before his time, his hatchet face fixed with a permanent scowl as if chewing on something sour.

Sasha didn't know much about the man, other than he had been with Oleg in the paramilitary back in the old country. Miros rarely used two words when he could use one, and did his best to say less than that. Roberto liked to call the driver 'the Mute', but never to his face.

Miros gave Sasha a silent nod of greeting and unfurled an umbrella before opening the door, moving it to keep the rain off his passenger.

Oleg rose out of the BMW's dark interior, and Sasha was reminded of a wrestler walking out of the shadows towards a floodlit ring. Easily old enough to have been Sasha's grandfather, Oleg had a broad, square face with hawkish eyes. A thin grey mane reached his shoulders down from his receding hairline, the colour matched at the even-trimmed bow of a moustache and light beard. He wore a heavy military-style jacket from some upmarket label, and Sasha imagined he selected those sort of clothes because they reminded him of his days as a soldier. Oleg was more comfortable in warrior's garb, and rarely wore the flashy suits favoured by his contemporaries from the gangs in Hamburg and Berlin.

He gave her a measuring look. 'You are unhappy that I am here,' he said, in a rumbling mutter. It was typical of Oleg to start a conversation this way, greeting her with a judgement.

'There was no need for you to come.' She glanced over his shoulder, in the direction of the terminal. 'I didn't want to put you at risk.'

He snorted. 'Risk of what, getting wet?' She opened her mouth to speak, but he talked over her. 'You worry too much, girl. No one knows I am here, our enemies are too short-sighted. And if they did, what could they do about it?'

At Oleg's side, Miros grunted at the notion, the closest sound he ever made to a laugh.

Sasha wanted to answer Oleg honestly, to tell him that it wasn't the local police that concerned her, but the Federal cops from Brandenburg who were constantly sniffing around Gorod's businesses. They knew exactly what he did and how much money he earned from his illicit dealings, but they could not prove it. All it would take for those dots to be joined was for Oleg to be in the wrong place at the wrong time. He knew this as well as she did, and still he was here, where his presence might be witnessed.

Instead she said: 'You have me to do these things for you.'

'I have you for lots of reasons,' said Oleg, and he reached out to touch her face. Sasha didn't flinch as his fingers caressed her cheek, finding the white scar. 'I grant you responsibility because you are loyal. But never think that gives you the right to dictate to me.'

'I am looking out for you,' she managed.

'I know.' Oleg's hand dropped away. 'I appreciate that. But I must be here for this, Sasha. It is a matter of principle.'

The tone of his voice told her this part of the conversation was over, and Sasha knew she would only trigger his anger if she returned to it. 'What do you want me to do?'

'Explain it to them.' Oleg walked into the hangar with Miros as his towering shadow, and Sasha followed on beside him.

Vincent, Roberto and the others stood silently, some of them exchanging nervous glances as Oleg found a place where he could observe the proceedings.

Sasha wondered what was going through their minds; all were guilty of some indiscretion, it was in the nature of men like them to think that they could get away with things. But now they were united in the same thought. *What have I done wrong?*

'We are in a privileged position,' began Sasha, as she scanned the men's faces. 'We are mongrels, strays and the unlucky.' That earned her some lukewarm chuckles from the assembled group. 'But we have our skills. Oleg has a talent for seeing the value in a person . . .' She paused, reframing her words before she went down the wrong path with them. 'A general recruits his soldiers from wherever he finds them.'

Sasha knew Oleg would approve of a military metaphor, and from the corner of her vision, she saw him give a nod. She continued on in the same theme.

'We came from different places, some of us lost, some of us looking for a fresh start.' She felt her skin prickle with recall triggered by her own words, and pushed down a raw tide of memories that threatened to rise. 'Some of us trying to escape.'

That brought mutters of agreement. *Good.* They were paying attention to her now, even Roberto.

'An army needs many qualities to operate effectively,' said Sasha. 'Unity and loyalty. Obedience and diligence. With those, any threat from an external enemy can be resisted.'

She let her gaze pass over Vincent, who recognised the signal. He moved closer to Roberto, anticipating what was to come.

'But the threat from the enemy within is the hardest to defeat. *Traitors.*' She let the word hang. 'Comrades who would turn on their own.' Sasha cast over their faces, dwelling on Roberto. The others noticed, and one by one they turned in his direction.

The burly man was slow off the mark and it took him a moment to realise what Sasha implied. 'You look at me?' His colour rose. 'The fuck you say? You call me a traitor?' Roberto spat on the concrete floor. 'You skinny bitch! I don't talk to any fucking cops! I don't talk to the Turks or the Arabs!'

With the exception of Vincent, the other men standing near to Roberto retreated, physically distancing themselves from him.

'You don't,' agreed Sasha. 'You haven't sold us out to our rivals or the police. We would know if you had.' She shook her head. 'You sold us out to your *greed*, Roberto. You have been stealing.'

'*Fucking bullshit!*' Roberto's shout echoed off the metal walls. He took a threatening step towards Sasha, but Vincent had a pistol in his hand before the burly man could make a move, and the skinny Frenchman jammed the barrel of the Czech-made semi-automatic into his kidneys.

'Don't be stupid,' said Vincent. 'Oleg knows about the money.'

'Roberto has been skimming from our transactions,' Sasha explained, for the benefit of the others. 'He abused the trust of his comrades to line his own pockets.'

'She's lying!' Roberto retorted. 'What money?' His eyes grew wide, fear warring with his anger and winning. Finally, desperately, he turned to the figure watching the scene unfold. 'Oleg,' he said, his voice cracking, his bluster dissolving. '*Please . . .*'

Oleg's frown turned to disgust. He looked away from Roberto and met Sasha's gaze. 'Bring him to me,' he said.

# FIVE

Kevin was in an odd state. Fatigued enough that he could have fallen asleep given the right conditions, but awake enough that his uneasy alertness pulled him back the other way.

He longed for somewhere quiet to retreat to, but the airport was too brightly lit, too busy with noise and activity.

There was no point waiting at the departure gate for the forty-plus minutes his flight had been delayed, staring out the window at the worsening rain. His eyes were too tired to finish the thriller in his bag and he didn't want to look at a newspaper, assuming that any doom-laden headline he might read would only depress him further. Kevin needed to lift his mood, to distract himself even for a while, just to get through the next few hours.

Some airports had quiet spaces or exhibitions of art where travellers could decompress. Barsbeker was too provincial to entertain those; the closest it came was a cluster of stores near the security area. But there was a display of elegant objects in there, in a manner of speaking.

Kevin didn't like the airport enough to have a 'favourite' part of it, but if pressed, he would have pointed to the glassy cabinets of a wristwatch shop on the concourse called Die Uhr. Airports, aviation, travel – they were inextricably linked to watches, from glamour shots of timepieces splashed over the pages of in-flight magazines to the weighty aviator specials on the wrists of passing pilots.

Kevin wandered up the line of softly lit cases, examining the faces of the watches laid out before him. He passed by the regular marques and into the expensive section, admiring designs from Tag Heuer, Panerai, Montblanc and the other manufacturers whose price tags were far beyond his limited means.

Some men were car guys, in love with Ferraris or Aston Martins. Others were dedicated to their favourite sports teams. Kevin Tyler's thing was watches. *Horology*, as the aficionados called it.

His fascination with timepieces came from a vintage Omega his stepfather had owned when Kevin was a boy. It was the man's pride and joy, something only brought out for special occasions – *like the one James Bond wears*, he would say – and for Kevin, that forever set the idea in his young mind that a successful man, a good man, *a hero*, was someone who wore a cool watch.

The first time little Kevin had seen *inside* a wristwatch, into that tiny, intricate universe of spinning cogs and fine, perfect gears, he had been determined to learn how they worked. That impulse made him become an engineer, and decades later he still held on to that fascination, although life had smoothed it down and dulled its lustre.

He looked at his own personal Mona Lisa, nestled on a cushion in the middle of the display. A Breitling Super Chronomat 44, a sleek sports chronograph made by the Swiss precision watchmaker, with a price well north of fourteen thousand euros. The idea that Kevin might have the disposable income to buy it was so remote as to be laughable, but he liked to indulge the fantasy of the lifestyle the 44 promised its owner.

*If I was rich, I'd have one like that for every day of the week.* Sadie accused him of being an idiot when he told her that, starting an argument that ended in some harsh words about the size of her shoe collection.

Kevin became aware of someone standing nearby, and he looked up. Mr Gold Card, his faint sneer in place, stood peering at a wide-faced dress watch with a rose-gold case. Kevin recognised it as a model by A. Lange & Söhne, and quite possibly the most expensive thing in the room.

'I'm surprised there's a market for these in a place like this,' the other man said airily.

The attendant who stood near the sales desk smiled politely, with the poise of someone used to dealing with rich people's manners, or lack thereof. 'Barsbeker is a refuelling stop for private aircraft travelling over the *Ostsee*,' she explained, using the German word for the Baltic. 'Clients of that calibre appreciate fine timepieces.'

Gold Card gave a short *huh* of amusement. 'I don't think oligarchs on the go would spend more time than they had to in a dreary dump like this.' He threw Kevin an arch look, trying to encourage agreement. When Kevin didn't give it, he left the dress watch and came to study the case of Breitlings. 'These are nice,' he said, 'if you like that sort of thing.'

The other man leaned on the case in a way calculated to make his cuff slip back and reveal the sleek Rolex around his wrist. It was a special edition worth more than what Kevin currently owed on his mortgage.

'If you can *afford* them,' the man added.

Kevin made a show of looking at Gold Card's watch. 'Great craftsmanship. You'd think it was real, wouldn't you? But there's only one "L" in "Rolex".' He walked away before the other man could respond, taking enjoyment in Gold Card's momentary dismay as he glared at the face of his watch to double-check the lettering.

It wasn't a fake of course, far from it. But the fact that the snob been made to believe so, even for a second, was a small victory that Kevin savoured on a day that had been otherwise absent of them.

At this end of the airport, a larger branch of the convenience store Relay had racks of last-chance purchase items for anyone who had forgotten to pack deodorant or who wanted a souvenir of their visit. Kevin searched past refrigerator magnets in the shape of the German flag, ornamental beer steins and lederhosen-wearing figurines next to collectable spoons and tins of gingerbread, looking fruitlessly for what he needed.

Suddenly, a sharp crack sounded behind him. He turned towards the source of the noise in time to watch a frantic young woman in a sweatshirt tumbling face-first to the floor.

50

Before she could cry out, she went down hard. The woman had a Pullman case like Kevin's, and some mistaken instinct kept her hand clasped around the handle as she fell, hauling it over with her. One of the Pullman's wheels burst out of its socket, violently arresting the movement of the case and transferring its kinetic energy down the unlucky lady's arm.

Kevin offered a helping hand, which she gratefully accepted. Rising, dusting herself off, the woman said something in heavily accented German that he couldn't follow, but it was clear she was thanking him. Together, they studied the broken wheel socket and the woman gave a sorrowful groan that transcended linguistic barriers.

Kevin couldn't help but feel sympathy. *Yeah, me too*, he wanted to say. He dropped into a crouch, finding the errant plastic wheel where it had landed. The axle had snapped and ejected it across the floor, turning the case into an immovable dead weight. By the look of the young woman's luggage, she had filled it to the limit, and her slight build would make it a serious effort for her to get it to the departure gate.

But mechanical problems like this were what Kevin did best. 'I'll fix it,' he told her, rooting around inside his shoulder bag. She gave him an odd look as he produced a narrow-gauge roll of duct tape – through force of habit, the engineer never left home without one – and he tore off a strip of the heavy-duty material. Kevin quickly fashioned a repair from the tape and bits of broken axle, reinserting the wheel and completing the makeshift patch-up. He gave it an experimental spin with his finger.

51

'There you go,' he said. 'That'll last you until you get home.'

'*Danke sehr aufmerksam,*' she said, with feeling. '*Sehr shlau!*' The woman waved and carried on her way, rushing to the gates.

He almost called out 'have a good trip!' but thought better of it.

Doing a fix on the fly was second nature to Kevin. He'd made a habit of it at home, bringing dead appliances back to life or jury-rigging custom playthings for Maddie when she was small, but Sadie had always hated him doing it. His ex-wife didn't believe in make-do-and-mend, complaining that it made them look cheap. He frowned at the memory as the tape went back into the bag and he returned to the store, resuming his search.

Next to plush bears and little remote-controlled toy planes, he finally located what he was after. Kevin deliberately purchased the most uncool postcard he could find, one showing a bland, washed-out photo of the harbour at Kiel inset with images of the surrounding countryside. Carrying it to a bench near an ornamental planter, he wrote down Maddie's address in New York from memory.

His pen wavered over the empty half of the postcard. *Dear Mads,* he began, *Hello from Pop.*

It was how he began every card he sent to her, how he had done it from when she was a little girl, through to the present day. It was their private thing, a shared greeting between dad and daughter, daughter and dad. Kevin had started sending the postcards half out of guilt, sublimating his regret at the work that took him away from home while his girl grew up. But Maddie loved to read and like most kids, she loved to get things in the post – especially bright, glossy cards covered with pictures of faraway places.

It was tradition. Kevin would send her a postcard, letting his daughter know he was thinking of her no matter where he went, and when Maddie was old enough to travel herself, the cards started to come back the other way. Kevin had a collection at home, filling a box in the corner of his study. The recent ones were adorned with pictures of yellow taxicabs and towering cheeseburgers, the neon of Times Square, the Empire State Building and Lady Liberty. He'd never been to America, but Maddie thrived there.

In a way, he felt slightly jealous – of a whole country, it seemed. He hadn't realised that at home, his daughter couldn't be herself, not truly.

The guilt about that weighed heavily. He hadn't seen the signs. He'd missed them, over and over again. And what did that say about him?

Kevin understood now, or at least he was trying to. It had taken the expanse of an ocean between them for Madeline Tyler to find the confidence to tell her parents she was gay.

*How are things*

Kevin scratched down the words, already frowning as he started to second-guess himself, fearful of repeating previous mistakes.

*How are things with you and Andrea? Are you doing OK?*
*I hope*

He lost his impetus and paused, staring at the card. At length, he blew out an exasperated breath and put aside the pen.

'Hope what?' Kevin muttered. 'I hope you don't resent me for being an idiot dad. For putting my stupid bloody foot in my stupid mouth every time I open it.'

He loathed the unkind truth that Maddie had gone halfway around the world to come out to him. He hated to think that she felt she couldn't tell him to his face. It was a father's job to give his child a safe place, free of judgement. But he'd failed in that.

Maddie told her parents who she was over a video chat call, a black-framed screen with three little pictures-in-picture. Maddie in the middle, like always. Kevin against the bookshelf in his tiny study, and Sadie sitting in some sunlit garden he didn't recognise. The knot in his stomach Kevin had felt that day twisted tightly now, as if it were happening right this second.

*This is Andrea*, said Maddie, and into the picture walked an athletic young Latina girl with long dark hair and a no-nonsense half-smile playing over her face. *She's ... My girlfriend. I've had time to think about a lot of things since I came over here, and Andrea's helped me understand them a bit better. I've figured out who I am and what I want.*

What he should have said was *good for you* or *fine with me*; but Kevin didn't think, and instead he blurted out *how did this happen?* As if he'd walked into the room and found something broken. And it got worse from there.

In retrospect, Sadie reacted in exactly the way Kevin expected, with histrionics, then confusion, and finally numb acceptance. She kept talking about how sad it was that Maddie wouldn't have kids, that she wouldn't get to be a grandmother, somehow forgetting the fact that there were plenty of same-sex couples with children.

But in the moment, all Kevin could think was that he had done something wrong. Was it his fault? He tried to comprehend. Had Maddie been turned off men because he had set a bad example for her? Was there something he had said or done, or *not* said or *not* done, that had set her down this path?

*It doesn't work like that*, Andrea snapped, breaking her silence. *It's who she is, don't you get it? She's here, we're queer, get used to it.*

The call didn't end well, the four of them negotiating a stop to it rather than parting on understanding. Inevitably, Sadie blamed Kevin.

But because they were family and they *did* love each other, they manoeuvred awkwardly around this new landmass in the geography of their relationships, without really acknowledging it. After that day, there was a new distance in place that, try as he might, Kevin couldn't bridge.

People weren't cogs and gears inside a machine, running to a rhythm. They were messy and difficult and contradictory, and he wished he had the blueprint for how it worked.

Kevin's ex-wife thought this was a phase that Maddie would pass through, but he had no such illusions. He knew his daughter too well. Andrea had been right; this was who she was.

He wanted to be the good dad, the understanding dad. His cheeks reddened as he replayed the video call in his mind, that and every other stilted conversation they'd shared since then.

*I am so bad at this*, he thought. *Am I using the right terms, the right pronouns? Am I doing this wrong?* He walked through an emotional minefield, and with each step he took he was worried he'd only make it worse.

It took him a while to figure out his mistake. He'd framed Maddie's announcement as if it was something that had gone *wrong* when in fact it was anything but. This was *right*. She had found her truth after hiding it away for who knew how long, and that was the best thing that anyone could have in their life.

Kevin didn't mind who his daughter loved. She was smart and she made good choices. He wanted her to be happy, and for Maddie to know that. But it felt like every time he tried to distil that intention down into actual words, it became a mess that he over-analysed, mismanaged and ultimately, *fucked up*.

Maddie forgave his clumsiness, of course. Because she was a kind person and a better daughter than either he or Sadie deserved. She let it go unspoken and they carried on. But now there was brittleness to their relationship, a sense of fragility so stark that Kevin would sometimes lie awake at night, alone in his bed, terrified he would make another mistake and drive her out of his life forever. It was why he had been ducking her calls. He felt paralysed, as if no matter what decision he made, the distance between them would only grow.

*You overthink everything* said Sadie's voice, rising up out of an old, bad memory, *always stuck in your own head.* He wanted to believe it wasn't as bad as he thought, but without looking Maddie in the eye, without being in the room with her, he had no way to be sure.

Andrea was another case entirely, brazen, unfiltered and briskly direct in that way that only Americans could be. Kevin saw, even across the miles, that Andrea loved his daughter fiercely, but despite the fact the two of them shared that strong, common ground, he couldn't connect with her. Andrea only saw Kevin's mistakes, and there were plenty of them.

'I want to say the right thing,' Kevin said to himself, staring at the half-blank postcard. 'Somebody *please* tell me what the right thing is.'

He crossed out *I hope* and wrote *I want you and your partner to know that* before he ran out of momentum and hissed through his teeth.

'This is a postcard,' he growled at himself, 'not a sodding formal declaration!'

Finding words that were not awkward or overwrought was difficult, and the more he thought about trying to encapsulate the *exactly correct thing* on an eight by eight centimetre square of cardboard, the further it withdrew from him.

In a quick flare of annoyance, Kevin swore under his breath and tore the postcard in two, then into quarters and eighths, turning the picture of the harbour into confetti. He dumped it into a rubbish bin and stifled the need for an exasperated shout.

That done, he took a calming breath and stalked back over to the store. He bought the exact same postcard again and returned to the spot by the planter.

Kevin pushed aside the noise inside his own head, and put the pen to work once more.

*Dear Mads,* he wrote, *Hello from Pop.*

# SIX

Vincent prodded Roberto with the pistol, and in the time it took the Frenchman to herd him across the hangar, the burly man's manner transformed from its usual bellicosity into something more suited to a terrified child.

To Oleg, it was a pitiful sight, but one he had seen many times. Even the toughest of men could be undone by fear. They would reach a point of no return, never aware how close they were to it until the fateful moment came, and they would crumble. Iron wills turned to sand, collapsing under their own weight. The biggest thug, the hardest warrior, reduced to a mewling parody of themselves.

It disgusted him. Oleg loathed the pathetic and the fragile. Roberto had disappointed him with his stupidity, believing he could get away with stealing right under Oleg's nose, and now he disappointed him again with this display of spinelessness.

Roberto tried desperately to convince Oleg that Sasha was lying, that there was no money, that he had done nothing wrong. His piggish eyes darted around as he searched for an exit, and Oleg knew that if it hadn't been for the pistol in his back, Roberto would have already fled.

Sasha maintained an air of indifference, but Oleg saw through it. She knew what was coming and a part of her was reluctant.

He frowned. No matter how hard he worked her, no matter what guidance he gave, there was a part of Sasha he was unable to expunge. A troubling kernel of dogged morality that clung to her like a barnacle on the hull of a ship, impossible to dislodge. He resolved to apply more pressure to her. It was important the men feared Sasha almost as much as they feared him. Without that, she was useless as his lieutenant.

His predatory gaze shifted back to Roberto, and Oleg raised a hand to make him stop babbling. The big man bowed his head, staring at the floor.

In the silence that followed, the only sound was the steady drumming of the rain on the tin roof above their heads. Oleg took a breath and continued the evening's lesson.

'When I was a young man,' he said, taking in his audience, 'during the war, there were more mistakes made than there were victories. My unit had the dirtiest of jobs. We would go from village to village, looking for collaborators and traitors, and when we found them ...' He paused, considering. 'We always did. We would kill them in the street. Sometimes with guns, sometimes with a machete. When we were bored and we wanted sport, we would make them kill each other, with their women and children watching. The settlement would be burned to the ground as a warning to the rest.'

The words triggered deep sense-memories. Bosnia and Eastern Croatia, a good thirty years ago now, Oleg and his comrades stalking the land like they were tigers, preying on anyone who was not Serb, who did not give tribute or show the proper respect.

He never remembered the faces, but the smell of petrol fires and horse manure was suddenly strong in his nostrils, that and the feel of grey mud beneath his boots. His hands tensed, the cold ghost-weight of a Kalashnikov assault rifle etched into the recollection of the sinews in hands. Had he closed his eyes, he would have been back there.

The colour drained from Roberto's round face. The burly man was ashen. His mouth trembled, but he dared not speak.

'There was a soldier in our unit ... ' Oleg gave Roberto a fatherly nod. 'He made a mistake. It was his job to vet intelligence from our informants, to prepare the men so they would know what to expect from each village that we targeted. The mistake was in his diligence. Everyone said he was lazy and self-interested, that he looked out for himself instead of the unit.' He took a breath. 'An ambush was waiting. The collaborators had grown tired of our retribution.'

Oleg remembered that day, he and the others striding into the tiny town square, they who controlled this land, the locals nothing but prey to be cut down. But a heavy machine gun hidden in the back of a cart opened up and snakes of tracer fire ripped into the unready. Four men were blown apart by the big Dushka's heavy-gauge bullets before someone killed the gunner with a grenade.

He told the story of how they died, and Roberto started to shake.

'Four men lost, because of one mistake.' Oleg gave a sigh. 'After, when we had taken our revenge, the soldier could have lied. He could have tried to blame someone else. But he did not.' Oleg gently patted Roberto on the shoulder. 'He admitted his fault. He took responsibility and pledged to do better. And because he was a good soldier, a *useful* soldier, his commander gave him a simple punishment and forgiveness.'

A glimmer of hope flickered in Roberto's eyes. 'You ... Were the commander?'

Oleg's lips thinned into a smile. 'I was the useful soldier.'

'I'm sorry for what I did.' The words gushed out of Roberto in a torrent, as he grasped desperately for a way out of his predicament. 'I became greedy, I took money, and I promise I won't do it again! I will make amends—'

'It was a lie, however.' Oleg continued, telling the story to Sasha, Vincent and the others, ignoring Roberto's entreaties. 'I did not make a mistake. I *knew* there was an ambush waiting for us. I was at the rear of the squad as we entered the square, and the men I disliked were at the front.' His hand dropped from Roberto's shoulder and he stepped past him.

Oleg remembered the taste of cordite smoke and the hard, punching report of the Dushka making shockwaves in the wet air. His smile widened.

'I knew exactly what I was doing. I owned my choice. Those men were in my way. I stabbed them in the back.' As Oleg spoke, he reached inside his jacket and his hand returned with a stubby combat knife in it.

Before Roberto could turn around, Oleg slammed the blade into him, burying it to the hilt. The knife went up under the big man's shoulder blade and pierced his heart.

Roberto staggered away, whimpering as he tried to reach around and grab at the weapon. Dark crimson fluid streaming down his jacket, he crumpled to his knees and then down on his side. He began to die, breath by panting breath.

Oleg crouched to look him in the eye. 'The commander was a fool. Killed a few weeks later in a NATO bombing raid.' He shook his head. 'I have never made his mistakes. You understand? All crimes against the unit, no matter how small, must be punished as if they were the most severe. In this way, discipline is maintained.'

Roberto's blood pooled on the concrete, and Oleg stepped back, careful not to get it on his shoes. He turned to Sasha and the others.

'Our business . . . It is not forgiving. We commit monstrous acts for our share of money and power, and the price is high if we fail.' He gestured towards the steel coffins, in which they smuggled drugs, money, diamonds and guns across the European continent, alongside the cadavers of the unlucky.

He nodded at a larger, box-like container at the rear of the hangar, a half-size version of the ones carried on cargo ships and freight trains. If someone looked inside, they would see the eye-bolts welded to the interior. Those fixed chains around the ankles of the women trafficked in from the Baltic States. It stopped the cargo from becoming troublesome. The containers had a faint reek of blood, shit and fear soaked into the metal that no amount of stringent cleaner could completely erase.

His eyes fell on Sasha. He had first seen her inside that rancid steel box, after a fight had broken out among a half-dozen Natashas plucked from the streets of Riga and Gdansk.

Defending herself, she had ripped off part of another woman's ear with her teeth, and to punish Sasha for damaging goods he could otherwise have sold, Oleg decided to make her pay back the debt. He put that feral edge of hers to work.

His instincts about the rake-thin Polish girl had been right. She had venom in her veins. It just needed to be correctly harnessed.

'I trust,' concluded Oleg, as Roberto's breathing finally ceased, 'my point is clearly made.'

'Get rid of this mess,' Sasha ordered, taking her cue. Roberto's friends exchanged worried glances, but they did as she told them, finding a body bag in which to place the still-cooling corpse.

Oleg walked away, massaging the hand that had wielded the knife. His fingers were stiff, the muscles plagued with aches. Age crept up on him in unexpected ways. He had never believed he would live this long, assuming that one day a rival's bullet would remove him from the world. But Oleg had surprised himself by growing into the role of survivor. He outlived his enemies by sheer doggedness, and made new ones in their stead. None had killed him yet. None were capable enough.

Sasha trailed after him, and Oleg knew she dwelled on what had just happened. She didn't need to voice her concerns. He had made himself a murderer again – not that he cared, for the count was high without Roberto's corpse added to it – and had a half-dozen witnesses to it.

But she would understand. Sometimes a leader had to hold the knife himself, to be seen to do the work.

Oleg gave a grunt of approval. He wanted tea, he decided. A hot drink to dispel the chill of the evening. Miros, dutiful as ever, had anticipated his boss's needs and led the way to the back of the hangar, where a heated samovar waited.

Oleg glanced over his shoulder, making sure Sasha followed. 'The other thing,' he began. 'Is it dealt with?'

'Working on it,' she replied. 'I'm waiting for the call.'

'Running late.'

'Cutting it close,' admitted the woman. 'He's pushing his luck, as usual. But Von Kassel knows what will happen if he doesn't obey.'

*True enough*, reflected Oleg. As tonight's lesson had affirmed, he made it his business to be sure that everyone he dealt with understood the price of non-compliance, and the glib politician knew that full well.

Another thought occurred. 'What about the *kerovi?*' Oleg used the derogatory slang for cops, a Serb word that meant 'dogs'. On the way in, he had seen an airport-security cruiser driving back to the shelter of the main terminal as the rain set in.

Sasha's lip curled, the action catching at her scar, pulling her expression out of kilter. 'We keep our profile low, they pay attention to other matters.'

She glanced back at Roberto's corpse being carried to Memoria Tranzyt's on-site mortuary. He would be dealt with later, via their usual channels for disposal. Murdering a man on airport grounds wasn't exactly *low profile*, but if no one spoke about it, who could say?

Sasha moved up to fall in step and she spoke again as she threw a look back at the parked BMW. 'You're not leaving?'

'In a hurry to see me go?' Oleg clicked his tongue. 'Not yet.' The clatter of the heavy rain became a drumming, rumbling chorus, and out past the open doors of the hangar, the downpour sluiced off the roof in curling ribbons of water pushed away by gusts of wind. 'I think I will remain for a time.'

'There's no need,' she said, framing a suggestion that would be something to do with Oleg returning to his nice, warm home instead of being out here in the cold.

He cut her off before she could continue. 'Don't tell me what is needed, and what is not.' He didn't raise his voice because he didn't have to. The careful, quiet censure in his words was more than enough.

Oleg had known hardships that would have killed these children around him. Frostbite and malnutrition. Gunshot wounds and blunt-force trauma. He resented the thought that Sasha and the others might look at him and see his advancing age instead of his experience. He would stay, he decided, because that too was a kind of lesson. A reminder of who and what he was.

And if this troubled Sasha, better he know now. She was the other reason Oleg wanted to remain, to observe her. Was she ready for more responsibility? Did she have the respect of the men? He needed answers for these questions, to be certain that the work could continue to prosper.

Oleg's earlier statement echoed in his thoughts once more. *Our business is not forgiving.*

*'KnightSky Air flight four-zero-four to London Gatwick is now ready for boarding. Passengers please proceed immediately to the departure gate.'*

Kevin was on his feet before the announcement made it past the fourth word, stuffing the unfinished postcard in the side pocket of his shoulder bag with one hand, simultaneously trying to juggle his passport and boarding pass with the other, all while dragging his wheeled case. He made the clumsy advance as rapidly as he could, but his heart sank as he came in sight of the gate.

If anything, the amount of people there was larger than before. The slow-moving mass of passengers oozed towards the bottleneck of the doors, waiting to be funnelled into the jet bridge and on to the plane, which had finally arrived.

He resigned himself to getting a bad seat, making peace with the fact. He'd probably be crammed in on a row that didn't recline, too close to the ever-present pungency of the toilets, with leg room that would be at best an afterthought, but at least he would be going home. It wouldn't be better there, but he could literally and metaphorically put Germany behind him, and start to pick up the pieces.

Kevin drifted at the rear of the group, shifting his weight uncomfortably, watching one of the gate crew giving a disabled passenger a temperature test, another handing out paper face coverings for those who needed one. He fumbled for the reusable mask in his jacket pocket; Kevin had his vaccination jabs up to date, but he didn't see the sense in taking unnecessary risks. In an open, well-ventilated spot like the terminal, he didn't bother with it, but sealed in a pressurised aluminium tube with what looked to be a cabin full of other travellers, Kevin wasn't going to chance it. Air travel always made him feel low-key ill, even before the threat of COVID.

As he unwound the mask's elastic straps, he heard the gate public address system come to life. '*Ladies and gentlemen, can I have your attention please? KnightSky Air regrets to inform you that due to circumstances beyond our control, flight four-zero-four to London Gatwick has been overbooked. At this time, any passengers willing to postpone their departure until tomorrow, could you please come forward?*'

A mutter of dismay spread through the waiting passengers, and not a single one of them moved. Everybody waiting to board the plane shared the same thought: *Miss my flight? You must be joking.*

They knew that KnightSky 404 was the last flight of the day to the UK, and surrendering their ticket would strand them here. Kevin looked out of the window, to where the Airbus A319 bearing the KnightSky Air livery sat amid the worsening downpour, and his jaw set. *Shitty seat or not, I'm getting on that plane*, he vowed.

The gate agent made the statement again, and when it became clear there would be no takers, her tone shifted from towards something more schoolmarmish. *'Be advised, if no one is willing to postpone their departure, KnightSky Air will be compelled to select passengers at random for ticket reallocation.'*

Having failed to appeal to anyone's civic-minded nature, the next step was to threaten involuntary disembarkation. That meant picking whatever luckless chump had made a last-second booking, typically someone travelling on their own.

'Ah, shit.' Kevin cursed quietly, as that realisation caught up with him. He looked at his boarding pass, where the text **Standby** was printed in large letters. The office had sorted out the flight for him after the collapse of the deal, and he hadn't thought any more about it, but he was certain he could sense the gate agent's pitiless gaze zeroing in on him.

The woman read something off a screen and raised the PA mike to her lips. *'Can the following passenger please make themselves known to a KnightSky Air staff member?'*

'Don't say my name.' Kevin stared at the floor and whispered the words like a litany. 'Don't say my name don't say my name don't say my name . . .'

'*Passenger Gregory Brent-Shaftoe, please come to the gate desk, thank you.*'

He looked up with a start, in time to hear a mumbled expletive as a figure detached from the front of the group. It was Mr Gold Card, and as Kevin watched, the man marched angrily to the desk, his face as thunderous as the sky outside.

Kevin couldn't help himself, and broke into a grin as the other man started an argument with the KnightSky staff. 'Couldn't happen to a nicer bloke,' he said quietly, as the plane started boarding and the passengers shuffled forward.

But his grin faded when the gate agent made another announcement. '*Passenger Kevin Tyler, please come to the gate, thank you.*'

The walk to the desk felt like a march to the gallows, and Kevin was conscious of everyone's eyes on him as he stepped up to stand beside Gold Card, who spared him a withering look. He offered his passport, but the gate agent barely considered it.

'I'm afraid this flight is overbooked,' she said, with the rote precision of a scripted performance. 'You gentlemen are the only single travellers on this departure. We only require one of you to accept a postponement and re-ticketing. There will be no charge for this service.'

'That's very generous,' said Gold Card, in a dismissive tone of voice that made it clear he thought it was nothing of the sort. 'I decline.'

Kevin stiffened. 'I, uh, *also* decline. Firmly.'

'Firmly?' Gold Card raised a mocking eyebrow.

Kevin saw an opportunity and seized it. 'You know they're playing us off against one another, right?' He nodded at the woman. 'If we both refuse to accept—'

The other man spoke over him. 'What do you think will happen, *Kevin*? You think they'll magic up another plane just for us, if only we show a little solidarity?' He snorted in derision and waved at the window. 'Look at the weather out there, it's touch and go *this* one will get off the ground!' He carried on, without giving Kevin time to respond. 'I'll tell you what. How about we play for it? *Rock-Paper-Scissors.*'

The gate agent remained stony-faced, interested only in the result and not the method. Kevin gave a wary nod, and on the count of three, he showed two fingers – *scissors*.

But the other man opened his palm, showing off that bloody frequent flyer's card again. 'Do you have one of these? No? What a shame.' Gold Card turned, pinning the gate agent with a hard look. 'Four hundred and fifty thousand, three hundred loyalty points,' he told her, barely pausing for breath, 'just below Platinum Status, which I will hit next month on a prestige-class trip to Singapore. Now, do you really want to turf a valued customer off this flight and have me complain about it to your European area manager when we play golf at the weekend, or . . . ?' He gestured in Kevin's direction.

Kevin bristled at Gold Card's superior tone. 'My money is as good as his,' he retorted.

'Oh, Kevin,' said the other man, with false sorrow, 'it really *isn't.*'

The gate agent wouldn't meet the other man's gaze, and he took that as confirmation, stepping straight into the boarding line and off to the jet bridge without looking back.

'I hope you will accept KnightSky Air's sincere apologies for this situation,' the woman told Kevin, the words *please don't make a scene* unspoken but heavily implied. 'I'm afraid that company policy prioritises our high status loyalty cardholders.'

Kevin barely heard her, his blood rushing in his ears as his colour rose and his cheeks burned hot. His fury rooted him to the spot, turned him into immobile stone. He wanted to shout down the unfairness of it, but he couldn't bring himself to do it. He stood there, rigid with impotent rage, unable to find a way to vent it.

Hands balled into fists, Kevin was only half-aware of the gate agent explaining that his ticket would be rebooked for the next flight at eight o'clock the following morning. She handed over a complicated reimbursement form, promising that KnightSky would cover the cost of a stay at the airport's tiny on-site hotel, before firmly asking him to step aside so the flight could continue boarding.

He drifted to a chair and sank into it, his bags between his knees, the form crumpling in one hand. By the time the gate doors closed and the Airbus pushed back from the jet bridge, Kevin raced the dying charge in his phone battery and the airport's spotty Wi-Fi service.

His run of bad luck remained true to form. Barsbeker's flug-hotel, with its miniscule, closet-sized rooms, was completely booked. His desperation increased along with the search radius for vacancies, hitting result after result that read 'Ausgebucht' in bright, unfriendly letters. When the search engine started recommending places several hours away in Hamburg, he knew he was wasting his time.

For a moment, Kevin entertained the idea of finding a different route home, but the handful of flights that would leave Barsbeker before the airport shut down for the night did not connect with anything that could get him into the UK any sooner.

The slow, inescapable reality of the situation settled on Kevin, pressing him deeper into the chair as if it were a physical weight. He had nowhere to go, no way to escape. Once more, his catastrophic, ruinous ill fortune had left him stranded with nothing to do but chew on his failures.

Outside, a ripple of distant sheet lightning backlit the clouds. Alone and dejected, Kevin watched his flight home rise off the runway into the embrace of the rainstorm, leaving him far behind.

# SEVEN

Turning the tumbler in a circle, his hand over the mouth of the glass, Lars Von Kassel watched the last lick of brandy swill around from left to right.

In the middle of his forties and, if one were honest, too well dressed for somewhere as provincial as Barsbeker, Von Kassel outwardly attempted to resemble the model of the modern, successful German. Everything he wore was handmade – the knitted woollen tie, the tailored suit imported from Savile Row in London, his spit-polished brogues. Even his spectacles were crafted individually by a company that made monocoque frames for Formula 1 racers.

But the clothes couldn't do much for the shape they hung from, a body that gave the impression of being too small for itself. A reporter for *Die Zeit* once mockingly described the politician as resembling a schoolboy who had gotten into his father's wardrobe, play-acting at adulthood, and that image had continued to dog Von Kassel throughout his entire governmental career. His pale face flushed slightly with the warmth of the brandies he had already imbibed, and his dull brown hair was out of place. But there was no one to see, he decided, no one of import out here in the flat backside of the country.

The last first-class passengers for the connecting LuftFluger flight to Paris had recently departed, leaving him alone in the executive lounge. The oak bar was empty, the artfully cramped seating areas completely vacant. Von Kassel remained the sole human in place, unless one counted the staff, which of course he didn't.

They hovered, distant enough to be beyond the boundaries of his personal space, with smiles that didn't reach their eyes and anxious manners betraying their real intentions.

They wanted him to leave. It was time for the lounge to close, for these menials to finish their dreary workaday tasks and return to whatever sort of home awaited them.

But Von Kassel was disinterested in that. His own needs were, as always, first and foremost in his mind. He wanted another drink.

He tossed back the remaining contents of the glass, set it on the bar and tapped it with a forefinger. 'One more,' he demanded, searching for and finding the bartender. 'Come, come, hurry, hurry.'

The young woman behind the bar, in a sky-blue shirt echoing the livery of LuftFluger's jetliners, threw a look in the direction of the man in the black jacket who had greeted Von Kassel on his arrival. A manager of some sort, he assumed, the jacket affording seniority.

'Herr Von Kassel,' he said smoothly, moving into range, 'we're grateful for your visit here today, but—'

He cut him off with an arch look. 'Come now. You can't serve me one more?' He chuckled, unfolding the affable smirk that he deployed at press conferences and television interviews. It made him appear harmless, congenial, as if he were sharing a long-standing joke between good friends. Von Kassel read a name off the metal badge on his jacket. '*Karl.* My man, please could you be so kind? I swear I will be on my best behaviour.' He gave a Boy Scout salute.

'Sir . . .' Karl-the-manager threw a look to where some of the lower echelon staff were dithering by a service door, clearly waiting to come in and start the business of cleaning up the place. 'We really do have to close the lounge.'

'I don't object,' Von Kassel said, with an accommodating smile. 'Clean around me! I don't mind!' He fixed the bartender with a firm look. 'One more and I promise I will fade away. Please, dear friends. My work in the Bundestag is so tiring, I rarely get a moment of peace to myself. I want to savour it.' He tapped the glass once more. 'May I?'

'Sir . . .' Karl tried again, and again Von Kassel spoke over him, firming up his words.

'It's just that a man of my stature, you understand, I can't be milling around out on the concourse. Awkward,' he admitted, shaking his head. 'Awkward for all of us.' The last few words hid the threat beneath the false bonhomie, the warning that Von Kassel might speak to someone senior to Karl if he did not acquiesce to his demands.

When Karl sighed, he knew that he had won this round. The bartender frowned and poured another measure, and Von

Kassel didn't look to see if Karl went away. His dismissal was clearly implied, and people like the manager were trained to know their place.

He watched the bartender do her work. The girl had a pretty face marred by her souring countenance. In her twenties, with something of a dash of Spaniard, Von Kassel guessed, she was trimly built and attractive enough that the politician's eye lingered over her body. In quick order, the bartender delivered a new glass of brandy atop a black paper napkin, and Von Kassel offered her a wan smile.

The young woman briefly met his gaze with a perfunctory smile of her own, a machine-made version of the expression that was utterly charmless. It set off a jagged splinter of recall in the back of Von Kassel's thoughts, pulling on the memory that had been lurking close by through the day.

*The same fake smile on another pretty face.*

*That pretty face, pale and inert against the carpeted floor.*

He drowned the memory before it could fully form with a heavy swig from the new glass, the taut fire of the rich brandy forcing the traitorous thought to retreat into the shadows. Von Kassel's mood darkened and he glared at the bar top. His eyes wandered to his satchel lying close by. Papers leaked out of the open flap, contractual documents with text so tiny and so dense it became a blur.

He adjusted his spectacles and peered at the contracts, leafing past the signatures at the bottom where the scrawl of his handwriting was visible. Scanned copies were already in his office, the deal done and complete. He should have been pleased, but the emotion was absent. Instead there was a hole where the brandy went, pouring in but not filling it.

Von Kassel made a negative noise and jammed the papers back into the satchel, rejecting the gloom gathering about him with a physical shrug and taking another pull from the brandy. He refused to allow himself to become bogged down by past events. They bored him.

*Look forward, only forward.* The politician had strolled into elected office on that slogan, and he returned to it now. The past – and past deeds – were for smaller minds to contest with, not of concern for a man with his face to the future. Lars Von Kassel had made a career out of being able to stay one step ahead of the mendacity he left in his wake, always slipping beyond the grasp of the consequences of his actions.

He did this by maintaining a perfect moral vacuum at his core – keeping his own needs, as always, first and foremost in his mind. Whatever deal needed to be made, whatever trade-off was required, he accommodated it. The alternative – to carry the burden of responsibility – was something outside of his experience, and he intended to keep it that way.

Fending off his boredom with an arch sniff, he reached for the burner smartphone concealed in the satchel's inner pocket, the device he used only for 'opportunities' whenever they presented themselves to him. With laboured, deliberate slowness, he began to punch in Dieter Boch's private number from memory.

The departure area in front of Gate Six had been empty since the departure of the flight to Madrid a few hours earlier, and the overhead lights were in low-power mode, giving the place a twilight feel. A family of West Asians waiting for their gate call had colonised one side of the space, near to where a shabby play area provided simple amusements for their children, but at the opposite end of the lounge area there was only one other occupant – a man in a dark suit, with a craggy face and unsmiling eyes, who poked grimly at the tiny screen on his phone.

Boch's natural aura of unpleasantness kept the family at bay, even the most curious of the scampering children, allowing him to do his job in relative peace. Using his index finger, he typed out a short message in English – COME AND GET IT – and sent the text to the number he had been provided by the woman who called herself Sasha. An animation of a winged envelope flying away played across the phone's screen, and he nodded to himself.

Under other circumstances, he would have risen from the seat and made himself scarce. If fact, if he had been doing this in the manner that *he* wanted to, Boch would have sent the message from the road, preferably several kilometres away from here.

But as always, his employer felt the need to get his hands on the details. Von Kassel had the irritating habit of listening to the objections Boch put to him, nodding thoughtfully as if taking it in, and then proceeding exactly as he pleased, ignoring any advice to the contrary. After a while, Boch had learned that his employer only ever feigned interest in other people's words, when he really just waited for them to stop speaking.

Von Kassel wanted *confirmation*. He wanted eyes he trusted to be sure that the exchange happened as it was supposed to. It had been a chore to convince the man not to be present here himself. In the end, Boch had appealed to the politician's vanity, the only ploy that was effective, in order to make him back off.

The phone trilled and Boch glanced at it, expecting to see a response from Sasha or one of her subordinates. He grimaced. The number on the screen was from Von Kassel's burner, which meant Boch did not have the luxury of ignoring it.

With a deep sigh, he pressed the **ACCEPT CALL** tab and raised the phone to his ear. 'Yes, sir?'

'*Is it over?*' Von Kassel spoke quietly, as if he did not want to be overheard. '*I'm four drinks in and my patience is waning.*'

'Everything is in place,' Boch replied. He looked in the direction of the entrance across the corridor which led to the toilets and washrooms in this part of the departure wing. From the angle of the seat he had chosen, Boch could observe everyone going in and out without making his scrutiny obvious. 'I am waiting for the pickup ...' He trailed off as a distant flash of lightning caught his eye from out beyond the terminal's rain-lashed windows. One of the children across the way gave a mournful wail, frightened by the storm-light. He heard the trailing rumble of thunder a second later, the noise doubling down the line from Von Kassel's handset. Boch unconsciously stiffened at the sound.

'*You are sure they will come?*'

Boch suppressed a sneer. 'With all that is at stake? I believe so, sir, yes.'

'*I suppose . . .*' Von Kassel sounded bored. '*After the trouble they have put me through, eh?*' He snorted. '*These blasted cloak-and-dagger games. Why can't we hand it over, face to face, and be done with it?*'

'It's better if there is no direct contact.' Boch wanted to remind his employer of the conversation where he had explained this fact two or three times, but he knew that would be pointless.

'*I'm going to come down there.*'

'No,' Boch said firmly, rising from his seat. He turned around to look off in the direction of the LuftFluger first-class lounge, finding the shaded entrance on the upper mezzanine level, half-expecting to see Von Kassel stepping out of the doorway.

'*What did you say to me?*' The politician's tone turned icy.

'Sir, we've been through this. You are my principal. It is my job to protect my principal. Let me do my job.' His tone became more urgent.

What he wanted to say was *stay where you are, idiot.*

Against reason, against logic, Von Kassel had insisted on coming along tonight, ignoring the plan Boch had set out for him.

Boch had arranged an afternoon flight, and someone to pick him up in Hamburg, even a dinner reservation at a popular restaurant, designed to give Lars Von Kassel a very visible, very public alibi that placed him nowhere near Barsbeker Airport on this day, at this time.

82

He dismissed it, insisting on remaining, as if events would grind to a halt without his presence to oversee them. The risk that entailed didn't register with Boch's employer. It was what Von Kassel wanted, and he was a man who had grown up in a world that had always bent to his will. He expected to be obeyed, as if it was against the nature of the universe to do otherwise.

Boch took a half-step in the direction of the first-class lounge, his gaze flicking back at the entrance to the washrooms. He couldn't keep both in sight at the same time.

'Sir,' he insisted, biting down on his annoyance and laying out his words with as much firmness as he could muster. 'If you are seen, here and now, it will draw interest that I promise you do *not* want.'

At length, Von Kassel gave a dispirited sigh. '*All right. You do have my best interests at heart, don't you Dieter? You know it's important to keep me out of harm's way. I appreciate that.*'

'It is my job,' he reiterated.

'*It is,*' agreed the other man. '*Because if anything untoward happened to me, well . . . It wouldn't go well for you either, would it?*'

Boch's fingers stiffened around the phone. 'No, sir,' he said tightly.

'*You keep me safe. I keep you safe . . . From certain truths becoming public knowledge.*'

The veiled threat was left hanging, and the line went dead. For a moment, Boch stood there staring at the device, allowing the resentment he felt for Lars Von Kassel to rise to the surface, loathing the man and what he held over him.

Boch's seething anger took all of his focus in that brief instant, and so he didn't see the Englishman from before, dragging his wheeled bag behind him, as he disappeared into the men's washroom.

# EIGHT

The coffee Kevin had imbibed had finally worked its way through his system, from sitting uncomfortably in his gut to filling his bladder, and he let his bodily needs drag him to the closest washroom.

Other passengers passed him going in the opposite direction, Kevin the only minnow swimming against the stream. They were on their way to board evening flights to Gothenburg and Copenhagen, most of them with the blank, fixed mien of the zombie business traveller, minds focussed on their destination more than their actual location. A lot of Barsbeker Airport's itinerant population were people who only stopped here to change planes, never leaving the bubble reality of airside, never setting foot outside.

Before today, Kevin had been one of them, one more element in the machine flowing from place to place along travellators, through jet bridges, into economy-class cabins. But now he felt disconnected, floating free and aimless inside the giant glass aquarium of the departure terminal. He had nowhere to stay, nowhere to go. The only resource he was rich in was time, and the empty hours ranging away towards tomorrow morning and the first flight out seemed like an infinity.

Musical tones sounded in the air, followed by voices in precise, cut-to-length German as they announced gate numbers and delivered prim warnings to latecomers. Each proclamation was immediately repeated, translated into flat, bored English, but Kevin no longer listened to them. The voices became background noise, merging into the occasional grumble of thunder loud enough to be heard through the triple-glazed windows.

He veered out of the middle of the walkway and made a beeline for the washroom, dragging his case in with him past grimy mirrors and cubbyholes full of fresh toilet rolls. There was a faint dampness in the air, and the reek of stringent industrial-strength cleanser warring with a day's worth of used urinals, but Kevin felt weirdly relieved to be in a smaller space. Out on the concourse, everything felt overlit, too open and exposed. He had a deep, almost primal need to be out of the way for a while, somewhere where the walls were close and no one else was around.

Whoever had used the first stall hadn't bothered with niceties like flushing, and Kevin pushed the door closed with a sour grimace. The second stall had a *Nicht Verwenden* out-of-order sign in place, so he sat in the third, locking the door and nudging the Pullman case up against it with his foot. Kevin hung his shoulder bag on a wall hook, and then slumped down against the wall with an exhausted exhale. The rigidity in his body faded away, as if draining into the toilet bowl he sat on.

He hunched forward, closing his eyes, catching his head in his hands, and gave a long, weary moan. Kevin smothered the sound in his palms.

'What … ?' he muttered to himself. 'What else can go wrong today?'

Prickling his skin, a bleak tide washed over him. Loathing, pity, anger and sheer bloody pointlessness threatened to consume him. Now he was in the quiet, there was no outside stimulus to drown out the drumbeat of his self-recrimination.

*You have no one to blame but yourself.* Predictably, the ghost-voice of Kevin's hectoring inner scold sounded exactly like that of his ex-wife. *You let the deal fail because you took your eye off the ball. Take a bow. You're one left carrying the can, like always.*

'Fuck off,' he snarled at nothing, banishing the voice. He opened his eyes, staring blankly at the floor. He needed some quiet, inside his thoughts as well as outside, some time to think about how to deal with this catastrophe.

'The deal of my career,' he said, his voice echoing off the walls of the toilet stall. 'Gone. Like morning bloody mist.'

Kevin hadn't been able to bring himself to look directly at the day's disaster in the hours that followed it. It was an ugly, open wound in his thoughts, too raw to dwell on. But he couldn't avoid it forever – and now, stuck in the airport, there was nothing but time to chew on it.

He shook his head. 'What the hell am I going to do?' The stale atmosphere of the stalls and the humming air conditioner provided no answer.

His gaze refocussed and Kevin found himself looking at an odd pattern of grey-white dust on the linoleum floor. He hadn't noticed it when he sat, but there it was, a powdery line half-compressed into the partial tread from a shoe. His mind clamped on to the pointless distraction, grasping at any stimulus that pulled him away from his ruminations.

Kevin cast around. There was more dust on top of the wall-mounted toilet-roll holder, and spots of it down the sides of the steel toilet bowl. Some instinct made him reach up and touch the back of his jacket. His hand came back with powdery grey particles on his fingertips.

He twisted in place until he sat on the edge on the toilet seat. Directly above the metal bowl, there was a panel set into the wall with a circular latch holding it shut.

He pressed it experimentally and it moved. The latch hadn't been properly closed, and more dust leaked out around the seams. The source of the powder had been discovered.

Absently, Kevin pressed harder, and without warning a grinding, cracking sound made him twitch back in shock.

The panel coughed out a cloud of dust and it fell out of the frame towards him, like a castle's drawbridge dropping open.

The modified Suzuki Carry van was barely larger than the odd-shaped cargo containers the ground crews loaded into to the jets, and in the stiff winds over the airfield, the light little vehicle juddered as it raced along the service road.

'Be careful,' Sasha snapped from the back, glaring at Vincent in the driver's seat. 'This isn't a race.'

'Really?' The Frenchman's reply was doubtful, light falling across his jagged face in sweeps as the van's windscreen wipers chased each other back and forth across the glass. 'We'll be happier when we are done with this. Don't pretend you like having Oleg around, watching like a hawk. Everyone's terrified they'll end up like that idiot Roberto.'

'An example had to be made.' Sasha's reply sounded half-hearted, even to her.

'No doubt,' said Vincent, 'but there are better ways to do it.'

Sasha scowled. 'I'll tell him you said that. Perhaps he will come to you for some advice.'

Vincent gave a nervous laugh and risked a look over his shoulder. 'You wouldn't do that.'

'Just drive.' Sasha folded her arms across her chest, bracing her legs against the floor and brooding. The narrow space was uncomfortable, designed to shuttle metal coffins back and forth to the Memoria Tranzyt hangar, not to carry live passengers.

She sighed. Any criticism of Oleg's brutal lesson back in the hangar felt like blame being hung on her, pushing culpability on to the woman for being unable to dissuade him from his murderous intentions.

It wasn't that she was a stranger to violence, or squeamish around it. Sasha's life had been a patchwork of brutality inflicted on her and those around her until she grew strong enough and clever enough to turn it back on her tormentors. She understood that violence was a necessary tool in the work that they did, and it would be a lie to say that she didn't sometimes indulge in it.

Her first kill had been a man on a lonely dirt track on Latvia, shot in the belly with a Makarov, on Oleg's orders. Sasha didn't remember his face, had not known his name. The only memories from that day were of the frigid air in her lungs and the echoing crack of the gunshot.

But Sasha did not take delight in it, not in the way that Oleg did. She saw it in his eyes, how a hateful sort of light came on in him whenever he was about to do someone harm. *The power of it*, she thought, *of life and death in his hands. That is his drug.*

She pulled her phone from the pocket of her jacket and thumbed it to life. The screen lit up, throwing illumination around the vehicle's dim interior. The text from the burner she had given to Von Kassel's man remained unchanged.

COME AND GET IT.

Sasha could hear the sneer in the message. The politician and his people liked to think that they were better than the criminals they dealt with, and for as long as that was useful, Oleg would allow them to continue in that mistaken assumption. Personally, Sasha didn't see any difference in either side. In her experience, all men were corrupt. It was only a question of the degree.

'Here we go,' said Vincent. The van's tyres hissed on the tarmac and it lurched to a halt by the main terminal building.

The rattle of the driving rain off the van's metal flanks eased as they pulled into the relative shelter of an elevated jet bridge, and Sasha hauled open the sliding door in the side of the compartment. The wind hummed in through the gap and she dropped out into it, zipping up her jacket against the damp cold. The heavy storm cell that stirred to life over the Baltic had crawled across the nearby shoreline and its inexorable advance would soon envelop the airport.

She looked around and up, finding the thick concrete turret of Barsbeker's control tower, where it rose from the opposite end of the terminal. In the dimly lit, faceted glass box at the pinnacle, a handful of air traffic controllers worked to get the last few flights out under the approach of the storm, before it took residence overhead.

Jet noise droned loudly through the downpour, a twin-engine airliner catching her eye as it leapt off the runway and thundered away, quickly becoming a blurry flicker of wingtip indicator lights as it vanished into the darkness.

Sasha watched it fade, wondering where it was bound. Sometimes she entertained the fantasy of slipping aboard one of the planes without knowing its destination, letting the fates decide where she would end up. But no matter where that might be, it would be within Oleg's reach. She'd known him to dispatch thugs halfway around the world to punish men who had wronged him, and nothing suggested that Sasha would be granted lenience where they had not. Oleg nurtured his grudges like they were his children.

'Here they come.' Vincent climbed out of the driver's seat, and he raised an arm in greeting as a trio of men in high-visibility vests approached the van. 'Remember to smile,' he added.

'Fuck off.' Sasha threw one last look in the direction of the hangars on the far side of the runways, back in the direction they had come. She imagined Oleg over there, watching her across the distance, judging everything that she did. Turning her back, Sasha put on a dispassionate expression and surveyed the new arrivals.

They were ground crew who worked on and around the airport apron, the people who handled the movements of aircraft and equipment, and these three in particular earned a decent benefit from Oleg's coffers on top of their regular pay. In return for that, they were his eyes and ears throughout Barsbeker Airport, the information they provided allowing Gorod's illicit imports and exports to operate in the places where security was thinnest on the ground. They were also useful for errands like tonight's task.

Sasha picked one of them at random, a brown-haired and otherwise unremarkable man with a pinched expression. 'What's your name?'

'Uh, Horst,' he began, rubbing his hand beneath his nose. 'I've been here a couple of years, I work in the—'

She silenced him with a look. 'I asked for your name, not your life story.' Sasha flicked at the screen of her phone until she came to the photo Von Kassel's man had attached with the text message. 'Take a good look at this.'

'OK.' Warily, Horst leaned in and peered at the picture. 'A bag? What about it?'

'Bring it to me,' she said, and explained the location of the item and what he needed to do with it. 'Do this quietly and carefully. Don't rush. Don't act suspiciously. And don't look inside. You understand? You do that and all three of you will get a nice bonus.'

'OK,' repeated Horst. She could see he was canny enough not to ask any questions about the bag's contents. 'What do I say if, I dunno, if I get caught with it?'

'Don't let that happen,' she said firmly. 'It won't go well.'

Horst's two friends exchanged glances. 'We were told there would be work for us.' The taller of them spoke with a shrug.

'There is,' said Sasha, pointing at the other two. 'You are collateral.'

'What does that mean?' Horst's nose wrinkled, as if he smelled something unpleasant.

'It means that if you're not back here in an hour with the bag, your friends here will be the first to pay the price.' Sasha opened her hands. 'We know where each of you live. We know the names of your families.' She pause to let that sink in. 'Do I have to draw you a picture?'

The tall man in the hi-vis vest turned to Horst and gave him a prod with a thick finger, his expression turning serious. 'You better not fuck up!'

'An hour,' Sasha repeated, looking at the clock on her phone screen. 'Get moving.'

Horst nodded and jogged off towards the terminal building. Vincent called after him. 'Don't rush, moron! Remember?' The other man nodded again and slowed his pace, his hands diving into his pockets.

'What are we supposed to do for the next hour?' The third man wearing a hi-vis vest broke his silence.

'Start by making me some tea,' Sasha demanded, and at length they followed Horst's friends back to a shabby static cabin that had been converted into a cramped break room.

When the two men were out of earshot and dithering over an electric kettle, Vincent glanced at Sasha. 'You know I could have dealt with this if Oleg had listened to me.' He shook his head. 'No messy hand-offs, no dirty money, no getting mouth-breathing idiots to be mules ...'

Vincent fancied himself as something of a technical expert, and among other jobs he handled the group's dealings with buyers on the dark web, and sourced new phones when the old ones became too risky to keep using. He and Sasha both knew that his work sat uncomfortably with Oleg, who still had one foot in the Cold War and a distrust of anything overly technical.

'Cash is always a problem,' he said. 'You know it and I know it. If we had done this shit with bitcoin, Oleg would never have had to get out of his chair.'

'I don't disagree,' Sasha replied. 'But I am not in charge, and neither are you.' She remembered Oleg's orders distinctly. *None of that fake computer money this time*, he had growled, *I want the cash. I want to take Von Kassel's real money from him. Rich men don't understand anything else.*

Vincent swore to himself, then leaned in close, his words becoming urgent. 'He's taking too many chances, Sasha. You see it too, I know you do.' He frowned. 'If he makes a mistake, if he goes down, we'll fall with him—'

'He *won't*,' she insisted, silencing him. 'And if you want to keep your throat un-slit, you'll shut your damned mouth.'

Kevin caught the panel halfway before it could slip out of his hands and crash loudly to the floor of the toilet stall.

His fingers gripped it tightly and his arms shook. He stifled a gasp as grey dust settled around him, and stared at what had been revealed. Behind the panel was a void maybe two metres square, a section of wet wall where the inflow and waste water pipes snaked around to each of the toilet stalls and urinals. Kevin could see the top of a plastic cistern, coated in a thick layer of cobwebs and more of the concrete-coloured dust.

A bulky black gym bag sat atop the cistern. The first thing he noticed was that the bag had no dirt on it. It looked pristine, practically new, as if it had been bought recently and placed there today.

It was so out of place that it took Kevin's mind a few seconds to catch up with what he was seeing. Then a torrent of questions came flooding in.

*What is that doing in there? Who would leave something in an airport toilet? Is it a plumber's tool kit? Or some thief hiding their stash? Is it drugs?*

*What . . . If it's a bomb?*

His gut twisted and his blood ran cold.

*Oh fucking hell, did I just find a fucking bomb?*

'Calm down,' Kevin told himself. He strangled the gush of panic and physically forced himself to slow his breathing and steady his hands. With care, he put aside the panel and took in the whole shape of the bag. There were no identifying marks on it beyond a red tag around the handle that noted it as cleared as a cabin carry-on. Turning over the tag, he saw it had the day's date printed on it, with a time index less than two hours old. This thing had been put in place around the same time Kevin had entered the terminal building.

He was suddenly sweating. How much explosive could you get in a bag that size? How much damage could it do? Didn't terrorists pack nails and ball bearings into these things, to cause the maximum amount of carnage? Kevin had no idea, as most of his knowledge of that kind of thing came from action movies and pulpy thriller novels.

*But a lot though, right?* He imagined bricks of C-4 explosive inside, with silvery blasting caps buried in them, wires trailing to some circuit board and the guts of an obsolete cell phone. Neon-red LED digits counting down to a cataclysmic detonation that would reduce the terminal to a pile of smoking rubble –

*– which made no sense when you thought about it, because why the hell would terrorists want people knowing when their bomb would go off?*

Kevin's shook off the mental image before his mind ran away with it, staring fixedly at the bag. He could see that the zip fastener had been partly drawn back, exposing something inside. Everything in him screamed to back off, to run away and find someone else to deal with this thing – but he was locked to the spot, trapped by his own curiosity.

With the care and precision of a heart surgeon, Kevin reached out and gently pulled at the corner of the bag to expose what was inside it.

A rectangular object the size of a brick fell out of the gap, off the edge of the open panel, and down past Kevin's legs, to land with a hollow splash in the metal bowl.

He threw himself backward off the toilet seat with a wordless bark of terror, scrambling madly for the stall's locked door, tripping over his bag, crashing to his knees in his panic.

But no explosion came. There was no tornado of fire and razor-sharp shrapnel. Kevin's heart hammered in his chest, and his hands shook as he pulled himself back up off the greasy floor. He craned his neck to look into the toilet bowl and saw the package sitting half-out of the dirty water.

His eyes widened when he saw was the object was made of. Wrapping a makeshift mitten of toilet paper around one hand, he plucked it back out and wiped it clean.

The packet was a wad of cash as thick as the paperback book in Kevin's shoulder bag. The notes looked worn, not pristine, pale yellow in colour with a picture of what appeared to be a bridge on one side, and an art deco window on the other. Kevin had never had one of them in his wallet, but he knew a two-hundred-euro note when he saw it.

His throat turned desert-dry, his moment of abject fright beaten into stunned silence. The packet in his hand had to be at least five, perhaps as many as ten thousand euros in used currency. Once again, he peeked into gap made by the open zipper and saw dozens more identical packets sandwiched between a set of corrugated plastic baffles.

It was more money in one single place than Kevin had ever seen in his life.

# NINE

The hissing in Kevin's ears was so loud he thought it might deafen him.

He swallowed hard, and as it abated he realised that it was the noise of blood rushing in his veins. His face turned hot and even though he had sat back down on the toilet, he felt light-headed, the floor moving like the deck of a ship in a storm swell.

In one hand he clutched the wad of money, a part of him still trying to square what he was experiencing with what was right in front of him.

It was hard to keep his thoughts on track. Each time he took a breath and tried to consider things rationally, he began to spiral. Competing impulses pulled him this way and that.

He wanted to *run*.

Jam the cash back into the bag and get out of the airport as fast as was humanly possible, *Oh god no*, in case whomever this belonged to came after him.

He wanted to *take*.

Plunder the bag and stuff as much of the contents as possible into his pockets, and *Why the fuck not?* To hell with whoever lost it!

He wanted to *hide*.

Fade away and crawl into some shadowed corner of the airport, *Please don't let me be seen*, and wait out the hours until this became a distant memory.

*Is this really happening?*

Kevin's breath came in panting gasps and it took a physical effort on his part to quiet his racing mind. Slowly and surely, he found his way back to something approximating calm.

As the mental dust settled, one question came to the fore. 'Where has this come from?' he wondered aloud and stood up on tiptoe, enough to look over the top of the stall door and make sure he was still alone. There was no movement in the washroom, and he sank back, weighing the money in his hand.

Kevin vaguely remembered a news story about a briefcase full of US dollars discovered in a South American airport's lounge by someone who had suspected it was a bomb. The police had later pieced together the truth, tracking down a courier working for a local cartel who had panicked and dumped their delivery after spotting what appeared to be Drug Enforcement Agency officers staking out the departure gate.

Was the same thing taking place here? It didn't seem real, but the evidence was right here in his hands. Kevin did the mental arithmetic and tallied up the potential total for the money in the black bag, assuming each wad was comparable to the pack of two-hundreds.

*At least a million and a half euros? Or more?* He sucked in a shaky breath.

'Fucking hell.' His voice echoed in the quiet. 'That's a lot of money.' Enough to alter the course of someone's life forever, it only they could get away with it. Enough that someone would notice if it was gone, someone who wanted their cash unseen, someone *criminal*. People had been killed for a lot less, he reflected.

*Put it back*, said Sadie's voice, *before you get yourself murdered, idiot*.

But if he did that, if he walked away . . . What would happen? Kevin had already tampered with the bag and the panel, and the dust would be impossible to clean up. How many places on the walls and the door handles had he touched and left fingerprints, not only in the stall but out in the washroom? He couldn't hope to conceal every single trace of his presence.

His stomach flipped over. Someone would be looking for this money. Maybe it was stolen. Maybe there was a reward for recovering it.

The glimmering of a decision started to form. What if he did the *right thing*? Not ignore it or run and hide, but bring it to the attention of people who could do something about it? That would be the proper thing to do . . . That would be what a good man would do, and Kevin Tyler wanted to believe that he *was* a good man.

The washroom door thudded open and two people entered, in the middle of a joking conversation. Kevin froze, waiting for one of them to hammer on the stall or kick it down to reveal some gun-thug intent on silencing him before he could report his discovery.

But nothing like that happened, and presently, after taking a piss and washing their hands, the arrivals departed again.

Kevin took deep breaths of the sour air to steady his nerves, and then put the panel back in to place over the black bag. The wad of money went into his inside jacket pocket and he cleaned himself up at the sink, splashing water on his face. Then, as an afterthought, he peeled the out-of-order sign off the neighbouring stall and stuck it to the door of the one he had just left.

He followed a group of young women as they left the adjoining female washrooms, keeping his head down and using them as cover as they meandered back out into the terminal proper.

*Keep moving*, he told himself, *keep walking*. Kevin felt hyper-aware of everything around him, as if the sensory input he'd largely ignored before was coming at him all at once. The voices of the laughing women sounded too loud and falsely strident. The cries of a fatigued, wailing child were like nails down a blackboard. The chimes and the babble of the flight announcements droned around and around, repeating and repeating.

Everything felt fake. Kevin had the sudden notion that he was walking through a movie set, the one and only actor who had no idea that he was playing a part.

He imagined himself as the hapless mark in the middle of some complex confidence trick beyond his ability to grasp, filmed for the delight of a guffawing studio audience. Kevin had watched enough local television in bland hotel rooms over the past months to know that in spite the dour stereotypes wrongly associated with the Germans, they absolutely adored a bit of low-brow comedy and would be only too happy to make fun of some down-in-the-mouth Brit.

He glanced around. No camera crews. No chuckling comedians. No joking.

What he did see was a figure turned away from him across the way, a broad man in a peaked cap and a black stab-vest with POLIZEI written across the shoulders.

As Kevin drew nearer, he saw that the police officer had a holstered pistol at his side, plus a radio and all the gear the real deal would carry. The policeman was giving an older couple directions to one of the departure gates – the same pair who had tutted and clucked when Kevin had cursed out loud at the taxi drop-off. They saw him coming and made the same judgemental faces, thanking the policeman as they walked away. The cop's task finished, he sensed Kevin's approach and turned towards him.

Kevin reached into his jacket, fingers touching the wad of money, mentally rehearsing what he was going to say.

*Officer, I saw something. Officer, I came across this in the toilet. Officer, there's something here you should see.*

'Oh. You again.' He was the stocky cop from the security line – Alfons, the one who had put Kevin on the spot with his bags and made him feel like a criminal. 'Has something blown up?' His terse manner suggested that he was not in a charitable mood.

Kevin's hand dropped away, and he lost his momentum. 'Wh-what do you mean?'

'Your luggage,' said Alfons, aiming a finger at the bag hanging off Kevin's shoulder. 'It hasn't gone *ka-boom*, I see. Very good. Please keep it that way.'

'Oh, right. Yes. I mean no.' Kevin's cheeks reddened again. Whatever he had meant to say or intended to do, he lost his grip on it, the words like sand falling through his fingers.

'You have missed your flight,' noted the policeman, without a hint of sympathy. 'Oh dear. *Wie schade.*'

'I, uh, um . . .' Kevin scowled, frustrated by his inability to get the words out. 'Can you, uh, help, I mean . . .'

Alfons gave him a narrow-eyed look. 'Perhaps you have mistaken me for a travel agent? Is it the cap?' His flat delivery did not mask his sarcasm. 'It is not my job to assist people who are late for their flights, that is your responsibility, sir. Take it up with your countrymen.' The policeman jerked his thumb in the direction of an empty KnightSky Air ticket desk.

'I wasn't late,' insisted Kevin, 'It wasn't my fault, that's not the problem—'

'Of course,' Alfons said over him. 'It never is. And yet it has been my experience that British travellers expect special treatment, even now.' He shook his head. 'I have dealt with more than enough of you today and I am afraid my tolerance is spent.' Kevin remembered the loutish pack of football fans from the security line, and realised that Alfons had lumped him in with them. 'You leave the club but you still expect the benefits, *ja*? *Nein.*'

'Wait.' Kevin held up a hand, once again wrong-footed by the police officer's manner. The last thing he expected was to be drawn into a lecture on the British government's decision to pull the country out of the European Union. 'That's not . . . I mean, I didn't vote for—'

'Strange how you all say that when you need something from us,' said Alfons, and he started to turn away.

'Officer . . .' Kevin reached out to grab the other man's arm before he could leave.

Alfons moved quicker than Kevin would have expected from a man his size, grabbing his wrist and twisting it, sending a jolt of pain up to his elbow. 'It is a foolish idea to put your hands on a police officer, do you understand?'

'Yes! Yes! *Ow!*' Kevin nodded briskly. 'I'm sorry! Please let go?'

Alfons released him and muttered something in German that Kevin didn't understand, but the meaning was clear. 'Unless you have something to confess, I suggest you find someone better suited to assist you,' he added in English.

The wad of money in Kevin's pocket felt like a brick of lead and he gulped in a breath of air, trying once again to reframe his words. Whatever intentions he had to come clean to the policeman now seemed no better than the worst of his choices. His gaze slipped to the heavy steel handcuffs on the policeman's belt, and he pictured himself manacled with them, being dragged across the terminal as he protested his innocence. Alfons glowered at him, and it was obvious that the man was unlikely to take anything he said on trust.

What Kevin heard himself say next was: 'My mistake. Sorry to bother you.'

\*

He dragged the carry-on behind him, walking without conscious direction up one wing of the terminal and then back along the other.

More and more of the departure gates were closing up, turning silent as the last aircraft out of Barsbeker made desperate runs to get out from under the storm. Monitor screens showing flight numbers and destinations dimmed. The elevated jet bridges were closed off, becoming dark corridors to nowhere, suspended up over the rain-lashed asphalt apron below. Distant lightning flashed, backlighting grey cloud the colour of oil-soaked wool, followed moments later by a sonorous grumble of thunder.

Kevin pulled the wheeled case on its aimless journey, the ticking of the plastic rollers becoming a metronome for the whole pointless endeavour. He was going nowhere, doing nothing, in danger of spiralling again.

When he reached the gate for the flight that had left him behind, he stopped and drew in a deep breath. He could feel the banknotes pressing into his chest, like the weight of guilt made real.

*But what do I have to feel guilty about?* The angry thought burned at the back of his skull, gathering there with the potency of a tension headache. *I'm not a criminal. Why the hell should I have to feel like I am?*

The money made the lie of that, though. He'd stolen something from something stolen – most likely – and one act didn't miraculously invert the morality of the other.

Truth be told, Kevin had done a few shady things in his past, but nothing on this scale, nothing that had ever been better than petty rule-breaking.

*How do I even know if it's real?* The question rose in his thoughts, pushing everything else aside. *Oh, shit, what if that cash is fake? How could you tell?*

An idea occurred to him, and his pulse raced. Kevin glanced across the way to where the Kaffee Tek coffee bar sat in its alcove. He could see Richie in the back, placing plastic jugs of milk in the tall refrigerator behind the barista machine. Blinds were already down over the displays of snacks and sandwiches. The server was starting the work of shutting up for the night.

Kevin rushed over, as quickly as he could without making it look obvious, and leaned on the counter, looking around behind the cash register and the credit card reader bolted to the worktop.

Richie reappeared from the back of the alcove, and Kevin glimpsed a dingy storeroom and a nondescript corridor beyond, stretching off into the backstage reaches of the terminal.

'Hey, mate,' he called, and Richie frowned at him.

'You still here?' Richie put down the box he carried and wandered over. 'Ah, man, I thought you'd already gone.' He made a flying motion with his hand. 'What happened?'

'They bumped me off the flight,' Kevin said bitterly. 'Overbooked. Gave my seat to some wanker with a loyalty card.'

'Shit, no?' Richie shook his head. 'But they gotta put you up for the night though, right? I mean, that capsule hotel thing they got here is weird, but at least you get a bed . . .'

'Full up,' said Kevin, and nodded in the direction of the empty departure lounge. 'I'm sleeping there tonight.'

Another lightning flash, this one much closer than the last, lit up the sky. The thunder chased it, the low rattle humming through the window glass.

'I hope you brought earplugs,' Richie said gravely. 'Ah, mate, that fucking sucks.' He paused. 'Look, I'm shutting up, but if you need a sandwich and a bottle of water or something—'

Kevin saw his opportunity and seized on it. 'I do,' he snapped. 'Yeah, I'm starving. Can you get me, uh, a couple of Ham and Swiss? And one of them cold coffee things?' In truth, Kevin hated the taste of the chilled coffee-in-a-can drinks, but he knew that Richie would have to go to the back to bring one to him.

'Sure. Give us a sec.' Richie stepped around the box and disappeared through the door to the storeroom.

Kevin had already peeled open the wrapping around the cash, and the moment Richie was out of sight, he pulled a note from the wad and leaned across the counter to snatch up a device sitting next to the register.

An ultraviolet lamp in a frame, the counterfeit currency detector activated by pressing a note on the pad at the base. The glow from the bulb would illuminate the UV ink on a genuine bill, showing up patterns normally invisible to the naked eye, and a handy information panel on the top of the detector told Kevin exactly what to look for in a fake. He had to half-climb over the coffee bar's counter in order to see clearly, but once he slid the money into place, the surface of the plastic note bloomed with orange stars in the shape of the European flag. He could see the hologram watermark as clear as day, and the metal thread bisecting the bill.

*It's real.* And that meant that the rest of the money in the bag was probably authentic as well. *A million or two of actual hard currency, sitting back there, waiting to be taken.*

'What the fuck are you doing?'

Kevin jerked away, dropping the detector, slipping back over the counter with the note scrunched up in his palm. Richie was standing right behind him, and he'd been so intent on the money he hadn't heard him return. 'Sorry, sorry, I, uh . . .'

Richie's expression turned cross and he swept a hard look around the register. 'You can't reach back here and fuck about, that's out of order. You trying to get into the till?'

'No. *No!*' Kevin held up the euro note. 'I have money right here. I wasn't trying to nick anything, I swear!'

To his surprise, Richie plucked the note out of his fingers. 'Well, you can pay for this then, can't you?' He dumped two pre-made sandwiches, two bottles of still water and a can of cold Arabica coffee on the counter, and proceeded to ring up the cost. Looking at the note, he frowned. 'Got anything smaller?'

'Yes!' Kevin took back the big bill and covered the cost with a twenty instead.

Richie handed over his change and folded his arms. 'I know we banter and shit, me and you, but you crossed a line, yeah?'

As Kevin swept his purchases into his shoulder bag, Richie drew an invisible barrier across the middle of the countertop with one finger. 'My side. Your side.'

'You're right, I took advantage.' Kevin nodded jerkily, and by way of apology he dumped his change into a nearby tip jar. 'I just found this, uh, on the floor.' He held up the two-hundred-euro note. 'My lucky day, right? I wanted to make sure it wasn't a fake.'

'You could have asked me to check it.'

'Yeah.' Kevin frowned. 'Didn't think. Sorry. It's just ...' He took a breath, and before he could stop it, a floodgate opened. 'This is the worst fucking day of my life, and I feel like I'm drowning in it.' Richie's expression shifted, annoyance giving way to confusion, but Kevin was already talking and the words started to gush out of him. 'You've seen me week in and week out flying into this place, working all bloody hours to try and get my deal, this fantastic deal, up and running. We were going to build a factory down the road from here, make bottles, recycled bottles out of paper, it was going to pay off, jobs for people and money in the bank ...'

'I don't ...' Richie was lost for words, uncomfortable with this unexpected tide of oversharing. But Kevin didn't let up.

'And I *need* it, man, I really need the money because I put everything I own into this deal, and ...' The words soured in his mouth, turning to ash. 'And it's gone. The whole thing. Today we were going to sign the contracts and get the green light ... And they pulled out at the last second. No explanation. No comeback. *Nothing.*'

It was the first time he had actually spoken the words out loud, and as he did, Kevin felt the horrible reality of the truth finally crystallise around him. Now he had said it, he had made it real. He couldn't hide from it or look away any more. The monstrosity of this fiasco, the ruin of it, was inescapable.

'Ah, mate,' said Richie, doing his limited, awkward best to offer some compassion. 'That's harsh.'

'I don't know what to do.' Kevin's voice echoed back to him as if coming from far away, and that hissing in his ears came rising once again. 'I don't . . .'

'Phone.'

'What?'

'Your phone,' repeated Richie. 'It's ringing.'

Numbly, Kevin reached into his jacket pocket and discovered his smartphone trilling away. In that moment, he had been so far inside his own bleak thoughts that he hadn't noticed.

The message on the screen of the smartphone read MADDIE CALLING, with the smiling face of his daughter displayed inside a glowing circle. On any other day, that smile could have lit up his world, but tonight it made Kevin sick with worry.

'Probably should answer it,' said Richie, as he went back to closing up.

# TEN

'Hot water's out again!' Andrea shouted over the hissing gurgle of the shower, her voice carrying along the hallway of the tiny apartment from the bathroom to the kitchen-dining space.

'I know,' Maddie called back, but her girlfriend didn't hear her over the rush of the water. She cradled her phone in her hand as she wandered to the threadbare beanbag at the window and dropped into it.

The phone screen read CALLING: POP and a cute animation of a cartoonish rotary phone emitted comical notes of music. Passing the third and fourth rings now, and her father still hadn't picked up. After no reply to her texts, she nursed a low-level worry that threatened to build into something more serious. Maddie knew this was the big day for the Luna Designs deal in Germany, but by now it should have been done and dusted.

Warm, late-afternoon sunshine spilled through the apartment's window, reaching in past the legion of potted plants Andrea had set up along the bright blue fire escape outside, which meant it had to be something like early evening over in Europe. She sighed, glancing out into the street.

Light traffic moved along Avenue B, a train of vehicles running south out of Alphabet City to the Lower East Side, and as she watched, a NYPD patrol car bolted past on the intersection with East 3$^{rd}$ Street, lights and sirens on full blast as it sped in the direction of the river.

Despite herself, Maddie smiled a little. The surroundings might have been cramped, cheap – and to be honest, not as clean as she might have liked – but the novelty of living in New York City was still as fresh and exciting to her as it had been the day she got off the plane at JFK. Andrea didn't get it, of course. Born across the East River in Queens, none of this was special to her, but Madeline Tyler had grown up in the monotonous, leafy suburbs of Essex on the outskirts of London, and to her the Big Apple was a magical place, even at its dingiest.

'No hot water.' Andrea padded into the room, swaddled in an oversized dressing gown, her jet-black hair still soaking wet and plastered to the back of her head. 'Second time this month.'

'I heard you.'

'You gotta talk to Hiram,' she continued, tapping her bare foot on the floor to indicate the presence of their landlord down below. The aging businessman and his wife owned the building and operated the mom 'n' pop deli-grocery at street level. While they were pleasant enough, they cut corners on the maintenance for their tenants. 'I can't do it,' Andrea noted. 'He's intimidated by me.'

'I can't imagine why,' Maddie said dryly, looking her up and down.

Andrea Bright – or *Bright the Fight* as her promoter liked to bill her – had made a decent go as a mixed martial artist in the bantamweight class, and there was a good chance she might go pro if things broke her way. Short but not tiny, she was toned muscle and sly smiles, the latter being the thing that first caught Maddie's eye about her. Later, she'd glimpsed the big heart inside that athlete's frame and fallen for the other woman.

'He thinks your accent makes you fancy,' Andrea noted. 'Like you're some kinda duchess or something.'

'I *am* a fancy duchess,' Maddie insisted, in her very best English Rose accent. They were the same age, but a study in contrasts. Against Andrea, she was taller, thinner, and she liked to joke that she had a ballet dancer's build, but the closest she had ever been to a *plié* was her dad reading her *Angelina Ballerina* bedtime stories as a child. Her smile levelled out into a frown again and she stared at the phone.

*Still ringing. Still no pick up.*

Andrea craned over to look at the phone in Maddie's hand, carelessly dripping water over her. When she saw who her girlfriend was calling, her expression hardened. 'Oh.'

'He didn't text back, so I thought I'd call him.' Maddie felt compelled to explain.

'Right.' The fewer words Andrea used in a sentence, the clearer it became that she was pissed off about something. Andrea's relationship with her own father was not a good one, and that simmering resentment always bubbled to the surface whenever Maddie brought up the subject of her dad.

'I wanted to check,' she added, as a thought occurred. 'Maybe his phone was switched off before.'

'Maybe.' In one word, Andrea made it clear how little stock she put in Kevin Tyler's reliability. She hadn't forgiven him for putting both feet in his mouth on the day that Maddie had come out to her mother and father, caught in the echo of her own experience with her family.

Andrea's own coming out was a sore point, to the degree that she hadn't spoken to her parents or her siblings in a long time. She often said that when Maddie came into her life, she had rescued her from loneliness, and that expressed itself over and over in her firmly protective manner towards her girlfriend.

'I'll try again later . . .' Maddie reached out to tap the END CALL tab.

'Forget him,' Andrea began, but before she could go on and before Maddie could hang up, the phone screen flickered and the line finally connected.

'*Hello? Mads?*' Kevin Tyler's tinny, faraway voice issued out. '*You there? Sorry. Didn't hear it ringing.*'

'Sure,' muttered Andrea, and she stalked away, grabbing another towel to vigorously dry off her hair.

'Hey, Pop,' said Maddie, relief pushing back her worry. 'How are you?'

'*Oh, so busy,*' he said, with a weak chuckle. '*Sorry I didn't message you. It's just . . . Everything's a bit manic.*'

In the background, she could hear the chimes of a public address system and a voice speaking German. 'Where are you?'

'*The airport.*' Then he corrected himself. '*Well, uh, just here to, uh, sort out some stuff.*'

'I thought you were going to be over there for a week.' Maddie's frown deepened. Her dad was being evasive, and that did not bode well.

'*Yeah,*' he said lamely, '*Plans change. But everything's fine though, don't fret.*' He paused. '*I know you. You worry about your mum and dad too much.*'

*Way Too Much* mouthed Andrea, nodding her head. She mimed a throat-cutting motion and gestured at the phone.

Maddie waved her away. 'As long as you're OK.'

'*Of course I am.*'

*Is that really true?* Maddie's gaze drifted to the window, out above the buildings and into the middle distance of blue sky and white clouds.

She tried to find the right words to cut through the banalities and go straight to what mattered, tried and came up empty. Something was amiss, but if she said that directly, her dad would get defensive, he would clam up and fumble out some excuse.

Whenever something wasn't right, her father's reaction was always the same – to keep it from her, his first instinct to try to protect her from the worst of the world. And while she loved him for that, she hated it too. Madeline Tyler was a smart young woman, not a child, and she didn't need him to shelter her. But she couldn't find the right way to tell him that with making it sound like a rejection.

From out of nowhere, a two-tone warble cut across the line, and Maddie heard her father curse under his breath. '*Now? Are you bloody joking . . . ?*'

She recognised the noise, her dad's phone warning him that someone else was trying to call him at the same time.

'What is it?'

'*I'm sorry, love. It's Colin. He's trying to get through to me.*'

'Right.' Without realising, she echoed Andrea, knowing what that meant. Colin Fish was her father's business partner, and work always came first with him.

'*I have to take this,*' he told her. '*I'll call you back as soon as I can. Love you.*'

'Love you,' she repeated, but the line disconnected before she got the words out.

Andrea balled up her towel and dropped it on the table with a deliberate *thud*. 'I smell bullshit.'

Maddie shot her a stern look, her sudden irritation finding something to vent at. 'Don't start.'

'Start what?' Andrea cocked her head. 'A *conversation?* Because you need to learn how to have one.' She made a sharp *tsk* sound. 'I know, like, British people are supposed to be reserved and all that shit, but can you ever actually say what you mean?'

'No, because unlike Americans, we actually have something called *tact!*' Maddie threw out the retort, and then immediately regretted it. 'Sorry. I didn't mean that.'

'Yes you did.' Andrea's tone softened and she came over, settling on to the beanbag with her, leaning into Maddie's shoulder. 'See? You *can* speak plainly when you want to.' She sighed. 'You and your dad do *not* know how to communicate. And believe me, I know how that goes.'

'You're not wrong,' admitted Maddie. 'Every time we talk on the phone, it feels so . . . So fake.'

'He cares about you,' Andrea said after a long moment, grudgingly conceding the fact. 'He needs to get out of his own way about it. Hell, you both do.'

'I think something's wrong.' Maddie met her girlfriend's gaze.

Andrea nodded again. 'You could be right. But until he gets to telling you about it, there's nothing you can do from this side of the Atlantic.' She leaned in and gently kissed her. 'It'll be OK. I got you, duchess.'

Kevin dragged himself back to the empty departure gate and sat heavily on one of the empty seats, leaning into the phone as he pressed it to his ear.

Switching out from Maddie's call to the incoming one from Colin Fish's phone, at first Kevin thought he had pressed the wrong tab and was listening to a voicemail message.

'*Hey Kev-oh, all right?*' said Colin, his tone heavy with the breathy, serious voice he always put on to show he was 'concerned'. The Welshman's accent softened to make it sound friendlier, but Kevin had seen him use that ploy before, whenever he tried to get something out of someone. '*You'll probably get this when you land, sorry I must have just missed you . . .*'

Colin was good at that, projecting a cordiality that sneaked past people's innate distrust, and it was a large part of his business strategy. He and Kevin had struck up a friendship at a dull-as-ditchwater networking event in Coventry a few years earlier, and that had led to their partnership and the founding of Luna Designs.

A few years Kevin's senior, Colin was overweight but not slow with it, never seen without a suit and tie, and always smiling. He remembered everyone's name and birthday, and always bought flowers to brighten up the office.

Underneath he was a shark, of course, but most people never saw more than a glimpse of that side of him.

Kevin caught up to what was happening. Colin had dialled his phone, expecting to leave a message, unaware that Kevin had been bumped off his flight and actually answered the call.

'I'm right here, Colin.'

'*What?*' Colin's shock was palpable. '*You're there? Oh, right . . . Uh, I didn't expect that . . .*' He could almost hear the other man mentally regrouping, rapidly changing gears to deal with this unexpected new wrinkle. '*Don't they make you turn off your phone on the plane?*'

'I'm not *on* the plane,' he said flatly.

'*But it just took off . . .*' Colin's voice faded as he held his handset away from his face for a moment, as if his attention was on something else.

*I bet he's looking the airport website. The departures screen.* That would have shown the details of when KnightSky Air flight 404 left Barsbeker, and there was no way Colin wouldn't have

120

known the facts of the journey. It was the job of their shared secretary Janet to arrange such details.

'The flight was overbooked, as if enough crap hasn't happened to me today. It doesn't matter.'

'*Ah.*' Colin grunted and made a quick attempt at levity. '*Never rains but it pours, Kev-oh!*' There was an odd echo under his voice that added distance to his words.

'Are you in the office?'

'*Oh, no.*' Colin sighed. '*Out and about, you know me! Gave Janet and the team the rest of the week off, eh? To, ah,* regroup.'

Kevin tried to fathom out what that was supposed to mean. 'Hang on a second, I need to top up my battery.' He pulled a plug and cable from a pocket in his shoulder bag and connected the phone to a power socket by the side of the chair. That done, he blew out a breath and tried to gather his thoughts.

He felt a stab of guilt as he realised that he hadn't begun to consider how the collapse of the German deal would affect their handful of employees at Luna's small UK factory. 'Have you told Janet and the others?'

'*Best to hold fire on that until Monday, I thought,*' said Colin. '*No sense giving people something to fret about over the weekend, get the cards on the table first.*'

Kevin leaned into his hand, trying and failing to rub the fatigue from his face. 'I did my best, Colin. I was ready to go! But then I walk into Montag's office and he gave me that hard-eyed look and said, *Nein, Herr Tyler.* Tossed back the contract, red lines through the signatures. Null and void.'

'*Bloody Krauts, eh?*' Colin gave a sniff. '*Always sticking the boot in.*'

Hugo Montag, the stiff and eternally purse-lipped scion of the Montag clan, had been the point man for his family's dealings with Kevin and Luna Designs from the start. The plan had been for the Montags to lease a parcel of the land they owned in the Rendsburg-Eckernförde area as the site of Luna's first European mini-plant, on top of making a substantial investment in the factory itself.

The Montags wanted to finance a green initiative, and Luna's recycled bottles were the perfect project, embraced not only by the local economy but also by progressive elements of the German government. Working in tandem with the UK factory, sharing knowledge, the project would bridge the divide caused by numerous Brexit deregulations and secure the fortunes of the company – and its investors – for years to come.

Not to mention doing some good for the environment by cutting down on the monstrous amounts of disposable plastics going into the ecosystem. Luna's biodegradable, Earth-friendly bottles had the potential to be a true game changer for the industry.

But Hugo Montag's prim good humour had been absent this morning. The deal was off, he said, each word of his dictionary-perfect English delivered with hard emphasis. According to him, the Montags had re-examined their liabilities in the deal at the eleventh hour and elected to drop out of the bottle-making endeavour for something altogether more conventional, in partnership with a German company.

'*Zett Holdings*,' explained Colin, '*I looked them up. They're going to put up a bloody textile plant, bloody sweatshop making cheap t-shirts or some such rubbish!*'

'I know, I know.' Kevin had done the same thing on learning the details, furiously Googling whatever he could find about Zett and the man who owned it. 'I don't get it. We made them a good offer. Money in the bank.'

But it made no difference. The Montags had made up their mind, and nothing would change it. Months of preparation from Kevin and the staff at Luna, months of pushing their coffers to the limit just to stay in the running, and now it was over and all he had to show was empty pockets.

'Montag wouldn't explain. He showed me the door. Can you believe it? He even had security there to escort me out, in case I got mardy about it.'

'Yeah . . .' Colin drew out the word. '*But what's done is done. Look, you know me, I hate to be the bearer of bad news . . .*'

'What the fuck now?' Kevin asked, without heat.

Colin chuckled nervously. '*Didn't reckon I'd have to say this, but uh, here it is, like. Turns out, the Montag family didn't keep their new partnership with Zett to themselves, see. Some of our other investors heard about the deal falling through and, ah, pulled their funding.*'

Kevin slumped back in the chair. He felt light-headed, as if the room was moving around him. 'Some?'

'*Well, actually, the lot of them.*'

'Oh, shit.'

'*Yes, shit indeed.*' Colin sighed again. '*And that impacts our operating capital. And by* impacts, *I mean, it wipes it out.*'

'We're done,' Kevin said, in a dead voice, as the reality settled on him. 'This was our one shot to stay afloat. What are we going to do? We're bankrupt!'

'*About the size of it, yes.*' Colin sucked in a breath. '*I hope you understand that I had to consider my own circumstances here.*'

'Yeah ... ' With everything swirling around him, it took Kevin a moment to register what the other man had said. 'Wait, what?'

'*Luna Designs is a dead man walking now, isn't it? So I've cashed out too.*'

'You bastard!' The blood-rush rumble came rising in Kevin's ears. 'You're leaving me to carry the can?'

'*Well, it was you or me, wasn't it? And let's be honest here. You were always the ideas man, the techie bloke, weren't you? All the engineering and that. Me, I'm the money bloke. And money walks, I'm afraid.*' Colin's falsely breezy tone made it sound so genial.

Anger crackled down Kevin's nerves in an electric surge. 'You gutless arsehole! You were going leave me a bloody voice message, you waited until now because you thought my phone would be off!' His voice rose, attracting the attention of the few travellers still moving through the terminal. But he didn't care. He felt the pendulum in him swinging back and forth between abject fury and desolate hopelessness.

'*That's true,*' admitted Colin. '*You know I don't like confrontations. But there's no friends in business. It's not personal.*'

'Go fuck yourself,' he shot back.

'*I can tell you're not taking this well,*' said the other man. '*I'll have my lawyer sent the appropriate paperwork around, all right? Best of luck to you.*'

The line went dead and Kevin's fingers tightened around the rectangular tile of his smartphone, knuckles turning white as he gripped it harder and harder, until the cheap anti-scratch shell around the casing gave off a cracking sound. A jagged sliver of broken plastic jabbed him in the meat of his palm and he let the phone drop.

Hands shaking, he pulled the plastic shard out of the shallow cut it had made and held a paper tissue to the wound before he started bleeding on the upholstery.

Now he was on the wrong side of it, Kevin had the sudden clarity of knowing that Colin Fish's betrayal had been an inevitability. *Fish the Shark*, he had once said jokingly, and in that moment the other man had given him a look that was pure animosity. Now Kevin wondered if the work Colin had directed him to do on the bottle design had been a deliberate ploy to keep him clear of Luna's money flow.

He had no idea of where he would even start without Colin's acumen to back him up. The other man was right; he *was* the ideas man, it was the reason he had been fronting the German deal, because his enthusiasm for the work was what had hooked the interest of the Montags in the first place.

On his own, cast adrift, Kevin could only see ruin. The collapse of the deal became the first falling domino, crashing into the next and the next, and every shitty thing that had befallen him today. Contaminated by his failure, radioactive with it, whatever he touched became toxic by association.

The bleak pit in his gut widened. His life was falling apart. He was going to lose his home. He was going to lose his company. He was going to lose *everything*.

Kevin drew his arms tight around himself and smothered a gasp that might have turned into a sob if had let it. His grip pulled tight and he closed his eyes.

And then he felt the pressure of a brick-shaped packet stuffed inside his jacket, remembering what was in it, and where there was more.

# ELEVEN

The rain kept up its assault on the terminal building's windows, the wind from the Baltic whipping it up into bursts that clattered against the panes with a sound like handfuls of gravel hitting the glass.

Alfons sighed manfully at the foul weather and decided not to bother calling his wife. Yuta would be in bed by now – she liked to turn in early as the winter months came on – and dragging her to the phone just to say he would be home late was pointless. He made such a habit of overtime and extra shifts, he doubted she would even notice his absence. The two of them had slipped into a comfortable sort of oblivion in recent years, more cohabiting the house than living in it as husband and wife. At some point, their lives had diverged from being a shared experience to something they lived in parallel with each other.

It sounded sad when he thought of it that way. But he didn't mind, and if Yuta did, she didn't make it clear.

*Would I even notice if she was unhappy?* Alfons dismissed the thought before it could take root. He was here, he was at work, and that was where his focus was meant to be.

Patrolling the terminal, he paused to admonish a child attempting to climb up one of the departure monitors and then turned his stern rebuke on the parent, a shrill woman with the look of a Berliner who dared to talk back to him. Alfons moved on, constantly scanning the mass of people moving through the airport, scrutinising them over the top of his spectacles with a peevish air.

The numbers were thinning out now, as Barsbeker reached the end of its flying schedule. It was Alfons's favourite time of the day, this and the moments after dawn, when the airport was almost empty, echoing with the promise of new places and new adventures. He liked the potential in that, even if he had never been one to travel, never really ventured outside of Schleswig-Holstein. He had lived in this part of the country since birth and never felt the urge to go elsewhere.

Berend Alfons was what that Berliner woman would call a 'small-town' man, loading up the comment with every negative parochial stereotype. But even if he was limited in one plane, he was wide-ranging in others. Alfons had an eye for people, most especially for their failings and their quirks, and it made others uncomfortable around him. A good talent for a policeman to have, some might say, but as he had learned too late in life, not one for a policeman who wanted to play politics and rise in the ranks.

He trudged on, following a meandering route. In these moments, the terminal reminded Alfons of a model building in the glass case of a museum. A perfect simulacrum of the real thing in miniature, empty of life, frozen in time. As a boy, he had spent hours staring into such replicas, picturing a tiny version of himself wandering those fake halls. Now he was the museum piece, if his fellow officers were to be believed, gradually gaining layers of dust.

A bright splash of neon-bright international orange flickered at the corner of his vision, and Alfons turned to put his full attention on a brown-haired man in the high-visibility vest of an airport ground worker, as he emerged from a staff-only door. He recognised the other man immediately: Horst was the son of someone Alfons had known at school, in his opinion a no-account type from a family of no-account types.

He watched Horst make a meal of looking around, and Alfons slipped out of sight behind a support pillar so he wouldn't be spotted. Eventually, Horst moved on, dragging a hand through his rain-wet hair and slouching away down the terminal.

The nagging sense of wrongness that Alfons had learned not to ignore pulled on him, like an annoying child tugging at the hem of his trousers. He pushed his glasses up his nose with a middle finger and made a sour face, musing. Horst had no business being around the public-facing part of the terminal building, his work was outside in the elements, and even the fact of the filthy weather didn't excuse him being there.

Barsbeker's management didn't like the vest-wearing types milling around where the passengers could see them, they preferred to keep them down on the lower levels or out on the tarmac. The indoor airport staff were kept better dressed, their clothes designed to mimic the smooth lines of flight attendant uniforms. Alfons wondered what would make Horst risk chastisement from his supervisor, and he decided to find out.

Alfons took a short cut so he would arrive in front of Horst as he passed the main departures board. He made it look unhurried, but the other man still saw him coming, and it was obvious as he slowed his pace.

'Horst,' began Alfons, with a nod of greeting. 'Late shift again?' He casually stepped into a position where the younger man couldn't easily walk by.

The nod was reflected back at him. 'Yes. Pay's good, right?'

'Is it?' Alfons tugged on the unnecessary admission. That was the thing about being police, the aura effect of the cap and the uniform. It made people talk, more than they intended to, and when people talked they told the truth. Even when they thought they were lying. 'I suppose it would have to be,' he said, gesturing at the rain outside. 'To work in that, eh?'

'Yes,' Horst repeated, becoming wary.

'Is your father well?' Alfons attempted a smile, trying to keep the momentum going.

'He said I shouldn't talk to you,' said the other man. 'Not even if you arrest me.'

Alfons chuckled. 'Why not?'

Horst gestured at Alfons's uniform by way of a reply. Then he frowned. 'Did you want something? Because I have a job to do.'

'Oh? What sort of thing?'

'Just ... A job.' Horst was smart enough not to supply any more information than he already had, and he knew that Alfons couldn't hold him up unless he had good cause. A sly smile pulled at the corner of the other man's mouth. 'You got a problem, take it up with my boss, yeah?'

Tellingly, Horst said *boss* and not *supervisor*. Horst's supervisor was a plump woman from Kiel who talked incessantly and always wanted to show off photos of her ugly grandchildren. His boss, though, was another matter.

Alfons knew the rumours that lurked beneath the surface of the work-side chatter, the stories about people engaged in the kind of petty crime and less-than-legal jobs that always orbited places like airports. The informal rule was that if it didn't inconvenience the passengers and it didn't mess with the planes, most minor infractions would go ignored. Frankly, the police and security assigned to Barsbeker were thin enough on the ground that they didn't have the manpower to deal with anything that wasn't a serious issue.

But there was another layer of rumours, one you would only find if you looked for it. Those stories hinted at darker truths, like certain men with influence who liked to go unnoticed while they plied their trade and gave bribes to idiots like Horst. Men who would stay out of the way and make life easy if you understood the way things worked; who would make you and your whole family disappear if you did not.

Horst must have seen the hesitation, the calculation in Alfons's expression, because then the power dynamic of the conversation flipped, and it was the policeman who unconsciously stepped aside to let the other man walk on.

Of course, young Horst could have been bullshitting the older cop, but that would have required a level of intelligence Alfons was sure he didn't possess.

Alfons thought about Yuta, asleep in their bed, and how much he cared about his wife, separate lives or not. It was too much to endanger her, even on an outside possibility.

He watched Horst disappear around a corner, and after a while, he convinced himself that there were more significant matters to occupy his time. Troublemaker tourists, militants and illegals, those were prey he could get to grips with, those were quantities he was expected to address.

Alfons turned away and carried on.


A choice could seem like an impassable mountain, a towering mass that you couldn't get past.

Then there were the other decisions that, once made, became obvious in retrospect. Some choices were really an open door that you were already halfway through, if only you could see them clearly.

This was the mantra turning around and around in Kevin Tyler's mind as he walked swiftly, back to the men's washroom on the main concourse. The energy that animated him was mostly anger and resentment, the dark bile of those negative emotions turned into the fuel he would need to propel him through the next few minutes.

The querulous voice in the back of his thoughts that warned him off was being drowned out by the drumbeat of his annoyance. What he was about to do was a gamble, a big one, but if he let the opportunity pass, then what would he be going home to?

Misery and ruin? An empty house and an empty life?

Every hour of this day had been one more punch in the face. Everything from the collapse of the deal down to the fact that the wheels on his stupid bloody case kept catching on the flooring, everything felt like the universe conspiring against him. From the significant to the trivial, the elements of Kevin's life were going the wrong way.

Nothing was ever smooth sailing. As hard as he tried, he could only remember the bad days, the good ones blurred out of existence by the weight of the rest. It wore him down, it soured his view of the world. Kevin couldn't wake up in the morning without asking himself the question: *What is going to go wrong today?*

And something always did. A spilled cup of coffee or a missed train, those he could shrug off. But the bigger matters, like a lying business partner or the rapacious banks calling in their loans, they sucked the good out of Kevin's life.

Today, whatever *could* go wrong, *had* gone wrong.

Kevin imagined his luck like a fuel gauge with a twitching needle, forever hovering over E for EMPTY, and no matter how hard he worked, how much he pushed, the needle barely moved.

*I'm sick and tired of living with that.*

So fuck Colin Fish and his shitbag investor friends, with their golf club ties and their surrogate-prick sports cars. Fuck Hugo Montag and the rest of his tedious, indifferent clan for stabbing Kevin's deal in the back. Fuck *this* country, and fuck *his* country, for making it so bloody hard for a man to make a good life for himself.

Kevin's jaw set in a hard line. He'd had enough of being the loser in every game, of always coming off second-best. There was an opportunity here, and if he walked away from it, if he didn't have the courage to grab it with both hands, the rest of his sorry little life would be cast in stone.

He saw it plainly. If he turned away, back to the departure lounge, and sat in that uncomfortable chair for the next ten bloody hours, then he would be admitting failure.

*Do that, and you're telling the world to keep on kicking you while your down*, he thought. *You'll be on your knees for the rest of your life, and you'll deserve it.*

If he walked on, if he seized the moment . . . It was taking the biggest chance he had ever known, and certainly it terrified him – but it would be the first real act of defiance Kevin Tyler had ever thrown back at his uncaring fate.

How could he *not* do this? The possibility would torment him for the rest of his days if he gave it up.

At the luggage store, Kevin bought a collapsible, soft-sided carrier that could expand to the same size as his carry-on, and tucked it down the side of his roller case. Then, following the back wall of the terminal, he navigated around a line of low planters until he was almost at the corridor leading to the washroom.

He waited until a high-sided electric truck rolled by, carrying a disabled gentlemen, his wheelchair and carer to one of the distant departure gates. As the humming vehicle crossed in front of the side corridor, briefly blocking the view of the entrance from the rest of the terminal, Kevin stepped out smartly in its shadow and disappeared into the public toilets.

The stale smell greeted him again as he stooped to make sure there were no feet visible along the floor level of the stalls. An automatic cleaning cycle started up in the urinals, spilling blue liquid detergent down the grubby porcelain, and the hissing sound made Kevin jump.

He held a breath and went to the third toilet stall. The out-of-order sign was still in place, and there were no indications that anyone had been in there since he had left.

He grabbed a few sheets of paper towel to wrap around his hands, and as quickly as he could, Kevin locked himself inside the stall. Taking care not to touch anything he didn't need to, he pressed at the panel above the toilet bowl, rocking it gently until the latch clicked and it yawned open.

Kevin half-expected to find the void behind the wall empty, as if the whole thing with the bag and the money had been some kind of bizarre, stress-induced fever dream. But the wad of euros in his jacket pocket was very real and the black bag was still there, heavy with the promise of its illicit millions.

*Take it.*

This time, he didn't recoil from the avaricious impulse. After grabbing a few dirty shirts from his wheeled case, Kevin unzipped the black bag and systematically shuttled brick after brick of tightly packed euro notes into the collapsible carrier, swaddling them in his soiled laundry to break up the shape.

He lost himself in the methodical action, moving back and forth, listening to sound of his breathing and the hiss of the cleaning nozzles.

He was almost finished when another thought occurred to him, and he halted, two bricks of money held in his paper-wrapped hands.

*I can get this on the plane,* he decided. *They won't open up a piece of extra luggage if I pay the fee to stick it in the hold.* But what would happen when he landed back in England? He was pretty sure that the bags wouldn't pass through another detector before they arrived at the reclaim carousel. *No,* he decided. *Whoever left this here did the hard work getting it through security. As long as some nosy customs officer at Gatwick doesn't decide to poke around inside, I'll be all right.*

Kevin wondered again about who the money was intended for, but pushed the question aside. *Their loss,* he told himself. *My gain. Think of it like the universe rebalancing itself. I'm owed a win, and if no one is going to give me one, I'll take it.*

A nervous laugh bubbled up inside him. He was going to do this, and by tomorrow, the boot on his neck from the debts coming due would be nothing more than an unpleasant memory.

'Clean slate,' he said aloud, looking at the notes. 'This'll get me free and clear, and then ...' Kevin trailed off. *And then what?*

*Worry about that later*, he decided, and went back to work.

Kevin had picked the collapsible carrier for two reasons – one, because it was the exact same colour as his wheel case, and two, because he could strap both pieces of luggage together and carry one atop the other. Someone would have to look twice to notice the case had doubled in size, and he was free to drag it after him across the floor rather than haul it around over his shoulder.

If he was going to commit a crime, then Kevin damn well wanted to look he was doing the exact opposite. He washed and dried his hands, conjured up an expression in the mirror that vaguely resembled nonchalance, then paused at the door.

It stood to reason that whomever had left the cash to be picked up would probably have a look-out somewhere close by, waiting to see who came out of the toilets carrying the gym bag – exactly the reason why Kevin had switched the money into something else, and been careful to conceal himself entering the washroom.

He pulled up the cuff of his jacket and checked his watch. Before he started, Kevin had noted the times on the monitor boards, finding the final international flight of the day out of Barsbeker – the busy 10.00pm departure to Stockholm. Right on cue, the airport public address system gave off its two-tone chimes and a voice announced that the fully booked AeroNordik flight was now ready for boarding.

From his end of the short-side corridor, Kevin saw people starting to move from the waiting areas and their seats in the food court, clumps of weary travellers and homeward-bound Swedes alike joining the flow of people heading out to the gate. He picked his moment, and with his head down and shoulders forward, Kevin emerged from the washrooms and merged seamlessly into the mass of the other passengers, moving away with the crowd towards the far end of the terminal and their waiting 737. He passed a man in a bright orange hi-vis vest going the other way, but deliberately didn't make eye contact.

The overloaded bags clicked against the floor, and with each step Kevin expected a heavy hand to descend on his shoulder, to be dragged roughly from among the group and slammed to the ground.

But that didn't happen. There was no shout of alarm, no cops or thugs to waylay him. *He was getting away with it.*

He walked on, dragging his prize behind him, waiting for the right moment to peel off from the crowd. Little by little, Kevin began to walk taller.

The phone in his pocket vibrated again and Boch swore under his breath before he even looked at it.

With a sigh, he leaned forward in his narrow seat so he could answer the call, while still watching the washrooms across the corridor from the departure lounge where he sat.

'Yes, sir?' He knew it could only be one person on the other end of the line.

'*Dieter.*' Von Kassel inserted a sing-song tone into his name, slurring it slightly. '*I'm being asked to leave again. Quite firmly now. It's very impolite. I don't think these peons know who I am.*'

Experience of his employer's habits allowed Boch to make a good estimate of how many more drinks Von Kassel had consume since they last spoke. He guessed one, perhaps two more glasses of expensive brandy, and grimaced. 'Just a little longer, sir,' he said. 'If I can ask you to be patient—'

'*I am not the one you have to ask,*' the politician retorted hotly. It was outside Von Kassel's experience to have the people he considered beneath him telling him what to do, and Boch imagined that the staff in the executive lounge had already been treated to a stiff-lipped tirade. '*Tell these damned contrarians!*'

His employer's rant went on, but Boch's attention was momentarily taken by a figure emerging from the corridor to the washroom. He frowned; he hadn't seen the man enter, but it didn't matter now. The mark was a young guy with short brown hair and a doleful manner, clad in the bright vest of an airport worker. Hoisted over one shoulder he had the black bag that Ansel Fuchs had delivered an hour or so before. He carried it with the carelessness of someone who didn't know what it contained.

'Sir, please. One moment.' Boch watched the man move off and disappear through a door marked for staff access only.

Satisfied with that, he gave a nod and rose to his feet. 'It's done,' he said, with a sigh.

'*What?*' Von Kassel was caught off-guard. '*It is? The ba*—'

'Don't say anything more,' snapped Boch, silencing him with his abrupt tone. 'You have fulfilled your obligations. It is time to leave.'

# TWELVE

Horst's comrades had taken up a spot on the far side of the break room, gathered around a portable television. Both of them were glued to an episode of *Alarm für Cobra 11*, but not so much that they ignored Sasha and Vincent. Every so often one of them would sneak a look in their direction, making sure they kept their distance.

Sasha was content with that state of affairs. It meant the men were afraid of her, and that Oleg's fearsome reputation did its job. Half of the work of intimidating people was letting them scare themselves into obedience, giving them just enough threat to envision the unpleasant consequences of non-compliance.

The prefabricated building was damp and poorly insulated, so she cradled a mug of black tea laden with sugar in her long-fingered hands, warming herself with it.

At her side, Vincent sipped from his mug and pulled a face at the taste. He opened his mouth to complain, but a grinding rumble of thunder sounded out at the exact same second a lightning flash blazed through the nearby window. On the television, the cop show's high-speed car chase briefly became a garbled mess of blocky, pixelated shapes, the sound replaced by incoherent squeaks and chirps.

'Shit.' The taller one of the two men leaned in and fiddled with the antenna cable. 'The storm is messing with the signal.'

'It's right on top of us?' His friend made the statement into a question and shifted uncomfortably in his chair, eyeing a spot on the ceiling where rain was dripping through into a grubby plastic bucket on the floor.

Sasha could guess what he was thinking, weighing up the difference between being stuck in here with Oleg's lieutenants, or being out there in the worst weather in months. She flicked a glance at a clock on the wall. Horst had been gone for over forty-five minutes, and his friends were getting nervous as the top of the hour approached.

Then the door banged open and the man in question came stumbling inside, drenched from head to foot despite the short distance he had covered from the terminal. Dragging a large gym bag with him, Horst slammed the door closed, shutting out the rain and the wind.

'This is it?' He panted out the words, stepping forward to drop the bag on the nearest table.

Sasha knew it was the correct item, but it was sensible to be thorough, and she double-checked it against the photo that Von Kassel's man had sent her. *All good.*

Vincent made a *shoo*-ing motion and dragged the bag towards him. Horst's friends rose from their chairs. They were eager to be gone.

'We're done here?' said the tall one. 'We'll get our, uh, bonus for this?' He gave Horst a tentative nod.

'You can go,' Sasha told them, '*after* we check it.'

'I didn't open it,' insisted Horst.

'I hope not,' she agreed. 'I hope you're not that stupid.'

The colour rose on Vincent's cheeks and he ground out a harsh curse in gutter French. He had the bag unzipped, and in a clawed hand he held up a large, rain-sodden clump of toilet paper. 'What the fuck is this shit?'

Sasha's gut tightened. The bag was packed to the seams with identical rolls of the cheap, institutional-grade tissue, the same kind the airport used hundreds of on a daily basis.

Sasha turned back to Horst and saw that he had gone as white as the paper. He put his hands up in front of himself, pre-emptively warding her off. 'I said I didn't open it!'

'I was mistaken,' she growled. 'You *are* that stupid.'

'Where's the fucking money, *cochon?*' Vincent shouted, and threw the wet paper at Horst, who deflected it away.

'I don't know anything about any money!' Horst shook his head. 'I did what you told me to!'

Sasha frowned, put down her cup, and walked over to the break room's kitchen area. She flicked the switch on the electric kettle and set the water inside to heat up. 'I was very clear about this job,' she said. 'Did you misunderstand me? Did you not take me seriously?'

Horst shook his head. 'I'm *not* stupid,' he bleated. 'I know who you work for! I do what I'm told!' He looked to his friends for support, but they were frozen where they stood, worried about how this might blow back on them.

'Just give it back, whatever you took,' said the tall one. 'Don't be an idiot!'

'*I didn't take anything!*' Horst shouted. 'You said go get the bag from behind the panel in the toilet, *I got you the bag!*'

'Did someone else put you up to this?' Vincent moved to block the door, in case the man tried to make a run for it. 'You'd better tell us.'

Horst shook his head, and sagged against a table. 'I'm not lying!'

Sasha studied him. Her first instinct was that Horst was too afraid to be hiding the truth, but there was always the possibility he was a far better deceiver than she realised.

A pennant of steam rose out of the kettle's spout as the water approached boiling point. 'OK,' she allowed, 'but you understand, I have to make sure.'

Horst blinked at her, not following her reasoning.

Sasha glanced at Vincent, and he took his cue. 'You two,' he said to the others. 'Get his arms. Hold him.'

Before Horst could react, his friends had come forward and snaked their arms around his, dragging him back to a standing position. The other men looked equally as terrified as Horst, because they knew that if they refused, it would be them who would be made to suffer.

Vincent looked Horst up and down. 'Is he left or right-handed?'

'Left,' said the tall man. 'I think.'

'Right!' Horst cried out. 'I'm right-handed!'

'Hold up his left.' Vincent gave the order, and Horst's friends reluctantly obeyed, forcing his arm out. The younger man struggled and began to whimper.

The kettle clicked off automatically as the water boiled. Sasha brought it to Horst's extended hand and let the searing hot plume of steam rise into his bare palm. He worked with heavy machinery, so he had tougher skin than most people, but he still moaned with pain at the touch of the super-heated vapour.

'Are you lying to me?' She asked the question, but the words were not hers; they were replaying from a memory years distant but still fresh. Where no one could see it, on the palm of the hand that held the kettle, Sasha's flesh bore old scars from healed scaldings.

Once, it had been her held to account for something that had gone missing, and Oleg Gorod holding the steaming kettle. Burning her to make sure she told no lies. Because only pain brought truth. Only pain removed doubt.

'I'm not lying!' Horst squirmed, trying to pull away his hand. 'Please!'

'I have to make sure,' she repeated, just as Oleg had told her all that time ago. 'There cannot be exceptions.' Then, she'd hated him for what he had done, but now she understood. *Pain brings truth.*

Sasha poured a gush of still-bubbling water over Horst's hand and across the cracked linoleum flooring. He screamed as it scalded him, but the thunder swallowed up the sound.

'*No no no!*' His face turned pink with agony and tears streamed down his cheeks. 'Please stop! I didn't do anything, *I didn't!*'

'I believe him,' said Vincent, with terse sniff. 'Look at him. He's pissing himself.' He stepped forward and gave Horst a shove with the heel of his hand. 'Get out. You're done.'

'D-done?' Horst cradled his twitching, heat-burned hand. 'But I—'

'I said *go!*' Vincent bellowed the order at them. 'Fuck off out of here and keep your mouths shut, or you'll get worse, *comprend moi?*'

The three men didn't wait for the Frenchman to further clarify his words, and they fled into the rainy dark outside, the break-room door banging shut in their wake.

When they were alone, Vincent turned pale. 'Ah, *shit.* Where's the money, Sasha? Oleg will skin us alive if we don't bring it to him!'

She nodded in grim agreement. 'That arrogant prick Von Kassel. I didn't imagine he had the balls to try something like this, but obviously I was wrong.' She considered the possibility. 'Maybe Oleg was right to come tonight.'

'Well, we need to move quickly,' said Vincent. 'We have to get our hands around this before it is too late . . . We can't go back to Oleg with nothing but excuses.'

'You have someone in the security office, right?' Sasha gestured at the air. 'What is his name?'

Vincent nodded sharply. 'Yeah. Imran, the Indian. He works on the monitor desk, with the CCTV cameras. I can get to him. Lean on him.'

Sasha drew a breath and scowled. She didn't like the thought of doing anything that could draw more unnecessary attention, but circumstances were in danger of running out of control.

Vincent was right about time being against them. Von Kassel had been seen in one of the lounges earlier that evening, and his man Boch was prowling around the terminal. If this business with the bag was some kind of idiotic ploy on his part, Sasha had to stamp down on it hard, before the politician took the upper hand.

'We need to find that asshole,' she said, 'find him and *explain* to him.'

'All right, I'll get it done.' Vincent made for the door, halting on the threshold. 'But we could use another set of eyes over here,' he added, as an afterthought.

'I know.' Sasha was already way ahead of him. 'Get the Indian to work, I'll deal with that.'

She sat down as Vincent rushed out into the heavy rain, and pulled out her phone, thumbing down the names on the contact list until she found the one she wanted.

Dialling: Miros read the screen, and within two rings the call connected. Sasha heard Oleg's driver breathing steadily but he didn't speak. 'It's me,' she said firmly. 'Something's come up. Tell Oleg I need you to help me with something over this side.'

Miros's reply was gruff and monosyllabic. '*What?*'

'I'll explain when you get here,' she told him. 'Do you have a clean gun?'

147

'*Yes.*'

'Bring it.'

In the airports Kevin had passed through, he'd often seen the sign that pointed towards the multi-faith room, and always wondered exactly what was inside it.

He wasn't the remotest bit religious, having grown up without any of that kind of thing in his life. To him, churches were places where you visited for weddings and funerals to mumble half-remembered hymns from school assembly, and the idea of voluntarily going to sit on some pew while a vicar read psalms was alien to him. But he had to admit to a sneaking sort of envy for people who had a strong faith. *It must be comforting*, he thought, *to have somewhere to put your problems. Somewhere to draw strength from.*

For Kevin, it didn't seem real. Life was too random, too chaotic to be part of some great cosmic plan. Because if there *was* someone in charge of it, it meant they didn't have much good in mind for one Kevin Tyler from Hackney.

*Or maybe not*, he considered, feeling the weight of his bags. *Maybe someone up there has finally decided to change my fortunes.*

Barsbeker Airport's multi-faith room stood on an isolated mezzanine level, up a set of stairs, behind an unassuming door with a narrow window in it. He peered inside, and saw the place was dark and unoccupied. Kevin dragged his bags in with him and closed the latch. He fumbled for a switch and turned on the lights.

He'd expected to find a space that resembled a chapel, but the area was a bare rectangle with plain walls and a worn beige carpet. It looked more like a function room in some low-rent motorway hotel than a place of worship and contemplation. A heavy curtain could portion the space in half, and there were racks for shoes by the door, and on one wall, a set of cubby holes filled with plastic boxes. Each box had a label with an icon on it, and the icons were repeated on a wide panel above the door. He recognised the Christian cross, Star of David, Islamic crescent-and-star, and the 'ship's wheel' symbol that denoted Buddhists, but the others were unfamiliar to him. At the end of the panel was a yin-yang and an empty circle, which Kevin guessed was meant to denote people who didn't have a faith, per se.

'All your theological bases covered, then,' he said quietly, instinctively pitching his voice down even though he was alone. Despite the ordinariness of the room, he still felt like he had to be deferential in it. His voice sounded flat and he realised that the space was soundproofed.

Under the boxes – which he now saw contained holy books, prayer mats and the like – were a dozen drum-shaped cushion stools. Grabbing one, Kevin moved to the corner of the room where he wouldn't be seen from the door and sat down, dropping the collapsible bag at his feet. On the floor, he saw a metal disc with an arrow on it pointing in the direction of Mecca, for use by any Muslim visitors. Kevin suddenly felt uncomfortable, as if he was disrespecting the space.

Greed was a sin for pretty much every religion, he reflected, but it was too late to walk back his decision now.

In the washroom, he had been too busy moving the money out of the gym bag to do more than vaguely register the full amount, but now he set to counting it. Package by package, Kevin unloaded and then repacked the collapsible bag, this time taking account of the denominations of the notes, and how thick the bundles were. There was nothing there worth less than a hundred euros, the plastic-paper currency tightly bound into shiny bricks. On some of them, the wrapping was peeling off, and he guessed that they had to be the older packs out of the lot. This money had been in storage somewhere, and by the look of it, not in a bank.

That underlined the undoubted origins of the cash. This was dirty, secret, criminal money. Not a bank heist take awaiting pickup, or some under-the-radar courier's load. This was *payment* for something, Kevin felt it in his bones.

And now he had stolen it, from god-knows-who, compelled by raw avarice and desperation. But Kevin couldn't stop himself from grinning. 'I'm fucking minted,' he whispered to himself.

There was more here than he had first believed. At best guess, the cash added up to around two million euros in used banknotes. That would be enough to not only drag Kevin's spiralling life out of the gutter, and kill off the debts slowly strangling him, it would leave him with a good chunk of change as surplus.

His mind raced, and he pictured what it would take to embrace the fresh start the money represented. He could sell the house and the car, cut loose and get a whole new roll of the dice. He could go see his daughter and her girlfriend, look Maddie in the eye and tell her how important she was to him. And this time, he could make absolutely bloody sure that he did it *right*.

Kevin had never had a second chance in his life. All of his opportunities had crumbled under their own weight, sending him lurching from let-down to let-down, barely scrambling to keep his head above water. He tried to imagine what it would be like to be comfortable for once, and not to feel constantly out of his depth.

*A day without feeling like I'm drowning*, he thought, marvelling at the possibility. *What would that be like?*

Dreaming it wouldn't make it happen, though. Kevin stared down at the cash and disconnected himself from the reality of it. 'Don't think of it as money,' he said aloud, his words flat in the quiet. 'Think of it as numbers. This is an engineering issue. Moving objects from one location to another, through a restricted channel.' Kevin parsed it mentally like an equation on a drawing board.

*IF cash money = £££*

*THEN problem = movement of £££*

*FROM here TO there MINUS detection.*

He could take his bags right now and walk out of Barsbeker's airside quadrant, back into the real world outside the airport's bubble. But the taxis on the rank out there were gone, fled back home before the storm set in, and the local busses almost certainly cancelled. The car rental offices would stay shut until tomorrow morning, the nearest village twenty kilometres away through a ferocious downpour.

All outgoing flights had now departed, and what remained were grounded for the night. For a moment, he wondered how much it might cost to rent a private plane. With the cash in the bag, he could afford it; but if the airliners weren't taking off, no biz-jet would brave the dark and turbulent sky.

*You can take the money . . .*

*But you can't run.*

He looked at his wristwatch. Eight hours until the Gatwick flight left the ground. All he needed to do was find somewhere to hole up and isolate himself, put the money somewhere safe and out of sight, then run out the clock.

Just do *nothing* for eight hours.

*How hard could that be?*

As long as he was careful, even if the people he had stolen from were in here too, sniffing around for their cash, he could make this happen. Kevin wasn't the only passenger being forced to wait out the night: dozens of other people had been bumped from their planes, and other flights had been cancelled entirely.

His ex-wife Sadie had teased him about his unremarkable nature. *You get lost in crowds with your face,* she chided. Tonight, Kevin could make that work for him. Blend in, become nobody, and *wait.*

Eight hours.

Four hundred and eighty minutes.

Twenty-eight thousand, eight hundred seconds.

*I can do it. Stay in here, be quiet, read some Bibles—*

The door to the prayer room rattled hard in its frame, and startled him, enough that it made Kevin jerk forward, almost slipping on to the floor.

Someone was outside. He could hear men's voices, stern and close at hand. They were working the handle, shaking it, trying to force it open.

The fragile calm Kevin had been hoarding since he entered the room disintegrated, and a new swell of raw panic filled his stomach.

Greasy, sickly terror gripped him as he frantically jammed the last few money bundles back into the collapsible bag and zipped it shut with shaking hands. The men outside the door called out, but it was hard to make out the words through the soundproofing.

Kevin kicked the bag into the deep shadows beneath the furled partition curtain, then dithered in the middle of the room. There was no other way in or out, and he feared that the men would break down the door if he didn't open it.

Struggling to keep his hand from shaking, he reached out and turned the latch, unlocking the door. It swung open and Kevin looked into the eyes of two young Muslim men, both clad in robes and taqiyah caps.

They were as shocked to see him as he was to see them. 'Sorry, sorry,' said one of them, a gangly youth with a well-kept beard. 'We didn't know someone was in here!'

'I thought the door was stuck!' said the other, with a nervous grin.

'I was, uh, *contemplating*.' Kevin blurted out the words, grasping for a convincing explanation and failing miserably. 'Contemplating, uh, *things*.'

'Oh.' The bearded youth nodded, slightly nonplussed by the reply. 'Are you . . . finished? It's just, my brother and I are late for *isha*, our prayers, and—'

'No, no,' Kevin shook his head, relief tamping down the fear as he realised what was going on. 'I mean, yes, finished.' He made a waving motion and took in the room. 'All yours.'

'Thank you.' The two men exchanged awkward looks, but Kevin gave them no time to dwell on his presence.

Gathering up his bags, he left as quickly as he could, his heart hammering against the inside of his ribcage.

*Eight hours,* Kevin reminded himself. *As long as I don't panic myself into a fucking heart attack.*

# THIRTEEN

'I expect better treatment,' Von Kassel said, as Boch trailed him through the terminal towards the main doors of the building, carrying the other man's satchel. 'Far better. But then I suppose one must make allowances when one is in the provinces.' The faint odour of brandy on his breath made the other man turn away from him.

Boch said nothing, half-listening, scanning for threats. This was the most dangerous moment, the time after the deal had been done, when any attempt to plant a knife in the back would surely happen.

Oleg Gorod's fearsome reputation also came with assurances that he kept his word, and with the money delivered, all should have been well.

But Dieter Boch had been party to many a situation where *all seemed well*, only to have it turn to shit in an instant. He lacked Von Kassel's ability to merrily carry on as if nothing could touch him. He didn't share the inane self-confidence that made the man believe he was bulletproof.

'And the staff there . . .' His employer said, waving a hand in the direction of the first-class lounge he had left. 'Rude. Distinctly unaccommodating.'

Boch made a noise of agreement, casting around for anyone suspicious or out of place. In this area, the airport was largely empty, with the nearby check-in desks now closed up for the night, with no one waiting around outside the arrivals gate for incoming passengers. Anyone loitering here would have stood out a mile, and he allowed himself to relax – but only a little.

Von Kassel halted short of the glass doors and frowned at what he saw outside. 'Oh my.'

Sheets of hard rain hammered across the road one after another, coming in sideways on as the high winds swept the downpour over the airport. Boch saw the poles of the street lights swaying, and as he watched, a discarded plastic bin of some sort migrated past the windows of its own accord, propelled in fits and starts by the gale. A moaning whine and a knife of cold air made it in through the seal between the doors with each new gust.

'Perhaps we should remain here,' ventured the politician. 'You can get them to reopen the lounge.'

Part of Boch wanted to agree, to retreat from the storm. The horrible weather brought only blurred, unwelcome memories he wanted to forget. But his own misgivings were unimportant. 'With respect, sir,' he said, 'I don't think that will be possible. Or sensible, given the situation.'

'Eh?' Von Kassel eyed him.

'You really need to be as far away from here as possible,' Boch said firmly, reiterating the statement for what had to be the tenth time that night.

The multi-level car park where Boch had left the car was less than a hundred metres away from the terminal entrance, but the rain would drench anyone who tried to cross the distance. Grimly, he started to button his jacket, and fold up the collar.

Von Kassel waved a hand in his direction, reluctantly accepting the situation. 'All right, then. We'll drive back to Hamburg tonight.'

'If that's possible,' said Boch, doubting the likelihood. 'With the state of this weather, the roads will probably be washed out. We'll be lucky if we make it as far as Kiel.'

'I don't care!' Von Kassel's mood shifted towards irritation, and he snapped at his driver. 'If you insist we leave, then get me out of here! Bring the car around, Dieter. I'll wait for you.' He tapped his foot.

Boch gave him a severe look. 'It is a bad idea for me to leave you alone, sir.'

'I'm not a child to be minded, I'll be fine,' he countered. 'Get the car.'

Boch continued as if he hadn't spoken. 'It's one thing to sit in a bar and drink brandy, another for you to be out in the open, without protection.' He leaned in. 'Gorod has people everywhere.' He didn't know if that was strictly true, but he thought it likely. 'If I stray from your side, I fail in my duties. I can't leave you exposed.'

'I suppose so,' allowed the politician, his crossness ebbing. 'Carry on, then.' He pointed at a rack near the doors, where umbrellas printed with the airport logo were left for inclement weather such as this.

Boch took one and unfurled it as they stepped up to the doors, and Von Kassel immediately crowded beneath the open umbrella as the pair of them ventured out into the rain's cold embrace. Boch's employer took up what little space there was under the fabric canopy, leaving his driver to face the wet with no cover of his own.

'Careful!' Von Kassel snapped at him again as they crossed the roadway, pitching his voice up to be heard over the wind. 'These shoes are handmade! I'm not walking through any puddles!'

'Yes sir, I—' Whatever Boch was going to say next was torn away by a thrumming gust that blew the canopy inside out. The wind wrestled with him and finally won, the handle slipping from his wet grip, the umbrella bolting away into the night.

Von Kassel swore and grimly marched the last few metres to the cover of the parking structure, cursing each step he took, and then finally they were in out of the rain once more. He muttered about the rain soaking the jacket and silk shirt he wore, but Boch was less interested in his employer's complaints than he was in the shadowed corners of the car park.

The space was too close-in for his comfort, the heavy concrete ceiling too low. There were thick supporting pillars, bad sight lines and poor lighting. It set off warning impulses in the former soldier's mind, and made him move as quickly as he could.

They were ten steps away from Von Kassel's jet-black S-Class Mercedes-Benz when Boch realised his instincts were ringing true. As he pressed the remote lock on the car's key-fob and the vehicle gave off an answering chirp, he became aware of two figures standing in the shadows.

The politician was so wrapped up in his own narrative about his waterlogged shoes that he didn't see the interlopers at first, not until Boch grabbed his arm. Dropping the satchel, his driver pulled him to one side and stepped between the potential threats and his principal, as they revealed themselves.

The first he didn't recognise, a glowering man with a face of hard, granite lines; but Boch *did* know the type. This one had the air of an ex-soldier about him, something indefinable in the way he carried himself, but to Boch, as obvious as if he had been wearing a uniform. He also knew the distinctive shape of the pistol in the man's hand – a Polish P-38 Wanad semi-automatic. *Eight rounds in the magazine,* he noted, *more than enough to kill us both.*

The second figure he was familiar with. The girl, Sasha, Oleg Gorod's cold-eyed messenger. Her presence confirmed what he already suspected. They were about to be double-crossed, and that talk about Oleg being a man of his word would be revealed as so much horse shit.

At his side, Von Kassel actually let out a snort of haughty laughter as he laid eyes on the gun. The fact that he was being threatened didn't seem to register. 'What do you think you are doing?'

'That is a question for you,' said the girl. Her tone was brittle and angry.

The man with the pistol took aim – not at the politician, but at Boch, showing that he knew exactly where the genuine threat lay here.

Boch moved slightly, inching towards the Mercedes. Thanks to the need to pass through airport security, he had been forced to leave his own pistol – a Walther PDP compact – locked in the car's glove compartment. It was highly illegal for a driver-slash-bodyguard like Boch to carry a firearm, but Von Kassel's influence had made sure that had never been an issue. Still, the weapon was little help to him now, though, unless he could somehow convince Oleg's thugs to let him access the vehicle.

He looked around, hoping to catch sight of someone else in the echoing parking structure, but they were quite alone, and it struck him that any sound of weapons fire would likely be lost in the rumble of the thunderstorm.

Von Kassel folded his arms up over his chest, one hand cradling his chin. He shook his head, behaving as if the gun was non-existent. 'No, no. You don't come here and threaten me. You know who I am. Oleg and I have an *agreement!*'

'You have a *debt*,' Sasha corrected. 'You need to pay it.' She nodded at the older man. 'One way or another.'

'No,' said the gunman, meeting Boch's gaze as the driver took another step. He gave a shake of the head, and his meaning was clear. *Stay away from the car or I will shoot.*

Boch looked up, spotting a security camera on the low ceiling, the device's unblinking eye looking directly at them. Whomever was on the other end of the camera's feed had a perfect view of what could would look like an armed robbery in progress, but the lack of any urgency from Sasha and her companion suggested that no help would be coming. Boch considered again what he had said to Von Kassel in the terminal: *Gorod has people everywhere.* It appeared he was right – how else had they known where to wait for them?

'You try to fuck us?' Sasha shook her head. 'After everything that has happened? Do you think that Oleg is not serious?' She took a breath. 'Do you *want* to disappear tonight?'

Von Kassel snorted. 'You can't do that to me. You don't have the authority.'

Boch saw Sasha's jaw harden at the other man's words, and he spoke up before Von Kassel could make it worse. 'The payment was made,' he insisted. 'I followed your instructions.' As he talked, another possibility became apparent. 'Maybe *you* are trying to fuck *us* over.'

He stared at the younger woman, trying to get a read on her. She wore the same clothes she had when they had met that morning, out at the site on the Montag property.

That conversation had not gone well. Sasha arrived with Oleg's final demands and the assurance that after the payment, the matter of the debt would be settled and they would be free to move on to other, more lucrative endeavours. Of course, Von Kassel could not be relied upon to keep his mouth shut, even when it was in his best interests, and he demanded to make the handover to Oleg himself.

Boch knew that would not happen. Oleg rarely showed his face in public, and he certainly wouldn't for something as sordid as Von Kassel's transaction. That, Boch reflected, was part of the problem. The politician considered himself to be an important man, and considered it disrespectful that the criminal would not meet him face to face. Von Kassel didn't grasp that it was best for all parties to maintain a distance, and he paid little attention to Sasha's warnings. *I don't deal with servants*, he had said, and left Boch to handle the particulars.

No matter what Boch did to disentangle his principal from this mess of Von Kassel's own making, the arrogant fool dragged him deeper into it.

He bit down on the deep-seated loathing for the rich man lurking in his own heart and concentrated on the moment. Boch had no desire to take a bullet for Lars Von Kassel's obstinacy.

'The bag,' said Sasha, 'it was a dummy. Where is the money?'

Boch licked his lips, and he began to entertain another, far more unpleasant possibility. 'I left the money behind the wall in the men's washroom, third stall from the right.' He spelled it out so there could be no misunderstanding. 'Just as you said. If it has gone missing, you need to question your own people, not blame us.'

Sasha and the gunman exchanged a look, a flash of doubt passing between them. But before either of them could continue, Von Kassel stepped forward.

'I will speak directly with Mr Gorod.' The politician spread his hands, his tone firm but reasonable, as if his demand had already been accepted. 'He and I will straighten this out.'

Boch turned to Von Kassel and leaned in to speak privately with him. 'What are you doing?' He hissed out the question. 'This is no time to play games, sir!'

'You do your work and let me do mine,' Von Kassel replied, returning the urgent whisper. 'I know how to handle these thugs! If Gorod wants to match wits with me, he'll find it a challenge.'

'Sir, *no*,' Boch insisted. 'You don't understand the kind of people we're dealing with—'

Von Kassel glared at him, his nostrils flaring. 'Never say *no* to me, Dieter, understand? Don't forget the consequences of my displeasure.'

The admonishment was like a punch to the gut. The bleak shadow of Von Kassel's leverage over Boch's life rose in his thoughts and he pushed it aside. At length, he nodded. 'I remember, sir. I'm . . . Trying to look out for you.'

'Good.' Von Kassel's smile snapped on like a light. 'But be a good soldier, do as you are told and get out of my way.' He stepped around Boch, and after casting a withering glance in the gunman's direction, he addressed Sasha once again. 'You won't injure me or my man. I'm worth too much for that.' His tone turned mocking. 'So act like an obedient little bitch and we'll trot along to talk to your master, yes? Get this dealt with like civilised men. No more guns and posturing!'

Boch could see Sasha seething in silence, and for a moment he wondered if Von Kassel had pushed his luck too far this time. In her shoes, Boch would have been considering how much pain it would take to make Von Kassel beg for mercy and spill his guts. But then the gunman gave her a wan shrug and let the pistol drop away to point at the floor.

'Get in the car.' Sasha bit out the words like she was spitting nails, angrily accepting the situation. 'You want to see Oleg? Fine. You can drive us to the hangar.'

'There! You see, Dieter? These people can be reasonable.' Von Kassel smirked around his answer, stooping to recover his satchel.

Boch said nothing. Breathing the same air as Oleg Gorod was exactly, precisely the last thing he wanted to happen, and it would be ten times worse if Von Kassel tried to play his games with the man. The politician was oblivious to the fact that they were putting their heads in the lion's mouth.

The gunman waved Boch towards the car with his pistol and Sasha climbed in the front passenger seat beside him, as Von Kassel and the other man got into the back.

'I'll tell you where to go,' she told him. 'Don't do anything clever or you'll regret it.'

'I already do,' Boch muttered, and started the Mercedes's engine.

Tucked away behind the travel pharmacy and beside another electronic departure board, the rack of left-luggage lockers resembled a wall of giant cubes. Each one was a featureless shape made of white-painted steel, and the lockers had no numerical identification on them, no visible handles or securing mechanism. If it wasn't for the touchpad control screen set at one end of the array, they could have easily been mistaken for some sort of modern art installation.

Kevin tapped the on-screen tab to show instructions in English, and with a few keystrokes, he selected a locker large enough to accommodate both his wheeled Pullman case and the collapsible bag. A swipe of his credit card confirmed the action, and of its own accord, one of the larger metal cubes opened along one side.

Kevin parked the luggage, dithering as he considered adding his shoulder bag. In the end, he decided to keep hold of it, and kicked the cube door closed with his foot. The touch-screen asked him for a passcode to secure the locker, and with a rueful half-smile, he typed in the first number that came to mind – 623343, his daughter's name spelt out on the alphanumeric keypad. The locker's magnetic bolts thudded home and he sighed. *Safe enough.*

Hoisting the shoulder bag's strap into place, Kevin slipped back through the pharmacy, doing his best not to be obvious about it. Thinking of Maddie brought her face to the front of his mind, and he pulled out his phone as he walked, waking the device.

Kevin had deliberately set the thing to silent mode after his conversation with Colin, but now to his dismay he saw that he had missed another call from his daughter. In the rush, he'd neglected to call her back.

Glumly, Kevin listed to the voicemail message she had left, kicking himself for his lack of consideration.

'*Hey Pop,*' she began, and the sad sigh in the words jabbed his conscience like a dagger. '*We didn't get to finish up, and, uh . . . I wanted to say love you, miss you, hope everything is OK over there.*'

In the background, he caught Maddie's girlfriend saying something terse, something like *wrap it up* and Kevin stopped, cradling the phone in both hands as he leaned against a support pillar. Even half-heard, he could pick out the edge of scorn in Andrea's words, and he imagined her making throat-cutting gestures, imploring Maddie to end the call.

'*Talk soon,*' she said, sounding distracted. '*Bye.*'

'Bye,' he echoed, to no one in particular. The impulse to call her back faded away. The familiar, ever-present fear was there again, the one that told him he would make it worse if he tried to explain it to her, the paralysis that always silenced him.

If Kevin was being honest with himself, a guilty, traitorous part of him was secretly relieved that he had missed Maddie's call. If he had spoken to her directly, he might have let something slip about his unexpected change in fortunes and the risks he was taking. And it was likely that his daughter would have tried to talk him out of it. He didn't allow himself to dwell on the fact that she might have succeeded, and what that meant for this whole chancy enterprise, instead convincing himself that he was looking out for her by saying nothing.

*The last thing I want to do is give Maddie something else to worry about . . . And give Andrea another reason to dislike me.*

With a sigh, he shrugged off the cloying negativity and set his mind to an upbeat attitude.

*I can do this. I* will *do this.*

*And when it's over, it won't matter how I got there.*

# FOURTEEN

Sasha's stomach twisted itself into knots as she climbed out of the Mercedes, stepping smartly from the vehicle, out of the rain and through the open doors of the Memoria Tranzyt hangar. She felt like a disobedient child called in to confess her misdeeds to a schoolmaster, and fought down the emotion.

Oleg stood waiting, arms folded across his chest and a look of stern, patrician displeasure etched over his grim features. Sasha hated herself for how she felt around him, pressed by the weight of an obligation she could not shake free of. Her brittle sense of self-worth, so strong when stressed in one direction, became fragile where Oleg's approval was concerned. Before him, there had never been anything in her life approximating a mentor, a father figure, a guiding hand, and try as she might to deny it, Sasha's misfortunes had inextricably linked her to the old soldier. She was bound to him in a way that she could not articulate.

Sometimes the men made jokes when they thought she could not hear them; they called her *the bastard's daughter*, mocking the twisted relationship between the older man and the young woman he had rescued from a life of slavery. Some of them offered lewd suggestions about the nature of Oleg and Sasha's connection, but none of them could understand. There was no sexual component to what tied them. Their bond was made of pain and fear, not just the experience of it, but the application of it on others. However twisted, it was the closest thing to a loving relationship her life had ever known.

She remained terrified of disappointing him. Oleg said nothing, taking in the unexpected arrival of Von Kassel and his driver-bodyguard with icy severity.

'Tell me you have good reason to let that idiot into my presence,' Oleg said in gutter Polish, aware that the Germans didn't understand a word of it. 'Make me understand why you have done this.'

'There was a problem with his payment,' she began. 'The money ... It wasn't where it should be.' Oleg's lip curled at that, but she pushed on before he could respond, grasping for an explanation he would accept. 'I couldn't allow him to leave. It would set a bad example.'

'True,' he allowed, switching back to English, the only language they shared with the Germans. 'I suppose you were right to bring this to me.'

'Herr Gorod!' Von Kassel came striding over to them, oblivious to Miros and his gun, and the other rough men milling around at the edges of the hangar. He extended a hand in Oleg's direction as if they were being introduced at some society dinner party. 'At last, we meet! I must say, I have been looking forward to this!'

Von Kassel's driver looked distinctly uncomfortable, his gaze darting around, trying to look in every direction at once. He had the air of a trapped animal searching for an escape route.

When Oleg didn't accept the politician's offer of a handshake, Von Kassel changed gears so smoothly Sasha almost didn't notice. Maintaining his high-wattage smile, the other man shifted to a mask of false bonhomie, one hand raking through his hair as he gave a self-deprecating chuckle. 'I know when I am playing the game and when I am being played, ha ha! And it is the wise, sagacious man who knows that he has been out-manoeuvred! I take my hat off to you, sir. I know, my appearance here makes this an unexpected turn of events, for both of us, but I truly believe that in each meeting there is the seed of opportunity, and solving tonight's issue affords you and I the chance to put our partnership onto a firmer footing!'

Sasha watched Oleg's manner stiffen by degrees as each glib word fell with machine-gun speed from Von Kassel's mouth, and the point when his tolerance for the other man's chatter ended came quickly.

Oleg brought up his hands in front of Von Kassel's face and smacked the palms together with a loud report, enough that the politician reacted as if he had been physically slapped, falling silent. Oleg drew a breath and ground out the next words he spoke like chips of granite. '*Where is the money you owe me?*'

Von Kassel cocked his head and chuckled again. 'Oleg! Come, come. No more games, *ja*? My man here did as he was told! You have what you asked for.'

Sasha quietly marvelled at how every word out of Von Kassel's mouth made it sound like he was in the position of power here, not Gorod. Nothing he said, not even the slightest gesture, admitted to the reality that he was the supplicant in this.

She took her cue to speak. 'Herr Von Kassel. This business with the money is not some ploy. If we do not have it, and you do not have it, then the problem is very much *yours.*'

For the first time, some measure of Von Kassel's spontaneous bluster wavered. He shot his driver a hard look. 'Boch!' He snarled the man's name. 'I delegated this responsibility to you!'

'And yet, you came here tonight in person, so the responsibility is ultimately yours,' said Oleg, looking him up and down. 'I know how men like you think. You see matters as games, as *sport*. And tonight, you thought you might play, yes?'

'Well, uh—' Von Kassel dredged up his practiced smirk again, affecting a comradely manner that failed to impact Oleg's dour contempt.

'Games are for children and imbeciles.' Oleg prodded him in the chest, ice forming on his words. 'What I do is wage *war*, Herr Von Kassel. War on your pathetic legalities. War on whatever you permit and fret over.' He paused to let that sink in, and in the moment that followed, a rumble of thunder rolled over the hangar roof.

Sasha watched Oleg study Von Kassel with a predator's eye, and at length, he showed a faint smile, changing tack.

'It is good you are here. *Yes.* This is a night for reminders, I think.' He glanced in the direction of the place where he had stabbed Roberto in the back. There was a scattering of absorbent granules in the spot, of the kind used to clean up spills of oil. Von Kassel had no idea what Oleg referred to, but Sasha and the others knew full well. 'Sometimes it is necessary for the man holding the chain to pull it tight.'

Von Kassel's head bobbed and he smiled inanely, as if he were humouring Oleg's musings. 'I suppose so.'

Oleg put a hand on Von Kassel's shoulder, and despite himself, the other man couldn't completely hide how he flinched at the touch. 'You wanted a meeting of equals, yes?' He grunted with amusement. 'That is not possible. You may be better dressed, better educated, better mannered. But you are still beneath me.'

The politician dismissed the insult with a nervous laugh, looking around for support and finding none. 'Now, let's not say anything we might later regret!'

But Oleg already had his hand on the small of Von Kassel's back. With firmness he pressed the other man in the direction of the hangar's rear wall, to where a window looked out on to the low woodland beyond the airport perimeter. Boch tensed as his principal was threatened, but Miros still had his gun out, and the driver-bodyguard was reluctant to intervene. Sasha stayed close, so that only she was within earshot of the quiet conversation between the two men.

Oleg's hand slipped up between Von Kassel's shoulders and he gripped the back of the man's neck, fingers digging in, forcing him to turn where Oleg wished. 'Look,' he said, quiet and intent.

Von Kassel squirmed, blinking at the rain-lashed view outside. 'I don't, ah, know what you want me to see.'

'The whore you killed is buried out there,' Oleg told him, in a matter-of-fact tone, and the atmosphere in the hangar deadened.

Sasha watched the politician's face turn pink. With his well-fed features, he reminded her of a colicky infant. 'Now, see here . . .' Von Kassel said hotly.

'I am not one to judge.' Oleg released his grip and the other man rubbed nervously at his neck. 'What man *wouldn't* strike a woman for laughing at his soft cock?'

'I . . . I . . .' Von Kassel blinked and stuttered, and then, as if a switch had been thrown behind his eyes, he sighed and took a moment to calm himself. 'Sometimes, mistakes are made,' he noted, and that was the closest thing to an admission of guilt he was capable of uttering.

'The grave is unmarked, but I know where it is,' Oleg said casually. Then he reached up to his neck and hooked the cord hanging around it with his thumb.

The former soldier drew out his old *matrikula* – what someone in the military would call 'dog tags' – a tin rectangle that opened up to reveal a folded card with details of name, rank and blood type. Hanging on the cord with Oleg's grubby, pitted tag was something out of place, a thin sliver of black plastic with metal pickups on one end. A memory card, like the ones in any common digital camera.

'I have pictures. Of you and her.' Oleg spoke quietly, running the memory card between his thumb and forefinger so Von Kassel could see it clearly. 'I keep them close at hand, for insurance's sake.'

For someone who always talked about himself as a man from an analogue era, Oleg's base distrust of modern technology no longer applied when it was to his benefit. Vincent maintained the card's contents for him, letting Oleg hold reams of blackmail material he had accrued over decades on one tiny shard of silicon.

The *kompromat*, to use the Russian term for it, wasn't only Von Kassel's potential ruin, but threats to the rich and powerful all over the continent. Photos, grainy videos from hidden cameras, scans of long-since shredded files; the gathered mistakes of a great many important men.

Sasha remembered the night when Lars Von Kassel's future became the property of Oleg Gorod. The politician liked his brandy and he liked women of a certain sort – not damaged goods like Sasha, but ones who were young and small of frame, with tight thighs and pale faces. And he enjoyed throwing them around in the bedroom during intercourse, making noise and wrecking the place.

It had been Sasha's unpleasant task on some occasions to make sure the right kind of girls were on his menu. In return for feeding his private appetites, Von Kassel's public government connections made certain problems go away for Oleg's people. Still, she loathed the man, even if he had his uses.

But on that night, the night of his *mistake*, the relationship had gone from merely transactional to something quite different.

The politician drank far too much, and when he couldn't perform, the companion he had taken for that night mocked him for it. Standing there, a naked, impotent child in a man's body, Von Kassel's apathetic backhand knocked the girl off her feet. She tripped and fell badly against a bedpost. The impact broke her skull, the injury fast and fatal.

Sasha recalled the sight of the dead girl after it happened, as she directed Oleg's men to gather the corpse and clean the up the bedroom. Her eyes hazy and unfocussed, her porcelain face slack and a fan of dark blood congealing around her nostrils. Von Kassel ignored them as he fretted and dressed himself at the other end of the hotel suite, as far away from his handiwork as he could be without leaving the room.

Vincent had the suite wired to film the liaison on Oleg's orders. They always did. But this turn of events provided a new opportunity which the old soldier exploited with a brisk, clinical accuracy.

*When a target commits an error,* he'd told her, *do not hesitate. Strike in the moment and take control. Such instants can change fortunes.*

Later, Oleg let something slip about the brandy that had been left in the suite that night, and what might have been added to it.

Sasha started to wonder if the girl's sordid end had been engineered from the start. The component pieces of a tragedy, put in place to achieve a result that would benefit Oleg far more than a few photos of some sleazy politician's face buried between the thighs of a sex worker.

Before, Oleg had a minor degree of leverage over Von Kassel. If he had used it, the results would be negligible – this was Europe after all, where permissive attitudes held greater sway than in other parts of the world, not like puritanical America with their squeamishness over fornication – and such a scandal might even be weathered by a man as slick as the unctuous politician.

But the girl's murder changed the conditions of Von Kassel's arrangement. She had been part of his stable, his property. There was a cash value attached to the corpse. And far worse than that was the footage showing the politician's callous, dismissive act of violence, captured in living colour. It meant Oleg *owned* him.

In the weeks that followed, the tasks Von Kassel was called to perform grew more complex, more frequent. There was also the matter of the debt incurred for the loss of earnings from the girl's clients. It cost a lot of euros to ship over the new ones, to keep them fed and dressed and clean.

When Oleg had dispatched Sasha to name the price to be paid, she thought Von Kassel might shit himself on the spot. But he had solemnly accepted, clinging to the belief that he could buy his way out of this mess he was in with a bag of used currency. Rich people always thought throwing money at a problem would make it go away, but that was a fallacy. In situations like this, you could only really buy time, not a solution.

He did his best to hide it, but defeat haunted Von Kassel's face. Sasha watched him stare out into the rain, watched the emotion slowly bleed away until he returned to the inane neutrality that was his default expression. 'You certainly know how to make your mark on a man,' he offered, forcing a grin. 'Kudos, sir.'

The compliment meant nothing to Oleg, but he let it lay where it fell. 'I am concerned you have forgotten your obligations,' he said. 'The seriousness of them.' He prodded Von Kassel again. 'Remember, I protect you. Only I can keep you out of a prison cell.'

Something in that statement made the politician shoot a hard look in the direction of his driver, but Sasha couldn't read the content in the glance. 'Yes,' he said stiffly, 'I suppose that is true.'

'Don't become an annoyance,' Oleg warned. 'Remain useful.' He patted the other man on the shoulder, showing him a cold smile. 'And all will be well.'

'Indeed, indeed.' Von Kassel's head bobbed, as he grasped at a straw of hope. He took a breath, and Sasha guessed he was marshalling some fresh, facile response. Oleg didn't give him time to voice it.

'If I don't have my money by dawn,' he told him, 'that dead whore will be the least of your problems.'

The phone in Sasha's jacket hummed against her ribs and she frowned, plucking it out of her pocket with long fingers, jamming it to her ear. 'Talk,' she said tersely, turning away from the other men.

'*It's me.*' Vincent's voice sounded flat, as if he were inside a small space. '*I found Imran. He let me into the security room.*'

Faintly, Sasha heard another man's voice. '*Hey, we're not allowed to use phones in here . . .*'

'*Shut up!*' Vincent snapped, off-mike, then came back to her. '*So tell me, what am I looking for?*'

'We will get to that,' she told him. 'The car park first. Make him delete the recording of us and Von Kassel.'

'*Already done*, chérie,' the Frenchman said smugly.

'I told you not to call me that. Do it again, and I cut off your prick.'

'*Forgive me,*' he said, back-pedalling. '*What next?*'

Sasha held the phone away and saw Boch watching from the sidelines. 'You. The bag. When did you deposit it?'

Boch's lip curled at her instant attitude. The man didn't like taking orders from her. He looked at his watch. '20:30 hours.'

She relayed the information to Vincent. 'Is there a camera that covers the entrance to the men's washroom on the concourse?'

'*Imran says yes,*' replied Vincent. '*He's not happy about being forced to do this.*'

'Explain it to him,' Sasha replied. 'Don't call back until you have something we can use.'

'She sounds, uh, *serious,*' offered Imran, as Vincent cut the call. The skinny East Asian security technician had been pretending not to listen to the conversation, but in the close quarters of the airport's CCTV monitoring room, he couldn't miss hearing her clipped responses to Vincent's words.

'Very much so,' noted Vincent, and decided to use the moment to his advantage. 'It would not go well for you if she had to come over here.' He shook his head, and ran a hand through his lank hair. 'Neither of us would want that.'

'Uh,' repeated Imran. He made the noise a lot, like a placeholder for when he had nothing better to say. His round, tawny face was too large for his skinny neck, and he had an oily, unhealthy complexion. Along with that, Vincent had the impression that the man wasn't the sharpest tool in the box.

He told Imran what he needed to see and what time index to search for. In front of the technician, one wall of the room was arrayed with video screens, each relaying a live feed from a camera inside the terminal. Some were static, others were moving in a slow back-and-forth pan, surveying passenger lounges and the duty-free store. A control panel with a stubby joystick and function buttons like that of a video player was mounted in front of them.

'We get a lot of trade there,' Imran noted, nodding at the feed from the store. 'Shoplifters. People try to sneak bottles off the display, hide it under a jacket.' He manipulated a dial, rewinding a few seconds of footage, then letting it play on.

'Don't care,' Vincent replied, with a sniff. 'Show me the washroom.'

'Uh. OK.' The technician consulted a floorplan displaying the locations of the terminal's cameras, each one designated with a numerical code. He punched in the number corresponding to the camera across from the washroom and the live feed appeared on a central monitor.

Vincent cocked his head, examining the view, the motion oddly birdlike. As he watched, an elderly man with a walking stick emerged from the men's room, adjusting his belt as he went. The camera's eye didn't see past the washroom's doorway. 'That's the best you can do?'

'Uh, yes.' Imran nodded. 'It's a static camera. Doesn't move.'

Vincent folded his arms. 'Show me this angle from eight thirty this evening.'

'OK.' The technician punched more buttons on the keypad, and the monitor view flickered. Now the time index ticking away in the corner was different, and the light quality had changed.

'Make it go quicker.' Vincent made a rolling motion with his hand, and Imran put the recording up to four times normal speed.

Within a few moments, the politician's man Boch passed across the frame, the sped-up replay giving him a cartoonish gait as he marched into the washroom, toting a heavy black bag. Vincent made a note of the time, scribbling it down on the back of his cigarette packet, and then again when Boch exited less than a minute later without the bag.

'Is that it?' Imran gave him a worried look, shooting a glance at the door. 'Only, you're not supposed to be in here, right? And if someone sees you, I get in a lot of trouble.'

'You think so?' Vincent leaned forward, forcing Imran to slide away from the control panel. Now he had watched the technician working the buttons and dials, he understood how the playback worked and he helped himself to it, dialling up the replay speed another few notches. 'You don't know what trouble is, my friend.' He didn't look away from the screen as he spoke, eyes on the men moving in and out of the washroom, one after another.

Then he saw the young guy with brown hair in the hi-vis vest enter empty-handed, and then exit a minute or two later toting the black bag over his shoulder. Vincent hit the pause button and noted the time index again.

'Uh, well . . .'

He sighed and shot Imran an uncompromising glare, before the man could utter another word. 'All it takes is one phone call to the BAMF,' said Vincent, using the term for the federal office for immigration. 'One call to have them check your papers. If they take a close look, what will they find?'

Imran broke his gaze and stared at the floor, saying nothing. The young man's papers were good fakes, bought and paid for to get him into Germany's welfare system, but they both knew they wouldn't stand up to an intense investigation.

Oleg's organisation didn't only traffic in sex workers and illegal commodities. They made a tidy profit on counterfeit papers as a side deal, and as a bonus sometimes those fake IDs put useful people in their debt. In this case, people like the hapless Imran.

Satisfied that the technician would remain quiet, Vincent returned to the monitor. He had the time where Boch had dropped off the bag and the time where Horst had recovered it. Somewhere between those two points, somebody else had entered the washroom and swapped out the money.

Vincent ran the footage in reverse, watching for someone walking backwards into the corridor, someone with a bag large enough to hold a couple of million euros in cash.

And eventually, he had his quarry.

# FIFTEEN

Sasha's phone buzzed angrily, indicating the arrival of a message. Flicking up the screen with her thumb, an image appeared before her. Captured by Vincent from the airport's security cameras, she looked down at a picture of a harried-looking white man in his forties approaching the washroom, caught in mid-stride as he dragged a Pullman case behind him.

The phone vibrated again as a second and then a third image appeared, other grabs from a monitor screen showing the same man at different angles. In these pictures, she could see him laden down with a shoulder bag and a third item of luggage, a large bag slung over the extendable handle of the wheeled case. She flicked back to the first picture again; in that one, the man only had the shoulder bag and the Pullman.

Sasha pulled at the corners of the clearest shot, expanding it until the man's face filled the screen. She had seen his expression before. That peculiar mix of fear and daring, that air of something to hide.

The phone buzzed once more, this time signalling a text message. *This is the one,* Vincent had typed. *Nobody else left washroom with different baggage.*

'What is it?' Oleg was at her side. He'd approached silently, ghosting up to her while her attention was on the screen.

She handed him her phone. 'Take a look.'

'Is this who stole from me?'

'That is what I will find out.' She paused. 'I don't know the face.'

'It matters little. Just another thief.' Oleg looked as if he was about to spit. 'Like flies on shit.' He turned and barked an order. 'Miros! Come here!'

His eternally dour expression unchanged, the older man approached, passing by Von Kassel's driver as he did so. Sasha thought of two dogs sizing each other up, growls ready in their throats. Oleg held Sasha's phone up so Miros could see the image of the man with the bags.

'That him?' Miros's lips thinned. 'Still here?'

'Vincent will be using the cameras to look for this man,' she offered.

'Search the airport for this wretch. He won't be going anywhere in this weather. Recover what belongs to me.' Oleg turned away and pressed the phone back into Sasha's hand, jerking his thumb at Miros. 'You send the pictures to him, yes?'

Sasha tensed, sensing the direction of the conversation. 'I will go with him—'

'You remain with me.' Oleg shook his head.

She started to protest, but Von Kassel – who had been hovering at the edges of the conversation – took the opportunity to insert himself into the discussion.

'You appear to have this in hand, I will leave this troublesome business to you,' he began, and he waved at the open hangar doors where the rain continued to hammer down in sheets. 'This storm! I really cannot remain, you understand? I'm expected in the office tomorrow . . .' The politician took a step towards his driver, nodding and smiling as if his decision to leave had everyone's approval.

'No.' Oleg's voice cracked like a whip. Sasha winced to hear the tone of it, unconsciously recalling the punishment that usually followed.

Miros took his cue and stepped in front of Von Kassel, his hand resting on the pistol in his waistband, and the politician halted. In turn, Von Kassel shot a worried look at his man Boch, who stood drawing his hands into fists. Sasha knew instinctively that unless the situation defused in the next sixty seconds, there would be bloodshed.

'I do not like repeating myself,' Oleg said carefully, addressing the politician. 'You will not leave my sight until your debt is in my hands. Would you rather stay out here, or shall I put you in there?' He inclined his head in the direction of the area at the back of the hangar, where the cold storage lockers holding the front company's corpses-in-transit were situated.

Von Kassel grinned weakly, but it didn't reach his eyes. Sasha was learning that this was his evasive reaction, to feign good humour when he was out of his depth or if he felt threatened. 'No need for threats, my friend,' he managed. 'But you must realise, matters of state take precedence—'

'Yes, yes,' Oleg cut him off once more. 'You are a very important man with very important things to do.' He sighed. 'Do you think that here, under my roof, that makes any difference to me?'

'The sooner we find the man who took the money, the sooner you can go,' Sasha told him.

A light snapped on in Von Kassel's eyes. 'All right. Yes!' He snapped his fingers as if he were summoning a waiter, and reluctantly his driver approached. 'Boch! Make yourself useful! Go with him.' Before anyone could complain, he nodded vigorously at Oleg. 'Two sets of eyes are more useful than one, yes? And what better way for me to prove to you that I had nothing to do with this unfortunate complication?'

Von Kassel's driver was reluctant, but he didn't argue. He and Miros exchanged another wary glance. 'I need to see the target,' said the politician's man, producing his own smartphone. 'Send me the picture.'

'All right,' said Oleg, at length, considering his next words. 'The money is the priority.'

Miros frowned. 'The thief?'

'Bring him back alive,' Oleg replied, thinking it through. 'Another example will need to be made.'

Boch tried to keep his expression neutral, but he knew his misgivings were writ large across his craggy features. As the woman in the leather jacket tapped at her phone to message the photos to him and Gorod's taciturn thug, he tried to catch Von Kassel's eye. His principal studiously ignored him.

*This is a bad idea.* Once again, the arrogant minister acted without reflection, making the choice that made him look best in the moment, never stopping to consider what ramifications it might have. *I shouldn't expect any less,* thought Boch. *He's built a political career on doing exactly the same thing.*

But this wasn't some abstract debate where Von Kassel could make hollow promises and then skate clear of any responsibility for them after the fact. This was an arena populated by violent criminals – perversely, men to whom someone's word was considered their bond. That notion was alien to Boch's employer. Von Kassel expected the truth to be whatever he said it was, even if it flew in the face of reality.

Boch knew there was a good chance the Lars Von Kassel would not be able to stay silent, that the man would infuriate Oleg Gorod without even knowing it. Oleg's foul temper was as notorious as his vicious nature. Everyone knew the stories about the atrocities the war veteran had committed in his native Serbia, back in the days of civil war and ethnic cleansing. Boch was a hard man by any measure of the term, but even he knew enough to fear Oleg's legendary capacity for brutality. He pictured Von Kassel saying the wrong thing, making one glib remark too many, only for the old soldier to lose patience and gut him like a pig.

It wasn't that Boch gave a wet shit about the politician's life. Under other circumstances, he might have snapped the idiot's neck himself. No, his concern was for what would happen if Von Kassel disappeared.

Just like Oleg and his memory card full of *kompromat*, Von Kassel had his stock of influence as well, hidden in some unknown place that Boch had been unable to determine. Clumsy by the Serbian's standards, the politician had still managed to secret away a few details that gave him leverage over others, details that would come to light if he were ever to suffer some sudden, unexpected misfortune.

Among that material was an accident report from the Autobahnpolizei, detailing a fatal collision on a storm-blasted night like this one. The report described a young mother and her six-year-old son, and how they were both killed instantly when their Renault spun out on the wet highway, crashing into the median strip.

It contained details of the black Mercedes-Benz that had rammed heedlessly into the vehicle at high speed, the erratic motion of the car that suggested the driver had been drinking heavily, and the telling detail of how the vehicle had failed to stop after the collision.

An old friend of Lars Von Kassel, now a senior police commander, brought the report to the politician because the Mercedes was registered to his office. Von Kassel himself had been attending a ballet performance at the time of the accident, but a key member of his staff had been behind the wheel of the car that night.

Dieter Boch remembered his hazy moment of inattention on that rain-slick road when the two cars struck, and the icy sensation as adrenaline shock burned through the vodka fogging his thoughts. The alcohol had grown to become a problem after his discharge from the army, and while at first he had been able to hide it well enough to get the driving job, it had grown to overshadow every aspect of his life. Until that night.

He gave up drinking the next day, and he hadn't touched a drop since. But that wouldn't resurrect the late Fraulein Gerda Kraft and her little boy Florian, and it didn't free her widower Anton from the despair Boch's weakness had inflicted on an innocent family.

He had been in the midst of packing a bag, contemplating a fugitive life on the run from the consequences of his actions, when Von Kassel found him. The politician knew the details, of course – he could show keen focus when he wanted to. But rather than throw his driver to the wolves, he made the whole sorry incident fade away. The police report that would have led investigators to Boch was not filed. The tragedy of the hit-and-run remained unresolved.

And in return, it meant Von Kassel *owned* him.

In his apartment on that fateful morning after, as Boch poured bottle after bottle of cheap booze into the maw of his sink, the politician watched and talked. And he said something honest, in the one and only time Boch could ever recall hearing Von Kassel speak the truth.

*I don't know how to engender loyalty from others,* he said, in a rare moment of self-awareness. *I barely know the meaning of the word. I can amuse, I can persuade and mislead and threaten. But I don't know how to make men willingly give me their allegiance. I only know how to take advantage of their worst natures.*

Von Kassel handed him the police file and explained that now he had two things that were unique in the world; one was the only other copy of the paperwork; the other was Dieter Boch's complete obedience.

Boch's reverie faded back into the moment at hand, and he regarded Von Kassel, and Oleg standing behind him. They were part of a pyramid of coercion, one preying upon the other.

The politician gave him a sage nod, ignorant of the driver's train of thought. 'You still have that pistol, don't you? Take it, in case you need to make a point.' He leaned in, his voice dropping. 'Don't let me down.'

A hundred different retorts boiled around in Boch's mind, but he stamped on them, and simply nodded as a good servant was meant to.

Time didn't pass for Kevin.

It oozed. It crawled. It dithered.

He tried to stop himself from lifting his cuff to look at his wristwatch every few minutes, but the action was turning into some kind of unconscious tic and he couldn't stop himself repeating it.

He peered at the sweep of the Promaster's minute hand, trying to perceive its motion. Nothing. Had he stepped into some weird pocket of oblivion when he decided to take the money? *Perhaps it's cursed*, he thought, with a weak smirk, *like the gold doubloons in that pirate movie. I stole the cash and now I'm trapped in a crappy municipal airport for eternity.*

As an iteration of Hell, this was an insidious one. Being stuck in Barsbeker was a mix of dry fear and mind-numbing tedium, and Kevin shivered involuntarily at the notion.

He let out a sigh, banishing the bleak fantasy. He'd taken the chair at the end of a row, in the lee of a support pillar to give himself some cover from anyone who passed up and down the main concourse. Not that many people were moving around now, of course. The airport had cycled into night mode, some of the lighting dimmed, all but a few of the shops and restaurants closed down until the morning and the departure screens blank. The aircraft at the stands outside were dark avian shapes in the haze of the rain.

The other travellers in the same boat as Kevin – those unable to get a hotel room, those stuck here for the night after missing a connection or the far-too-early arrivals – were scattered around in ones and twos up and down the empty departure lounges. Across from him, a thickset young man with the look of a student sat staring into the flickering light of a movie as it spooled out over the tablet computer in his hands. He wore oversized headphones that made him look like a cartoon character, and now and then he sniggered wetly at whatever he was watching. A few seats down, an old, tweedy couple were camped out around their luggage, both fallen asleep against one another. Mouths open, they snored in gentle unison, lost to the world.

Kevin envied them. The thing keeping him alert was at the opposite end of the spectrum; *raw, cloying anxiety.*

Out of nowhere, the storm decided to remind them of its presence with a flash of sheet lightning that backlit the clouds. For a flickering instant, the dull grey sky above the airport became a wall of dirty white. The moment of daylight brightness faded, consumed by a long moan of thunder that rolled down the length of the terminal, rattling the windows.

In the passing of that moment, Kevin's eyeline snagged on the sight of two men he hadn't noticed until now, the pair of them walking purposefully up the middle of the concourse.

His hackles rose. Both were dressed in good suits and if you saw them from the corner of your eye you might not take a second look. But if you did look twice, you would see their watchful gazes sweeping back and forth. They were hunting.

He had the impression of a pair of wolves squeezed into human clothing, stalking on their hind legs. The closest man looked like the older of the two, his worn face carved into a hangdog expression. The other one, Kevin had seen earlier that day at close hand – the broken-nosed German in the green jacket, the one who had barged right into him when he had first entered the terminal.

*They're looking for me.* He knew it instantly, with the hard conviction of a prey animal catching sight of an apex predator.

'I don't see him.' Boch pressed a finger to his earlobe, where a wireless earpiece burbled quietly.

Connected to the phone in his pocket, he had an open line to Oleg's man Vincent up in the airport's security room, as the Frenchman directed their pursuit. He looked up, finding one of the glossy black domes fitted into the ceiling of the terminal. Dozens of them lined the concourse, and behind each one was a camera feeding video back to the monitors. But not every eye was being covered all the time. There were still opportunities to slip by unnoticed – but there was no way for someone down here to know when a live feed was being scrutinised and when it was not.

At his side, Miros gave a grunt, affirming the same lack of a target. He too was listening to the conversation through a wired headphone snaking up to his ear.

'*He must be close.*' Vincent's voice sounded tinny and nasal. '*I'm looking at footage from twenty minutes ago, showing him entering that area. He hasn't left it.*'

Miros inclined his head, indicating his intentions, and wandered away in the direction of a row of vending machines, scouting the perimeter of a waiting area. Boch nodded in agreement and pulled out his phone once again, to fix the face of their target in his mind's eye.

He couldn't shake the sense that had seen this man before, earlier today. Just as Vincent was doing with the security recordings, Boch mentally rewound his memories of the day, sifting them for the target's face.

*The Englishman.* It came back to him in a rush. *Yes. The one he had nearly knocked down hours earlier, the one who seemed familiar.* An itch at the back of the ex-soldier's skull turned into a nagging tension. There was a connection here he wasn't seeing, a piece missing from the puzzle of the night's events, and it irritated him. But he would have the facts if he located this man, he was certain of it. The Englishman didn't look like the type who could withstand Boch's style of questioning for long.

'*Found him.*' Miros muttered the words into the microphone tab hanging off the cord at his throat. '*Far corner.*'

Boch's head snapped up and he looked, spotting Miros advancing towards the lounge area. Tracking his line of sight, he zeroed in on what the other man had spotted.

Hidden half out of sight behind a thick pillar a few hundred metres away, the Englishman had one hand up to his face, making a poor attempt to conceal his features. Miros deliberately let his jacket fall open, and only Boch and their target saw the glint off the shiny, nickel-plated pistol in the man's belt.

*Idiot!* Instead of approaching carefully, Oleg's thug tried to intimidate the Englishman from across the room by flashing the presence of his weapon.

'Cover that up, moron!' Boch snarled into his headset, but the damage had already been done.

Spooked, the target sprang to his feet, dragging his shoulder bag up with him, and quickly moved away. He deliberately took a path that wound past the other civilians dotted around the open-plan lounge, forcing Miros and Boch to double back and around rather than follow.

'*Do you have him?*'

'He's on the move,' Boch said into the microphone.

'*Be careful,*' Vincent called back. '*There's still a* flic *patrolling around there. If we do this quietly, they'll never even know it.*'

*If I run, they will kill me.*

Kevin's hands went into his pockets to stop them from shaking. He felt the eyes of his pursuers boring into his back, and with each step he took he was afraid a kick would drop him to his knees, or a shove would knock him into the wall.

He veered into the compact maze of the duty-free store. The store was arranged into sections with paths that snaked from one to the other – the whiskey stocks leading into gin and vodka, tobacco products to watches and sunglasses, perfumes adjoining colognes and so on. Kevin had entered through the latter, passing through the faint aromas of dozens of spent tester sprays, then jackknifed into the booze section. Reflected in a tower of schnapps bottles, he glimpsed a dart of forest-green, the jacket of the craggy German somewhere behind him.

Kevin thought about snatching up a heavy, square-sided decanter to use as a weapon, but the idea was foolish, pointless. All of his half-baked plans to hide and run out the clock until the morning were crumbling. Unless he could get away from these men, it would be over. He shuddered as he thought of what they might do to him when they caught him.

Kevin stifled the screaming, accusing voice in his head that railed against the impulsive choice he had made, trying to push down the panic rising in his chest. Desperation, stupidity, avarice, conceit – all of them had put him where he was now. What mattered in this second was the choice he made next.

He turned right, pushing past a temporary no-entry barrier closing off the cabinets of cigars, and past a startled custodian in the middle of mopping the floor.

A formidable-looking sales assistant behind the counter saw him and called out in hard, strident German. '*Dieser Abschnitt ist geschlossen!*' She came rushing after Kevin as he strode quickly across the wet floor, deliberately ignoring her, making for the opposite exit.

As he passed back on to the concourse, he risked a look over his shoulder and saw the two men arguing with the assistant, the woman making *step-away* gestures as she blocked the path to follow him, forcing them to double back again.

Instead of taking the obvious route, Kevin followed the low planters that took him towards the food court, staying close to a line of support pillars for cover. Week after week of travelling through Barsbeker during the drawn-out negotiations for the Montag deal had given him a mental map of the airport terminal's layout – mostly for the shortcuts to the departure gates that allowed Kevin to shave a few minutes off his boarding time. Now that knowledge was coming in useful, knowledge he guessed that the man in the green jacket and his grim-faced companion didn't share.

He passed the stairwell leading up to the mezzanine and briefly considered going back to the multi-faith room. He shook his head. It was too far and even if he made it there, with only one entrance he would be boxed in. The thought of being trapped in that soundproofed room with the two thugs hunting him made Kevin's gut flood with ice.

The smarter option would be to put himself where there were lots of people around, but at this hour the terminal's transient population was thinly spread. That left the dubious option of approaching the security point and gambling that the presence of any police and customs officers would deter the criminals – but that was back in the opposite direction.

As clever as Kevin's brief detour had been, he was quickly running out of room to manoeuvre. If he wanted to get through this in one piece, he needed to *think* his way out of it instead of *reacting*.

*It's a flow problem*, he told himself, switching back to his engineering mindset. *Find a different path. Bypass the blockage.*

Kevin skirted the edges of the food court, circling around. The restaurants and service counters were shut, metal mesh barriers closing them off, their inner spaces darkened even while the open seating area before them was still brightly lit. He looked for shadows but there were none.

The food court had several entrances, and at the last moment, Kevin turned away from his intended path, towards the closest one in the lee of a large animated billboard. He hesitated on the threshold, and that pause saved him.

The German in the green jacket and the grim-faced thug were waiting near the next entrance along, the very one he would have stepped through had he kept going.

*How did they get ahead of me?* He shrank behind the billboard, peering through a gap. *How did they know where I was going to come out?*

As he watched, the man in the jacket looked up at the ceiling, revealing the black plastic comma of a wireless headset in his earlobe. He was talking to someone, and Kevin followed his line of sight.

The German was looking directly into a black hemisphere embedded in the acoustic tiles overhead.

*Security camera.* The chill in Kevin gut worsened as the truth became apparent. *They have someone watching me.*

# SIXTEEN

'He's not here.' Boch growled. 'You said you had him.'

'*I said he was moving that way,*' Vincent retorted, his voice rising into a whine over the open channel. '*He must still be in the food court.*'

'Saw us,' said Miros, shaking his head. Before Boch could stop him, Oleg's man left the spot where they were waiting and strode into the empty dining area. He drew his gun, keeping it down along the line of his thigh as he moved.

'Put that away!' Boch hissed the demand at Miros's back, but the other man ignored him, stalking though between the vacant tables and chairs.

'*There's a service door about twenty metres away,*' said Vincent. '*He could have slipped out there.*'

'Where does it lead?'

'*A stairwell to ground level, and out to the runway apron.*'

Scowling, Boch left Miros to his own devices and strode to the windows looking out over the empty jet bridges and storm-lashed tarmac. Torrential, driving rainfall flowed across the parking apron in dense sheets, the deluge coming down so hard that even he would have baulked at the idea of going out in it. His instinct about the Englishman told him the man wasn't desperate enough to risk such foul weather. 'No. He's still in here with us.'

Boch looked back at the food court. Miros stood in the middle of the space, peering under the tables.

'*Wait* ... ' Vincent went off-mike for a second and Boch heard him berating someone. '*No, idiot, bring up that one! There!*' When he came back on, his words came with rapid-fire speed. '*I see him! He must have spotted you: he doubled back around!*'

'Which way now?'

'*He's taking the path through the store ... Maybe to the main entrance?*' Vincent trailed off. '*It's hard to tell. He's avoiding the cameras. This one is smart, he's looking for blind spots.*'

'Not that smart,' Boch muttered, turning the thought over in his mind. 'I know where he's going.' He gave a shrill, purse-lipped whistle to attract Miros's attention, and the other man looked his way. 'You follow, I'll get ahead of him. We'll catch him between us.'

Kevin's instincts told him to run.

But if he ran, he would become obvious, he would be picked out by motion alone, and he had no desire to find out what would happen if he was caught by the men pursuing him.

Was there still a way out of this that ended with him keeping the money? He wanted to believe there was, but with each minute that passed, that possibility receded further into the distance. As he walked briskly towards the security area near the airside entrance, Kevin dismantled the problem in his mind as if were a piece of faulty machinery.

Only he knew where the money was at this moment, and only he had the code to open the locker where it was hidden. If he could put himself somewhere that was just as safe for the next few hours, there was still a chance he could make it to freedom. But first he needed to get rid of the criminals, either drive them away or force them out into the open.

Up ahead, no more than a few hundred metres distant, Kevin saw a pair of customs officials in conversation with a man in the uniform shirt and vest of a German police officer. The cop had his cap in his hand, toying with it as he spoke.

Kevin's heart sank. It was the same man who had given him a hard time at the security checkpoint, the same one who had almost twisted off his wrist when had made the mistake of putting a hand on him.

He faltered, his pace slowing. Seeing the cop – *Alfons, that was his name* – was almost enough to make Kevin lose his grip on the whole situation. If he came clean to the police officer about the whole situation, how likely was it that the man would give him an honest hearing?

He ran through other options, from the basic to the ridiculous; what if he picked an argument with the cop, or did something to deliberately provoke a reaction? Would Alfons take him in the back somewhere, maybe lock him in a room and give him a talking to? Kevin shook his head. *Too risky.* There was a chance the German might decide to actually arrest him, and if he was searched, if the wad of money in his pocket was discovered, how the hell would he explain that away?

No, the only way this was going to work was if Kevin could somehow make Alfons get in the way of the man in the green jacket and his plug-ugly friend.

*I can do it,* he told himself. *I'll tell him I saw something unusual.* He remembered the message on the poster on the wall at the checkpoint – *if you see something, say something.*

But then a flash of green caught his eye and Kevin saw the man in the jacket walk right in front of him, stepping up to drop a piece of litter into a waste bin, as casual as anything. Once again, the man in green had made an end run around him, cutting him off from safety.

Kevin stopped dead in the middle of the concourse. He was no more than a hundred metres from Officer Alfons, who continued on in his conversation with the customs agents, blithely unaware of the drama unfolding behind him. Directly between Kevin and the policeman, the man in the jacket stood watching, looking him up and down like a butcher appraising a disappointing cut of meat.

Then slowly, he met Kevin's gaze and shook his head. The gesture silently communicated the warning. *Don't do anything stupid.*

The urge to scream formed in Kevin's throat. He took a breath, forming the words in his mind, playing out the moment.

*Help! Help! He's got a gun!* He'd yell it at the top of his lungs and run for cover, leaving green-jacket there to be dog-piled by Alfons and his friends.

Except it was likely this man *did* have a weapon. His colleague certainly did, Kevin had seen it stuffed in his waistband, and he had no doubt that other thug was somewhere close by.

If he cried out, what would stop the man in the green jacket from shooting up the place? The cop had a pistol too: most of the German police force carried them as a matter of course. What if opening his mouth lit off a shoot-out, right here in the middle of the terminal? There were a dozen other people around them, other travellers waiting out the storm, oblivious to the danger among them. The thought of bloody violence erupting in here made Kevin feel physically sick.

One of the customs men said something that made Alfons burst out laughing, the sound of his chugging guffaw so loud and so abrupt that it made the man in the jacket twist around in surprise.

Kevin seized the moment of inattention and strode away, taking the only other path open to him. He couldn't go back – the thug with the gun had to be behind him; he couldn't go forward, not with green-jacket in the way; so he walked as quickly as possible around the line of the support pillars and down in the direction of the KnightSky departure gate.

He sped up into a jog, glancing over his shoulder. Green-jacket followed, his pace measured, and as Kevin watched he saw the other thug approaching from another angle. They had him now – all they needed to do was trace the concourse to the farthest departure gate. This wing of the terminal ended in another silent lounge and a wall of windows looking out on to a parked airliner. Aside from a couple of travellers stretched out and asleep across the chairs, this area was practically empty.

Ducking behind a departure board screen, Kevin broke line of sight with the men and shifted the carry-on bag on his shoulder. He looked at the doors beyond the KnightSky desk, the same doors he should have walked through to board his flight earlier that evening. An elevated jet bridge beyond them led to nowhere, but a set of stairs vanished down to the ground floor service areas. He ran to the entrance, but the doors remained firmly locked shut, knocking him back when he tried to force them open.

*No escape that way.*

He threw another look over his shoulder. Any second now the two men would appear around the side of the inert departures screen, and the chase would be over.

Then Kevin's gaze caught on the shuttered front of the Kaffee Tek counter in an alcove across the way, and his adrenaline spiked. There was still one more thing he could do. There was still one person here he could trust to help him.

*This isn't over yet!*

He rushed to the coffee stand and grabbed the shutters, pressing his face to the gaps in the panels to look through and inside. A few lights were still on in there, and Kevin banged the flat of his hand on the shutters, calling out. 'Richie! Richie, mate! You in there? I need help!'

'What?' A voice filtered out from the back of the coffee stand's tiny kitchen.

'It's me, Kevin!' He pulled at the latch that would open the shutters, but it wouldn't budge. 'Please, you have to let me in!' His voice rose with the pitch of his panic.

The shutters rolled up a half-metre and Richie's wide-eyed face appeared in the gap. 'You can see I'm closed, right? Seriously, I shouldn't even be here myself—'

'Don't care!' Kevin shrugged off his shoulder bag and shoved it through the open gap, then followed it himself, sliding up and over the counter, down into the serving space.

'Hey, no! My side, your side! I told you before, you can't do that!' Richie held out his hands, trying to stop the invasion, but it was too late. Kevin reached back and slammed the shutter down into place, fumbling for the bolts that would lock it closed.

'I'm sorry, I really am . . .' Kevin's voice dropped into a low whisper. 'But you're the only person I can count on right now.'

'What?' Richie recoiled at his statement, wavering between surprise and annoyance. 'What the fuck are you going on about? You high or something?'

'There's two blokes out there looking for me. They find me, I'm in a lot of trouble . . .'

'Cops?' Richie shook his head. 'Get out! I don't need that kind of heat!'

'No, not police,' insisted Kevin. 'Worse than that.'

Richie pushed past him and returned to the shutters, looking out through the gaps in the metal panels. Kevin looked over his shoulder and caught sight of the man in the green jacket and the gun-thug, the two of them loitering by the empty departure lounge, scanning the space like hunting dogs.

'Oh. Right.' Richie's attitude shifted, turning from annoyance to something Kevin couldn't read. 'I get it.'

A question rose in Kevin's thoughts. 'Do you know them?'

'Nah,' said the other man, lowering his own voice. His back was turned so Kevin couldn't see his face. 'But I ... I know the type, yeah? Well enough to wanna stay the fuck out of their way.' At length, Richie looked around. 'Did you piss off someone nasty?'

'Something like that.'

'You said, like, you make water bottles. How's that get you into trouble with them?' Richie retreated away from the shutters, moving deeper into the back of the coffee stand's narrow confines. 'Or was that a load of bollocks?'

'No, but I ... ' Kevin hesitated on the verge of letting out the whole story, then held it in at the last second and shook his head. 'It's complicated.'

'Yeah, I bet.' Richie sized him up, and Kevin had the uncomfortable sense that the other man was weighing his options, considering the risks he would run in hiding his regular customer. 'This ain't like me giving you a free latte with your tenth cup,' he went on. 'This is well dodgy.'

Kevin looked past the other man, to the door that led into the back areas of the terminal, his mind racing. 'You have a car, right? Like, out in the employee car park?'

'Well, yeah,' admitted Richie. 'But I wasn't going to drive back to my flat any time soon. I mean, have you seen that rain out there? That shit's *biblical*. Road'll be washed out.'

'But you *could* drive,' Kevin insisted, seizing on the idea. 'If you were willing to chance it.' Before the other man could reply, he continued. 'I can pay you. Get me out of the airport and I'll make it worth your while.'

'Oh yeah?' Richie raised an eyebrow.

'What do you make? Ten euros an hour?' Kevin honestly had no idea what the going rate was for a barista, and he plucked the number out of the air. 'I'll give you, uh, a *thousand*.'

*The money is safe and hidden in the left-luggage locker*, he thought, *I could leave it there for days, weeks even. Come back when things have calmed down and pick it up. I just need to get away right* now.

'I'm not a taxi, mate,' Richie retorted. 'Shit, you probably need a fuckin' boat out there tonight, not a car!'

Kevin heard voices from the other side of the shutters, and footsteps approaching. His desperation rose. The hunters were closing in. It had to be now or never. He made the only choice he could.

'Look, do it and I'll give you this.' Kevin tore the pack of banknotes from inside his jacket and held it out to the other man. Richie's eyes widened in shock at the sight of the inch-thick wad of euros. 'You drive me out of here and it's yours.'

Seconds seemed to lengthen into hours, then Richie gave a nod and snatched the money out of his hand. 'Yeah, right, come on then.' The cash vanished into his pocket.

He shoved Kevin towards the back door as the shutters rattled loudly against their frame. Fingers appeared around the gap where the low edge met the countertop, grasping for purchase, and then the whole thing shook violently as the men outside struggled to get it open. To Kevin's horror, he saw the blocky silver muzzle of a handgun thrust through the gap, the black eye of the barrel sweeping left and right.

'Move!' hissed Richie, propelling him out through the door.

On the other side, in the section where passengers were never meant to set foot, the neat and clean spaces of the airport terminal building were replaced with drab concrete walls, echoing metallic corridors and harsh industrial lighting. Kevin let himself be guided into a service lift with a drop-gate door. As Richie sprinted in after him, the other man slammed the heel of his hand against a control panel and the door clanked shut.

It was only as the lift started to descend that Kevin realised he was missing something. In a hot burst of dread he snatched at his shoulder, grasping for the strap of his carry-on bag. It wasn't there.

'Oh *fuck*!' He dived for the lift controls, mashing the buttons.

'What are you doing?' Richie pushed him away.

'I have to go back!'

'Are you mental? A second ago you were begging to leave!'

'My bag!' Kevin shouted the words at him. 'I left my bag up there!' In the rush and the panic of their escape, he hadn't remembered to pick it up from where it lay on the coffee-shop counter.

'Have to leave it, then,' Richie said, matter-of-factly, his eyes suddenly cold. 'Unless you want to see that gun up close, yeah?'

\*

The call came in with the number of the burner phone Sasha had given to Boch, and she raised her handset to her ear, anticipating what the driver would say. She had done her research on the man, as Oleg always expected of her, aided by Vincent's skills on the dark web and the extended network of contacts under the influence of the Gorod organisation.

Boch was an ex-soldier, with a solid if unremarkable history as an infantryman and then a *Feldjäger*, the military police of Germany's armed forces. But there were blank spots in his background that couldn't be accounted for. Sasha suspected the hand of his patron, Von Kassel in that – the politician was cunning, making sure there were no visible levers of influence outsiders could use to pressure the man in his employ.

She gave the man a narrow-eyed look, which he met from across the room with a jaunty wink. Sasha tapped the CALL ANSWER tab and turned away. 'Do you have him?'

'*Not yet*,' said Boch. '*He's not acting alone. Someone is helping him. Someone working at the airport.*'

'Who?' She frowned at the thought. Oleg's organisation had its tendrils spread widely in this part of the world, and that included more than a few people working throughout the complex. Imran the security technician was only one of them.

Whomever was foolish enough to believe they could steal from Oleg and get away with it would share the same fate as that idiot Roberto.

'*I have a lead*,' said the driver. '*In his haste to run, he left behind a bag.*' She heard the sound of metal fasteners being opened, of papers being leafed through. '*There are files . . . I don't see a passport.*'

'I want it,' she replied. 'Tell Miros to bring it back to the hangar. In the meantime, you keep looking for this man and his ally.'

'*Miros won't like that.*'

'He'll do what he's told if he knows it came from me.'

Boch considered that for a moment. '*A slip of a girl like you . . . How* do *you get soldiers to toe the line? Or is it Oleg they're afraid of?*'

'Everyone should be afraid of Oleg,' she retorted, her resentment rising. 'As for me, I have my own methods of encouragement.'

'*I don't doubt it.*'

Her jaw stiffened. She didn't have time for this thug's insinuations. 'Find the thief,' Sasha repeated. 'You were a *bulle*, yes?' She used the derogatory German slang for policeman. 'It should be easy for you.'

Before he could reply, she jabbed at the End Call tab and then dialled another number. Vincent answered on the second ring. '*Oui?*'

'The thief has gone into the service areas,' she told him. 'He has a friend. We're looking for two people now.'

'*Understood,*' said the Frenchman.

Vincent raised his shoulder to hold the phone between the crook of his neck and his ear, as he leaned in over Imran and tapped on the monitors. 'You have cameras in the corridor behind there, right?'

'Uh, yeah,' said the technician, shifting uncomfortably. 'Look, how much longer is this going to take? Because I haven't had my break yet and, uh, I need to eat something . . .'

Vincent waved him into silence. 'We'll be done when I say we're done.' He tapped the screen again, more insistently this time. 'The corridor?'

'OK.' Imran punched in a few numbers and the display flicked to a grey passage, the only signage a series of coloured bands on the walls which provided directions to the backs of the different concession stands and lower service levels.

The metal doors of an industrial elevator were visible in the corner of the frame. 'Where does that go?'

'Down to ground level,' said Imran. 'The, uh, tarmac. And the sublevel, but that's storage, I think.'

'You think?' Vincent shot him an acid look. 'Do you know what initiative is, Imran?'

'No,' said the other man, with a dull blink. Vincent was reminded why it was Imran had needed fake papers to get him a job.

He hissed through his teeth, and Vincent turned to the technician, cueing up a threat vicious enough to make Imran understand how serious this was. But before he could put the fear of god into the other man, the door to the security room opened and a police officer walked in, fingers fiddling with the band of the uniform cap in his hand.

'Oh, hey.' Imran gave a wan smile to the new arrival. 'Hello, Berend.'

'I am making the rounds, checking in,' said the cop. 'And please, you will address me as *Officer Alfons*,' he added, in a way that suggested he'd said this many times before to Imran.

'Everything is, uh, fine,' Imran noted, but he didn't sell the lie one bit.

The policeman's gaze switched to Vincent and locked on to him like a radar tracking a target. 'And who are you?' His suspicion coloured every word.

Vincent made a split-second calculation. It wasn't a problem when he was here and no one knew about it, but there was a fine line between what he could get away with as one of Oleg's 'employees' and what might upset the balance. *Keep a low profile*, Sasha always said. This whole situation was attracting too much interest, and this nosy *flic* getting involved would make matters worse. He couldn't afford to have Alfons start asking questions. That would lead inevitably to a decision he didn't want to make.

'Boyfriend,' Vincent said brightly, and he leaned in and planted a chaste kiss on Imran's cheek, much to the surprise of the other man. 'Later, *chéri*.' He offered Alfons a demure smile on his way out, and slipped through the door and into the corridor as quickly as possible, disappearing around a corner before the cop could come looking.

# SEVENTEEN

The service elevator's doors folded back with a metallic clatter, and Kevin spilled out into the grubby corridor beyond, his face flushed with colour, his hands cutting through the air in anxious motions.

'Stop a second,' he insisted. 'Wait.'

'What?' Richie followed him out, his tone turning hard-edged. 'Seriously?' He jabbed a finger in the other man's chest. 'You pull me into whatever shit you're swimming through, and now you've got, what? Cold *fucking* feet?' He folded his arms across his chest and shook his head.

Kevin could see he was losing his grasp on the situation and desperately tried to reframe things, fighting down his own rising panic with a gulp of air. 'Look, you're right . . . I'm sorry. But—'

Richie wasn't listening to him. 'This is the way.' He started moving again, towards a T-junction further down the service passage.

Behind the clean facia of the airport's customer-facing spaces, Barsbeker's internal corridors were workmanlike, hard lines and walls painted a dull institutional green. The barista's footsteps echoed flatly on the scuffed linoleum flooring, and back here the air had a chill to it that felt like rain-damp.

Kevin cast around, finding a number stencil-painted on one wall, indicating that they were now on a sublevel below the main concourse. He wondered where that put them on the map of the airport as a whole.

Sensing his question, Richie pointed and frowned, aiming a finger at the junction ahead. 'Bear left, that takes us under the arrivals area and back up to the staff car park. That's where you wanna go, right? Out?'

'Yes.' Kevin nodded, then immediately shook his head. 'I mean *yes* but *no*. I mean, I can't go, not yet.'

Richie gave a sharp hiss, sucking his teeth in a gesture of frustration. 'For fuck's sake, forget your bag or whatever. Not worth it. Those arseholes chasing you probably have it now, right? Whatever's in there is as good as gone.'

'That's just it!' Kevin retorted. 'I can't let them keep it! There's stuff in the bag, papers . . . ' The colour drained from his face as a terrible possibility occurred to him, and his hands slapped at the pockets of his jacket. To Kevin's relief, his now-redundant boarding pass, his vax paperwork and passport were still there – but that didn't put him in the clear.

The voided contracts for the Montag deal were in his luggage, and in the text were details of his name, Luna Design's office address, and a dozen other facts that someone could use to discover the details of his identity.

He thought about the photo of him in the 'corporate team' section of Luna's company website, shining a forced grin in his freshly pressed suit and tie, arranged beside a block of text that talked about exactly who he was and what he did for a living. It would only take someone with a bit of internet savvy a few short steps to find out all about Kevin Tyler. A sickly sensation washed over him as he thought of the mess he was in spilling out beyond the confines of the airport and engulfing his life. He had to recover the bag before that could happen.

'I need it,' he insisted. He planted himself in the middle of the corridor, refusing to take another step. 'I won't leave without it.'

Richie turned around and stalked back towards him. All the chummy, good-natured banter the other man usually showed evaporated, and in its place Kevin saw some of the swagger and menace he remembered from the rough kids that haunted the housing estate where he had grown up. 'Look, man, you want to leg it, I'll get you out of here. You made it worth my while. But we have to go right now.' He jerked a thumb in the direction of the concourse above. 'I know them blokes, yeah? I've seen them around, doing their thing, and I don't want them knowing I'm helping you out. Let me tell you this straight, you don't get a second chance with those people.'

'I believe you,' Kevin admitted, 'but that doesn't change anything.'

Richie threw his hands up on the air and made an exasperated noise. 'You're a nutter!' He shook his head. 'Fine. Go back up there, get yourself in deeper. You're on your own, and I'm keeping the readies.' He patted the wad of money Kevin had paid him as his exit fee.

The other man walked away, picking up the pace as he made for the end of the corridor. Kevin watched him go, and he knew that without someone on his side, this moment would be the end for him. Perhaps he'd been foolish to consider Richie as anything approaching a friend, but right now the other Londoner was the closest thing he had to an ally – and he needed all the support he could get.

'I can pay you more.' Kevin heard himself say the words before the thought had fully formed in his mind. 'Help me get the bag back and I'll double what I gave you.'

Richie stopped dead, his trainers squeaking on the scuffed lino. He didn't turn around. 'Double?'

'That's right.' Kevin's mind raced and he licked his lips. His throat was dry. 'After I get the bag.'

'This better not be hooky cash,' Richie said warily. 'That why you were mucking about with the note tester at the till?'

'It's not counterfeit,' he confirmed.

'And it's not yours, is it?' The other man turned back a second time, pacing out the thought, his eyes narrowing. He made a winding-up motion by his head. 'Yeah. You ripped off those prats upstairs, didn't you?' He didn't wait for Kevin to admit it. 'That's fucking ballsy, man. I wouldn't reckon you'd got that in you, but shit . . . '

Kevin tried to keep his expression neutral and give nothing away, but a good poker face had never been his strong suit.

Richie laughed humourlessly. 'So, here's the thing. You're going to give me *four* times the cash.' He held up the fingers of one hand. 'And you're gonna do what I tell you, or we're both screwed. You get me?'

'I get you.' Kevin sighed, momentarily disappointed at himself for caving in to this new demand so quickly. But it wasn't like he had a lot of options at this point.

'Where's the cash now?' Richie looked him up and down. 'You ain't carrying it on you, obviously.'

'It's ... In a safe place.' He caught himself before he said the words *in a locker*. Richie might know what and where he meant by that, and Kevin couldn't give up what amount of leverage he still had.

'OK, yeah. Play it like that.' Richie nodded. He paced back past Kevin, wandering in the opposite direction to the T-junction. The corridor ahead that way wasn't as well-lit as the other path, and the floor sloped downward in a slight incline marked with patches of damp. 'I know where those blokes hang out,' Richie added. 'There's these private hangars on the other side of the runways, yeah? For cargo and shit? It's where the rich dicks park their planes.'

Kevin accepted that with a nod. He'd seen the hangars Richie described on numerous occasions, catching glimpses of them from the air when he flew in and out of the airport. The cluster of buildings were isolated out where the border fences met the woods beyond.

'If they're gonna be anywhere, that's the place.' Richie shrugged. 'But you got no guarantee they'll bring your stuff there. It's a long shot.'

'I'll take that chance,' Kevin said firmly, with more conviction than he felt.

'I know a way over,' continued Richie, 'but if it ain't there, that's it, we don't hang about, right? I don't care if you pay me ten times as much.'

Kevin nodded, but at the same time he wondered exactly how much the other man knew about the gun-thugs and whatever they did at Barsbeker.

He was forming that thought into a question when the service elevator behind them clanked into life and began to rise back up to the concourse level. If the men hunting him had figured out where he had gone, they might be intent on following him down into the airport's sublevels.

'We gotta motor,' said Richie, and he broke into a jog. 'C'mon, hurry the fuck up!'

Soaked from the heavy rain, Miros stalked into the hangar with the manner of a pissed-off cat, his perpetual grimace deeper than usual and his eyes like stones. He held out the recovered shoulder bag to Sasha, but before she could take it, he deliberately let it drop to the floor with a damp thud.

The act was a small gesture of disrespect calculated to get a rise out of her. Miros didn't like it when Sasha gave him orders, even when she worked in Oleg's stead, and more so when it meant he had to trudge back across the airport grounds through one of the worst thunderstorms of the year.

She didn't give him the satisfaction of letting her irritation show, gathering up the bag with a balletic sweep of the arm.

Oleg approached, sparing Miros a nod of approval as she peeled open the bag's flap to reveal the contents.

'That looks too small for my money,' said Oleg, casting a hard look in Von Kassel's direction. Attracted by Miros's unexpected return, the politician made a poor job of pretending not to be interested, orbiting closer to the others as the conversation progressed.

'Files. Papers,' Sasha noted, leafing through the contents. Aside from a zip-case containing men's toiletries and a dog-eared paperback book, the bag had nothing in it that immediately caught her attention. The papers were in English and German, dense blocks of text in a tiny font that went on and on in impenetrable legalese jargon. Oleg followed her to a nearby workbench and watched as she emptied the contents of the bag, spreading them out. 'I am not sure what I am looking at.'

'Contracts?' Oleg wondered aloud. 'Or perhaps something meant to distract us from the truth.' He looked at Von Kassel again, his suspicion undimmed. 'I do not enjoy having only half of the picture.'

Sasha thought for a moment, and was about to suggest she accompany Miros back to the terminal once more when Oleg stepped closer and guided her away with his hand.

He lowered his voice, clearly unwilling to let Von Kassel listen in on what he was saying. 'The man who attempts to steal from me without someone to watch his back is a fool of the highest order. Roberto was such a man and he paid for that. But this ... ' Oleg gestured back at the bench and the discarded bag. 'There is more going on, I feel it in my blood.'

'You think Von Kassel is involved?'

'We know he likes playing his stupid games,' Oleg noted. 'I would not put it past him. Men of his ilk are accustomed to gambling and writing off their losses as if they mean nothing.'

Sasha watched as Von Kassel wandered over to the workbench, craning his neck to look at the contents of the rain-soaked shoulder bag. 'What does he gain from having someone steal back his own money?'

'It is *my* money,' Oleg snapped. 'It is what I am *owed*. If I find that idiot has been interfering with this night's work from some ill-judged intention to out-manoeuvre me ... I'll gut him and bury him next to the whore.'

A murderous light glittered in Oleg's eyes, and it was hard for Sasha to look away from him. It had been a long time since Oleg shed blood with his own hands, and she had forgotten how much he relished the prospect. Dispatching Roberto earlier that night had rekindled something in him, she realised, the dark thrill of killing a man. Like a drinker who strayed too long from the bottle, one sip wasn't going to be enough to slake the old soldier's renewed thirst; the consequences were secondary to Oleg, echoing in murder how Von Kassel acted with his riches.

'We don't know for certain he is involved,' ventured Sasha, finding herself in the curious circumstance of defending the smug politician, if only for the sake of caution. 'Von Kassel has more than enough enemies who would be happy to see him ruined.'

'True.' Oleg reluctantly considered the possibility. 'But even if this is some opportunist taking advantage, there is still more to it than what we've seen.' He nodded to himself, reasoning out the situation. 'Somebody is helping the thief. That much is certain. Someone who knows this place. Someone who knows *us*.'

'Who would take that risk? Anyone who knows us, knows the price they would pay for crossing you.'

'Ah, but greed makes men stupid, Sasha,' said Oleg, with an icy smile. 'They think they are bold, but they become thoughtless.' He studied her with a long, measuring look. 'That is why I have you close to me. Women don't carry that taint . . .' He tapped her on the arm. 'Women know how to be content with their lot. Men never are.'

Sasha couldn't be sure how to respond to that, so she gave a brisk nod, and that appeared to satisfy him. She changed tack. 'What about Von Kassel's man, the driver?'

'Miros left him to keep searching the terminal, yes? That works in our favour. As long as Von Kassel's attack dog isn't here for his protection, he will rein in his undisciplined tendencies.'

'I don't like him.'

Oleg snorted with bleak amusement. 'Which one?'

'Both. I know Boch's kind. A pig that wears the skin of a man.' Sasha remembered the corrupt cops who would chase her down the dingy streets where she had grown up, and the price they exacted when they caught her. 'And him . . .' She nodded on Von Kassel's direction. 'He is worse. Not a pig but a jackal.'

'All true,' admitted Oleg. 'But never forget, we only tolerate these people as long as they are useful. When the time comes they prove useless to me . . .' He hesitated, as if seeing that terminal moment in his mind's eye, and relishing the prospect. 'I will dispose of them, discard them. Best that way, to bury what has no value and do not look back.'

He met her gaze again, and in that hard and pitiless void she saw nothing but the certainty of a killer.

While the attention of Oleg and his thugs wandered, Von Kassel decided it was his duty to take the initiative, and he homed in on the bag the skinny woman had left discarded on the workbench.

He threw a sideways look at Sasha and Oleg as they colluded in whatever scheme the old soldier had at hand. They were a peculiar pair, by turns like a commander and his aide, or a stern father mentoring an errant child. Von Kassel wondered idly if the old man ordered the woman around in his bedroom as much as he did elsewhere – or was it the other way around, perhaps? For a moment, he pleased himself by imagining Oleg Gorod trussed up in some ridiculous sex game get-up, and the thin girl spanking him into tumescence. It entertained him to speculate about other men's perversions. In his experience, the richer you were, the more freedom you had to pursue them.

With a sigh, he put aside that crass thought and concentrated on the contents of the shoulder bag. Predictably, these criminals

224

hadn't given the papers more than a cursory once-over, leaving open an avenue of investigation that the politician could exploit.

He had always been gifted with a keen eye. Even as a youth, Von Kassel had learned to parlay that particular skill into something valuable. Just a quick glimpse at a document left on a desk or a paper facing the wrong way, these he could parse in a moment, searching for some detail that might be of use. People around him had learned the hard way never to leave out anything that could possibly be injurious or worse, *incriminating*, because Lars Von Kassel would see it, squinting down through his rimless spectacles, taking it in and storing it away for the day when he needed some leverage.

He turned the same eye on the material before him. He discarded the trashy English-language thriller novel after giving it a withering look – some pulp about a lone protagonist from a special military brigade, with a cover showing a muscular soldier clutching a rifle and running down a dusty alleyway in a nameless Arab country. The book was his first clue to the identity of the bag's owner, and most likely, the person who had interfered with the payment of Von Kassel's debt.

*A man, obviously*, he decided. *Someone with a limited and commonplace life, who fantasises of being the same sort of hero lionised by his undemanding reading matter.*

Searching the bag's inners and the zipped pockets lining it brought no new rewards other than a clump of receipts held together by a paper clip, and a smaller bag containing deodorant, shampoo and a few other travel-size toiletries.

The items were from characterless English brands, of a cheap quality that Von Kassel would not have dreamed of putting on his own skin.

*British, then.* He considered that, amusing himself with his analysis. *Helping themselves to all they see, of course. How tediously predictable.*

Von Kassel left the paperwork until last, but when he scrutinised the pages, what he saw there swiftly killed the complacent sneer on his face.

He shifted nervously, instinctively moving to shield the documents from anyone else who might look over his shoulder, and he carefully reread the section that had alarmed him.

*The Montag Foundation.* There it was, the name in unmissable black letters at the head of the voided contract document. For a moment, he wondered if this was some ploy by Oleg to wrong-foot him, but then he dismissed the notion. The criminal was too blunt, too direct for that kind of subterfuge. No, somehow the complications of Von Kassel's private business ventures had become enmeshed in this night's troublesome events. He read on, trying to fathom out the details.

Gradually, the reality came into focus. The names on the voided contract documents – the signatories Colin Fish and Kevin Tyler, a company called Luna Designs – meant little to him, but the matter of the deal was very familiar indeed.

He saw that the land parcel in the local area owned by the Montag family had originally been destined to end up in the possession of these Englishmen, and he allowed a sly chuckle.

'Well, well . . .' he said aloud. 'How remarkable.'

Von Kassel hadn't been interested in who the other party was in the Montag deal. He had only cared about ousting them and forcing the family to make the sale to *him* instead. The factory he had planned would give a comfortable swell to his portfolio and let him bolster the fiction that he was investing in the district. Given the dip in his recent polling numbers, he needed to appear supportive of the working class out in the provinces, even if the jobs the factory would create would actually go to cheap immigrant labour rather than Germans.

Through Zett Holdings, his shell company, the politician had ordered his people to apply as much pressure as required to get the Montags to sell to him instead of any foreign interests – and after months of secret manoeuvrings, and less-than-legal gambits, the original deal was undone at the eleventh hour and usurped by Von Kassel's.

He had been vaguely aware that the other party in his little game was based in Britain, but now fate brought him face to face with those he had beaten to the prize. Von Kassel thumbed through the worthless contract papers, weighing this new information in his thoughts. *Is this some attempt by them to get back at me,* he wondered.

It would complicate matters with Oleg if the Serb found out about it. He wouldn't accept any talk of coincidence. There was only one way to deal with this, and that would be to find the thief *first*, to have Boch deal with the Englishman and recover the money before Oleg discovered this troubling connection.

*I need to keep control of this*, Von Kassel decided. *But in a way that the Serb believes he is still in charge.*

It didn't escape him that he was playing a dangerous game, but as always, he relished the thrill. Opportunity always came wrapped in risk, and he was not a man to shy away from it.

Something in the side pocket of the bag attracted his attention and he reached into the space, finding a rectangle of card. An *ansichtskarte*, a picture postcard sporting a bland collage of images from the nearby town of Kiel, laid out in a vain attempt to make the place look interesting. Von Kassel examined the pictures and sniffed, supremely unimpressed.

He turned it over. While the card had been addressed, there was only the beginning of something written on it. *Dear Mads*, read the words in an untidy, overlarge hand. *Hello from Pop.*

As with much he came across, Von Kassel's first thought about the card was to consider how he could use it to his advantage.

'What are you doing?'

He couldn't stop himself from jerking back in surprise. Oleg stood right behind him, once more exhibiting his disconcerting ability to approach without making a sound.

'Looking for a way to speed this along.' Von Kassel covered with a weak smile and pushed the contract papers away, out of sight. The postcard disappeared into his pocket before Oleg saw it. 'I wonder if things would move faster if I could play a more proactive role?'

'Such as?' Oleg very deliberately pulled the papers back out from the bag where he had tried to conceal them, and leafed through the pages.

Carefully, Von Kassel tapped a finger on the contracts. The last thing he wanted was for the man to actually *read* them. 'There are names here. It could be nothing, but they might provide us a clue as to the identity of tonight's interloper.' Oleg looked up, searching Von Kassel's expression for mendacity. He did his best to appear truthful. 'Let me contact my people in Hamburg. I have assets you do not, my friend. I may be able to uncover something useful.' He had no intention of doing that, of course, but the Serb would never know.

Oleg pursed his lips as he chewed on the idea, then at length, he gave a nod. 'Very well. But you will inform me of everything you learn.'

'Of course!' Von Kassel's fingers clamped around the contracts, but Oleg wouldn't release them. 'I, ah, will need those papers.'

Oleg hesitated; then he let the contracts fall into Von Kassel's hands. 'Don't make me regret this decision,' he growled.

# EIGHTEEN

Kevin trailed close behind Richie, who moved with a certainty that he found a little unsettling, and the service corridors gave way to concrete tunnels that echoed with mechanical noises and rumbles of wind filtering down from the aircraft apron above them.

Harsh industrial lights behind metal cages threw poor illumination over lines of steam pipes that followed the ceiling like the roots of a massive tree. Safety signs in terse German made it clear in no uncertain terms that no one unauthorised should be down here.

The barista took turns seemingly at random, pushing through heavy fire doors or doubling back when they came upon locked security barriers. He clearly knew where he was going, but that didn't do anything to settle Kevin's nerves.

He decided to speak up. 'You know your way around.'

'Yeah,' said Richie, with a brisk nod. 'Come down sometimes with the lads, y'know, for a bit of . . . ' He made a smoking gesture with his fingers, miming taking a long drag from a phantom joint. ''Cos the smell don't carry, right?'

'You get away with that?'

'What management and the cops don't know don't hurt 'em,' he replied.

Up ahead the passage ended in another heavy door, but unlike the others this one wasn't locked. As Richie shouldered it open, an arctic blast of wet air rushed out, and Kevin flinched.

Pulling his jacket closed, he took a step forward, but Richie didn't move, hesitating on the threshold.

'This,' he said, rapping on the door with his knuckles, 'this is like your actual point of no return, right? You get me?'

Kevin stiffened. The roiling churn of his doubts filled his belly: a black and oily stew of fear would easily overtake him if he let it. He sucked in a breath and nodded. 'Let's do this, and then we can get the hell out of here.'

'Better be worth it,' Richie added, as he pushed the door wider.

Kevin said nothing. He thought about the bag of money back in the locker and tried to focus on that. *It* will *be worth it. Just hold your nerve.*

'Keep up.' Richie broke into a jog and Kevin fell in step, following him into another long, square-walled corridor that ranged away into the dimness.

'What are these tunnels for, anyway?' He threw the question at the other man's back as they reached a junction and turned right.

'Maintenance,' said Richie. 'Like, for the lights on the runway, innit? And there's the steam pipes.' He slapped the palm of his hand on one of the thick tubes above his head as he passed beneath it. 'Not using them now, but in the winter, they keep the tarmac warm. Melts the snow so the planes can land.'

'Right.' Another low moan of wind came down the passage as Kevin's guide executed another turn at another junction. He tried to estimate how far they had walked, and overlay that onto what he knew of the airport's arrangement.

By Kevin's estimation, they had to be under the main runway by now, running parallel with the terminal building. A steady pressure of cold air came down the tunnel after them, carrying the force of the storm above. Lightning flashed, sending thin shafts of white light through service grates in the ceiling. Then thunder rumbled up there, and with nothing to attenuate the sound, it boomed off the runway and resonated into the passage below. Kevin felt the pressure in his skull, the same kind of tension that grew and grew before his ears popped on an outbound flight.

His guess about their location was confirmed when he walked past an alcove containing electrical switching gear in a yellow-painted locker. He looked up and past it to see an orange glow bleeding down from above, where a marker light poked up through the airstrip's asphalt. A steady streamer of rainwater made its way down through gaps around it.

'Watch your step,' offered Richie, but the warning came too late.

Looking up, not paying attention to where he was walking, Kevin stepped right into a deep puddle that lapped over the top of his shoes and soaked into his socks. 'Ah, bollocks!' Gamely, he moved to the side, but the damage was done, and cold liquid squelched around his toes and the soles of his feet with each new step.

'Gotta be careful,' said Richie. Kevin could feel the tunnel floor sloping slightly, and he noted the damp in the air was more noticeable here. 'When it belts down like this, some bits get flooded, yeah?' Richie halted, pointing along a side passage.

It was dark in there, but Kevin smelled dirty water and saw the shimmer of light reflecting off an ink-black pool that could have been metres deep.

'I heard a bloke drowned in there,' said Richie. 'On a night like this.'

Kevin scowled. 'Let me guess. *And his ghost still haunts these passageways.*'

Richie spread his hands, his face the picture of seriousness. 'You said it, bruv, not me.'

'Don't take the piss.'

'Hard not to.' The other man gave a rough chuckle. 'Come on then.'

They passed other side tunnels, some of them as waterlogged as the 'ghost passage', others that led to alcoves filled with hardware or metal ladders extending upward to ground level. Amid the heavy odour of the constant rain, and an ever-present whiff of spent jet fuel, Kevin smelled the acrid tang of ozone and oiled machinery. They continued across a couple more four-way junctions, each one labelled with a letter and number combination that corresponded to the tunnels branching off from it.

Only after they had moved away from under the main runway did Kevin realise he hadn't been paying enough attention to the route they were taking. If he was down here on his own, it would be easy to become disoriented – every tunnel looked like every *other* tunnel, the non-sequential marker numbers on the walls practically meaningless to him. He quickened his pace a little, falling back into step with his guide.

When they passed under the airport's secondary runway, Kevin knew they were close to their destination. The smaller strip of tarmac was positioned at an angle from the main runway, connecting to it at the eastern tip. Beyond it lay the cluster of private hangars and support buildings, the last part of Barsbeker airport before the perimeter fence and the low woods beyond.

Richie made another turn and stopped at a dead end. 'Up here,' he said, indicating a ladder that would take them out of the under-levels.

Kevin peered up at a metal hatch. Rainwater came down in thin sheets where the edges of it didn't meet its frame, and the rungs of the ladder were wet. 'You first,' he said.

Richie grunted irritably. 'Yeah, 'course.' He started the short climb. 'Don't forget your brolly, right?'

Kevin said nothing, and stepped quickly between the curtains of rain sluicing down. Just as Richie reached the hatch and shouldered it open, a new blaze of lightning lit up the sky above and for a split-second the whole scene was illuminated as bright as daytime.

Following him up the slippery ladder, taking care not to lose his footing, Kevin rose into the teeth of the downpour and the answering roar of more thunder. From inside the terminal building, even from down in service tunnels, the rain hadn't seemed as bad as this, but Kevin's jacket soaked through even as he emerged into the freezing night air.

Richie hadn't waited for him by the manhole cover across the ladder well. Kevin cast around and saw a shadow lurking a few dozen metres away in the scant cover of a fuel bowser parked near a small, darkened hangar.

He kicked the cover shut, and on the wind he caught Richie calling out something indistinct. It was hard to hear over the rushing hiss of the rainfall. The other man waved urgently, like he wanted him to get in out of the rain.

*Too late for that*, Kevin thought glumly. *The only way I'd be any wetter is if I jumped in the sea.*

Out of nowhere, a new wash of hard white passed over Kevin like the sweep from a lighthouse. He blinked in surprise, but too late he caught up that the illumination wasn't the flash of more sheet lightning.

He twisted around. The headlights of a vehicle on full beam roved across the tarmac as a cargo van swerved off the service road and back in Kevin's direction. Whomever was driving the vehicle out in this filthy weather had definitely seen him.

Kevin's fight-or-flight instincts kicked in and he chose the latter option. Splashing through puddles on the cracked asphalt, he sprinted across wide helicopter landing circles painted on the apron, making for the shadowy deeps of the hangar. He spotted the other man disappearing inside the barn-like structure through the gap between the towering doors, and ran in the same direction.

He was at the entrance when the headlights caught up with him, throwing a bouncing, monstrous shadow of his running form into the hangar interior. Kevin dared a look over his shoulder and wished he hadn't. The van powered towards him at a fast clip, intent on running him down.

'*Oh shit!*' Kevin found an extra gear he didn't know he had and ran as fast as he could though the hangar doors and into the shadows beyond.

He jackknifed right, clipping his head against the wing of a parked Cessna, ducking around the nose of the light aircraft as he sought cover.

Behind him, the van came to a halt with a squeal of brakes on the threshold of the hangar, the headlights throwing a column of white down the middle of the building. Kevin heard the vehicle's door creak open, and a new, skeletal shadow moved across the floor as the driver entered.

He dropped down behind a tool rack and held his breath, straining to listen. Kevin picked out the odd footstep here and there, but for the most part the sound was drowned out by the constant drumming of the heavy rain on the hangar's roof.

'Hey!' The shout echoed off the walls. '*Ich sehe Dich!* I saw you go in here!'

Kevin fought the impulse to peek out from behind the rack and concentrated on his breathing, trying not to pant. Each lungful of air he took sounded like a wheezing gasp to his ears, and he was petrified that it would give him away.

'You can't hide,' said the voice. 'Show your face. Don't make me call security!' He had an accent, but not a German one. *French maybe?*

It slowly dawned on Kevin that this guy, whomever he was, didn't know that there were actually *two* of them in the hangar. That meant if Richie had his wits about him, they still might be able to get out of this in one piece. But if the other man was thinking the same thing, he gave no sign.

For a moment, Kevin wondered if the guy from the van was someone unconnected to the grief he was going through, but when he gave in and finally dared to look up from cover, what he saw in the man's hand told him otherwise.

The tall, angular figure had a thin stiletto-bladed knife in his fingers, the light from the vehicle catching the edge of it.

'You have no way out,' he called.

Kevin didn't recognise his face. He wasn't one of the two who had come after him in the terminal building, but the man with the knife had to be part of their group. He watched the guy cast around.

Then, to Kevin's alarm, the guy picked a path and started walking slowly in the direction of the Cessna and the tool rack.

Vincent moved carefully, placing his feet as quietly as he could, trying to sift the sounds around him for some inkling of where his quarry had gone to ground.

The glow from the van's headlights threw long fingers of shadow up the walls of the hangar, making it hard to see who might be lurking in the far corners. He remembered that this building belonged to some local flying school that had fallen on hard times during the pandemic. Both of their light aircraft were chocked up and half-dismantled, engines cowlings open to the air. Nothing in here was worth that much to anybody, hence the lacking security.

Vincent considered seeking out the switches for the lights, then dismissed the idea. For all he knew, the hangar didn't have power, and even if it did, this side of the airport was supposed to be empty at this time of night. If he started running up the floods, someone on the night shift in the control tower across the way might notice the activity and come looking. Sasha's earlier admonishment about keeping a low profile echoed in the Frenchman's thoughts and he sighed.

He *was* sure of one thing. The man he had followed in here was the thief. In that brief moment the runner had turned back to look at the van as Vincent came after him, his face was brightly illuminated by the headlights. It was the same person he had watched on Imran's monitor screens, sneaking out of the men's room with Oleg's money.

*What's he doing out here?* He'd seen the man climbing out of the maintenance well. Nobody was going to sneak across the airport that way without a good reason. *Oleg will want answers.*

Vincent moved to the closer of the two small planes, where the shadows ran thicker, the place where anyone hoping to hide would have the best chance of it. Rain finding its way down through holes in the roof spattered off metal in ringing notes like the click of a metronome, and his grip tensed around the handle of the knife. He didn't often have call to use it, but he wasn't afraid to get bloody when the situation demanded it.

*Cut first, ask questions later,* he decided. *That's how to handle it.*

Still, he wondered if it wouldn't be a good idea to have some backup. The idea of bringing in the thief on his own had its appeal, to be sure – Oleg would be impressed – but he didn't want to take any chances.

With his free hand, Vincent pulled his phone from his pocket and flicked it to life. The screen blinked on, illuminating his face, and he momentarily dropped his eyes to the device as he thumbed down to call Sasha.

In the same second, a piece of the shadows broke off and he heard someone make a grunt of effort. He reeled back in shock as a bright crimson fire extinguisher came swinging up and around out of the darkness, right at his head.

Kevin put his weight into the attack, hauling the extinguisher from a rack on the wall and towards the man with the knife, swinging it with both hands. Rolling his shoulders like an Olympic shot-putter, he tried to slam the metal cylinder into the other man's head, but his adversary was more nimble than he looked, dodging out of the way before the blow could connect.

Kevin couldn't correct his clumsy assault once it was happening, but chance favoured him as the extinguisher fell into the downswing and he clipped the other man's hand – the one holding the knife. He lost his grip on the cylinder and it clanked away across the hangar floor, but the passing hit had also disarmed the skinny man, smacking away his blade.

That didn't slow him down, however, or stop him from cracking a fist wrapped around a phone into Kevin's face.

He rolled with the hit, the hard impact sending spirals of pain behind his eyes, and his brain chose that exact moment to dredge up a famous quote that Colin Fish had been fond of repeating. *Everyone has a plan until they get punched in the mouth.*

*Mike Tyson.* The voice of Kevin's inner critic, the one that sounded like his ex-wife Sadie, reminded him of who had dropped that nugget of immortal wisdom. *But you're not him, are you?*

The other man surged forward and grabbed at Kevin's jacket, shoving him back into the Cessna's fuselage. The plane rocked on its undercarriage and before he could stop him, the skinny Frenchman pushed his forearm up against Kevin's throat, choking off his breath.

Kevin tried to look past the other man, desperately searching the gloom for any sign of Richie. This was the perfect moment for the barista to ride to the rescue, but it rapidly became clear he wasn't coming to help.

'Prick,' gasped Kevin, and the Frenchman thought the curse was for him.

He smacked Kevin's head with his free hand. 'Who the fuck *are* you?' He demanded. The man still gripped his phone in the other hand, and the light from its screen gave his face a ghostly cast. His eyes were wide and angry, and Kevin could smell stale coffee when he exhaled. 'Where's the money, *connard?*'

All of Kevin's bottled-up frustration exploded out of him in an angry shout. '*Up your fuckin' arse!*' His fury temporarily stripped away the polite veneer of the professional English businessman at large and for a moment Kevin regressed back to the North London lad he had been in his misspent youth.

The Frenchman blinked in shock at the sudden change in his manner, and Kevin seized on the momentary distraction, ramming an underhand punch into his gut. The blow landed where he needed it to, more by luck than judgement, and it winded the other man. He staggered back and coughed, his arm dropping away from Kevin's throat.

Kevin Tyler hadn't been an actual fight with another person for over a decade, maybe even two. The last such engagement he could remember was some bleary-eyed drunken scrap in a pub car park, where he'd come off worse. He tried to stay in trim – more or less – with sporadic trips to the gym, but even a generous observer wouldn't have called him *fit*, at best *average*. Someone with serious bulk and muscle could probably have twisted him into a knot, but fate was on his side right now, presenting him with an adversary who had less meat on him than a vegan curry.

Kevin knew he didn't have skill, and he certainly didn't have strength, but what he did have was a day's worth of being royally fucked-off. Gritting his teeth, he channelled every last drop of that indignation into going at the Frenchman like a wild man, slapping and clawing at his face, keeping him off-balance and on the defensive.

A dim memory from childhood Judo classes popped up in the back of his thoughts, and Kevin stepped in, hooking the other man's ankle with his foot. He applied the move in the right place, and to his surprise, it actually *worked*.

The Frenchman overbalanced and stumbled, Kevin's lucky hit aided by a skid on a wet patch of flooring. He went down backwards, falling against an empty engine hoist, cracking his head against the overhanging jib.

Kevin loomed over him, fists cocked, ready to throw out another punch but not really sure how to do it. The other man didn't rise, letting out a weak gasp, going slack.

At the sight of his handiwork, Kevin's anger dissipated and he felt a little sick, wondering for nasty second if he had accidentally done some irreparable damage to the other man. Sure, the bloke had come at him with a knife, but Kevin hadn't woken up that morning in the Kiel Komfort Lodge intending to end the day by crippling some stranger.

Warily, he crouched down and touched a finger to the other man's throat. He was out cold, his breathing fluttery but his pulse steady. 'Oh, thank fuck for that.'

'You didn't top that guy, did you?' Richie's voice led him out of the shadows, the barista choosing his moment to emerge from behind part of a cut-off wing.

'No.' Kevin shot him an acid glare. 'No thanks to you!' A little of his earlier annoyance came back. 'Were you going to hide over there and watch us smack each other about?'

Richie said nothing, stooping to pick up the fallen man's weapon from the floor, holding it by the point of the blade. 'You were lucky,' he noted. 'Look at this. He would have splashed you, given half a chance.'

'Yeah.' Kevin sobered at his own admission. 'Well, cheers for no sodding help.' He stepped away from the man on the floor, panting with exertion, and rubbed a hand over his face.

'Gonna leave him there?' Richie's question was loaded with nasty implications. He aimed the knife at the unconscious man. 'What if he wakes up?'

'We're not going to stab him, if that's what you mean, *shit*!' Kevin shook his head. 'Give me a minute.'

'Whatever you say, man.' Richie shrugged and folded closed the flick knife with an unpleasantly casual familiarity, before pocketing it.

Kevin searched inside the tool case and grabbed a roll of duct tape that he used to tie the Frenchman's ankles together, and his wrists behind his back. He put another strip over the man's mouth, in case he came to and started crying out for help. As an afterthought, Kevin used more tape to secure the guy in a sitting position against the frame of the metal engine hoist. Someone would find him eventually, hopefully after Kevin and Richie were long gone.

'He wouldn't have done that for you,' Richie remarked, watching him work.

Something in the barista's tone rang a warning note with Kevin. 'How do you reckon?' He made the question a challenge. 'You know this bloke, then?'

'I know his type, don't I?' Richie deflected, turned away and started walking. 'C'mon. The big hangar's next door. If they have your gear, that's where it'll be.'

# NINETEEN

When the second call went straight to Vincent's voicemail, Sasha began to have concerns. He never ventured anywhere without his phone, he barely even put it down to take a piss, so this sudden silence put her on edge.

*Did we finally cross one line too many,* she wondered. *Are the authorities on their way?*

An unpleasant scenario unfolded in her mind's eye – the Frenchman waylaid by airport security, or worse, by one of the cops who patrolled Barsbeker. Locked up in some overlit room, being grilled for whatever he knew. Sasha wondered how long it would take for the Frenchman's innate sense of self-preservation to override his fear of Oleg Gorod.

She sighed. Their operations at the airport were predicated on an unspoken agreement between the criminals and the locals. As long as Oleg and his people didn't do anything too flashy, as long as they stayed well below the radar, they didn't draw attention.

Sasha understood the trade-off – the security contingent were understaffed, underfunded and under-motivated, so why would any of them want to risk their well-being over crimes that wouldn't affect their lives? In her experience, ordinary people could overlook anything as long as they didn't have to see it up close. They only needed an excuse.

Trafficking, smuggling, those sort of enterprises went unseen, like someone walking down a city street and ignoring a homeless beggar camped in a doorway. People's gazes skated over these things if you gave them an out, if even the thinnest veil covered it up. She knew that too well from personal experience. Sasha's arms drew close over her, unconsciously hugging herself against the chilly air inside the hangar.

Once, *she* had been the unseen, lost in alleyway shadows or behind the doors of a dingy brothel. She knew what it felt like to be invisible. In the beginning, she had resented it, but now she understood the power that status gave her. Ordinary people would see the savage look in her eye, the scarring on her face, and they would look away. She could sense them writing their own story about her in their heads, feel their compulsion to gloss over her presence and move on. She made it work for her.

But it was a fragile thing, as delicate as a soap bubble. Push too hard, take too much advantage, and the bubble would pop. Once seen, *truly seen*, Sasha and the others could only be considered a threat, and that would bring their enemies to bear.

Tonight, the veil was starting to slip away, the bubble straining to hold. Once again, her gaze strayed to the spot on the floor where Roberto had breathed his last. *We've pushed too far*, she told herself.

When she looked up, Oleg was there. He gave her a quizzical look. 'What now?'

'Vincent has gone dark.' She didn't try to deny anything. Oleg could see through her as if she were made of glass, and even the smallest of falsehoods would earn his ire. 'It's not like him. I think something is wrong.'

'Something *is* wrong,' Oleg retorted. 'We are being fucked with.' He shook his head grimly. 'This is what I get for stepping back from the work. Without supervision, the chain of command loosens. Mistakes arise.'

She wanted to tell him that tonight's problems were nothing to do with that, but Oleg had his narrative and nothing she said would deflect him from it. Over the past few months, Oleg had drawn back from having his hands in every element of the group's dealings, and until tonight, Sasha had thought he was settling into the new reality. Now she was catching up to how far from the truth that really was.

She tried a different approach. 'With respect,' Sasha began, 'if moves are being made against us, it is tactically unsound for you to remain here. The risk of exposure is grave.' She had pushed this argument more than once tonight to no avail, but she hoped that re-presenting the notion in military terms would get through to the old soldier, get past his vanity to his cooler, more strategic mindset. 'Let me deal with this, sir.'

Oleg's lips thinned, his grey-white beard twisting around his mouth. 'Why does everyone think I need protecting?' He whispered the question, as if talking to himself. 'The old man should stay home, eh?'

He chuckled, but Sasha knew that the false humour was a trap. 'Not what I meant—'

His eyes flashed with renewed resentment. 'You think I am incapable of meeting my enemy face to face?' Colour rose in Oleg's cheeks. 'Go home? *Go home?* Do you know what I do *at home?*'

Sasha searched for the right thing to say, to mollify Oleg before his towering anger grew. But any words she uttered, no matter how sincere or calculated, would be the wrong ones.

'I sit in my nice, comfortable home and I count my money, girl.' He nodded, seething at the thought of it. 'I want a drink? I have the best, I have it immediately, at the snap of my fingers. I want a woman? I screw whomever I want.' Oleg drew himself up, tugging on the line of his coat. 'And all the while, I get fat and I get slow and I get old. People say the dog has lost its teeth.'

'No one says that,' Sasha said quickly. 'You command respect.'

'Not enough!' Oleg's tone rose. 'There was a day when men trembled at the mention of my name! Now conniving shits like Roberto and that fuck Von Kassel think they can abuse me? Think I have forgotten!' He jabbed her in the breastbone with an iron finger. 'Forgotten what it is to be hungry, hateful.'

A sinister light grew in his eyes once again, a savage and predatory glitter that Sasha recalled only too well. She couldn't stop herself from flinching. The memory of that look on Oleg's face and the times he had hit her, disciplined her, came back in full force.

'There is no lack of clarity here. Someone stole from me, it is no different from what Roberto did. And as he paid, so will they. In paper and in blood.' Oleg leaned in close to her and his voice dropped to a husky whisper. 'I will not lose face, Sasha. Not over this. Not *ever*. I will slit a thousand throats if I must, and let the cops come to see it.'

Despite her fear of him, in that moment Sasha's frustration slipped past the gates of her self-control and she spoke without thinking. 'Your reputation is meaningless if you are in a prison cell!'

The blow came from out of nowhere, a powerful back-handed slap that sounded louder than the thunder rumbling overhead. Sasha reeled, fireworks bursting across her vision, her face stinging with pain.

'Don't question me because I favour you,' growled Oleg, flexing the hand he had hit her with. 'I will reopen that scar on your pretty face, take it all the way down your throat to your belly.'

She blinked back tears of pain and nodded woodenly. He was right, of course. She had spoken out of turn and paid for it.

A voice in her head railed against his abuse of her, but it was so distant and Sasha smothered it easily, as she always did.

'Did I make a mistake granting you authority?' Oleg's voice was low and loaded with menace.

'No,' she replied, killing off her moment of weakness and meeting his gaze. 'I did not think before I spoke. It won't happen again.'

At length, the ghost of a smile formed on his lips. Her contrition pleased him. 'Good. I give you latitude, Sasha, because you are special to me. But do not misuse the privilege.'

She tried to manage a small smile in return, but the pain in her face made it impossible.

The largest of the buildings on the far side of the airport were a cluster of connected metal sheds painted with a sign that read *Memoria Tranzyt* and a logo of a dove of peace. Kevin followed Richie's lead, keeping to the shadows where the few exterior lights didn't reach, moving under the scant protection where the arched roofing deflected away the rain.

He looked up into the cloudy night. 'Is this ever going to stop?'

As if in reply, the storm above them let out a grumbling snarl of thunder that rolled from horizon to horizon. Richie smirked at that, pulling his collar tight and beckoning Kevin to a roller door at the back of an outbuilding.

'In here,' he said, dropping into a crouch. The roller door opened for trucks to back up to and drop off their cargo, and Kevin could see that the mechanism was old and poorly maintained. Richie peered through a gap, then with a nod, he lifted it up just enough to squeeze under and inside.

Kevin did the same, catching his jacket on the door. He swore and fumbled at the material, finally extracting himself, but not before getting an icy trickle of falling rainwater right down his collar.

He rose up inside the building and blinked, his eyes adjusting to the dimness. A bone-deep chill prickled over his hands and his face. 'Is it actually *colder* in here?' Kevin's question wafted into the air in a pop of vapour, answering itself.

'Yeah,' said Richie. He moved up past a loading dock to another door, pausing to press his hand against it. 'Listen. Past this, you gotta be as quiet as a bloody church mouse, you get me?'

'I do.'

Richie jabbed him with a finger, unsatisfied with his reply. 'I mean it! I'm not getting topped for you, money or no money.'

'I said *I do*,' Kevin shot back.

Richie muttered something under his breath that Kevin didn't catch, and then with care, he slowly opened the door. A draught of polar air came out through the gap, and Kevin couldn't stop a shiver running through him. It felt like someone walking over his grave.

They passed through an unlit anteroom and into a larger space where the wintry cold hung in the air like it was something physical. As if he could reach out and grasp it.

'Keep to the wall,' Richie whispered. 'And don't touch nothing.' Then he pointed at another door at the far end of the room with a wire-lined window. Kevin could make out the lights of the hangar beyond.

They moved quietly, but Kevin's pace slowed as a thought nagged at him. There was something familiar about the room they were in. It wasn't as if he had been here before, it was more like he had looked at pictures of the place, or seen it in a movie.

And then he had it. The clues were right there. A floor of white tiles. A pair of rectangular metal tables in the middle of the room, with their grimy steel surfaces and drain grates in the centre. The wall on one side that was lined with rows of metre-square doors three tiers high, each with a pull-handle like you would find on an industrial fridge.

Kevin looked at the closest of the doors and saw a clipboard hanging off it, a bill of lading fixed in place. The German word *verstorben – deceased –* was visible on the paper, caught in the light falling from the window.

He froze. 'This . . . is . . . *a mortuary.*' Kevin's skin crawled along his arms and his back, as if trying to escape from him.

Ahead, Richie's shadow gave a perfunctory shrug. 'Well, yeah.'

'Mortuary.' Kevin said it again, trying to grapple with the idea. There were dozens of the locker doors within arm's reach, and he felt his stomach flip over and knot up as he considered what might be behind them. Dead bodies, siloed in each of the chillers, corpse after corpse stacked up and waiting . . . for what?

'You got a phobia or something?' Richie sniffed.

'Or something,' echoed Kevin. 'Dead people freak me out! You could have warned me!'

As a boy, on the occasion of his Great-Aunt Ruby's funeral, little Kevin Tyler had made the mistake of wandering off during the wake, only to accidentally lock himself in the dining room where the old dear's embalmed body had been laid out for the mourners to pay their respects. Trapped in there for what felt like hours, he couldn't forget her pale, sunken features and the wraith-like cast of her flesh. Forty-plus years later, that indelible childhood horror still lurked in the corners of Kevin's memory.

'Deal with it,' whispered the other man. 'It's this way or through the front, and you don't wanna do that, right?'

'No.' Kevin steeled himself and kept moving forward. 'But why the hell do they have a morgue out here?'

'They ship 'em home, don't they? Die on holiday, get posted home, *bish-bosh*.' Richie shrugged. 'Not everyone wants to be planted where they drop.'

'I suppose not.' Kevin kept his eyes on the door ahead, concentrating hard on not thinking about the dead bodies around him awaiting repatriation.

Richie gave a low snort of derision, mocking his obvious discomfort. 'See, that's why it works. No one likes mucking about with stiffs, innit? So it's easy to slip some gear in with the coffins.'

'They do that? Smuggle contraband with the bodies?' Kevin shook his head.

'Better than using some unlucky twat as a mule,' Richie noted, and he patted one of the lockers. 'And they don't rat to the Feds if they get caught, do they?' He stopped by the door, and tilted his head to look through the window. 'I see some blokes, but they're way over on the far side. Still want to do this?'

Kevin was asking himself again how it was a guy who sold coffee to overtired airline passengers knew about this particular bit of criminal infrastructure. He put that aside and took a deep breath. 'Come this far.' His jolt of old, clammy terror about the corpses faded away, replaced by a different stripe of fear – fear for his life, and his future.

The hangar was as wide as the terminal building, and at a push it could have housed a mid-sized airliner. Currently, the only residents were a sleek-looking business jet and a few parked cars, along with maintenance gear, storage racks and a couple of cargo containers.

There was more than enough clutter for Kevin and Richie to find cover behind, and with most of the hangar's overhead lights concentrated around the jet and the cars, they had the benefit of shadows as well.

'You see it?' Richie hissed.

'I'm looking . . .' Kevin crouched behind a stack of wooden forklift pallets and searched the space for any sign of the shoulder bag he had left behind. Now that he was here, facing up the reality of his situation, the full weight of it was coming to bear.

They had come out here on the thinnest of possibilities. For all Kevin knew, the men who had pursued him around the terminal had taken the bag and destroyed the contents, or worse, already gleaned what they needed from them. But he couldn't let go of even a slim chance to get it back intact. Escaping the confines of Barsbeker Airport, with the money or without it, would count for nothing if these thugs could track him down.

There were a handful of men busy at the far end of the hangar, moving around and stacking crates. In the other direction, closer to where Kevin and Richie hid, there was an isolated workbench piled with items he couldn't see clearly at this distance. *Is that it,* he wondered?

Kevin looked away again, towards the parked cars – and tensed. One of the hunters was there, the tall, grim-faced one who had flashed a gun back in the terminal. He loitered near a BMW parked at the entrance to the hangar, occasionally shooting looks in the direction of two others near the offices at the back of the building. Kevin made out an older man with long, grey-white hair and a military bearing, who stood holding an intense conversation with a short-haired woman in a shiny leather jacket. He could only pick up a faint mutter of their discussion from this distance, but it was clear from their body language that whatever was being debated was a serious matter.

'*Oh my days . . .* ' Richie said to himself, barely breathing the words as he spied the couple. The younger man paled.

'You know them?' Kevin shot him a look.

'No.' The denial came too quickly to be true. 'We need to go . . . '

But then a figure stepped out from behind a black Mercedes-Benz S-Class parked near the other car, and Kevin forgot about everything else.

'What,' he growled, 'is *that* oily little bastard doing here?'

Lars Von Kassel. Businessman, politician and most recently, the bane of Kevin Tyler's life, ambled around out there as if on an evening stroll.

In the aftermath of the implosion of the deal between Luna Designs and the Montag family, Kevin had briefly tried to stop his emotions yo-yoing between abject fury and crushing sorrow by digging into the reasons behind it, trying to find some meaning to the sudden calamity.

What he had learned from a few hours of indignant internet sleuthing was that this unctuous man – this greasy-pole climber opportunist, this two-faced schemer – had swept in at the last moment to destroy any chance of Kevin's company building a biodegradable bottle plant in the German heartland. And in doing so, Von Kassel had kicked over the first domino shoving Kevin down into the shit he was currently in.

It was unreal. Not for the first time today, Kevin wondered if fate was making sport out of him, if some invisible hand had grabbed the threads of his life and scrambled them into a messy, unsolvable knot. He glared across the open space of the hangar floor at the other man, watching him stroll around the Mercedes, arms flapping at his sides as he idly attempted to warm himself.

Kevin's bile and venom, forced into quietus by the drumbeat of fear, churned back up to the surface when he looked at Von Kassel. This man was the root of everything going wrong in his life, and if Kevin had held a stone in his hand, he would have hurled it at him.

'We gotta go! These guys will kill us—' Richie grabbed at Kevin's sleeve, but he shrugged him off with a sharp jerk.

'Fuck him,' Kevin hissed, but Richie didn't seem to know who he was talking about. Propelled by his frustration, Kevin crabbed forward, staying low. He slipped into the shadows, circling quickly towards the workbench.

Doing his best to keep the gear racks between him and the others in the hangar, he felt a flash of elation as he closed in on his target. The bag lay discarded atop the bench, the flap hanging open with a few papers visible inside.

*Not far now.* The soles of Kevin's shoes crunched on particles of oil-absorbent gravel, but the sound didn't carry under the constant clatter of the rain. He made it to the bench and dropped to a knee.

Extending one hand, staying down so he wouldn't be spotted, he reached up across the bench and found the shoulder bag's strap. Fingers closing around it, he pulled. The bag moved, slow and steady, before finally sliding off the edge, dropping into his lap with a thud.

The contract documents were damp from the rain but they were there. Kevin leafed through the papers, his heart hammering at the inside of his ribcage. He could hardly believe it. Everything looked to be intact. *He'd done it.* Now all he had to was leave the way they had come and get the hell out of here.

'*All right?*' Richie's voice suddenly called out from across the way, pitched up and loud as if greeting someone from the far side of a street.

Kevin looked around the side of the workbench, bewildered by the younger man's insane decision to announce his presence. He saw Richie walking out into the middle of the hangar, hands raised in a *we-are-all-friends-here* gesture.

'What is he doing?' said Kevin to the air, and for a moment he wondered if Richie was deliberately distracting the thugs so he could make his escape.

The girl in the leather jacket was on the man in an instant, her face twisted in annoyance. She said something he couldn't hear, and Richie nodded at it.

Then Kevin's chest tightened when Richie turned to point in his direction. His next words were carried right to him.

'Yeah, he's over there.'

# TWENTY

Miros punched the Englishman in the belly so hard that he collapsed on the hangar floor, coughing up a streamer of spittle that ran down his shirt and pooled there.

Sasha let him land a kick as well, then waved off Oleg's driver with a terse gesture. Miros backed away, so she could step in to take a good look at the thief. It was absolutely the same man from the security camera footage, the same pasty face and the same pale blue eyes. He didn't look like much, but Sasha had learned from experience not to underestimate people she did not know.

Still, with the way he clutched at his gut and gasped for breath, it was clear the man was either a long way out of his depth or a good actor. She would find out which soon enough.

Sasha took a moment, marshalling her thoughts, considering the best way to get what was needed from him. Somewhere behind her, Von Kassel stalked left and right, hands playing around his face as if shielding himself from this sordid business. Oleg, for his part, hung back to watch her work. This was another opportunity for him to judge her, of course, but she pushed that notion aside and concentrated on the matter at hand.

Silence was a powerful tool of intimidation, if correctly wielded, and Sasha used it now: but it didn't appear to be working. Instead, the Englishman stared daggers at the man who had turned him over, incomprehension and near-panic warring across his features.

'*Why?*' Ignoring Sasha, he shook his head and demanded an answer from his betrayer. 'Why did you give me up?'

'You really are a fucking chump, ain't you?' The younger, skinnier Englishman shook his head mockingly. 'You had your chance but you kept on pushing it, yeah? *Why didn't you listen to me, eh?*' He shouted the last sentence into the other man's face, making him recoil.

'I thought we were . . .' The thief couldn't finish the thought.

'What, *mates?*' The other man's derision cut through the cold air. 'Because I sold you cups of coffee and gave you a nod when you walked past? You fuckin' joking?'

He leaned in, and Sasha could see a long-buried resentment rising to the surface. She decided to let the moment play out, to see where it would go.

'We're not mates, you twat,' Richie snarled. 'You and me? We're not alike, *Kevin.*' He put acid emphasis on the other man's name. 'You reckon 'cos you come from London too you fucking know me?' He shook his head. 'Blokes like you are all the same. Cruising around in your nice suit with your flash watch, acting like you're the dog's bollocks. I gotta smile and say *all right, how's it going* 'cos the money I get is shit and I need the tips. And all the time, you're looking down your nose at me, *oh yeah, Richie the coffee guy loser with his dead-end job, not smart like me.* I know you think it.'

The thief opened his mouth to speak, but he couldn't find the words. Sasha could see the truth in his eyes, the understanding creeping over him. He'd been foolish enough, arrogant enough to think that the other man had been a kindred spirit, perhaps because of their shared upbringing. But he hadn't sensed the bitterness beneath. Like many who were born outside true want, beyond real poverty, he'd missed the signs. It was easy to be blind to the reality of those on the rungs of ladder beneath you. This Kevin really didn't know the other Englishman at all.

Sasha did, at least to a better degree than the man sprawled on the floor. Like several of the low-tier workers at Barsbeker Airport, Richie's employment there had been helped along the way by people who worked for Oleg. She recalled something about how the skinny young man was wanted by the Spanish cops for some drug crime he'd committed in Ibiza. Oleg's influence had made sure that problem didn't follow him to Germany. For a price, of course.

Men like that one had to be watched, because they were avaricious. But when push came to shove, they would always end up on the side that kept them out of trouble.

'What you said . . . I never thought that,' managed Kevin.

'You never thought *anything* about me,' Richie countered, and the fact of that was damning. 'Not until you wanted something.' He snorted. 'I never fuckin' liked you. You reckon I'm gonna get myself in the shit for you 'cause you put some spare change in the tip jar? Piss off.'

'Our friend here is a poor judge of character!' Von Kassel had drifted into the fringes of the conversation, and he couldn't resist the opportunity to impose himself. 'Terrible trait for a businessman to have, *ja?*' He spoke in English so he would be understood, unwilling to let his barbed comments go unappreciated by the captive audience.

'I know you,' Kevin retorted, his voice hollow as he tried to gather himself. He rose to a sitting position, eyeing Miros in case the thug came in to knock him down again. 'You've ruined me.'

'Oh.' Von Kassel pulled a sad face. 'Have I? I don't recall . . .'

'Seriously?' Despite the moment, Kevin gave a snort of contempt. 'The Montag deal?'

'Oh. That.' The politician played at scrutinising the other man, narrowing his eyes owlishly. 'Yes. Of course. I didn't recognise you at first . . . But then I seldom pay attention to the little people, it must be said. And I do ruin a lot of things that get in my way. *Entschuldigung.*' His head bobbed and he ran a hand through his hair. 'Rest assured, it is nothing personal.' Already losing interest, he pulled out his phone and started tapping out a text message to his driver, turning to Sasha. 'This regrettable incident finally appears to be in hand. I'll have my man Boch come back and we'll be on our way.'

'You will depart when I permit it,' growled Oleg, his voice carrying as he approached, his words rimed with icy menace. 'And not before.'

*No matter how bad it gets*, Sadie had once told him, *somehow you're always capable of fucking it up even more.*

Kevin's ex-wife had a way with words which meant that even after years apart, her pithy, damning insults remained embedded in his brain. He could almost hear her voice ringing off the walls of the chilly hangar, and in this moment he was hard-pressed to disagree with it.

*Look how wrong you are*, he said to himself. *You thought you were on top of this, but you were never close. And now these people are going to kill you.*

Practically everything Kevin had been aiming for with this ill-advised adventure had blown up in his face. He had recovered the bag, but now that meant nothing. The men he had fled from had him by the throat. He felt betrayed by Richie, not only because the other man had literally given him up to save his own skin, but also betrayed by his own mistaken assumptions about the other guy. His cheeks burned with shame. How had he ever fooled himself into thinking he could do this and get away with it?

Arrogance? Stupidity? Desperation? In the cold light of realisation, he saw it was all three.

*You should have left that bag and walked away*, accused the Sadie-voice. *Now look what you have done, idiot.*

'Get up.' The man in the big jacket with the long grey hair gave him the order, and Kevin obeyed. He drew himself up to a standing position, the bag he had risked so much to get back dangling awkwardly from its strap over his shoulder.

The other man studied him with an intense loathing that Kevin had never experienced before. It made him want to shrink back, but he sensed that any show of weakness would only worsen his situation. He did the only thing he could, and kept silent.

Then slowly, the man in the jacket turned towards Von Kassel – who, despite being dismissed a moment earlier, continued to hover nearby. He acted like someone on the edge of a conversation at a party, trying to break into a discussion when the other participants didn't really want him there.

'*This* is who you let steal from you?' The man in the jacket shook his head. 'This amateur? *Pathetic.*' The comment barely registered with Kevin. He was too afraid to be insulted by the implication.

'My dear Oleg—' Von Kassel forced a smile and started to speak, but the woman in the biker leathers silenced him with a look.

'Do not say his name,' she hissed.

'Step aside,' said the man called Oleg, dismissing the politician with a wave of his hand. 'You should wait in the office.' He gaze returned to focus on Kevin. 'You may find what happens next distasteful.'

The ominous suggestion hung in the air. Kevin's gut twisted and he feared he might lose control of his bladder.

'There are options other than violence,' Von Kassel began, his tone irritatingly reasonable.

'Know your place.' Oleg ground out the words, and Kevin watched him reach for something on a chain around his neck, holding it up to dangle it in front of Von Kassel's face. The politician visibly recoiled, like a vampire being shown a crucifix, the smarmy smirk on his lips crumbling.

For a moment, Kevin wondered what could possibly elicit such a reaction, but then he saw a square of black plastic hanging off the chain. *A memory card.* Whatever was on the thing, it made Von Kassel shit himself.

Kevin had clearly put his foot right in whatever messy business was going on between the two men. *I have to tell them,* he thought. *Maybe if I come clean, they won't kill me. If I give back the money, if I beg for my life, they'll let me go.*

Kevin started to trade off the idea in his thoughts. How much would he be willing to accept to make this ordeal end? Letting them beat him black and blue? How far would they go? He wondered if it would end up like in those Japanese crime movies, where they would slice a finger off an offender's hand as a warning to others. Or would they cut his throat and be done with it?

What if the money was the only thing keeping him alive?

'You.' Oleg called out again, and Kevin looked up, but the man in the jacket was pointing at someone else. At Richie. 'You know him?' he said, nodding in Kevin's direction.

'*Yeah*, uh, I mean *nah*. His name's Kevin. Buys coffees from my stall, innit?' Richie's entire manner and attitude had totally changed. He was diffident and respectful when Oleg spoke to him, barely willing to meet the older man's gaze.

'Look at me when I talk to you.'

'Yeah. Sorry.' Richie stiffened, raising his head. 'I saw him today. He missed his flight, didn't he? Then he came back later, said something about fake cash.'

'Money.' Oleg seized on that. 'What money?'

'He had a two-hundred-euro note,' said the barista, shifting nervously. 'Thought it was fake but it wasn't. Real deal.' He eyed the other people standing around him, the girl in the leather and the hard-faced man who had worked Kevin over.

'So you helped him?' Oleg cocked his head, waiting for a reply.

'Not really ... ' Richie's hand drifted to his face. 'I mean, like, he said he'd pay me to get him out of the airport.'

'How much?' The short-haired girl took her cue and Kevin tensed as Richie reluctantly reached into his jacket and pulled out the wad of euros he'd given him.

'This is ... ' Richie didn't finish the sentence. The girl snatched the money from him and thumbed the notes. She threw Oleg a nod.

'That looks familiar,' offered Von Kassel, attempting a light tone. 'What was lost has been found.'

'Where is the rest?' Oleg took a step closer to the younger man, and Richie backed off, bumping into the woman, who pushed him away.

'I dunno.' Richie shook his head. 'Straight up.'

'You helped him.' Oleg repeated the words, venom dripping from each one. 'After all we did for you?'

'I paid my way for that . . .' Richie tried and failed to show a modicum of defiance. 'I didn't make any trouble. *I paid!*'

Kevin didn't know what that payment was for, but he could take a guess. The oblique comments that Richie had made about the illegal activities that went on at the airport were taking on a new dimension.

Oleg glanced at the woman. 'You see, Sasha? How greed makes men foolish?'

'I wasn't—' Richie started to speak, but before he could get any more words out, Oleg reached across to the hard-faced thug standing at his side and pulled something from inside the other man's jacket.

Richie's hands rose in front of him as Oleg levelled the nickel-plated pistol at his forehead. Von Kassel made a gasping noise and stepped back, pursing his lips in dismay.

'You.' It took a second before Kevin realised that Oleg was talking to him again. 'The coffee he makes. It is good?'

Kevin tried to find his voice, but there was nothing there. He managed a shaky nod.

'Where,' Oleg began again, turning his attention back to Richie, 'is the money?' The gun did not waver.

'I don't know!' Richie cried, flushed red with exertion. He jabbed a finger at Kevin. 'He knows, I don't!'

'Then what use are you?' The shiny pistol bucked in Oleg's hand with a thunderclap crash and Richie spun away, crimson mist and brain matter jetting from the back of his head as he fell.

Kevin watched him go down as if the moment was in slow motion. The young man toppled, crumpling at the knees, becoming a loose, doll-like thing instead of a person. He hit the hangar floor in a sprawl of limbs, a twitch running through him. A halo of shimmering red pooled around the ruin of his head, his face cored inward by the point-blank hit.

The woman – Sasha – reacted to the murder not with shock, but with grim acceptance, tutting to herself as she noticed that some of Richie's blood had spattered on her jacket. Oleg handed her a kerchief to clean it off, and then he moved in Kevin's direction, the silver gun catching the overhead lights as it swung at the end of his arm.

Kevin had nowhere to go, backed up against the workbench where he had found the bag. A strange sensation washed over him, his senses becoming hyper-sharp as the pistol came up before him.

He registered every little detail with perfect, unflinching clarity: Oleg's well-trimmed beard and his granite-hard eyes; the machining down the slide of the pistol; the drumming of the rain on the roof; the tang of spent cordite and blood in his nostrils.

'You understand now, I am serious.' Oleg gestured at the man he had murdered, an awful satisfaction in his tone. 'Yes? So tell me where my money is.'

*You tell him you're dead you tell him you're dead you tell him you're dead.*

The litany of panic rolled around and around in Kevin's head. His jaw worked but no sounds emerged. He knew, with absolute and total certainty, that the moment he gave Oleg what he wanted, the next bullet in that gun would end him.

*You tell him you're dead you tell him you're dead you tell him you're dead.*

Part of him wanted to fall to his knees and plead for mercy, to grasp hold of some slim possibility that this man, this stone-cold killer, might forgive Kevin's folly and let him get his life back. He almost said the words, his lips quivering with the shapes of them.

He stared into the dark void of the pistol's muzzle, the black hole of it absorbing light and sound, the power within a heartbeat away from destroying him.

*You tell him, you're dead.*

'I will not ask again,' said Oleg.

His hands trembling, his quaking voice barely a whisper, Kevin managed a shake of the head. 'N-no.'

Oleg leaned in. 'What did you say to me?'

'No.' Kevin shook his head again, sweat falling from his brow, and the refusal was the only word he could utter. '*No.*'

Then pain exploded across his face with such force that for an instant Kevin was terrified that Oleg had shot him. He was down on the floor again, with no memory of falling, hands splayed against the painted concrete, a gusher of blood streaming from him.

Shakily, he reached for the burning centre of the agony. His nose was out of shape, crooked and swollen. The blood came from his nostrils, down his lips and chin.

Oleg stood over him, rendered into a shadow by the overhead lights, the silver gun held butt-first in his hand. Kevin had a flash-frame memory of the weapon coming at him, Oleg pistol-whipping him for daring to show some backbone.

'Very well,' said the older man, nodding briskly. 'You want to do this the hard way? I will oblige you.'

He stepped back, and Kevin tried to straighten up, but the racking pain encircling his head was too much. He probed at his broken nose again and gave a whimper.

Powerful hands grabbed him by the shoulders, hauling Kevin up, his bag dragging on him like an anchor, and he was shoved to the rear of the hangar. The hard-faced man who had knocked him around forced Kevin into a stumbling march, and behind him, he saw Oleg talking to the woman with the short hair.

The woman looked his way, and her face was absent of any mercy.

Oleg frowned, examining Miros's pistol in his hand. Sasha could see he hadn't expected the thief to defy him, and now his frustration had nowhere to go.

Her eyes flicked to the new corpse cooling on the hangar floor. *Another one to deal with,* she thought to herself. *How many more will we have before the sun comes up?*

Oleg examined the gun, which still had blood on the frame, and then pocketed it. 'Make him talk,' he said, glancing after Miros. The big man disappeared towards the cold room, pushing the Englishman in there ahead of him. 'I need answers.'

A few metres away, Von Kassel chuckled quietly. 'Surprising . . . That one might be tougher than he looks!'

'Be quiet.' Oleg didn't look in the other man's direction, and continued giving his orders to Sasha. 'Go in there, deal with it. Miros can make himself useful cleaning this up.' He nudged the dead man with the tip of his shoe.

'What makes you believe he will talk to *her*?' Von Kassel had not taken the hint, and continued to act as if he was a part of the discussion.

'Because Sasha has a unique understanding of how to cause men pain,' Oleg replied. 'Don't you?'

'Yes, sir.' Ever since he had 'rescued' her from a cargo container full of trafficked women, Oleg had tried to mould Sasha into his ideal of the perfect soldier.

He commended her when she was ruthless. He brought her a parade of traitors and men who had wronged him, and had Sasha hurt them in lengthy, horrific ways. What the old man had taught her was dark and terrible, and yet she had done what he asked without question. At first, out of fear for herself, then later, because he praised her, and she was so starved of affection that she would accept any scrap of it, no matter how twisted. She knew this was true, but she saw no way to change it.

Von Kassel cleared his throat, stepping gingerly around the dead man. 'If I may ... ?' he ventured, then carried on without waiting for permission. 'Of course I understand the need to compel this fellow to reveal the whereabouts of our, ah, funds, but the matter of his identity does create complications ... For me.'

Sasha eyed him. Typically, Von Kassel viewed the situation through the lens of his own self-involvement.

The politician took on an imploring tone. 'If you . . . do away with him? It would look bad for me. I could be implicated!'

'Because of the contract with the Montag family.' Oleg gave an arch sniff. 'I am aware of your project. I am aware of how you do business.'

'Then you see,' Von Kassel said firmly. 'He turns up dead, looking like he's been tortured to within an inch of his life, that draws attention to my business! And attention to *me* may become attention to *you*.'

Oleg's lips thinned at the politician's barely veiled threat, but he said nothing.

Von Kassel gave Sasha a quizzical look. 'At least you could try to make it look like a suicide?'

'Don't tell me how to do my work,' she snapped. 'I won't tell you how to be an arrogant pig.'

'He makes a good point,' Oleg allowed, drawing a triumphant smile from the other man. 'Do as he says.'

'It is too late for caution now.' Sasha spoke without thinking, and she saw Oleg's eyes widen with annoyance, realising she had overstepped her bounds once more. Doing so in front of the politician only made it worse.

Oleg slapped her across the face, then turned away, this time refusing to grant her any more consideration than that. 'Get to work,' he grunted. 'Make yourself useful.'

# TWENTY-ONE

The hard-faced man shoved Kevin back into the chilly space of the mortuary and he slipped on the tiled floor, losing his balance.

Without saying a word, the man grabbed a metal chair and dragged it across to a point beneath an overhead light. He yanked the shoulder bag off him, tossing it to the floor, and landed another meaty punch in Kevin's belly. There wasn't any anger behind the blow, just a workmanlike effort meant to keep him weakened and afraid.

It hit hard, and Kevin crumpled, breath gusting out of his mouth in a wet, strangled gasp. Before he could recover, the bigger man put a hand on his chest and forced him backward. Kevin collapsed into the chair and rocked against it.

'Wh-what are you going to do?'

The big man didn't answer, didn't give the slightest indication that he had heard the words, and for a second Kevin wondered if he actually understood English. Or perhaps the violent-silent act was meant to ramp up Kevin's panic level. *It was working.*

From a pocket, the man produced long, thin strips of black plastic, deftly looping them around Kevin's wrists. They pulled tight with a buzzing rasp, and he realised they were ordinary cable ties, the same kind of thing they had in toolboxes back in the workshop at the Luna Designs factory. The man secured each of Kevin's wrists to an arm of the chair, twisting them so that his palms were facing upward.

The careful, deliberate way he did that was, strangely, the most terrifying thing yet. Kevin's mind raced with the horrible possibilities of what might be coming next, and his gaze dropped to the floor. He spotted a stainless steel drain grate amid the grid of grubby tiling, and couldn't stop himself from picturing a stream of watery blood – *his blood* – winding down it.

He forced himself to look up. Sitting on the chair in the dimness, with the walls of chiller lockers surrounding him on both sides, he felt like he was trapped inside a metal cube, the bone-deep, wintry cold of the room leaching the hope and the life out of him.

*You're going to die in here.* He heard Sadie's voice, as frosty and as matter-of-fact as the hard reality around him. *This will be the last thing you ever see.*

A groan escaped Kevin's lips, but it became lost in the creak of the door opening. The woman with the short hair stepped in from the hangar and said something in a language Kevin didn't recognise. *Russian? Polish?* He couldn't tell. But the tone of it made it clear she was dismissing the big man. He gave her a sullen nod, and she held the door open so he could leave, then let it swing closed on its own.

276

The woman studied him for a long moment. Her blank gaze was unnerving. Kevin felt a compulsion to say something, *anything*, to fill the menacing silence, but he clamped his jaw tightly shut, biting down on the impulse. He tested the ties around his arms, but there was no give in them.

He remembered something from the pulpy thriller novel that had been his in-flight reading, about how police investigators and military interrogators used the absence of questions to get their subjects to talk. People under stress were naturally inclined to fill quiet moments with words, and if allowed to speak unhindered, they gave away details they didn't intend to.

*Say nothing. Give nothing.*

He forced himself to look away from her, finding a blank spot on the far wall to concentrate on. Kevin focused on the cracks in the plaster, digging deep inside to find what precious scraps of determination might still be hiding inside him.

She zipped up her jacket, frowning at the chill, and walked across to a sink fixed to the wall. She ran some water from the hot tap, testing the temperature with her fingertips as faint wisps of steam rose. Kevin tried not to watch, but he couldn't keep his gaze from straying.

The water's heat didn't satisfy her, so she moved to a cabinet nearby and rooted around inside. Presently, she came back with a bright, surgical steel instrument, like a hacksaw. Weighing it in her hands, she seemed to make a decision, before coming his way. The sharp teeth of the saw caught the light as it moved.

Kevin suddenly became very aware of the bare skin of the palms of his hands, forcibly offered up to the air like those of some worshipper at prayer. The woman halted in front of him, and he could sense her considering her options. She was considering the best way to cause him the most pain. Sickly dread coiled in his belly, and once more the tide of blank panic began to swell.

Kevin sucked in a breath and fought for control of the reaction. *This is it,* he told himself, *this is where it is going to end . . . Unless I can stop it.*

Every second that passed, every inhale and exhale of breath took him closer to the end of his life.

He had to resist. He had to hold on and keep the fatal moment from happening. Every second he was still breathing, there was still hope. Still a tiny, fractional chance that he might survive this night.

Swallowing his fear, he looked up and deliberately made eye contact with the woman. He remembered something else from the novel, about how to survive when taken hostage. *Make your captors empathise with you. Make them see you a human being, not just a prisoner.*

He saw the first bloom of new bruising on her face, the ruddy shade of it familiar to him. 'Your name's Sasha, right?' Kevin blurted out the question, stumbling over the words in his haste to get them out. 'He . . . He hits you, doesn't he?'

There was no need to clarify who *he* was. The woman hesitated, her gaze boring hard into Kevin.

Another precious second ticked by, another moment for Kevin to take a breath and stay alive. If he could get her to talk to him, if he could keep her from hurting him, there was *still a chance.*

But there was only one thing Kevin could say, and the thought of it frightened him. He realised that he would have to give up a truth that he rarely spoke of to another human being, something even his daughter didn't know about him.

'Never talk about this, never do, always kept it down deep, in the box,' he babbled, 'you know the box, I bet? The box where you keep things people mustn't see.'

She dropped into a crouch, her face level with his. Her expression fell somewhere between despondent and curious. She cocked her head, and Kevin took that as tacit permission to carry on.

'I know what it's like when people say they care about you, but then they hurt you. My dad ... My *real* dad ...' It was hard to form the words. He blinked, fear and old, painful memories misting his vision. 'He hit me and my mum, when I was very little. Said it was for our own good. Because he *cared.*' Kevin shook his head, as a dark abyss of long-buried childhood memories reopened beneath him. 'But he didn't care. People like that don't know how to care about anything but themselves.'

He'd kept those bleak years locked up tightly so the poison of them couldn't leak out, kept them pushed down so far that he convinced himself they could not rise again. But now here they were, raw and real. Called back into being as if it had happened yesterday.

He remembered screaming and the kiss of a leather belt across his back. His mother cursing his father. The crack of blows landing. The horrible powerlessness of being too small, too weak to do anything to prevent it.

Kevin had vowed never to be that man as long as he lived. When his biological father had walked out on them, it was like the ending of a prison sentence. Mum soon married again, and his stepdad turned out to be everything the other man was not. The scars healed but they didn't fade.

'People who hurt you,' he managed, finding the words as he went, 'they do it to get what they want and then they abandon you.' Kevin nodded at the door. 'Him out there. That's what he is. That's what he'll do.'

'You may be right.' Her voice was smoky, her accent rough with Eastern-European intonations. 'But that changes nothing.'

She leaned in and pushed up on sleeve of Kevin's jacket and the shirt underneath, exposing his forearm. Then, with slow precision, she drew the saw across the surface of his skin, cutting a shallow, ragged line of crimson from left to right.

Kevin let out a sharp cry of pain and his body stiffened against the metal chair. He tried to twist back, away from the cut, but she pressed down on his wrist, putting her whole weight into holding him in place.

Sasha moved the bloody saw to a different spot on his forearm and did it again, each tiny razor-sharp tooth of the blade tearing into him. Rivulets of red ran down and soaked into the cuffs of his shirt, dripping off the chair to tick against the tiled flooring.

Kevin's breathing came in hard, pulsing chugs as she leaned back, giving him a moment's respite. The wounds on his arm sang with agony, open to the cold air. He smelled the metallic odour of his own blood and bile burned in his gullet.

'Please stop . . .'

But she didn't. Sasha moved to his other arm and repeated her actions, pulling up his sleeve, resting the bone saw on his bare skin, pressing down his arm. He shook his head, beads of sweat flicking off him despite the chill of the room.

She drew the saw blade across, making more shallow incisions to mirror the first. Kevin howled and shook against his restraints, the cable ties biting into his wrists where they held them firmly. He felt the shuddering of his body echo down through the chair's metal legs, and they scraped against the tiles.

He rocked forward, panting, his arms on fire. Sasha stepped back, and without taking her eyes off him, she unzipped the cuffs of her jacket and bunched up the sleeves.

The woman showed him the pale skin of her forearms. A hashing of stark white scars drew lines across her wrists, and there were other, longer lines that traced up towards her elbows. 'Cut this way,' she said, making a left-to-right motion, 'and it means you want to hurt yourself, to bleed.' Then she traced the course of the lengthy scar over her vein. 'Cut like *this*, and it means you really want to die.'

Kevin tried to speak, but the pain turned it into a moan.

'I know how deep to cut,' she told him. 'To hurt or to kill. I will stop if you tell me where Oleg's money is.'

He fought past the agony. 'If I tell you, will you let me go?'

Sasha's expression became a blank, and she didn't reply. She didn't have to.

'No!' Kevin answered for her. 'I say anything, I'm dead!' He was too consumed with fear to try and play dumb. It was far too late for any kind of subterfuge. All his effort was set to enduring the pain, leaving little else behind.

'You should have thought of that before you stole from him.' Absently, she flicked his blood off the saw and studied him anew, considering what she would cut next.

'I'm desperate!' he yelled back at her. 'And stupid, yeah! But my life is falling to pieces, I saw an opportunity and I took it! I . . . I had no choice.' Kevin tried to steady himself, shifting uncomfortably in the chair. 'He's making you do this. Oh god, he killed Richie in cold blood, that poor fucker. He's making you do that to me!' When she didn't respond, he cried out to her. '*Why* . . . ? Why do this for him? Hurt people for him?'

'I have no choice,' she echoed, and Sasha looked away.

A horrible moment of understanding swamped him as he saw emotions he recognised cross her face. He saw himself, the little boy trapped in the cycle of violence, not knowing how to get free of it.

Kevin had been lucky. Fate had pulled him away from that bleak reality and into a better one. But the woman in front of him, she was the end product of that dark path, a person damaged and abused by what she had endured.

'Someone who hits you doesn't love you,' he said, gasping for breath, tensing through the throbbing agony. 'They hate you, no matter what they say . . . ' He choked back a sob of pain. 'They want you to be the victim.'

The saw blade dipped slightly, pointing away to the floor. Sasha stared at nothing, her expression turning stony and unreadable. Had he pulled on some cord of truth, maybe got through to her in this one desperate moment?

*Every second she hesitated, he was still alive.*

Kevin wondered if he could really convince her to free him, but it was a desperate fantasy. Even if he had found some fraction of common ground, he didn't have the ability to make it work in his favour. He wasn't a gifted talker like Colin Fish, able to win people around to his side with a few clever words and some false humility. Machines he could deal with, their problems and solutions he could understand. But the chaos and mess of emotions always left him lost and uncertain.

'Whatever you say does not matter,' said Sasha, her tone distant. 'The only thing that does is whatever Oleg wants.'

Then from out of the silence that followed came a trilling electronic tone. The phone in her pocket was ringing.

As she reached for it, a hot rush of adrenaline surged in Kevin's veins. He was past the point of thinking clearly, his fear at the wheel. He reacted, allowing desperation to propel him.

Kevin pushed up off his feet and came forward, dragging the metal chair with him, diving at Sasha in the brief moment her attention was split. Hurling himself across the gap between them, he had no conscious plan in mind, just the frantic impetus to strike out, to do something, *anything* to save himself.

He almost had her, but even though Sasha was slight, she was quick. The woman dodged his clumsy attack, kicking out at his feet to trip him before he could get up momentum.

With the phone's warbling, insistent call still echoing off the walls, Kevin let out a whining grunt of despair as his balance faded and he crashed to the floor. He landed on his right side, crying out again as he trapped a bleeding arm beneath himself against the cold tiles.

He looked up as Sasha loomed over him. Kevin expected to see fury and disgust on her face, but her expression was one of disappointment. 'What you said about your father . . . A lie. To make me lower my guard.'

'No,' he managed, new jags of pain lancing through his limbs. 'True. All true.'

She considered that, then raised the phone, glancing at the name on the incoming call screen. 'The difference between you and me . . .' Sasha turned and started to walk away. 'I am a survivor. But you will always be a victim.'

'That's . . . What they want you to believe . . .' Kevin gasped out the words but she was already at the door, stepping back into the hangar, the phone at her ear.

He slumped against the floor as the door creaked shut. Alone in the room, Kevin felt gravity dragging on him, as if the force of it had abruptly doubled. He clenched and unclenched the hand trapped beneath him, the slippery patina of his blood sticky against the tiles.

Then his arm slipped off the chair and he realised that the bite of the cable tie around his right wrist was no longer there. He rocked against it, rolling away, and his arm flopped down. In the hard impact with the title floor, the shock had cracked the plastic clip holding the tie shut. *His arm was free.*

Gritting his teeth against the pain from the cuts, Kevin reached over with numbed, blood-slick fingers to the other restraint around his left wrist. Fumbling, he worked his fingernail under the other cable tie's clip. He struggled and felt it loosen slightly. Kevin pulled furiously at the restraint to widen the gap, tearing the skin over his knuckles as he dragged his other hand free.

Panting, he lay on his back in the fallen chair and stared at the door Sasha had exited through. She could come back at any second, and if she found him like this, things would only get worse for him.

He scrambled to his feet, grabbing the back of the metal chair. There was a lock on the door but it secured from the other side, so he wedged the bloodstained seat beneath the handle as a makeshift barrier. It wouldn't hold for long against anyone determined to gain entry, but it was something.

Kevin went to the desk where the bag – the damned thing that had put him in this shitty situation – lay discarded on the floor. He gathered it up, swinging it up over his shoulder by its strap. To his relief, there was a first aid kit in the cabinet containing a few rolls of gauze bandage.

As he wound the gauze around the cuts on his arms, he looked away to avoid staring at the damage done, into the shadows at the far end of the mortuary. The door leading back out to the rear of the hangars was there, the same one he and Richie had used to sneak inside.

Kevin visualised the next steps to take. Out of the door, find his way back to the ladder well, follow the tunnels back to the terminal building. Even now there would still be people there, police and security guards he could implore for help, someone to patch up the burning cuts on his arms.

He would have to tell them the whole story, of course. The money. The choice. What he had done, what he had seen. All of it. But right now, Kevin wanted nothing more than to get out of this place alive. He wanted to run and keep running until this horrible day was a bad memory.

The need to flee was a physical thing, trembling through him. But he knew that as much as he needed to *run*, he needed to *think*. Blind panic would end him as quickly as the bullet that had killed Richie.

Kevin's gut twisted as the callous murder replayed in his mind's eye. Nothing could have prepared him for that kind of heartless, casual brutality, the horror of it tinged with an unreality that made everything nightmarish and dreamlike.

*Think first*, he told himself, fighting to hold on to the notion. *Use your head . . . Or you're a dead man.*

# TWENTY-TWO

'Speak.' Sasha studied the bloodied saw with distaste, and at length she slid it into the pocket of her jacket, before wiping her fingers on a kerchief.

She heard a nervous cough on the other end of the line, and pressed her phone closer to her ear. *'Uh, it's me,'* came the reply. *'Imran.'*

'You are interrupting me in the middle of something!' she barked at him, directing her annoyance at the hapless security technician. 'What do you want?'

*'Vincent gave me this number. You're Sasha, right?'* His voice had an odd echo to it, as if he had his head in a bucket.

'What,' she repeated, each word a straight-razor, 'do you want?'

*'I don't have much time, I said I had to go to the toilet, but, uh, he'll notice if I'm gone too long . . . The cop, Alfons I think his name is, that's who I mean. He's hanging around the security centre and he won't go away!'*

'Why should I care?' As she spoke, Sasha saw a familiar figure entering the hangar. Striding in from the rain, Boch's expression was fixed in a grumpy, irritable mask that didn't change when he nodded at his employer. She watched Von

287

Kassel move into the other man's orbit, as if he thought that might give him some measure of protection.

Sasha scowled. The *bulle*'s presence could only make this night worse.

'*The cop is looking through the CCTV footage from this evening,*' said Imran. '*He keeps on going back to the same bits, watching playback from the terminal concourse. He knows something's going on. What do I do? And where's Vincent?*'

The fact that Imran had no idea where Vincent was as well did not sit well with her, but Sasha said nothing. Talking to the dim camera operator about that would only confuse the issue. But then if Imran had not seen him, it was likely that the airport authorities hadn't taken the Frenchman into custody or something equally troubling. It irritated her that she was forced to deal with this without an ally to back her up. Reluctantly, she put the matter of Vincent's absence aside and concentrated on what was imperative.

'Pay attention. You will keep your mouth shut. If this man asks you anything, you will play dumb. I know you can do that.'

'*I don't know, uh, anything,*' Imran replied, starting to whine. '*Am I going to get in trouble?*'

'Only if you talk,' she warned him, and cut the call as Boch came striding over. His unlovely face creased in a deep grimace, and it was clear that being out in the rain had only worsened his mood.

'He's in there?' Boch pointed past her, at the door to the mortuary. 'The little shit who took the money?'

'I am dealing with it,' she told him.

Boch looked at the bloody kerchief she held and raised an eyebrow. 'Is that right? Then let's see your handiwork.'

Sasha pushed at the door, but it only moved a few inches before it ground to a halt and jammed in place. Momentarily confused, she drew it back and tried again, only to get the same result.

Boch shoved her out of the way and with an angry growl of effort; he slammed his shoulder into the door with a loud crash. It still didn't give, but the noise drew Oleg's attention, and he came looking. Miros trailed at his heels like a protective guard dog, having rearmed himself with a stubby pump-action shotgun from the boot of the BMW.

Boch's second shoulder charge dislodged the door and it banged wide open. Sasha saw the metal chair – the *empty* metal chair – spin away into the gloom and her heart sank.

She followed Boch into the cold room and swore under her breath. The Englishman was nowhere to be seen, and as she cast around, she saw the bag brought back from the terminal was missing as well. The blood spattered on the tiles was the only evidence the captive ever been there.

'This is *dealing with it?*' Boch grunted. Then he raised his voice so it would carry back into the hangar. 'He's gone.'

'There.' Miros had followed them in, and now he pointed into the gloom at the other end of the room. The far door was open, and Sasha could see a damp, bloody handprint on the frame.

'Go after him!' Oleg bellowed the command, loudly enough to make everyone jump. He stood on the threshold behind them, rendered into a black shadow by the light falling in from the hangar.

Miros didn't hesitate to obey, and he started moving at a run. Boch paused long enough to throw Sasha a dismissive look and followed along with the other man, vanishing out of the far door.

Sasha's body caught up with her frozen thoughts and she started after them, but she had barely taken a step when Oleg's voice rumbled behind her. 'Not you.'

'This is my error,' she said, imploring him. 'I should not have left the prisoner on his own—'

'It is *my* error,' he snapped, talking over her. 'Expecting something you are not capable of giving.' Oleg turned away. 'Once again you disappoint me.'

Sasha ran after him, back into the bright, open space of the hangar, the door groaning closed behind her. 'Sir! Give me a chance to make amends.'

Oleg didn't grace her with a look, just a terse shake of the head. 'You will remain here. Where I can watch you. Discipline must be enforced in full for every mistake.'

'Oh dear . . .' said a voice from nearby. Von Kassel was, of course, unable to observe in silence, trailing the pair of them as they walked to Oleg's BMW. He feigned concern. 'This is a troubling development.'

'*Fuck off!*' Sasha couldn't stop herself from snarling at the politician, who watched her with an air of smug superiority. 'This does not concern you!'

'I believe it does,' he said. 'Oleg has made that clear.' Then he tutted. 'I can empathise. It is so hard to find reliable staff these days.'

She bit down on the impulse to punch Von Kassel squarely in the middle of his pudgy schoolboy face, and forced herself to turn away. When she looked back at Oleg, the old soldier had Miros's pistol in his hand, the hammer cocked.

He examined his reflection in the silver frame of the gun. 'Much has become clear to me tonight.' Oleg was almost talking to himself. 'Weaknesses I have been unaware of. Flaws in my organisation ... In my judgement. I am paying the price for delegating to those who lack the will to do what is necessary.'

Fear jumped and twisted in Sasha's chest. She had known Oleg's rage too often, his thunderous anger demonstrating itself in outbursts of sudden, brutal violence; but there was another dark shade to him, a stony, clinical kind of fury that only surfaced on the rarest of occasions. At the thuggish extreme, he might beat a man to death or cut his throat – but at the other end of the scale was the soldier, the cold-blooded killer who had boarded up a village of refugees and then burnt its buildings to the ground with them trapped inside.

The glimpse of him she saw now, this was the Oleg who murdered indiscriminately, who had killed women and children with mortar shells loaded with mustard gas, who would sacrifice his own allies if it suited his needs.

And as he spoke, she saw clearly the lie of the times he had showed her affection, saw it for what it really was. Another weapon in his arsenal, a tactic to be deployed and then discarded when no longer useful.

Oleg cradled the pistol in his hands, and Sasha waited for him to raise it, anticipating the thunder that would end her.

But then the politician broke the moment's tension with a stage-managed clearing of his throat. 'I realise emotions are running high, but might I offer an alternative that could be useful to all of us?' He smiled slightly. 'If you will permit me, of course?'

Still holding the gun, Oleg glanced in Von Kassel's direction. 'You've done nothing but talk, but you say little of value.'

'Guilty!' He said the word with a sing-song lilt. 'Call it an occupational hazard. So much my daily life is spent dissembling, sometimes it is difficult to remember how to be ... *direct.*' Von Kassel reached for something in the pocket of his suit jacket. 'It's not that I lack confidence in my man Dieter and your fellow ... Miros, is it? But it does no harm to have a contingency plan. And I think we can all admit that this Englishman has been quite difficult to pin down. I would like to suggest a more efficient method of applying pressure to him.'

The object in Von Kassel's hand was a nondescript postcard, a bland collage of photos on one side, a scribble of text on the other. He offered it to Oleg.

'This is meaningless.' Oleg frowned at the card.

'On the contrary.' The politician pointed at the writing. 'There is a name there, you see? An apartment number and a street address.'

'Avenue B,' Oleg read aloud in English. 'East Village. New York City. United States.'

'I recall you have contacts in America,, yes?' Von Kassel's ingratiating manner made Sasha stiffen, but Oleg didn't appear to notice.

'A cousin,' admitted the old soldier. 'And some men who owe me favours.'

'Perhaps you could reach out to them?' Von Kassel produced his phone and offered it to the other man. 'Please. Feel free to use this.'

Sasha knew the men in New York. The cousin Oleg spoke of was not actually his blood relative, but another of the 'tigers' from the days of the civil war, a wolfish killer called Rodovan. He had been sent away to America because the murders he had committed in Europe were attracting too much attention from local law enforcement.

Oleg's leaden gaze found Sasha and his eyes were unreadable. He gestured at her. 'Make the call. Show me you are capable of following that simple order, at least.'

'Yes sir,' she said, looking down at the floor.


The shaking could have been from the cold or the terror. All that mattered was that Kevin remained silent in the close, dark confines, his jaw clamped tightly together to stop his teeth from chattering.

He strained to listen, pressing one ear to the metal wall. There had been raised voices, angry shouts and heavy footfalls – some of them so near to his hiding place that he was convinced they knew exactly where he was, that his plan had been blown before it even had a chance to begin. But now everything was silent and the only sound he could hear was the endless drumming of the rain resonating through the frame of the building.

He waited, hemmed in on all sides by the chilly metal borders of his confinement, lying on his belly in the pitch dark, his nostrils filled with the sharp stink of harsh chemical cleaning agents. Kevin turned his bandaged arm, and the faintest aura of light from the glowing hands of his watch became visible. The glass face was smeared with his blood, but it was still ticking.

The watch told the story. Only a couple of minutes had elapsed. His sense of time was out of synch, exaggerated by fear until each passing second took an eternity.

He couldn't wait any longer. In the darkness he couldn't see the walls around him, but he could *feel* them closing in, the reeking steel coffin shrinking, threatening to trap him there.

With a panicked flurry of movement, he punched forward and forced open the thick metal hatch holding him in. The clasp gave and the hatch swung wide, revealing shadows outside. Kevin clawed at the body tray beneath him, kicking, almost wedging himself in place in his haste to get out. He tumbled out of the narrow, deep cabinet, landing in a heap in front of the wall of mortuary lockers.

The others in the cluster he had chosen were occupied by the recently deceased, and that had been Kevin's gamble, hoping that Oleg's people would buy the lie of his panicked escape out the far door. Hoping that they wouldn't check the refrigerated compartments for someone who was still breathing.

It had taken more courage than he knew he had not to run, to climb inside one of the corpse lockers and stay quiet while the people who wanted him dead were right there, cursing his name. He imagined the pallid bodies crammed into those other tight spaces and reeled at the thought that he still was dangerously close to becoming one of them.

*So now you're running again.* His accusing inner critic rose out of the silence. *What are you going to do now, Kevin?*

'Shut up,' he whispered, and listened for voices. He could hear the faint sound of talking in the hangar, but it was far away. He had a window of opportunity to flee, with his pursuers looking in the wrong places for him, but it would mean nothing if he didn't act on it *right this fucking second.*

Grabbing the shoulder bag from where it had fallen, Kevin padded to the open door and peered out. He saw the darkened corridor beyond, windows streaked with rain. And at the far end, a way out into the storm.

He ran and didn't look back.


'Something here.'

'What?' Boch followed the sound of Miros's voice across the floor of the neighbouring hangar. He didn't get any other information than that, and he grunted his annoyance. He had quickly discovered that Oleg's pet thug had a limited vocabulary that didn't extend beyond sentences longer than two words, and it was a waste of time trying to get more from him.

'Here,' repeated the other man. 'Look.'

In the shadows behind one of the decrepit flight school's old Cessnas, a man had been trussed up against an engine hoist with strips of grey duct tape. Boch remembered his face from earlier in the evening. The French punk with the sly grin. He wasn't grinning now, his face swollen from a beating.

*Did the Englishman do that?* Boch hadn't thought the man capable of such a thing, and he quietly re-evaluated his estimation of his quarry.

He stripped the tape off the Frenchman's mouth and slapped him lightly around the cheeks. 'Hey. *Hey!*' Boch snapped his fingers in front of the semi-conscious man as his eyes fluttered. 'Wake up! Who did this?'

Boch's question earned him a mumbled moan but the answer was unclear. He spat and stepped back, gesturing at Miros. 'What is he saying? You talk to him.'

'Vincent.' Miros leaned in, taking the Frenchman's chin in hand. Then he looked up at Boch. 'Free him?'

'Do what you want,' Boch sniffed. This Vincent character showed signs of a concussion, and clearly he would be of no help in their search for the thief. He walked away, using the flashlight app on his mobile phone to illuminate the dim corners of the smaller hangar. He knew in his gut that there was nothing here, and that instinct was rarely misplaced.

A nagging thought kept returning to him – that he had missed something significant back in the mortuary, some clue as to where his target had gone to ground.

*To ground.* The notion pulled on him, and Boch turned back the other way, jogging quickly to the open doors at the other end of the smaller hangar. Outside, the sheeting rain turned the tarmac a glossy black.

When he had lost the Englishman's trail back in the terminal building, he knew there had to be some escape route he wasn't aware of. The manhole covers appearing regularly along the line of the aircraft turning apron told him he was right. There were tunnels under the runways, and if his target had used them once, there was a good chance he would do so again.

Someone with training and experience would not make that mistake. If their roles were reversed, Boch would know to find a different escape route. As he stepped out into the hissing downpour, he heard the faint clatter of metal on stone and he knew his instinct had been right.

*There!*

A few hundred metres away, on the edge of the grassy median strip, a low concrete wall surrounded a ladder well that descended into the maintenance spaces beneath. He saw a figure shouldering open a manhole cover, their fingers slipping as they fought to dislodge the metal hatch.

Boch pulled his Walther PDP and brought the gun up in both hands, drawing a bead on the figure. It *was* the Englishman.

He had managed to get behind them as they swept the hangars and outbuildings – commendable for an amateur, Boch had to admit – and that fact reinforced the driver's determination to take him. He had been right that something was amiss after all.

He advanced slowly, aiming his pistol through the rain, weighing his shot. If he hit a vital organ, he could kill the thief outright and lose any hope of locating the money. Oleg and his people would not be happy if that happened. The outcome would be bloody, to be sure.

He would need to get closer, to take the target unawares if he could, or wound him if he couldn't.

Sheetlightning flared over the terminal building, briefly turning the stormy night into an instant of watery daylight, and he took a good look at the Englishman. He had the manhole open now, dithering over the ladder leading down into the dimness.

Boch cursed his luck as the man glanced up, just as the light faded and thunder called across the low cloud overhead. The two of them locked eyes.

'*Shit!*' The other man's startled curse carried to him on the breeze.

Boch made a split-second decision and squeezed the Walther's trigger, deliberately aiming a few degrees off true. His shot kissed the low concrete with a singing ricochet that pulled another string of swear words from the Englishman.

'Do not move!' Boch shouted, over the rush of the rain. 'The next one goes in your belly!'

But for the second time this night, he realised he had underestimated the other man when the Englishman stepped forward and dropped straight down the open manhole.

He broke into a run, making splashy steps across the tarmac as he raced the last few metres to the ladder well. He was aware of Miros coming up from behind, probably drawn by the report of his weapon.

Boch pulled out his phone again and used the flashlight, sending a cone of bright illumination down the manhole. The ladder was shorter than he expected, the tunnel floor a couple of metres down, and there was no sign of the Englishman lying crumpled in a heap at the foot of the rungs.

*But then he's been through there once tonight*, he thought, *he knows how deep it goes.*

Boch jammed his gun into his belt and swung around the top of the rain-slick ladder, sliding down into the tunnel. He hit the floor with a wet smack. A ripple spread out before him across an inch-deep layer of rainwater, a clear sign that the drainage in the passageways struggled to cope with the unseasonable deluge from the storm.

The ladder vibrated as Miros came down with heavy, thudding bootsteps. 'Here?' he asked, as he reached the bottom.

Boch panned the phone's light around the featureless sides of the square-walled channel, catching a flash of movement at a junction up ahead.

'There,' he snapped, and took off in pursuit.

# TWENTY-THREE

Jagged, aching impulses raced up Kevin's legs with each smacking footfall across the concrete floor, the icy rainwater swamping his shoes as he fled. He veered into the nearest tunnel and ran as fast as he could, breath gushing out of his mouth in pops of mist.

The pathway extended into darkness, yellow light thrown in pools from bulbs strung every few metres. He had to duck to avoid cracking his head on clumps of piping hanging off the low ceiling, skidding on the floor as he lost his footing.

A ragged oval of white swung across the walls, the beam of a flashlight cast from somewhere behind him, and Kevin heard an angry shout. It was the same man from out by the hangar, the craggy-faced German who had taken a shot at him.

He almost stumbled as he looked back. There were two figures in the distance, their shapes distorted by the dazzling light, one of them aiming a weapon in his direction.

Kevin heard the roar of a shotgun's discharge and he cried out in fear, flinching away from the sound echoing down the tunnel. A cloud of lead shot clattered off the walls and he surrendered to his panic, letting it give him the burst of adrenaline he needed to flee.

He ducked into the first side-tunnel he came to, then took the next turning without stopping to consider where he was heading. His shoulder bag bounced and slapped against his back as he ran.

The voices behind him sounded off the concrete walls – definitely two men, arguing in fast, angry German – and the warped acoustics of the maintenance passages made it hard to gauge their distance. One moment, they were far away; the next, Kevin thought he was right on top of them.

He forced himself to a halt, bunching his hands into fists to stop them from trembling. Kevin's breaths were coming in rapid panting gasps, and he tried to slow each inhale and exhale, but his body did not obey. Each lungful of air was sore and rasping, and the muscles of his chest burned, resonating with the pain down his face and arms.

He strained to listen. Over the constant rush of the rain and the heavy dripping of water falling off the pipes overhead, he picked out the scrape of boots on wet concrete. It sounded like they were moving off.

*But which way?*

A horrible dread settled on him as he realised that he was well and truly lost down here. He'd reacted instead of thinking, running heedlessly in a desperate attempt to escape pursuit, and now he would pay for it.

Kevin looked around, searching the walls for the indicators he had seen while following Richie out to the hangars.

Eventually, he came across a string of numbers stencil-painted near the last turning he had taken, but they were different from the ones he had seen before.

Without some frame of reference, the legend *MON 12M E 45* had no meaning; it might as well have read *U R FUKD* for all the help it gave him.

'Think . . .' he whispered to himself. Kevin closed his eyes and tried to visualise the path he had taken, and slowly he understood that things were worse than he thought. To get back to the route Richie had followed from the basement of the terminal building would mean going back the way he had come. Into the path of the men with the guns.

He winced, touching at his newly crooked nose, and Kevin's fingers came back sticky. His wounds burned, joining the chorus of pain from the lacerations across his forearms. His energy leaked out of him, draining away into the cold water at his feet. Fatigue reached up and took hold. It was as if he had been awake for days on end.

Then a growling voice from somewhere close by said '*Diesen weg*,' and Kevin's exhaustion faded against the thudding of the pulse in his ears.

*They're coming this way.*

He pushed off the wall and sprinted down the tunnel, hunched forward and arms up to guard his head as he ran and ran. The slick of light from the torch blazed over the walls again and he heard the voice rise into an urgent shout. They had seen him.

The passage ahead was damp underfoot and he could see no sign of any tunnels branching off it as it dropped to a shallow slope. But to go back would be a fatal mistake. Kevin kept waiting for the burning impact of a bullet in the back, but it never came, and vaguely he wondered if they had decided to take him alive.

Dead, he couldn't give them anything – it was why Oleg had ordered the woman to torture him, to force Kevin to give up the whereabouts of the money.

*They want me in one piece*, he thought, *so they can cut me until I talk.*

Then without warning he was running into deepening water, sliding to a stop with the icy cold of it lapping up around his shins, soaking into his trousers. Blinking into the dark, he could make out a black, rippling mirror reaching away. The sloping tunnel ahead was filled to the ceiling with the overflow from the punishing rain, the deluge too heavy, too torrential to drain away quickly.

*Gotta be careful.* Kevin remembered what Richie had told him earlier that night. *When it belts down like this, some bits get flooded.*

Behind him, the light from the torch bobbed as the figure bearing it approached. He heard the oiled snap-clack of someone working the slide of a shotgun, ratcheting a fresh shell into the weapon's breech.

'Come back,' called the gruff voice, in terse barks of English. 'That is a dead end.' The man with the gun let that sink in. 'You do not want to die here.'

Despite the tension of the moment, Kevin felt the bitter urge to laugh. *Die here? Or die somewhere else?* It would make no difference.

'Fuck it!' He took three fast, deep breaths, filling his lungs with as much air as he could. On the last inhale, Kevin threw himself forward and hit the dark water with a heavy, echoing splash.

The harsh cold enveloped him and the muscles in his body reacted with a shuddering shock, as if the floodwater itself wanted to eject him from its icy grip. Kevin was a regular if average gymnasium swimmer, but the occasional holiday dip in the sea was the sum total of his experiences in waters like this. Pain and cramping bloomed along his arms and legs as his feet scraped the slanted bottom of the flooded corridor, and he flailed, making clawing motions as he tried to pull his way forward. A gush of silvery bubbles flowed from his mouth.

There was only darkness before him. The light behind spilled from the flashlight in his pursuer's hand, and to go back that way meant the end. The raw, powerful dread that had made him run before came back tenfold, but this time Kevin took control of it, used it to motivate him. He pushed off the floor, fighting to hold in his remaining breath, feeling himself rise.

His hands slapped the pipes lining the ceiling and he knew that he was in the deepest part of the corridor, where the floodwater had filled it completely. Grabbing the metal bolts holding the pipes in place, he used them as handholds, pulling himself away. The shoulder bag slipped down across his chest, drawing on him, but after too many heart-stopping seconds, Kevin's hands cut back through the surface of the water.

The incline of the corridor rose by degrees, and with it the floodwater dropped away. Soon his feet were on the bottom again and his head was out of the bitterly cold liquid.

Shivering and gasping with each laboured exhale, Kevin dragged his soaked, freezing form out of the water. His nostrils were filled with the stink of rain-damp and machine oil, and it was all he could do not to drop to his knees and collapse. Behind him, the dark space of the flooded corridor shimmered, but no light followed him.

He staggered to a squelching halt where the side tunnel joined a main access way and stared at the black water, incredulous that he'd managed to make it through. Only someone crazy would try to follow him. He gave a shaky chuckle. *Only someone crazy would have gone through there in the first place!*

Glancing around, Kevin spotted an alcove where machinery from the airport's steam heating system vented plumes of hot vapour, out on to the runway above. Drawn to the warmth like a moth to a flame, he stumbled towards it.

Boch panned the beam of the phone's torch across the rippling surface of the floodwater and mentally counted off the seconds. At his side, Miros shifted uncomfortably, the pistol grip of his short-frame shotgun in one hand, the other's clawlike fingers kneading the pump-action slide. When the Englishman didn't come back out of the water, Miros let the gun's muzzle drop, and gave Boch a questioning look.

'Drowned?'

'We need to be sure.' Boch put the phone away. 'I am not ruining my suit to go in there and check. You?'

'No.' Miros's unpleasant features creased in a sneer.

He looked around, searching for a branching tunnel. 'This passage leads back to one of the main paths.' Boch had a head for directions, part of the skill set that made him a good driver. He rarely needed to consult a map once he had his bearings, even in a maze like this. 'We'll find another way around.'

Miros nodded and waited for Boch to lead the way. He had the measure of Oleg's bodyguard now, he decided. The man had a soldier's manner to him that Boch recognised from his own time in the armed forces, but he was a follower more than a leader. Miros was the type of man to be content when he was being given orders, and lacking direction from Oleg, he automatically deferred to Boch to tell him what to do.

'Follow me,' ordered Boch, and Miros returned a nod, stepping into line.

The apartment was quiet without Andrea's presence, and without the comfort of her to give Maddie some stability, she had set to tidying the place up as means of distracting herself. But she attacked the chores listlessly, trying to focus on the laundry or the washing-up piles in the sink, and failing.

Every other moment sent her thoughts drifting back to her conversation – such as it had been – with her father. She glanced up at the digital clock on the microwave oven in the little kitchen. Evening here in New York meant it had to be the middle of the night in rural Germany. Maddie hoped that her dad had been able to find somewhere to rest out the hours, but she couldn't shake off the memory of his voice down the line from Europe.

*Why couldn't he say what was wrong? And why couldn't I just ask him?*

It sounded easy when laid out in those terms, but years of awkward silences, hurt feelings and obstinacy were not so easily overcome.

There had always been a fragility between father and daughter in the Tyler family, maybe a reaction against the smothering, always-on presence of Maddie's demanding mother . . . At least, until she left them both for someone else.

Maddie was conscious of the fact that she wasn't the kind of daughter Sadie Tyler had really wanted. Sadie craved a little girl pal she could mould in her own image, a protégé, and so the more Maddie had shown signs of developing her own identity, the more their relationship became strained.

Unlike her mother, her father had never judged the choices she'd made, but he hadn't really backed them either, and by the time he realised his mistake and tried to undo it, it was too late to overcome the inertia of the roles they had settled into.

Had she been here right now, Sadie would have told her daughter to bury any concerns about her father's problems in Germany and focus on herself, but Maddie wasn't capable of turning her empathy on and off like a light switch. She loved her dad and she worried about him, even if it was at times a hopeless endeavour. It was like a law of the universe, unbending and unchangeable.

She sighed. Andrea would be back from sparring practice at the Mountain Gym down by the East River in an hour or so, and then they would go out to the cinema. Maybe Maddie would be able to lose herself for a while in the flickering images on the movie screen, and maybe tomorrow she could try again to talk to her father. Really *talk* to him, like Andrea said, instead of skipping around the difficult subjects as if they didn't exist.

Abandoned on the table across from the kitchen, Maddie's phone began to ring and she started towards it, tossing aside the dishcloth in her hands. But she had only taken a step when it fell silent again.

She frowned, rocking on the balls of her feet, unsure if she should pick it up or go back to the sink. Maddie turned away and it rang again – twice this time before falling dark again.

She crossed the room, snatched up the device and tapped the screen. An alert informed Maddie of two missed calls from her dad's number. Then, even as she was registering that, the phone buzzed in her hand. He was still trying to reach her, but something wasn't right, the connection wasn't happening.

'Hello?' she answered, flicking the phone to speaker mode. 'I'm here.' There was nothing but dead air on the line, and then the call ended. When Maddie tried to dial back, she got a busy signal.

The loud, hard double-knock on the apartment door came out of nowhere and made her jump, enough that she dropped the phone on the table.

'Madeline Tyler?' A man's voice with a low Brooklyn drawl called out from the landing. 'NYPD. Can you come to the door, please?'

*The police?* A dozen unpleasant scenarios flashed through Maddie's thoughts. *Has something happened to Andrea? Or is this to do with Dad's calls?* She moved in hesitant steps down the narrow hallway ending in the front door, her hands coming together before her.

American cops intimidated Maddie, with their uniforms and their guns and their swagger. And while she had never been on the wrong side of them, her Latina girlfriend had more than a healthy disrespect for the New York law-enforcement community. Andrea had drummed it into her: *don't talk to cops, not without a lawyer.*

But she couldn't sit here in silence and hope they went away. If the police were here, it meant something was wrong.

The knock came again, two sharp bangs of a fist on the centre of the door, hard enough that she saw the cheap wood quiver under the impacts. 'Miss Tyler,' said the voice again, 'are you there? We need to talk to you.'

Her feet were bare, so she padded silently up to the door and peered through the spyhole. She had a warped fisheye view of a young guy with short blond hair in a cheap suit jacket, standing with one hand propping him up on the door frame. He looked to the side, and Maddie saw the indistinct shadow of a second person out of sight.

Taking a deep breath to steady her nerves, she spoke up. 'Can I see some ID, please?'

'Sure, no problem.' The blond man produced a wallet and flashed a gold badge at the spyhole. *Gold means a detective*, she thought, recalling that detail from some crime show she had watched. 'Can you open up?'

Maddie secured the safety chain and pulled the door back a short way, enough to get a better look at the man and his companion.

The blond man smiled thinly and bobbed his head, but the person behind him had a stony, forbidding face of sharp lines that made no pretence at warmth. He was wiry, with a closely shaven pate and he reminded Maddie of something dog-like and predatory. She instinctively took a step back and the other man broke eye contact, throwing a look down the stairwell to the floors below.

'Hello there,' said the blond man, his tone conversational. 'You're Madeline?'

She nodded a yes before she could stop herself. If Andrea had been here, she would have chastised her for admitting even that simple fact to this stranger.

'Just you in there?' He tried to look past her into the apartment.

She deflected the question with one of her own. 'What's this about?' Her gut instinct told her to slam the door in the man's face, but she didn't move.

'Can we come in?' The blond man gestured at his colleague. 'Trust me, this isn't something you want us talking about where your neighbours can hear.' His smile became an insincere grin.

'I don't—' Maddie was halfway through her refusal when her phone sounded again, drawing her attention back to the kitchen. She saw it on the table, the vibration of each ring making the device shudder in little skips of motion.

What came next happened in quick, brutal succession.

'Wasting time,' the other man said irritably, in a thick accent less Upper East Side and more Eastern Europe. He pushed his companion away, slamming into the chained door with the heel of his hand.

The cheap safety chain gave way with a high-pitched *ping* of breaking links, and the door flew back on its hinges. Maddie wasn't quick enough to get out of its way and it struck her across the cheek.

Firelight and pain shocked through her and she stumbled back into the hallway, aware of the two men storming in after her. She tripped over the rough edge of an ugly, threadbare rug that Andrea had rescued from a yard sale that summer, losing her footing. As she hit the floor, Maddie's brain caught up to her predicament and she sucked in a breath to scream for help. But instead of air, she inhaled a mist of droplets with a cloying, medicinal taste.

The blond man stood over her, one hand clamped over his nose and mouth like a makeshift mask, the other working a small pump-spray bottle in her direction. 'Shit, Rodovan, what the fuck happened to *be subtle*? I had the badge, I was handling this!' His muffled tone rose into a whine.

'Too slow,' said the other man.

'Fine. Close the goddamn door, will ya?' The blond man's voice sounded strange, turning fluid and faraway.

Where the mist touched Maddie's face, lips and nostrils, her skin numbed. She tried to speak, but her tongue became a heavy, leathery mass. Her vision blurred and objects around her transformed into fuzzy blobs of colour and light.

*Drugged.* The thought slid through her mind, its progress ponderous and slow.

Once, some nasty little prick at a bar in Greenwich Village had tried to slip Maddie a roofie in her drink, but when the first tingle hit, she'd thrown it in the guy's face before the effect could fully kick in. This was far, far worse.

That time, Andrea had been there with some of her friends from the gym and the guy had got off lightly with a pair of black eyes. But Maddie was alone here, and she felt her body becoming a piece of slack, deadened meat. Whatever was in the spray, it was potent and fast-acting.

'Help me get her up.'

The walls turned around her and Maddie was dimly aware of strong hands under her armpits, carrying her forward. Her head lolled against the jacket of the shorn-haired man and she smelled cheap cologne and cigarettes.

'The van in the alley?' The conversation orbited around her, coming from everywhere and nowhere.

'Yes.'

'Take her down the back stairs. Do it quick.'

Maddie could still hear the warbling ringtone of her phone as her feet clipped the doorstep and scuffed the chilly tile floor out on the landing. Her arm jerked, her fingers clasping at air, as if she could still reach out and grab the phone.

She tried again to speak, but all that emerged was a hollow gasp of air.

*Dad*, she cried silently. *Andrea. Someone.*

*Help me!*

# TWENTY-FOUR

The stiff breeze pulled Kevin's voice from his mouth as he cursed at the phone in his hand, watching the screen fade out and shut down for the fourth time.

The device had been deep in a jacket pocket when he braved the freezing water in the flooded tunnel, and he'd staked his hopes on it being able to work despite being temporarily submerged, but that was clearly in vain.

Admitting defeat, he leaned back against the wide black tyres of the parked airliner sheltering him from the storm above. Tucked in the shadows of the plane's stubby undercarriage, he was out of sight from anyone on the rain-lashed runway or up in the terminal building. It had been a long sprint from the ladder well over by the turning apron, and the AeroNordik jet was the first piece of cover he had come across.

There was nothing between his hiding place and the entrance doors leading to the terminal's ground floor, but the space was brightly illuminated by overhead floodlights, and he feared being caught in the open. With the noise of the raging storm, someone could take a shot at him out here and the sound would be smothered by the thunder.

Kevin's hands trembled. Was is possible to get hypothermia from wet clothing? He had no idea, but he was chilled through, and it made him sick to the stomach. If he stayed out in the elements, he was going to be seen or he was going to freeze to death.

The men chasing him had to know where he was heading. They would be looking for him inside the airport proper, watching the entrances. He needed to find another approach, he needed to stop *reacting* and start *thinking*.

Down by the airliner's tail, a set of covered mobile boarding stairs were mated up to the rear exit doors. Kevin had seen people moving around inside the lighted passenger cabin, and he guessed that a service team were on board, deep-cleaning the aircraft in preparation for its departure the next day.

He craned around. At the front of the plane, the elevated jet bridge connecting it to the departure gate on the first floor of the terminal was still in position.

It was a way back into the airport that might not be watched. His only problem would be avoiding the cleaners, but the jet was one of the larger ones at Barsbeker, a medium-haul Boeing, so the odds were favourable.

Kevin dashed to the base of the mobile stairs, then thudded up them two at a time, looking around nervously as he moved. Crouching by the rear exit, he listened for voices inside the aircraft and heard nothing.

The service team had to be up at the front, in the business-class cabin. *While I'm dumped back in economy, as usual,* he thought. He squeezed in through the half-open exit door, closing it behind to find himself in the airliner's aft galley.

Past a partition curtain, a narrow cylinder of empty seats ranged away from him towards the front of the plane, but Kevin hung back, searching for something. Finally his gaze landed on a nondescript panel that most passengers would have completely overlooked, but to someone who was a frequent flyer, someone whose ex-wife had been a flight attendant in a past career and loved to reminisce about it, it was an open secret.

Kevin pulled a handle on the panel and it clicked aside, revealing a couple of shallow steps leading to a low-ceilinged space beneath the passenger cabin. He ventured down, taking care to shut the panel behind him, and emerged in the airliner's crew compartment.

On long, transatlantic flights, this was where the cabin crew could take their breaks away from the demands of people wanting extra peanuts, blankets and chicken-or-beef. Here they could catch some sleep, dozing on shallow bunks beneath the feet of the passengers above. He remembered that Sadie had particularly enjoyed his discomfort when she relayed bawdy stories of what reckless, bored flight attendants did in spaces like this one.

He sat heavily on one of the mattresses and let out a long, weary sigh. For a moment – for what seemed like the first time in forever – Kevin felt safe enough to stop and gather himself.

Peeling off his damp jacket, he then methodically emptied the waterlogged contents of the shoulder bag on the bunk opposite and grimaced at the stale reek coming off the matted, ruined contents. Everything there was a mess, the contract papers a gummed-together clump of unreadable, ink-smeared pages, his toiletries split and leaking, and the unfinished novel he'd been reading bloated like a water-soaked sponge.

Kevin had been so blindly focused on getting the bag back to save himself, so afraid that Oleg and his people would find the threads of his life hidden in it, that he hadn't considered what could go wrong. And it had, in ways far worse than he could possibly expected.

*That man Oleg killed Richie right in front of me. And for what? To prove a point?*

Fear for his own safety had kept thoughts of the other man's demise at bay while he was on the run, but now Kevin had stopped moving the horrible reality caught up with him.

By rights, he should have been angry at the other Londoner for giving him up at the worst possible moment, but it was hard to feel anything other than dread and sorrow. Kevin had foolishly believed that there was some connection between hem, based on the vague thread of their similar upbringings – but looking at that fact in the harsh light of what had happened, he could see now that it meant nothing.

Desperate and friendless in a foreign land and a hostile situation, he had grasped at the closest thing to an ally, deceiving himself into believing that Richie would be on his side.

*But why would he be?* Kevin shook his head glumly. *I didn't really know him. I bought coffee from him. He was civil to me because it was his job, and I saw something that wasn't really there.*

Richie had betrayed him to save his own skin, and it had been for nothing. Everything the barista had said, those asides that made it appear like he knew more than he admitted, it made sense. *And now he's dead.* A piece of meat, not the easy-going person he had pretended to be, smirking and making chirpy jokes. Just a corpse like those filling the cold lockers back in the hangar.

If Kevin had left the bag behind and run the risk, Richie would still be alive. They would be in the man's car right now, most likely miles away from here trying to navigate the drenched country roads, but more importantly *gone.*

He stared at the bag and its contents, shivering quietly, then emptied his pockets. His passport and wallet were in a similarly ruined state. Worthless, all of it, but paid for with a man's life.

Kevin held in a despairing groan and pushed off the bunk, pulling open the plastic concertina-doors across the storage spaces in the crew compartment. Inside he found spare items of clothing kept there for the airliner's flight attendants – shirts, jackets and blouses, skirts and trousers in AeroNordik's uniform colours on hangers in orderly rows – he searched through them until he located something in his size. There were blankets in another locker, which became makeshift towels to dry himself off, and in a third was a soft-sided zip case containing a fresh first aid kit.

Dead-eyed and robotic in his movements, Kevin stripped to the waist, then cleaned and bandaged the lacerations on his arms and wiped the blood from his face. Cupping his damaged nose between his fingers, he took a deep breath and reset it with a jerk. New pain blasted through his skull and he howled into his hands to smother the sound.

He waited for the agony to subside, then changed into some of the clean air crew garments, staring into nothing. When he was finished, he kicked away the heap of his bloody, sopping-wet clothes, and sank back against the curved wall along the line of the narrow bunks.

The cold in his flesh had migrated into the depths of his body, into the bones and marrow. Kevin hugged himself for warmth, tilting his head down onto his chest. A fuzzy, thickening sensation pressed at the inside of his skull. He felt so utterly *exhausted*. He needed to rest, if only for a little while.

Kevin closed his eyes, and –

*'Hey, Pop.'*

Her voice echoing, Maddie's long fingers brushed against his cheek and Kevin blinked into awareness. Despite the fact that the crew compartment had no windows, it was suddenly daylight-bright in there. The air was warm and filled with floating motes of dust, drifting like summer pollen in the faintest breath of wind.

Kevin tried to move, but the mattress he sat on was unwilling to let him up. The foamy mass of it held him gently but firmly, as if he had sunk half into it like it was made of quicksand.

Maddie reclined across the compartment from him in a cross-legged settle, fingering the damp pile of papers by the bag. 'I can see your name on this,' she said. Her hand came away wet with crimson.

*Don't touch those.* He tried to speak, but his lips wouldn't move.

Kevin managed a gasp as a surge of emotion rushed through him. He was afraid and elated, his desperate wish to speak with his daughter unexpectedly granted. He was willing to give it all up for one more minute with her, to be able to look Maddie in the eyes and confess his mistakes.

But when he tried to tell her that, the sounds that left him were warped, strange echoes that bore no relation to words. He tasted sand in his mouth and his hand rose to his face. To his slow horror, Kevin felt his teeth crumbling into powder.

'You should have told me the truth, Dad,' said Maddie, shaking her head ruefully, unaware of his distress. 'But it's too late now, isn't it?' She toyed with his dead phone. 'Everything's broken. We can't talk. But we never really do, do we?'

As Kevin watched, more sand spilled out of the phone's metal case, glittering in the diffuse light. He took a breath and it was almost a sob.

'I know what you're going to tell me.' Maddie nodded sadly. 'You have done so much wrong in your life.'

She didn't say it with accusation, but with sorrow. Maddie had never judged him before and she wasn't doing it now. It was more that the daughter could articulate what the father wanted to tell her, better than he ever could have done himself.

'And you keep moving forward,' she went on. 'You try so hard, but instead of getting better, you keep making *new* mistakes.'

Rendered mute, Kevin nodded slowly, accepting the damning truth. He wanted to tell Maddie about why he had married her mother, about how they had loved each other back then and how it had gone away. He wanted to explain why he had gone into business with a man like Colin Fish despite the warning signs. To tell her about the petty, stupid little grifts and risky schemes he had stumbled through over the years that she had never known about. To make Maddie understand why he didn't leave that bag of bloody money and walk away.

He wanted to explain how *that* choice, and the others, had seemed like the right idea at the time.

'Or maybe it's because I'm a sodding idiot.' For once, it wasn't his ex-wife's voice admonishing him this time, it was his own. The words poured out him in gushes of powdery sand. 'And today's the day my luck finally runs out.'

'That man Oleg is going to kill you,' said Maddie. 'You can't let him.' The compartment distorted around her, elongating, becoming too bright to look at directly. 'The money is covered in blood, Dad. You see that, don't you?'

He nodded. 'Yeah. I do.' Kevin's eyes prickled with tears as Maddie began to recede from him, as the golden light took her. 'Please, Mads, don't go. Don't go. I'm sorry. Everything I did was for you. I'll be better. I mean it.'

'You always say that.'

'*I always mean it!*'

Kevin shouted himself awake, and the shock of it made him rise up and smack his head against the low ceiling of the crew compartment in the seconds before he remembered where he was. The cloying grasp of the vivid dream hung on to him like the reek of smoke and he had to sink back to the mattress, steadying his breathing before he could carry on.

Kevin's pulse drummed in his ears and he was shaky. Panic – his constant companion throughout this entire night – rippled down his gut, but he crushed it before it could grow anew.

*I fell asleep?*

The tight stiffness in his muscles and the pain in his joints made that clear enough. Exhaustion had pulled him under, plunged him into a dreaming abyss, but for how long? In the dim light of the compartment, he angled the face of his watch to look at the hands. At first he thought he'd misread the time.

*Hours had passed.*

How was that possible? It felt as if he had shut his eyes only a moment ago, but if the watch was to be believed, he had been taken away into nothingness for the better part of the night.

Kevin's hand touched his lips. He knew it was his weary mind playing tricks on him, but the arid, rasping taste of the sand in his mouth had been so real, he needed to reassure himself that he still had his teeth intact.

Checking himself over, he was whole if unsettled. Distantly he registered the thought of what might have happened if he had been discovered by Oleg's hunters while he was dead to the world. The notion of waking up with a knife to his throat or a gun against his temple made him shiver.

He strained to listen, but no sounds carried through the fuselage of the silent aircraft. That was one good thing. The cleaning crew would be gone by now, making it easier for Kevin to sneak off the jet and back into the airport.

'If I'm still here,' he muttered. He'd been out of it for long enough that the plane could have taken off and flown somewhere else by now, with Kevin out cold in the crew compartment like some erstwhile stowaway.

The shoulder bag and the papers that he had risked so much to recover, he left stuffed into one of the storage spaces, along with his wet clothes and the bloodstained debris of his used dressings. Carrying it with him would only remind Kevin of how much had gone wrong tonight.

There was only one way for him to bring this dreadful situation to a close, one final card he had to play. He couldn't run, he couldn't fight, and he couldn't hide in here forever. The only other way out was to surrender.

It was dark in the passenger cabin when he emerged from the galley, but the spill of light through the oval windows in the airliner's fuselage gave him enough illumination to navigate by.

Kevin leaned across an aisle seat to peer out at the night. The rain still fell, the droplets flickering off the flat surface of the jet's wing, but it was a desultory downpour now, lacking the power of the earlier deluge. The storm had finally moved on, leaving broken cloud scattered in its wake across a pre-dawn sky. Nearby, the lights of the terminal building blazed, and Kevin picked out a lone figure moving around on one of the upper levels. There were still people in there, ticking off the hours until Barsbeker awoke from its slumber and the planes began flying again.

He picked his way to the front of the aircraft. The mobile stairs at the rear were gone and the door there sealed shut, but the jet bridge was still in place. Kevin paused in the forward galley, rummaging through the drawers and compartments until he came across a tray loaded with tiny bottles of booze. Skipping over whiskey, gin and vodka, he stole a couple of brandy miniatures and bolted them down in quick order. Partly it was to warm him up a little, but mostly he hoped it would serve as a little liquid courage for what he would do next.

Kevin read the instructions for working the door off the safety card in a nearby seat back pocket, and to his relief it opened without setting off the inflatable escape slide. He climbed out into the darkened jet bridge and made his way down the corridor, finally emerging at the arrival gate inside the terminal.

He took a second to get his bearings. He was at the far end of the building from the KnightSky gate, but close to the security area. Kevin moved to the glassed-in balcony and hid in the lee of one of the terminal's giant concrete support pillars, using it to conceal him as he scanned the level below.

The store fronts were shuttered now, the duty-free section closed off by honeycombed roller gates that blocked off any means of entry. Only the newsagent remained open around the clock, doggedly offering snacks, fizzy drinks and overpriced souvenirs to an empty concourse and waiting areas populated by passengers dozing fitfully in their chairs.

From here, he could see the clump of coloured cubes housing the left-luggage lockers where he had deposited the money. Kevin tried to put himself in the shoes of the criminals. What would they have been doing while he slept out the hours on the airliner? He knew that they had to have a contact working in the CCTV room, so he could assume that if he was spotted by a security camera, the criminals would know about it in short order. He looked around, finding the shiny black hemispheres set into the terminal's ceiling.

*Had they already seen him?*

He imagined watchers in reach of the exits, waiting for Kevin to show his face before the sun came up. The woman with the saw, the tall thug with the gun, the brute who looked like a boxer, waiting for him to resurface.

Or would their boss be cannier than that? Would Oleg wait for Kevin to recover the money, then take both in one fell swoop?

*The money.* Kevin recalled the texture of those wads of cash in his hands, the density and the weight of the bills as he had counted out one bundle after another on the carpeted floor of the multi-faith room. The flame of old, reckless greed rekindled briefly in him, as he thought again about what he could do with that kind of money.

*If I take it.*

*If* he was willing to follow this whole thing through to its most dangerous conclusion. He might succeed – there was still the slimmest of chances – but failure would be the death of him, and the monumental weight of the odds loomed large.

Kevin wished he'd had the foresight to grab a couple more miniatures of brandy. Stone-cold sober, it was a battle to get past the fear that rooted him to the spot.

Then he saw a familiar face, as a stocky man in a POLIZEI vest with a cap in one hand came wandering into view, patrolling the edge of the concourse with the bored but watchful air of a hunting dog lacking any prey.

*What was the copper's name?* Kevin racked his brain, dredging up the information. *Alfons! That was it!* If he could get to the man, he could turn this whole situation on its head.

He didn't care any more if the German policeman dragged him away in cuffs, anything was better than the prospect of a bullet through the skull. Kevin made up his mind to spill his guts to the authorities and trust that these local plods would be smart enough to call in backup from Kiel.

*I'll tell him everything*, he decided.

Kevin waited until Officer Alfons passed beneath the balcony where he was hiding out, and bolted out of cover. He sprinted to an open stairway leading down past the mezzanine level to the concourse, taking the steps two at a time, his stolen flight crew jacket flapping against him as he ran. Kevin forced himself to slow to a walk as he reached the lower level and trailed after the policeman. He cleared his throat.

Suddenly, he didn't know how he would draw the man's attention, or exactly what he was going to say when he had it. He wondered if he would have to take a swing at the man, try to make Alfons arrest him, anything to get out from under the all-seeing eyes of the CCTV monitors.

'All right.' Kevin drew himself up and took a deep breath to steady his nerves. 'I'm doing this.'

A soft chime sounded from a speaker in the ceiling above, heralding an announcement over the airport's public address system. Kevin halted, surprised to hear it go off when there were no flights to be called, and no errant passengers to be admonished about running late.

The PA voice was a clipped, computerised approximation of the tones of a young woman with a *Hochdeutsch* accent. Usually, she relayed her messages first in businesslike German, but this time it was English only, and what she said rooted Kevin to the spot.

*'Attention please, paging passenger Kevin Tyler. Will passenger Kevin Tyler please pick up the white courtesy phone immediately? There is an urgent call from your daughter.'*

'Maddie?' Her name jolted him out of his moment of stasis, and Kevin cast around, spotting a telephone unit on a service desk a few metres away across the concourse. As he rushed over to it, he was aware of Alfons looking his way. The cop had to be wondering what was going on, and why the PA call had been sounded.

Kevin flexed his hands to stop them trembling and snatched up the handset, pressing it to his ear. 'This is, uh, Kevin Tyler. Hello?'

*'Bitte warten sie einen moment.'* The synthetic voice asked him to wait, and in the moment of silence before the line

connected, Kevin turned his face to the wall, trying to make himself less visible.

His thoughts raced. Maddie knew what airport he was at, she knew about the flight delays, so it wasn't beyond the realm of possibility that she had called Barsbeker directly when attempts to reach him on his ruined phone failed.

*It's got to be that,* he told himself. *Please, let it be that.*

But the next voice he heard was a rough, smoker's growl. '*Tyler*,' began the man, over-enunciating his name. '*Listen carefully. We have Madeline.*'

# TWENTY-FIVE

In the middle of the wide, long room, there was a mismatched collection of furniture around a folding card table, a couple of old lawn chairs, a threadbare barstool and the decrepit sofa that Maddie had awakened upon.

Her first impressions of the place were the odours of the old couch, where her face rested against it, the smell of dog hair and Chinese food baked into the thing.

Her captors had spared every expense with the location they kept her in. It was the gutted shell of an office on the second or third floor of a converted warehouse, the plasterboard walls slumping and the lining paper peeling off in sheets. Old floorboards creaked when anyone walked around, and across from her were arched windows heavy with grime, most of them covered with taped-up pages from old copies of the *New York Post*.

When she came to, her first reaction was understandably one of silent terror. Being drugged and abducted from one's home wasn't something any normal person would be able to shrug off. But a long time ago, Madeline Tyler had vowed to herself that she would not be a victim, no matter what happened to her, and now she reached inside and dug deep to find her bravery, remembering that promise. Her grogginess wore off gradually, leaving her with a cloying medicinal taste at the back of her throat and a stiffness in her limbs.

To her relief, the men who had taken her hadn't done anything else other than tape her wrists together and deposit her on the sofa. She had some blurry, half-formed memories of being dragged out of the apartment, the smell of fresh air and diesel, and then the muddy sounds of traffic.

She had been in a vehicle. *A van?* She dimly recalled someone talking about that.

The two men who had impersonated the police to get Maddie to open the door were in here with her, but they weren't invested in her well-being. When she tried to talk to them, they ignored her, and she had the impression that they weren't really sure what to do with her.

*Is that a good or bad thing?* Maddie had no way of knowing.

But she did have an unpleasant inkling as to what the root cause of this whole situation might be.

When she was twelve, her father had taken her aside and told her that he had a very special thing for her to do. He'd been sporting a black eye that day, and laughed it off when she asked him how he got it.

*Listen, Mads. If some strangers you don't know come along and ask you about your dad, if you're at home or on the way to school, you tell them he's gone away on holiday, all right?*

He made it sound like a joke, like a funny game, and she'd gone along with the ruse. She never did see any strangers asking questions, but soon after Maddie had made the mistake of mentioning the conversation to her mother, and that had set off a vociferous argument. At the time, Maddie had believed she was the cause of it, but years later she had come to understand what had really gone on there.

She loved her dad, but he made bad choices. Maddie had hoped that sort of thing was behind them now, but sitting there on the couch and listening to the two men grumble to one another in some language she couldn't understand, she could only wonder what new trouble her father had become caught up in.

The angry-looking one, the one the fake cop had called 'Rodovan', checked a message on his phone, before throwing her a cold glance. He stalked away to the far side of the room, dialling a long number as he went. She watched him speaking to someone, but his tone was too low to make out anything.

Maddie's attention was snatched away when she heard the whoop of a police car's siren passing close to the building. She sat upright, her body automatically tensing, but no sooner had it sounded, the noise faded away as the patrol car raced by without stopping. Dejected, she stared at the windows, trying to see through the film of dirt to what was outside. She thought she heard children's voices outside, making out the tops of a couple of trees and the low, boxy shape of another building with a brightly painted facia. There was something familiar about it.

She *knew* that place. Had she been there? *Yes!* But when?

It was exasperating, remembrance drifting just out of reach, half-recalled and ghostly. All Maddie could be sure of was that it wasn't far from the apartment, somewhere on the East Side, somewhere she and Andrea had visited on a hot summer day.

*Cold drinks in their hands and flip-flop sandals on their feet. Birds chirping in the trees. Kids from the block yelling and playing. The birds had been so loud.* The disparate threads of her memory floated apart, refusing to mesh into a whole.

The man who had flashed the counterfeit detective's badge noted her shifting around and wandered over. Maddie instinctively retreated into the corner of the couch as far back as she could go, her moment of reverie lost.

He looked her up and down. 'You sit there, keep quiet, this'll be over soon.' His tone was companionable and chatty, as if he were some neighbour from down the hall talking about the weather, as if his part in kidnapping her was trivial and unimportant.

She gave a shaky nod. 'What do you want from me?'

'Oh, this ain't about you, hun,' he replied, deepening Maddie's suspicions. 'Don't do nothing stupid, you hear? We'll get you back to your boyfriend and it'll all be good. Just . . .' He made a *close your mouth* gesture with his fingers.

That comment about a boyfriend made it clear that these men didn't know much about Madeline Tyler's personal life, and that was some small comfort. It meant that Andrea probably wasn't mixed up in this mess.

*Andrea.* Maddie's chest tightened as she thought about her. Judging by the fading daylight through the windows, not much time had passed between them taking Maddie from the apartment and her awakening here. That meant that Andrea would soon be home from her sparring practice at the gym.

Maddie felt ill as she thought about how Andrea would react. The two of them never went anywhere without letting the other know in advance, she'd even leave a note if she was skipping down to the bodega for a bottle of milk. Maddie thought of Andrea finding the broken door chain and signs of a scuffle, and imaging the absolute worst.

*I'm fine I'm fine I'm fine . . .*

Maddie closed her eyes and concentrated on the words, trying to send them to Andrea across the distance, hoping she might sense it.

*But you're not fine.* She heard the phantom reply in Andrea's curt, serious tones. *Maddie, you are so* far *from fine it's unreal.*

'Tyler.' She turned in the direction of the voice, picking her surname out of the air as Rodovan spoke into his phone. But the man wasn't addressing her. 'Listen carefully,' he said. 'We have Madeline.'

'Dad . . .' she gasped. 'Are you talking to—?'

The blond man was on her in an instant, putting one foot up on the sofa. 'I said be quiet.' His false good nature evaporated. 'My buddy here wanted to tape your mouth shut, but I said no . . . You gonna make me regret that?'

Maddie knew that he expected her to be submissive, but she refused to give this creep the satisfaction. 'Sod off,' she told him, in a defiant voice.

He snorted with derision. 'I love that Brit accent. Makes everything sound, I dunno, *super-classy.*' Then his eyes narrowed and ice formed on his next words. 'Don't push your luck, though.'

Maddie could hear the tinny burble of someone on the other end of Rodovan's phone, and she recognised the cadence of her father's voice. The hard-faced man made a spitting noise and spoke over him. 'It is simple,' he growled. 'Give back the money and the girl lives.'

*Money?* She seized on the word. *Oh, Pop. What did you do?*

Then Rodovan held the handset out to her. 'He wants to speak to you.' Gingerly, she took the phone and stared at the long string of numbers on the screen, and the blinking call icon. 'Make him understand the situation, eh?'

Maddie took a deep breath and raised the phone to her ear. 'It's me,' she began.

'*Mads.*' Her father put a lifetime of regret and sorrow into that single word. '*Oh, sweetheart, this is my fault. I'm so sorry you were pulled into this, I tried my best to keep it under control and it's . . . It's gone wrong . . .*' He sounded as if he was on the verge of tears, and Maddie gulped down a sob of her own, mirroring the emotion.

'Dad, what happened?'

'*I did a stupid thing, Mads. I was desperate and greedy and I did something I never should have. But I will fix it, I mean*

336

*it. They won't hurt you if I give them it back; you'll be OK. I promise you.'*

'Tell me what you did.' Maddie Tyler had always known that there were secrets her father had kept, not only with the stories about rough men asking questions about him, but other matters he wanted to protect her from. 'I need to know.'

And as she sat there on that reeking, tumbledown couch, it spilled out of him.

She listened in silence. He told her about the last-second collapse of the big German deal, and how it was going to ruin him and his company, about his debts and his deadbeat partner. He talked about a bag of money and a risky opportunity he was too desperate to pass up, and then stumbled over his words as he told her about a man who had been killed right in front of him.

Maddie sat rigidly, staring at the dirty windows, letting his words wash over her. She was terrified for him and furious at him all at once. She wanted to shout and to sob. But more than that, she wanted him to be safe and far from the brutal madness he had fallen into. Kevin Tyler was flawed and he was a fool but he was the father who had always provided for her, always shielded her from her mother's mood swings, who always tried his best to do the right thing ... Even if it he went about it the wrong way. She loved him deeply, and always would, whatever came between them.

*'I'm sorry, Mads,'* he said again, a tremor in his voice. *'All I've ever done is disappoint you. I didn't want that to happen again. Please forgive me.'*

'Dad, no . . .' Maddie felt tears cutting down her cheeks, and she took a deep breath. Rodovan had been talking quietly to his comrade while she spoke with her father, but now he came back her way, and she knew she only had moments before the phone would be taken from her. 'Listen to me,' she said, with more conviction than she felt. 'Just do what they say and . . .'

She blinked away tears and suddenly the brightly painted building across the street was steady in her view. *I do know that place. I know it!* The recollection snapped into focus like the turning of a kaleidoscope and she had it, right there on the tip of her tongue.

Maddie spoke rapidly. 'We can go out like we did last summer, to the pool where the kids were playing and the birds wouldn't shut up. Just across the street.' She heard her father make a questioning noise, but it was too late to stop. 'Just across the street,' she repeated. 'Not far away. Do you remember?'

'Enough.' Glowering suspiciously, Rodovan leaned in and snatched the phone from her hand, shoving her back against the couch. He stalked away, raising the handset again.

'What did you say to Daddy, huh?' The blond man folded his arms across his chest and eyed her. 'He knows what's gonna go down if he screws with Oleg again, right?' Maddie had no idea who *Oleg* was, but she could take a guess. 'Won't be fun for you,' he added.

'He understands,' she said.

*But he won't,* Maddie told herself, the grim reality of it settling on her.

*No one knows where I am.*

*'Just across the street,'* said Maddie, *'not far away, do you remember?'*

'I don't ...' He couldn't find the words, and Kevin trailed off mid-sentence. One moment she had been making sense, the next his daughter was babbling about *birds* and *kids* and a *pool* and he felt like he was coming unglued from the conversation. 'Mads, what are you talking about?'

When she didn't reply, his heart leapt into his mouth and Kevin was afraid that Maddie had been forcibly silenced. The next words he heard were from her captor, the growling Eastern-European man.

*'Now we are clear, yes? You know the stakes.'*

'Yes.' He bit out the word.

*'Oleg is watching. If you disobey, if you try to run, if you don't have the money, she dies.'*

Kevin felt heat rising on his cheeks and tension gathering in his limbs. 'I'll give it back. If you let her go.'

'Sir.' From behind him, a firm and commanding voice demanded his attention. 'Are you all right?'

Kevin turned, knowing the origin of the clipped, stern diction before he laid eyes on the speaker. Alfons, the German police officer, was standing right behind him. His arms were folded behind his back and he watched Kevin with a serious, measuring gaze, studying the stolen AeroNordik jacket he wore with more interest than was wanted.

'Do you need assistance?' he added.

'*Who is that?*' demanded the voice on the phone.

'No one,' Kevin said, then shook his head. 'I'm fine, officer. Thank you.'

'*A pig is there?*' The other man's manner hardened. '*You get rid of the cop right now or I cut the girl.*'

Kevin's hand stiffened around the telephone. 'Fine,' he repeated, fighting to keep a fixed expression on his face.

'Are you sure—?' Alfons went on, sensing something amiss.

'Can't you go away and leave me alone?' Kevin almost shouted the words at the police officer, cutting him off before he could finish. His voice carried across the quiet of the terminal concourse, drawing even more attention from the few travellers scattered around. 'Please,' he said, trying to backpedal from the outburst. 'I want some privacy!'

The policeman's expression darkened. 'Of course,' he said coldly, and strode away without another word.

'He's gone,' Kevin panted, trying to keep calm. 'I made him leave.'

'*Why were you talking to a cop?*'

'I wasn't!' He fought to hold his voice level. 'It wasn't anything!' Silence followed his assurances, and although it only lasted a few seconds, to Kevin it felt like forever. He held his breath, terrified that the next sound he heard down the line would be screams.

'*Listen carefully,*' said the voice, and Kevin finally exhaled. '*These are Oleg's orders: get his money and bring it to the hangar. He said you know where that is. Return the money, she lives. Oleg said if you try to be clever again, if you run away again, the daughter pays the price. You have one hour.*'

The line fell silent and Kevin closed his eyes, wanting nothing more than to disappear into the darkness.

Half in shock, Kevin paced to the nearest waiting area and sank in an unoccupied chair, his hands clasping at his wristwatch. His only company was another man across from him, a guy around his age in a business suit who dozed peacefully, his hands wrapped around the strap of a carry-on bag.

He felt a momentary surge of hot, irrational hatred for the stranger, briefly consumed by jealousy for someone who appeared to have nothing in the world to worry him.

*Lucky fucker*, he thought.

Kevin fiddled with his watch, setting its timer function to a fifty-minute countdown. He studied the tiny digital display under the broken sweep hands, watching the seconds fall away. He wanted to jump to his feet and run, run as fast as he could to the locker to recover the bag of money, but he knew that was the wrong play.

Kevin had the sad benefit of having been a mark more than once in his life, and he knew the signs. Oleg and his people were dialling up the pressure on him, cutting off his options, giving him no time to think, forcing him to respond on instinct.

But it wasn't his life on the line any more. These people had Maddie's future in their hands. If there was even the slightest chance that she could come out of this alive, Kevin had to do all he could to make it happen.

*I have to make amends. I have to fix this.*

*I have to* think.

He would give Oleg what he wanted, that wasn't a question any more. But Kevin had absolutely no guarantee that the brutal criminal would keep to any bargain. He needed an insurance policy.

The man in the opposite seat grunted and mumbled something in his sleep, shifting position. His movement revealed a phone poking out of his breast pocket, and Kevin saw an opening.

Making certain no one would notice, he stood up, pretending to stretch, and snatched the phone. To Kevin's relief, the device had a facial recognition lock screen, and after positioning it in front of the sleeping businessman's head, the phone activated.

He moved to a secluded corner of the empty lounge and leaned over the device. From memory, Kevin typed in the international dialling code and country codes for America, followed by the number for Maddie's apartment. He held his breath again.

On the third ring, the line connected and he heard Andrea say his daughter's name, her voice thick with emotion.

'No,' he said quietly. 'This is Kevin. Madeline's, uh, dad.'

Andrea said nothing for long seconds, but he could hear her breathing, composing herself. When she did speak again, her words were laced with venom. '*I get home today and my neighbours say some shit has gone down at our place, shouting and yelling, and she's gone, and there's a mess here . . . You better not tell me this is your fault,*' she said firmly, '*because if it is, I swear I will cross the goddamned ocean to beat the shit out of you!*'

'It is my fault,' he said, in a dead voice.

'*Motherfucker!*' Andrea roared the curse at him, and he recoiled. '*You lousy son of a bitch, she loves you like anything and you get her into, what? Some sketchy bullshit? Where is she? Where's my Maddie?*' The young woman's anger trailed off into furious sobs and guilt twisted in Kevin's chest.

'I'm sorry.'

'*The way I hear it, you're* always *sorry,*' she managed. '*How's that working out?*'

He let the question pass. 'Look, I pissed off the wrong people and they'll hurt her if I don't pay them back.'

'*So pay them!*'

'I will! But you need to go to the police . . . ' The words tumbled out in an urgent rush. 'It sounded like she was inside a big building . . . ' He concentrated on the memory of the call, and the odd echo he'd heard in the voices on the line. 'A warehouse? I'm not sure.'

'*The cops are useless,*' Andrea said grimly. '*It'll take days before they do anything. People like us ain't exactly a priority for them.*' She hesitated before speaking again. '*You know how many were there? Neighbours said two guys came around.*'

'I heard one man. Eastern European. Maybe another one in the background.'

'*You talked to them? To Maddie?*'

'Yes.' He took a breath. 'Andrea . . . I know you don't think much of me. And you're right to. I'm a fuck-up. I don't deserve a daughter as good as Maddie. But she's the best thing I ever did, and I'm half a world away and my only child is in danger *I* put her in.' Tears prickled Kevin's eyes. 'I'm begging you. Please help me.'

Andrea was quiet again, composing herself. '*Was she OK?*'

He nodded. 'I reckon so. She said I would be all right if I did what they told me.' He gave a brittle chuckle. 'That's like her, isn't it? Always looking out for other people first.'

'*Yeah,*' Andrea said softly, '*it's why I care about her.*'

'At the end, the last thing she said . . .' Kevin struggled to remember the exact words. 'It didn't make any sense.' A cold shiver passed through him. 'She was trying to tell me something.' He screwed his eyes shut, willing himself to remember. 'About last summer. A pool where kids were playing. And birds. Birds that wouldn't shut up.'

'*Oh, shit,*' breathed Andrea. '*I remember that! The public pool on 10th . . . It's a few blocks from here, we went there . . .*'

'She kept saying "just across the street". "Not far away." What does that mean?'

'*It means my girl is smart,*' she said. '*There's a building across from the pool. Used to be for storage. Like a warehouse.*'

'That's where she is!' Kevin was suddenly on his feet, elated by the revelation, but then he hesitated. The primal parental impulse he had to run to his child's rescue would do him no good here. He took a steadying breath. 'We can get her back.'

'*Yeah, we can,*' said Andrea, and he could sense she was making a decision. '*As long as the creeps holding her don't get spooked.*'

'I'll do my part,' he promised. 'I'll do whatever I can to make her safe. That's what matters to me.'

Once again, Andrea was quiet for long seconds. '*You do love her, don't you?*'

'More than anything in the world.' He paused, thinking it through. 'And you feel the same, right?'

'*Truth.*' She sighed. '*How 'bout that? You and I have some common ground after all.*'

'I trust you, Andrea,' he said, casting a glance out the terminal's windows at the cloudy sky. 'Maddie wouldn't be with someone who didn't deserve that.'

'*She has a big heart,*' came the reply. '*So don't prove her wrong, Kevin. Be the father she thinks you are.*'

# TWENTY-SIX

'Report,' said Oleg, his eyes tracking Sasha like twin gun barrels.

She stepped away from the hangar's entrance and gestured with the phone in her hand. 'I spoke to Rodovan. The girl is secure. He did exactly as you asked, sent the message, spoke to the thief.'

Oleg nodded to himself. 'He is a good soldier. Reliable. Competent.' *Not like you.* The last part was unspoken, but Sasha knew the old man was thinking it.

'Your money will be here by the top of the hour,' she added, keeping her tone level. 'The thief knows he has no choice now.'

'There is always a choice.' As usual, Lars Von Kassel wanted to offer his opinion on this and every other discussion. He dallied nearby at the side of his Mercedes, drumming his fingers on the bonnet. 'But only for those of strong character. The Englishman could still take the money and flee.' He considered that possibility. 'Given his performance so far, he might even escape.'

'Don't mistake luck for ability,' said Oleg.

347

Sasha should have ignored the other man, but the politician irritated her so much she couldn't stop herself from engaging. 'If he does run, Rodovan will kill the daughter.'

Von Kassel shrugged. 'But some men would make that trade. Pay that price and not look back.'

'Men like you?' Sasha couldn't keep the sneer from her tone.

'In my experience, greed beats guilt.' He didn't respond to Sasha's jibe, and glanced at Oleg. 'Tyler's weakness is his attachment to his family. He's trapped by it, forced into the outcome that benefits us.'

'For once, we agree on something,' Oleg allowed.

'Very promising!' said Von Kassel. 'I must say, despite the tribulations we have faced tonight, I do feel richer for the experience. Shared misfortunes are a strong basis for mutual respect, don't you agree?'

'You see him?' Oleg pointed out Miros to Von Kassel, who stood off near the BMW, sipping at a steaming cup of black tea. Off the politician's nod, Oleg continued on. 'I once watched him dig a rifle round out of his own belly and patch up the wound. He had only a lock-knife and a bottle of bad vodka to help him. *That*, I respect. You?' He smiled thinly. 'Not so much.'

'Perhaps I will surprise you.' The other man coloured, and forced a bland smile. Von Kassel's own bodyguard was nowhere in sight, and his absence made his employer nervous. 'I am curious about one detail,' said the politician, running a hand through his unkempt hair, attempting to change the subject. 'You make much of being a man of your word, Oleg. If the thief comes here on bended knee, begs for mercy, pays back what he took . . . Will you keep to the terms of your bargain?'

'The Englishman dies,' snarled the old soldier. 'No one steals from me and lives to talk about it.'

'That is not what I asked.' Von Kassel's lip curled.

'If you refer to the daughter, Rodovan will dispose of her once I have my money.' Oleg dismissed the matter with a shake of his head. 'There can be no loose ends. Besides, women disappear all the time from city streets.' He looked at Sasha, as if reaching into her soul and pulling the old, buried memories of her abduction out of the bleak past.

A dim beat of emotion stirred in her, faint as a guttering match in the hollows of an abyss, a cry of pity for the woman in New York. Sasha's deadened empathy briefly rose and then faded again. She had been in her place. She knew exactly what Tyler's daughter would be feeling at this moment. *The fear. The nauseating, creeping terror.*

Sasha had convinced herself that she didn't remember those emotions, and that Oleg's tutelage had purged them from her, but it was a lie. The frightened, beaten-down runaway that Sasha once was had not been transformed into the cold-eyed assassin Oleg wanted her to be. The runaway was still in her, wrapped in the lie of the killer, peeking out through the cracks in the shell of her new self.

'I asked you a question.' She snapped out of her introspection. Oleg was addressing her directly, inquiring about Vincent's condition.

'Miros brought him back from the flight school hangar across the way,' she said quickly, and jerked her thumb in the direction of the offices. 'I put him in one of the rooms, but he has a concussion. He needs to go to a hospital.'

'The Englishman did that?' Von Kassel made a face. 'Well, I suppose I shouldn't be surprised. They are common brutes under the skin.'

'Check on him,' said Oleg, each word leaden. 'No one leaves until I have what I am due.'

'I'm not a nursemaid—' Sasha began to protest half-heartedly, but Oleg held up a hand in a warning she knew well. She fell silent.

He leaned close to her, and whispered in her ear. 'Have you forgotten your discipline, girl? Is it necessary for me to correct you?' Oleg nodded in the direction of the metal cargo containers in the far corner of the hangar, the same as the one he had hauled her out of an eternity ago, and he made the threat that she feared the most. 'I can always put you back where you were found.'

Sasha closed her eyes, and for a second she could smell dried blood, machine oil and human waste. She was back there, back in that steel box, waiting to die.

'As you order, sir.' Sasha heard herself say the words, felt herself march on to carry out Oleg's command. But parts of her were breaking away from the woman he had turned her into, questioning everything he demanded of her; and it terrified Sasha that the old warrior's hawkish gaze would see it in each step she took.

The plan – if he wanted to be generous enough to call it that, because it was more like a loose assembly of bad ideas – was to start with what Kevin Tyler knew best.

*Every problem is an engineering problem*, his lecturers used to say. *It's only a matter of figuring out how far back to stand so you can see it.*

Still, it was hard to mentally make the distance, to study it clinically. His thoughts drifted back to his daughter and if he let it, Kevin's mind ran away with the absolute worst possibilities for what might be happening to her.

Mentally, he gripped the steering wheel of his racing, fear-fuelled thoughts, and pulled them back to coherence. To get everyone through this in one piece, he would have to draw on what skills he had and push them to their limits.

*I can fix this*, he thought. *All I need are the right parts.* Like a malfunction at the factory, like the wheel on that woman's Pullman case, he could solve the problem with what he had to hand. He just needed to fathom it out.

Kevin returned to the only store still open in the terminal, the bigger branch of the Relay news-stand and convenience store chain. A bored young man in a Sikh turban watched him with disinterest as Kevin cruised up and down the short aisles, pushing his selections into a collapsible carrier bag.

Nine-volt batteries. Disposable lighters. Dental floss. A German-language gossip magazine.

All the items were innocuous enough on their own – even the lighters, which passengers couldn't bring in their own through security but could buy when airside for use in the smokers' area. He ticked them off a mental list, ending with a nail-care kit containing a metal file and two of the goofy remote-control toys he'd seen on display hours before.

The man at the register gave him an odd look as he ran up the total, and Kevin tried to appear unremarkable.

His stomach gurgled loudly, drawing both men's attention. Kevin's cheeks coloured, and he reached over to a chiller cabinet, dumping a can of energy drink and some wilting packet sandwiches into the pile.

The sleeping businessman who had unwittingly donated his phone had not been careful with his security settings, allowing Kevin to use his banking app to pay for the purchases. With someone else's money spent, he tucked his goods under one arm and made his way to the nearest men's room.

It was only when Kevin stepped inside that he realised where he was; the place where this sorry odyssey had begun, the same washroom where he had stumbled on the bag of Oleg's dark money.

With a sigh, he kicked open the door to the stall and locked himself in.

Time wasn't on his side, but he had a job in front of him now and that made him focus. He drained the energy drink and stuffed the sandwiches down him, chewing mechanically as he worked.

Kevin cracked open the casings of the toys – bulbous parodies of airliners too chunky to fly, designed to roll around on the floor making whooshing jet sounds – and gutted their electronics. The lighters he attacked with the metal nail file, exposing their strikers and fluid reservoirs. One of them he kept back to heat the solder on the circuit boards from the toys so he could rewire them for a totally different end purpose. It was fiddly work, akin to doing a jigsaw or a crossword, taking the bits he had and fitting them together in new ways.

When he was done, Kevin had broken plastic leftovers he dumped in the rubbish bin and a parcel wrapped in magazine pages carried in the shopping bag. The other part of his jury-rigged creation went into a jacket pocket, hidden from view.

There was no way to test what he had built. It would either work, or not. Kevin imagined he wouldn't be in any position to do anything about it if it didn't.

With under thirty minutes showing on his wristwatch's timer, he splashed water on his face and walked back out into the terminal. He didn't look up as he passed beneath the black domes of the security cameras.

*Oleg is watching*, the man on the phone had said, and Kevin didn't doubt it. He kept his pace steady, watching the edges of his vision for any sign of the men who had hunted him through the building hours before. If they were there, they were keeping out of sight.

The bright lights along the concourse made the view outside look darker, but as he walked Kevin could see that the clouds overhead were breaking up, allowing through fragments of sky. Off at the horizon, towards the distant treeline at the perimeter of the airport, the first pale glow of the coming dawn had begun to gather.

'What am I doing?' The question was a murmur, barely a breath from his mouth, directed at nothing. A familiar, unpleasant tension gathered in the pit of his stomach – that *not-knowing*, the crippling uncertainty that threatened to paralyse him. It only took a slight push of perspective to make everything Kevin was doing seem like the worst possible option, and his fear gripped him tightly. More than anything, he wished for someone to tell him how to navigate this chaos of his own creation.

'Tell me the right thing to do,' he whispered. 'Show me how to solve this.'

But there would be no sudden flash of amazing insight here. Kevin's situation was wrapped tight around him, and only he was going to be able to unpick the mess of it.

He thought about the effortless, bulletproof heroes of the movies he loved to watch, who never had to reckon with the untidy disorder of the real world. Collateral damage didn't happen to them, but out in the everyday it was impossible to make a move without pulling on the threads of someone else's life. Kevin had put this whole thing into motion believing he could come through it cleanly, and reality had punished him harshly for that conceit.

The closest thing to being a hero he could do now was to try and undo that. His blood chilled when he thought about what might happen to him, but if it meant Maddie would be all right, the trade would be worth it.

At the left-luggage lockers, he tapped out her name on the alphanumeric keypad and the relevant container dutifully popped open. The bag with the money hung over his shoulder and he pulled it in tight, taking the weight. He half-expected someone to jump him and snatch it away then and there, but nothing happened.

*-They won't do that,* said the voice in his head. *Easier to grab it and kill you back the hangar, isn't it?*

The blunt truth of that pressed down on him, heavier than the wads of cash in the bag. He checked his watch again. Fifteen minutes to go.

On the wall next to the lockers was a backlit information poster, the same one he had seen at the security checkpoint.

**Wenn du etwas siehst, sag etwas.**

*If you see something, say something.*

Kevin pulled out the stolen phone as he moved on, thumb-typing the police hotline number displayed along the bottom of the poster.

From the spot where she had been observing the entrance to the four-floor Store-It building, Andrea spotted the beat-up blue Camaro as it grumbled to a stop past the corner of East 10th and Avenue D. She sprinted across the street to meet Deon and LaShawn as they climbed out of the car.

Deon, with his tall and gangly hoop-shooter physique, already had his arms up in a gesture of exasperation. 'Yo, Bright, what the hell?' His voice was loud and it carried. 'You text, expect me to come running?' Light-toned and made up of wiry muscle, he had the quickest hands of anyone down at the Mountain Gym, but he lacked stamina – something that Andrea regularly reminded him of.

'Dee, use your inside voice,' she snapped, stepping close to the pair. Andrea threw a worried look over her shoulder at the ugly, grubby building across the street.

Deon made a spitting noise and scowled. 'Girl, I ain't at your beck and call.'

'Don't call her *girl* less you want her to kick your ass again,' said LaShawn.

In contrast to the skinny man, Andrea's frequent sparring partner was a thick-set, densely packed young woman who could hit like a freight train when she wanted to. LaShawn was darker skinned with a scalp of tight black cornrows and a full face that usually held a smile for every occasion, but she wasn't smiling now. Andrea had made the situation clear to her on the phone, and the other woman looked grim.

Deon gave an exaggerated shrug. 'I let you win,' he retorted.

'Not the time,' said Andrea, and her tone shut down that line of discussion. She drew them into the cover of some trees near the fence around the swimming pool, backing up until they were against the chain-link but still able to see the Store-It.

The pool behind them was open but sparsely populated, with a clump of grade schoolers splashing about in the shallows, and when Andrea caught sight of them, she had to tamp down an unexpected surge of emotion.

She and Maddie had spent one of their best days in that place, laughing and joking, enjoying the sheer joy of getting to *be* with one another, and the memory was precious. The bleak possibility that the love of her life would be snatched away from her forever made Andrea's hands tighten into fists, it made her angry and terrified.

'It'll be OK.' LaShawn always knew the right thing to say, like it was her superpower. She placed a hand on Andrea's shoulder and squeezed. 'We're can deal with this.'

'*We* can?' Deon cocked his head.

'No cops,' Andrea said firmly. 'They'll charge in there and fuck this up.'

'So, what, you're gonna kick the door in instead?' He made a snorting sound.

'No, we're gonna do it,' said another voice, as Isaac jogged up to meet them from the other direction. He'd gone around the block to scope the place out, and now he was back, his expression did not bode well.

Isaac was the nimble one, the product of a Korean-American family from the same part of town where Andrea had grown up, and they'd known one another since they were kids. He always claimed that watching old Shaw Brothers movies together after school had led them both into Mixed Martial Arts, and his loyalty to his friend was the reason why Andrea had called him first.

Isaac and Deon exchanged fist-bumps and then the new arrival set to his explanation. 'There's a van in the alley round back, but no way in I could see,' he said. 'It's padlocked up, big heavy-duty shit. Front door's the only access.'

Andrea took that in with a curt nod. 'Any clue how many of those *pendejos* are in there with her?' Isaac shook his head.

'Blake says some sketchy-ass dudes took over the place a couple months ago,' LaShawn noted. Her brother delivered pizzas for Mike's Best Italian down the street, and he knew most of the goings-on in a six-block radius around the restaurant. 'Three or four wise guys most of the time. He says they're shitty tippers, look like some punks from Jersey.'

'Everyone from Jersey is a punk,' said Isaac, with a smirk.

'Man, fuck you.' Being from the Garden State himself, Deon couldn't let the jibe pass, but the moment of brief levity faded when he met Andrea's gaze and saw the fear in her eyes. 'Bright . . .' He frowned, his hands falling to his sides, his tone turning serious. 'I know it's not like me to be the adult in the room, but are we really gonna roll up on some mafia shit in there?'

'You owe me.' Andrea said the words to Deon, but it was true of all of them. Andrea had got Deon to the hospital when a back-alley bout had almost killed him. When LaShawn's mother was desperately ill the previous winter, it was Andrea and Maddie who had looked after her. And Andrea had bailed Isaac out of trouble so many times that they didn't bother keeping count any more. Now she was cashing in that debt – *every debt* – for the most important person in her life.

Deon sighed. 'I know she's your girl: we love her too, but we gotta *deliberate*, cuz.' He made a gesture that took in the four of them. 'In the cage, this crew? I have no doubts. But there ain't no referee here, no bell, no tapping out. We walk in there, it could go to hell.'

'He's right,' Isaac said reluctantly. 'We need to be smart.'

'Every second she's gone, it's killing me,' Andrea said, staring into nothing. 'We wait too long, she's lost. Maddie's not made for this. I mean, she's strong, right? But she's not a fighter. I'm supposed to protect her, I'm supposed to . . .' Her words choked off.

'Hey.' Isaac tapped his fingers against his chin, looking at LaShawn. 'So Blake drops off over there, right?'

'Yeah, sometimes.'

A grin split Isaac's face. 'I have an idea.'

The banging on the door brought Mort across the hallway, the stubby shotgun in his hand trailing at his back like an afterthought.

He didn't like being forced to take guard duty, but it wasn't like that asshat Swey was going to do it, and Mort was too afraid of Rodovan to complain about it. He didn't like the way the Serb looked at him, as if he was imagining of a way to get into his skull through the holes in his face.

Mort put down the shotgun on the bench near the metal door and peered through a mesh grille. A Latina woman stood out on the sidewalk in a green vest and a baseball cap with the words MIKE'S BEST emblazoned on it, and she held a large pizza box atop one hand. She saw him and gave a curt smile. 'Got your order,' she sing-songed.

'What?' Mort frowned. He hadn't ordered anything, but it was possible that Swey had got something and not bothered to call down about it. 'Wait a sec.'

He turned and yelled up the stairs, calling out about the food, but no reply came.

'What is it?' Mort added, stalling for time while he considered what to do next.

'Super-large, double extra cheese, double pepperoni,' said the woman. She cracked open the box to show him a glimpse of the contents and the rich aroma of spiced meat wafted in.

Mort's mouth watered and he licked his lips. He hadn't eaten since lunch, stuck in the van while Swey and Rodovan had been out dealing with the girl they'd been told to bag. Suddenly, a hot slice sounded like a great idea. 'OK,' he decided, and pulled back the heavy steel bar holding the door shut. 'Let me have it.'

'Sure thing,' said the woman, stepping up to him.

Then a fist like a trip hammer exploded through the bottom of the box and the pizza itself, hitting Mort square in the face.

His nose crumpled in blast of agony and he fell, showered with bits of salami, cheese and hot crust. Mort was still reeling from the shock of the punch when the Latina grabbed him around the throat and pulled him into a chokehold.

'Where is she?'

'Wha . . . ?'

The woman tightened her grip and spots danced in front of Mort's eyes. He clawed uselessly for the shotgun, but other people had followed her in, a short black woman and an Asian guy who swept up the weapon before he could reach it. He could make out a fourth figure on the street, scanning right and left.

'Where's the English girl?' Mort felt his assailant's hot breath on his face. Her muscles bunched like steel wire against his throat.

'Up,' he managed. 'Stairs.' Mort struggled, his initial surprise turning to fury. 'You know who you're messing with?' He glared at the others in front of him.

'Do *you?*' growled the woman holding him down, and then Mort couldn't breathe any more.

His vision greyed, and the last thing he knew was the reek of grease filling his nostrils.

# TWENTY-SEVEN

Painted in a deliberately brash checkerboard pattern of black-and-yellow squares, the Volkswagen Golf support car was probably the most conspicuous airport vehicle that Kevin could have borrowed, but in the end it had come down to this one because the keys were still in the ignition.

Usually, the car would be out if an arriving airliner needed to be guided to a specific parking area, and the flashing yellow strobes and giant FOLLOW ME sign on the back made it visible clear across the runway, but then again the time for a stealthy approach was well and truly over. He and Richie had tried that already, and the end result was grim and bloody.

Coming back to the Memoria Tranzyt hangar, this time Kevin had the chance to look around and get his bearings, impossible during the dark of the night and the lashing storm. The dawn was rising behind the building, the glow turning the low treeline behind it into sharp, spiky silhouettes. He could see the hangar doors were open wide now, with two vehicles parked near the entrance. Lights inside picked out figures moving around, taking up positions as he approached.

*Last chance to run*, said the nagging voice in his head, and the thought put weight on his foot over the accelerator pedal. He imagined stomping it into the floor and gunning the engine.

'Moment of truth,' he said to himself, reaching for the parcel in the shopping bag on the seat beside him. Kevin grasped for it, touching the metal of the gutted drink can and the lashed-up makeshift works inside. He swung the support car past the open hangar, deliberately bringing it around in a wide turn to halt near the black Mercedes-Benz, so that the parked vehicle would screen him as he climbed out.

Keeping the shopping bag low and out of sight, he approached the hangar, and before he came fully into the view of the men inside, he dropped it near the Merc's front wheel, kicking it under the engine as he passed.

The five of them were waiting for him, along with two or three others who hung around at the back wall of the hangar, like hyenas afraid to come too close to the lions.

The predators in this case were all faces Kevin had come to fear tonight. The stinging wounds on his arms reminded him who the woman Sasha was. He expected her to look at him with loathing for slipping out of her grasp, but her gaze was distant and wounded, and the fire he'd seen in her before was absent. Sasha stood in the shadow of Oleg, the man's military bearing cut with a savage grimace on his lips. He flexed his fingers into fists as he watched Kevin approach, in a way that promised more violence to come. Oleg was flanked by one of the hunters, the hard-faced one with deep-set eyes who held a shotgun over his folded arms like a father might cradle a baby.

Then, clearly separate from Oleg's clan, was Lars Von Kassel and his brusque, streetfighter thug, the one who had dogged Kevin through this chaos, almost from the moment he had arrived at Barsbeker. The politician gave his best impression of being bored with the whole thing, stifling a yawn and peering at the watch on his wrist. Kevin recognised the distinctive timepiece, even from a distance, as an ugly, overblown Hublot model that had the same lack of subtlety as the man who wore it.

'Right on time,' said Von Kassel, with a wan smile. 'You British can be prompt when properly motivated.'

'Stop there,' said Oleg, when Kevin was a couple of metres away. 'Open your jacket.'

Kevin did what he was told, lifting it up to show he didn't have anything hidden.

'You worry *he* would have a weapon?' Von Kassel's thug said it with a sneer, as if the mere idea was ridiculous.

'I have learned to be cautious,' Oleg said tightly.

'Overly so, some might say,' noted Von Kassel, with a sniff. 'Can we *please* get this over with? I have been stuck in this damp, provincial backwater all night and I have had quite enough of it.'

'Where is my money?' Oleg turned his full attention on Kevin, pinning him with a steely glare. 'In the car?'

That was *exactly* where it was, but for this to go how Kevin wanted it to, he had to convince Oleg otherwise. He deliberately looked to Von Kassel before answering, as if seeking guidance, before responding to Oleg's question. 'I stashed it. Let my daughter go and I'll tell you where.'

'Was I unclear?' The old soldier's expression hardened. 'The money, here. Or the girl dies.'

Kevin put every ounce of his very real fear into what he said next. 'This isn't what we agreed!' He glared at Von Kassel, continuing on as the politician's face creased in dismay. 'I did what you said . . . But my daughter isn't part of this, why did you have to bring her into it?'

'What is this man babbling about?' Von Kassel made a dismissive gesture.

'Don't act like you don't know me!' Kevin turned his frustration and dread into a shout. 'I'm only here because of you!' And that was, in many ways, the truth.

There was a long second when Kevin felt certain that Oleg had seen through his subterfuge, but then the older man's hawk-eye glare turned slowly on Von Kassel.

Before, in those moments after Richie had given up Kevin to save himself, he had seen the enmity and distrust seething between the ex-soldier and the politician, and now he used it, turning that into a wedge to drive between them.

'You're not seriously listening to this?' Von Kassel's bodyguard took a step forward, and automatically Oleg's man did the same. 'He's lying to protect himself.'

'Is he, Herr Boch?' Oleg shot a look at Sasha, then back at Kevin. 'Your employer told me he knows this man.'

'I don't know him!' Von Kassel's instinctive reaction was to lie. It was as automatic to him as taking a breath, and the moment the words left his mouth, it dialled up Oleg's distrust by one more increment. 'I mean, not socially!' The politician tried to back-pedal. 'Until today, I had never seen him before.'

'But you knew who he was,' pressed Sasha. 'Did you know from the start?'

'Please, I just want my daughter back ... ' Kevin let his hands drop to near his jacket pocket.

'Shut up!' The man called Boch shouted the command at him.

'No.' Oleg reached inside his coat and drew a gun. 'I want him to speak.' The weapon's muzzle swung at Kevin's head. 'This is the final time I will ask this question. *Where is my fucking money?*'

It took all of Kevin's resolve to stand his ground. He remembered the times he had watched Colin Fish use this tactic as a negotiating ploy, playing the role of the man with the weaker hand, letting others underestimate him so he could use that against them. 'He killed the deal I had here ... Everything I worked for. I had to do it!'

'Oh, *mein gott*, this is utter shit!' Von Kassel threw up his hands, losing his patience. 'Just punch him or something, make him say where he hid it!'

'Miros.' At the call of his name, Oleg's hatchet-faced thug raised his shotgun and aimed it – not at Kevin, but at Boch and Von Kassel, ratcheting a shell into the chamber with a jerk of the slide.

'He told me he'd give me a cut if I took the cash,' said Kevin. This was the core of the lie, so to make it ring true he folded some reality into it. 'I have nothing left back home, only debts and empty pockets waiting for me. I ... I was desperate ... and stupid.'

It hinged on this one moment, if Oleg bit down, if he was willing to assume the absolute worst about Lars Von Kassel and have his biases confirmed.

'I am not sure I believe this man's story,' said Oleg, and Kevin's heart sank. But then the soldier's pistol veered away from him towards Von Kassel. 'But I *do* believe that you are a traitorous, self-serving animal, and more than willing to make a fool's bargain if you would profit from it.'

In response, Boch's gun cleared its holster and suddenly Kevin was in the middle of an armed stand-off. One single second, one instant of tension away from a salvo of gunfire.

'What did he say?' The man called Rodovan glanced away from the window out over the city streets, throwing a disinterested look at his compatriot.

The other man shrugged. 'I dunno.' They had heard the muffled yell from the floor below, but neither of Maddie's captors were in a rush to address it.

She shifted uncomfortably on the threadbare couch, straining to listen. Rodovan had switched on a police band radio scanner, and the crackling voice of the dispatcher was a constant background mutter. She guessed he was listening out for any mention of this building, any indication that someone knew where she had been taken.

'Go look,' he demanded.

'You go look.' The blond man fiddled with a lighter and a fresh cigarette. 'I don't like talking to that guy, he creeps me out.' He mimicked a bug-eyed, leering face.

'Swey. *Go look*,' repeated Rodovan, his tone making it clear he expected to be obeyed.

'Fine. Whatever.' Swey pocketed his unlit smoke and exited the room. She heard him call out to the man downstairs from the landing. 'Mort, you ugly fuck. What are you bitching about?'

Rodovan returned to the police scanner. When he lent forward to fiddle with the volume knob, Maddie saw the heavy shape of a revolver in his waistband. The radio grew louder, and she couldn't help but listen, praying for someone to say that a unit was on its way, for the promise that a rescue was coming.

But the only person who knew her location was half a world away, and he had no idea what her panicked clues had been about. She wished her father was here, so she could embrace him and tell him she loved him for what might be the last time. The possibility she would never see him or Andrea, or anyone else she cared about again made her heart turn to stone.

She worried at the thick duct tape binding her wrists together. Her fingers prickled from loss of blood flow.

'Stop that,' snapped Rodovan.

'It's too tight,' she retorted.

He came marching over, his mouth twisting into an angry scowl, his hand coming up to strike her. But before he could follow through, a loud thudding noise sounded from out in the corridor, like a sack of cement being thrown against the wall.

Rodovan spun away, ripping the revolver from his belt. In the same instant, the door blasted open and Swey came stumbling back in as if he had been kicked by a horse. A stocky black woman with cornrows and a wild glint in her eyes was right on top of the blond-haired thug, landing punch after punch on him, her arms moving like pistons.

*LaShawn.* Only a few days ago, she and her brother Blake had invited Maddie around for Sunday dinner. Behind her came Andrea, and Maddie's heart swooped through highs and lows in the blink of an eye. Rodovan raised the pistol in her girlfriend's direction, and Maddie reacted.

She rocked back on the couch, bringing up her bare feet, and kicked the gunman as hard as she could with her heels in the side of his knee. He cried out in surprise and stumbled into a half-fall.

Andrea moved like lightning, using a low table in the middle of the room as a step up, kicking off it and throwing forward, arms out wide. Maddie had seen her do this move before, a flying grab that lent more to the showy theatrics of a WWF match than the curt, controlled power of her usual bouts.

Andrea collided with Rodovan, coming down hard as he struggled up, hitting him square on with a powerful body-check. The big revolver discharged with a catastrophic, thunderous bellow, the sound-shock of the wild shot hitting Maddie as a physical blow. She screamed as Andrea and Rodovan fell into a messy scuffling heap, arms and legs moving violently.

Without considering her own safety, Maddie scrambled to right herself and get off the couch. She was aware of glass breaking, of LaShawn bouncing Swey's head against the plasterboard wall. A hand grabbed her; Andrea's friend Isaac was pulling her out of the melee.

'No!' He was trying to get her away from there, to someplace safe, but Maddie wouldn't go. She couldn't leave Andrea.

The gun sounded again and Maddie cried out. Turning back, dread filled her as she anticipated the sight of something horrible.

The second shot had gone wild like the first. Rodovan and Andrea were on their feet again, in close, wrestling for control of the weapon as its muzzle aimed at a new hole in the ceiling. The man was winning, pressing his strength into pushing the revolver's smoking muzzle towards Andrea's face.

And to Maddie's horror, Andrea let it happen. The gun dropped, but in the second before Rodovan could pull the trigger a third time, Andrea brought down her forehead and butted him. Dazed, the gunman lost his balance, and Bright the Fight followed through to end this match with her signature uppercut. Rodovan collapsed against the wall and dropped again. This time, he didn't get up.

Isaac cut off the tape around Maddie's wrists and went looking for the rest of the roll to use on the two kidnappers, but she only had eyes for Andrea.

Blood trickled down her face from a cut on her forehead, but she grinned that wildcat smile that always made Maddie's heart leap. They embraced and fell into a lingering kiss.

'You rescued me,' Maddie said, her vision misting.

'No,' Andrea shook her head. 'You rescued me *first*, girl. I'm returning the favour.'

She smiled through the tears and ran her hand over Andrea's face. 'Oh. You're a mess.'

'I'm still pretty,' Andrea smiled briefly, but then it faded. 'Listen, your old man . . .'

'Is he all right?'

'Kevin called me.' She paused, searching for the right words. 'We came to an understanding, I guess. Smart what you did, giving him that message.'

'It's how we knew where to find you,' said Isaac, as he trussed up the semi-conscious Rodovan. LaShawn had already dealt with Swey, taping him to a pipe protruding from the wall.

Maddie clasped Andrea's hands. 'But he's still in trouble over there.'

'I get the idea he's smarter than he looks.' Andrea pulled her phone from a pocket. 'You better message him. Tell him you're OK.' She threw a nod at LaShawn and Isaac. 'C'mon, you two. Cops'll be coming and we don't want to be around for that.'

'What about these jerks?' LaShawn gave Swey another kick for good measure.

Isaac gestured around the room. 'Guns. Police radio. Wanna bet that's not the only illegal shit they got in here?'

'Hey!' Deon's voice carried up the stairwell. 'I hear sirens!'

'Let the trash take itself out,' said Andrea, leading Maddie by the hand. 'We gotta jet!'

Maddie followed along, tapping furiously at the screen of Andrea's phone with her thumb.

*Hey Pop*, she wrote. *I'm safe. XOXOX.*

Kevin hadn't thought to silence the text message alert tone on the phone he'd stolen back in the terminal, so when it started to sound, for a few seconds he had no idea what it was.

The tone was the *bing-bong* chime of an old-school electric doorbell, and in the middle of an armed stand-off, so incongruous that it almost made him laugh. He looked up, his expression becoming awkward as he met the steely gaze of Oleg and the others. 'I, ah, need to take this.' Slowly, he moved his hand to the pocket of his jacket.

The black maw of Miros's shotgun panned in his direction, even as Boch and Oleg kept their pistols squarely aimed at each other.

'Oh, by all means, let us indulge this idiot even further.' Von Kassel spat each word. 'Am I the only one with the intelligence to understand that this shit-stain is lying through his teeth?'

Kevin slid the phone out and held it up to show it wasn't a weapon. He tapped an icon to open the messaging app.

'Can you prove that?' said Sasha.

'She makes a salient point,' Oleg agreed. 'Why was Tyler at the airport tonight, at the same time as you?'

The message tab opened, and above a string of texts that obviously belonged to the phone's sleeping owner, there was a sentence sent from a number with an American country code prefix.

*Hey Pop. I'm safe. XOXOX.*

Kevin could scarcely believe it. *Andrea did it.* A wave of relief broke over him and he physically sagged, but no one noticed as he held on to his brief, precious moment of reprieve.

'I suppose you could call it bad luck?' Von Kassel gave a shrug, eyeing Oleg severely. 'Do you expect me to keep track of every single person who gets in my way?' He gestured in Kevin's direction. 'Do you? I rarely concern myself with such matters. It is beneath me.'

Perhaps it was fatigue, or the politician had grown bored pretending to be civil to those he saw as inferiors, but as he continued his tone grew strident.

'You people,' he sneered, 'you have to understand this sordid world *you* live in isn't *my* world. I operate at a higher level and I resent being dragged down to yours!'

'Sir, you should stop talking,' Boch said, from the side of his mouth.

'No!' Von Kassel's voice rose to a reedy shout, as if he was making a scene in some upscale restaurant about an underdone steak. 'I am not a criminal, I am an elected government official, and I will not be dictated to! I will not be accused of falsehoods by the likes of common foreigners! I demand respect!'

'Sir,' Boch said, exasperated, 'please shut the fuck up!'

'I will *not* be silenced!' roared the politician.

'What is that?' When the man called Miros broke his silence, his voice sounded like the snapping of dry twigs. He stared as Kevin pocketed the phone and pulled out another object from a different pocket.

Everyone looked in Kevin's direction. The thing in his hand resembled an old TV remote, a bulbous cylinder of injection-moulded plastic in jolly colours, with a little whip antenna at one end and two bright buttons labelled *Stop* and *Go*.

Kevin had the sudden desire to say something adroit and pithy, but his mind had gone blank. His cleverness had already been spent on the cobbled-together pieces of scrap under the wheel arch of Von Kassel's car.

He pushed the *Go* button with his thumb. The toy remote control gave off a buzz and made a whooshing sound, but nothing else happened. Miros's permanent scowl deepened and he advanced on Kevin, leading with the shotgun.

Panicking, Kevin mashed the *Stop* button instead, and for one terrible moment he cursed his own handiwork for failing him.

But then the bag under the front of the black Mercedes gave off a sizzling noise like a pan of frying bacon. The incendiary device Kevin Tyler had jury-rigged from a kid's toy, dental floss and a bundle of butane lighters, detonated with a flat crash of combustion, loud enough to echo clear across the runway to the main terminal building.

# TWENTY-EIGHT

'What is this about?' Uwe Braun, Officer Alfons's counterpart from Barsbeker's security contingent, demanded an answer. The cluster of uniformed officers waiting around the vehicles on the airport apron parted before him as he marched up to face the policeman.

He was a perpetually irritable man in a heavy-weather coat that looked like it was a size too large for him, and predictably, Braun was not happy about being summoned from his nice warm office and into the pre-dawn chill.

*Probably asleep up there*, Alfons thought, but he chose not to voice that particular suspicion and went straight to the matter at hand. 'We have a situation, Uwe.'

Braun rocked his head in some approximation of a denial. 'I know the night shift isn't the most challenging of assignments, Berend, but do you really need to spice it up by chasing terrorists that don't exist?'

Alfons's moment of restraint snapped. 'As opposed to what you do, turning a blind eye to whatever criminals pass through here?'

The men around them stiffened. Everyone working at Barsbeker knew that Berend Alfons took his job far more seriously than he needed to, and they also knew that Uwe Braun – to put it diplomatically – had a light hand when it came to enforcing border controls at the airport.

'You watch what you say,' growled Braun. 'You think I don't know what you've been doing all night? Stalking around the terminal, alarming the passengers?'

'There have been some reports,' Alfons began, 'people acting strangely.'

Braun looked at his watch, ignoring the comment. 'Your shift ended hours ago. Why are you still here?' He didn't stop to allow Alfons to answer that, and kept on without taking a breath. 'I'm not having you pulling people away their posts at the crack of dawn for no good reason!'

'I have a reason.' Alfons stepped over to a nearby patrol car where the light was better and showed Braun the screen of his phone. On it was an image that had been sent via the airport's anonymous tip-line, of a mess of wires and plastic connected to a set of batteries. An attached text message in English read BOMB INSIDE THE HANGAR.

'What is this supposed to be?' Braun raised his hands. 'It looks like a lot of rubbish.'

'I believe it is an IED,' Alfons said firmly. 'An improvised explosive device. This is a warning. We need to get over there right now.'

For the first time, Braun's bluster faded and he took another look at the picture. 'You're not serious. A bomb threat, *here*?'

He waved his hands around, gaining momentum again. 'I hate to break it to you, Berend, but this has to be some sort of hoax. Barsbeker is little more than a spot on Germany's backside, why would anyone want to—?'

With sudden brightness, a flash of incandescent orange bloomed hundreds of metres away, close to the hangar complex on the far side of the runway. A fraction of a second later the thud of combustion blew past the assembled group and rattled the doors of the terminal.

'Still doubtful?' said Alfons, recovering quickly.

To his credit, Braun knew not to debate the obvious. 'You heard Alfons, move, move, move!' he yelled, shouting at the other officers until they piled into the cars and set lights and sirens going. 'And someone call the fire unit!'

'I always appreciate your support, Uwe,' Alfons deadpanned. He climbed into the driver's seat of a patrol car, with Braun following suit, and floored the accelerator. The other man barely had his seatbelt fastened as the vehicle peeled out and raced away, slaloming around a parked Airbus and across the runway.

Sasha recoiled as a tongue of orange fire rolled up around the front of Von Kassel's car and into the engine compartment, burning through fuel lines, starting in on a blaze that would consume the vehicle in short order.

She threw up her hands to shield her face from the heat-wash and any possible secondary blast, instinctively ducking away from the hot chemical stink of the flames.

*The thief did that.* She knew it was the only possible option, that the device he'd produced was some kind of remote detonator. *But how is that possible? He's a civilian. He's nobody.*

Or perhaps Tyler's claim about his connection to Von Kassel was the truth, but with the eruption of sudden chaos around her, Sasha didn't have time to parse this new bit of information.

Everything happened at once. She saw the thief sprinting back the way he had come, out into the dim light before the coming sunrise. Miros's shotgun barked after Tyler's fleeing form, but he was way off the mark, the cloud of shot serving only to frighten his target instead of put him down.

She glimpsed Oleg taking cover and Boch raising his pistol, shoving a complaining Von Kassel behind him. The muzzle of Boch's weapon swung past Sasha and settled on Miros.

She yelled the driver's name, but her cry was stifled by a loud double report as the politician's bodyguard shot twice. Crimson pennants of blood burst from Miros's face and throat.

Oleg let loose a string of violent swearwords in his native language and shot back, cursing Von Kassel for what could only be his predictable betrayal.

Boch took a glancing round across one bicep as he forced Von Kassel into cover, but he returned fire, and Sasha dived to the floor to avoid getting hit. She scrambled to Miros, who lay with his ruined face turned away from her in a growing puddle of dark blood.

The stub-barrelled shotgun had fallen from the man's nerveless fingers, and she snatched at it, coming around to pump a fresh shell into the breech.

Sasha saw the flash of yellow lights as the *Follow Me* car out on the apron jerked into gear and sped away with the fleeing thief at the wheel. There were other flashing lights out there, and sirens too, more vehicles approaching at speed from the other side of the airport.

'Police,' she said, uttering the word like a death knell. The exact thing she had been warning of all through this damnable night was coming to pass, the veil of secrecy over their criminal enterprises collapsing because of unchecked violence and bloodshed.

Looking back through a thickening pall of fire smoke, there was no sign of Boch and Von Kassel, but she found Oleg crouching behind a trio of oil drums, reloading the pistol in his hand.

He looked up at the skirl of the sirens and spat on the floor. 'Fucking vultures, now they come?' He pitched up his voice, shouting at the few remaining men he had at the back of the hangar, ordering them to find Boch and his employer. Instead of obeying, Sasha watched the others make the more pragmatic choice to flee from the imminent arrival of law enforcement.

That abandonment heaped insult upon insult for Oleg and he swore vile curses on their lives and those of their families. Sasha had seen his towering rages before, but this was something else. Oleg Gorod was becoming wild, unhinged, burning with an indignant fury that bordered on lunacy. His men knew that, and they deserted him.

Oleg wavered between the objects of his anger, and she knew he was weighing the need to murder, to take out his violent urges on the fleeing Englishman or the venal politician. He came down on the choice she expected him to make, the prize he had been obsessed with from the start.

'I want my money,' he snarled, lurching at her, dragging Sasha to her feet. He pushed the woman towards the driver's side of his BMW. 'Get in there! We go after him. No one steals from me and lives!'

Sasha nodded dumbly, her ingrained reactions forcing her to obey. The parts of her that recoiled at Sasha's unquestioning obedience to this cruel old man screamed in her mind, but she still did as she was told, unable to break the inertia. Oleg had beaten compliance into her long ago and as much as she wanted to resist him, she couldn't.

Placing Miros's weapon on the front passenger seat, Sasha gunned the BMW's engine and the car screeched away from the hangar, slamming the burning Mercedes aside as it passed.

In the back seat, Oleg lurched from side to side, dropping the back window and aiming a pistol out into the dimness. 'Faster,' he yelled, his eyes wide. 'Run that piece of shit into the ground!'

Dieter Boch reacted, as he often did, more out of blind, vicious instinct than from conscious thought.

He killed Miros first because the man with the shotgun represented the most obvious tactical threat to the life of Boch and his principal, but it was a close call and it cost him, taking a wound from Oleg's pistol as the price.

The half-dismantled engine near the private jet in the corner of the hangar provided cover for Boch to catch his breath and examine the shallow wound. It burned like a bastard but he was heartened to see that the shot had only kissed his bicep, tearing several layers of skin without hitting the muscle. Blood itched as it trickled down his sleeve, soaked the cuff of his shirt, and ran over his fingers, but it wasn't his gun arm that had been hit, so he chewed on the pain and balled his hand into a fist.

'He's gone!' Von Kassel hid under the wing of the executive aircraft, having been stymied in his attempts to climb inside to seek a more comfortable setting to cower in.

The politician pointed and Boch frowned as he watched Oleg's dark green BMW drive out of sight, speeding away towards the far end of the runway.

'I cannot be here,' said Von Kassel, as he gingerly emerged from his concealment, automatically seeking the path of self-preservation. 'If I am forced to deal with the local police, there will be too many unpleasant questions . . . I need to disappear before they arrive!'

Boch nodded, glancing over his shoulder at the approaching patrol cars. They would be at the hangar in less than a minute. 'We'll find another vehicle,' he began, but Von Kassel shook his head firmly.

'Dieter, dear fellow, I am afraid this requires rather more than that.' He held up his hand. 'You will remain. I will have to find my own way.' Von Kassel grimaced at the thought of having to do something for himself for a change. 'It is imperative you distract those policemen for as long as possible.' He put a hand on Boch's chest and gave him a gentle push. 'If you need to go out shooting, I will understand . . .'

It was one thing for Boch to accept he was an unwilling vassal, forced by blackmail into serving the other man, but he had tolerated that status quo by knowing that at least if he kept Lars Von Kassel in one piece, he would survive as well. Now the politician demanded a sacrifice that even Boch wasn't willing to give.

'I do that and I'm a dead man!'

'I will not be connected to these criminals,' Von Kassel insisted. 'I can't allow it.'

'Allow it?' Boch snarled the words back at him, and the bile he had been bottling up for months burst out and overflowed. 'You entitled shit! I won't die for you!'

'Your job is to protect me!' The retort was incredulous. 'This is how you do it! So *do it!*'

'Fuck yourself!' Boch's iron-clad self-control, years of it layered deep and strong, cracked open. Not since the days when had sucked down a bottle of vodka every night had he felt so out of control, and so ready for violence.

Flashes of yellow and blue light flickered around the walls of the aircraft hangar, but Boch's focus was consumed completely by his disgust for the man standing before him.

Everything Boch had done to keep Lars Von Kassel out of the public eye, the sordid tasks he had performed, the clean-ups and the pay-offs he had handled, the secrets he kept, they counted for *nothing*. There was no gratitude, no respect for the work that had been done. Just the other man's arrogant assumption of his deferent compliance, no matter how stark the request.

Boch turned the Walther on Von Kassel, aiming the pistol at the fuming politician, and at last he saw the first inkling in the other man that he had gone too far.

'Now then,' he said, forcing a grin. 'Don't do anything foolish, Dieter. You're my strong right arm, my loyal man, remember?'

'Loyalty?' Boch's hand tightened around the gun. 'You told me yourself. You don't know the meaning of the word.'

Alfons, Braun and the others streamed out of the cars, advancing on the Memoria Tranzyt hangar. Those with weapons had them drawn, and for the aging policeman, the situation felt surreal.

He peered past the burning Mercedes as it boiled out black smoke through the open doors of the hangar. Part of him had never really believed that a place like Barsbeker would ever become the target of real danger, and perhaps he'd even hoped for that dull, uneventful reality to remain unchanged. In a world like that, he could always be safe, forever watchful and always in the right,

But this was happening, this was *real*. A bomb had gone off on his watch. They'd heard the gunfire crackling through the pre-dawn air as the cars sped across the tarmac. The long night's fatigue had been blasted away by a surge of adrenaline and Alfons could hear his heartbeat drumming in his ears. It had been a long time since he had drawn his gun in the line of duty, and even though he made sure to regularly requalify with the firearm, it was a struggle to keep his racing pulse from running away with him. He held his pistol out at the ready, tensing to keep it steady.

'Police!' Alfons shouted as loud as he could. 'Come out with your hands raised!'

A voice called out from behind him. 'Over there!' Kurtz, one of the other officers assigned to the airport, pointed at a cluster of figures sprinting for the chain-link fence behind the hangars. 'Runners on foot!' she yelled, and beckoned to a few others to follow, splitting the team as she dashed after the fleeing men.

Alfons continued on, past the burning car, squinting as the acrid stink of boiling plastic and rubber filled his nostrils. He was aware of Braun behind him and he waved the man away. 'Stay back!'

With his bright yellow hi-visibility vest, Braun was an obvious target, and he didn't object to letting Alfons take the lead. The security man retreated, waving to the approaching fire tender as it sped towards them.

Alfons entered the hangar and heard a gruff voice on his right. It sounded like somebody swearing a curse on something they hated, and the policeman moved in that direction.

He saw two men against the pearl-white fuselage of a private jet. One was a cowering form with his hands up as if to ward off a threat, and the other a stocky figure taking aim with a pistol, like an assassin about to deliver a kill shot.

'*Put down the weapon!*' Berend Alfons gave the mandatory command and his training took over.

The man with the pistol did not obey. With a jerky, surprised motion, he pivoted in place and the compact semi-automatic in his fist came rushing around to point in Alfons's direction, the gunman's finger tightening on the trigger.

The moment stretched like drawn wax, and Alfons thought of Yuta, fast asleep and alone in her bed. He imagined his wife awakening to the news that he was dead, and the brittle distance between them melted. He wanted to hold her, to remind her who loved her.

Before the other man could get off a shot, Alfons fired twice. It was a textbook-perfect grouping, centre mass in the gunman's torso, knocking him back and down. Alfons came forward, kicking the other man's weapon away from where it had fallen.

The shooter gasped out his last, lying there beside the wing of the jet, staring blankly at the roof arcing high above his head. Alfons rode a wash of nausea, but he kept his weapon at the ready.

The cowering man leapt to his feet, and he almost got a bullet of his own for his trouble. 'Officer! Oh, thank god. You came! You, uh ... You rescued me!'

Alfons blinked and refocused on the other man. He knew his face, but for a second he couldn't place it, finding him here in an unexpected context.

Then with a jolt, he had it: Lars Von Kassel, the smooth-talking politician whose speeches Yuta always turned off whenever the man appeared on television.

Despite himself, Alfons grimaced. Of the events that had happened tonight, discovering this venal self-promoter in the middle of it was the most incongruous.

Von Kassel edged away, distancing himself from the dying man. 'Can you believe this, my own driver ... ? He, uh, he abducted me!'

Alfons looked down at the man he had shot, and in the last breath before his eyes lost focus, the fallen gunman twitched with impotent fury and then fell still.

'Criminals! They forced me to come to the airport,' Von Kassel said, speaking quickly. 'I dread to contemplate what they had planned for me!'

'Abducted,' repeated Alfons, turning to follow him. His deep, ingrained sense for a lie curdled in his gut. It was part of the reason why he could not stomach watching this man speak. Every word that came out of Von Kassel's mouth sounded like some shade of falsehood, and here, unexpectedly in the flesh, it was no different. 'But you were in the executive lounge tonight. Drinking there despite it being closed?' Karl the lounge manager had made a point of complaining to Alfons about the politician's boozy interlude earlier that evening.

Von Kassel stopped, mouth half-open, and Alfons had the sense that the man had let his tongue outpace his brain with whatever explanation he was concocting on the spot. Then he closed his jaw with a snap and smiled thinly, wiping sweat from his brow. 'We can be discreet about this, yes? You know who I am, of course.' He peered at the policeman's ID card. 'Officer Alfons, is it?'

'I know who you are,' Alfons said flatly.

He was the man whose self-serving policies had cut this district's public budgets to the bone, shutting schools, doctor's surgeries and council offices, putting dozens out of work. That included Yuta, at an age where she would likely never find decent work again, forcing Alfons to take on his extra shifts to cover their bills.

He was a liar, a snob and a philanderer, and if Von Kassel thought he would be able to charm or bully the policeman, he was sorely mistaken.

'I consider it best to take you into protective custody, sir.' Alfons flicked out his handcuffs, and before Von Kassel could object, he had them snapped around the man's wrists. 'For your own safety.'

The politician set into a series of vociferous protests, but Alfons wasn't listening as he led him away, past the firefighting crew as they doused the burning Mercedes in retardant foam.

Braun did a double take as he laid eyes on Von Kassel, tearing his gaze away to address the policeman. 'Berend, we have another problem. The tower radioed, there are cars on the runway!'

'Then we have to get them clear,' said Alfons. 'Close the runway.'

Braun pointed up into the early morning sky, at a distant cluster of brightly glowing lights framed high against the dawn. 'It's too late for that.

# TWENTY-NINE

Kevin had the service car's accelerator mashed to the floor, pressing on it so hard that it was in danger of going through the firewall.

Ahead of him, the flat surface of the wet runway extended into the middle distance. Lines of white lights across it sped past under the Golf's wheels with a thudding cadence, as he raced to put as much distance as he could between himself and the mayhem at the hangar. Flashing strobes blinked in the wing mirrors but he ignored them, concentrating on figuring out the path he was going to take.

There were thin strips of asphalt that connected Barsbeker's primary and secondary runways to a loop of service roads girdling the airport, and if he could find the right one, he could get through the gates and out to the landside zone. Once there, Kevin could ditch this massively conspicuous vehicle and find some other transport.

Kevin remembered the affable cab driver who had brought him to the airport, in what seemed to him like another life. Maybe he was out there, sitting in the taxi rank, sipping a cup of coffee and waiting for his first fare of the day. He imagined slapping a wad of euros into the cabbie's hand. 'Get me the hell out of here,' he muttered.

The fantasy dissolved in a white flare of light as the headlamps of a big car came on behind him, reflecting off the rear-view mirror. Kevin risked a look, jerking his head around to see the muscular shape of the dark green BMW coming in fast. The bright chrome grille on the car's prow had the look of bared teeth, and Kevin reflexively twisted the Golf's steering wheel, skidding into a sideslip to veer away.

He had the momentary impression of Oleg leaning out into the air, the old soldier's shoulder-length hair blasted out behind him by the wind into a mad, leonine mane. Oleg had his gun, and he fired, blasting a fist-sized hole in the middle of the FOLLOW ME indicator mounted across the Golf's rear.

Kevin flinched, ducking in his seat as the car cut through curls of morning mist coming in off the sea, tyres squealing through puddles as he took it dangerously close to the edges of the runway. Orange indictor markers blurred by like hot flares of tracer as the BMW fell into the Golf's slipstream, gaining on it by the second.

The other car was larger and had more horsepower under the bonnet than the service vehicle Kevin had appropriated. In a straight-line run, there was no way he would be able to outpace it. The BMW grew in the rear-view, seconds away from slamming into the rear of the smaller vehicle.

Kevin tugged on his seatbelt to make sure it was locked tight, and grabbed the Golf's handbrake. *Mirror, signal, manoeuvre*, he told himself – although the stunt he was about to pull borrowed more from a misspent youth of long-gone Saturday nights doing doughnuts in car parks than anything in the Highway Code.

Wrenching around the steering wheel, he put in the clutch and yanked the brake hard. The car screeched into a skidding turn, but Kevin had been overly aggressive with it, and the Golf bounced into a spin.

As the BMW roared past, he glimpsed the scarred woman Sasha at the wheel, her eyes wide with surprise. Oleg fired again as the two cars passed, and Kevin cried out in terror as a bullet hit the windscreen, turning it into a spider's web of fractures.

The Golf settled, pointing back the way they had come, and with his hands still shaking, Kevin switched gears and floored the accelerator again. The vehicle started to pick up speed but it was sluggish and the other car was already fishtailing around to pursue.

'Come on, you bastard!' Kevin shouted at the Golf, hunching forward against his seatbelt as if that would give it an extra jolt of impetus.

Back at the far end of the runway, against the approach of the dawn's light, he could see the flashing strobes of emergency vehicles and a coil of black smoke pulled away by the stiff morning breeze.

The radio mounted on the service car's dashboard burst to life in a buzzy crackle and Kevin flinched in shock at the sound. Distracted, he heard a strident voice barking at him in German, saying something about *stop* or *wait.*

The BMW slammed into the rear right quarter of the Golf with a teeth-rattling impact, hard enough to knock Kevin's hands off the steering wheel. He cried out again and snatched back at it, but at speed on asphalt still wet from the deluge of the night's storm, it was enough to steal control from him.

Kevin felt the two cars collide again and the lighter Golf trembled, slewing left and off into the shallow ditch running alongside the landing strip. The rear of the service vehicle briefly lifted from the road and ground against the BMW's bonnet, and as Kevin felt gravity whip him around against the door frame, the other car lost control as well. Sasha had come in too fast and misjudged the shunt.

Both vehicles lurched off the runway and crashed into the rain-saturated banks of muddy grass alongside. The Golf slammed front-first into the deepest part of the ditch and lodged there, airbags deploying inside with blasts of noise and powder. The mass of the bigger BMW worked against it and the other car flipped on to its roof, gouging a black furrow through the wet earth for several metres before it came to rest.

Dazed and wracked with pain, Kevin could only slump in the driver's seat and fight for his breath. A heavy, fibrous mass pressed against him, and he grabbed at it. Kevin's hands touched nylon cloth. The bag filled with the money had bounced out of the back seat and come forward to wedge him into the door.

'Bastard,' he repeated, shoving it away. With slow, agonising movements, he struggled to extricate himself from the groaning, hissing wreck.

One moment, Sasha had the thief in her sights, coming up to give the *Follow Me* car a vicious kiss with the BMW's front bumper.

The next, everything slipped away. The other car was forced aside, but she had overcommitted the BMW and couldn't pull back on to the runway fast enough. Hitting the grass and mud at an oblique angle transferred the power of the car's engine into a kinetic shock that flipped it up and over.

Sasha's world rolled around her for one dizzy instant and then the BMW landed on its roof, the force of impact blowing out the windows and crumpling the top of the car onto her. The emergency airbags triggered and pain screamed through Sasha's body, a numbing force grabbing her torso like it was held in iron pincers.

She blacked out for a few seconds, and the dislocation of her thoughts made Sasha panic when she blinked back to awareness.

The BMW's engine was still roaring, it wheels spinning at nothing. She smelled hot oil smoke, wet earth and the aroma of spilled petrol.

Fumbling for her slide-knife, Sasha slashed at the sagging white airbags, deflating them with weak, stabbing motions. Her whole body was in pain, blood trickling over her mouth and into her nostrils from a cut on her chin.

It was hard for her to breathe. At first she thought it was only the safety belt that held her securely, hanging upside down in the driver's seat, but the relentless agony around her chest bit hard after she sawed through the strap.

'I cannot ...' she wheezed, hearing movement from the passenger seat behind her. 'Cannot move ...' Sasha's voice quavered as desperation filled her.

Part of the car's dashboard had become dislodged in the impact and distended inwards, forming a giant bear-trap that held the woman in place, pressed against the seat. Sasha braced her hands against the panel, she pulled and twisted, but that only brought more waves of pain. One whole side of her body was going numb where the panel was cutting off the flow of blood.

Oleg swore as he extracted himself from the mess of the BMW's rear seats, and she heard the passenger door creak open as he kicked it with both feet, the car shifting slightly. Cursing, the old soldier crawled out and dropped to one knee in the black mud. He panted like an animal, great gusts of vapour escaping his mouth with each exhalation.

Sasha could see him, out of arm's reach, his face a horror-mask of bloody streaks from dozens of scratches on his face, his wild hair flickering in the wind. Somehow he still had the pistol in his hand – even in the melee of the car crash, the soldier had not let go of his weapon – and Oleg used the gun to prop himself up.

'Oleg.' She had never called him by his first name, but Sasha was frantic to get his attention. 'I can't breathe ...

Please, can you . . . ?' Her voice came out in a tight wheeze. She extended a hand in his direction, through the broken frame of the driver-side window.

He gave her a cursory once-over, a pitiless calculation working behind his eyes. At length he looked away, to the other car in the ditch. 'Don't beg,' he muttered, rising slowly to his feet, grunting with the effort. 'It shames you.'

As he ignored her, Sasha made another straining effort to pull herself free, crying out in pain. Her body moved a couple of degrees and then no further. She felt nauseous as blood pooled in her head. Soon she would black out again, and Sasha feared she wouldn't wake up.

In the middle distance, the door of the smoking, wrecked FOLLOW ME car fell open with a crunch of metal, and a ragged shape dropped out on to the muddy ground. A large black bag, big enough to be filled with millions of euros in cash. Attracted by the sound, Oleg began to walk in that direction, limping and grimacing with every step.

*He was leaving her behind.* Despite knowing in some inner part of her soul that this moment was always going to come, it was still a shock to Sasha as she watched her erstwhile mentor deliberately turn his back on her.

There was an innocent girl buried in the depths of the damaged woman she had become. That version of her had attached herself to Oleg Gorod in spite of his abuses, because in Sasha's pitiless world his occasional, offhand benevolence was the closest she had ever come to someone showing her kindness. That desperate version of Sasha had clung to the thin thread of hope that Oleg, in some warped fashion, actually *cared* about her.

The hope betrayed, the thread snapped. He was leaving her to die, discarding Sasha as callously as the men she had watched him murder in cold blood.

'*Help me!*' She shouted out the cry, and the exertion made her dizzy.

'The weak are of no use to me.' Oleg halted, turning to look at her, disappointment writ large across his creased features. 'Help yourself. If you cannot . . .' He sucked in a breath and turned away again. 'I can always buy another of you.'

Sasha's vision blurred, and the hissing of blood in her ears became deafening.

In steady pain and weathering the first signs of a concussion, extricating himself from the wrecked car became a challenge for Kevin akin to climbing a sheer mountain face.

First he pushed the heavy nylon bag off him and shoved it out on to the ground, then he had to lever himself up across the front seats of the vehicle, where the ruined Golf lay at a steep angle in a ditch filled with icy brown water.

He had the top half of his torso hanging out, trying to boost himself the rest of the way with his feet, when iron talons bit into his bony shoulder. Kevin was dragged bodily out of the car and fell face-first into the mud with a wet squelch. Coughing and gasping, he kicked away and rolled over.

'Worthless mongrel.' Oleg loomed, his hot-and-cold fury running icy as he threw out the insult. He was tired and labouring the words, but to Kevin's dismay the pistol in the old soldier's hand remained rock-steady. 'Who *are* you? What gives you the right to piss over my business? You are *nothing*!' The fire rekindled and he bellowed the next words. '*You are nobody!*'

'I'm nobody,' Kevin muttered, bobbing his head. 'Yeah, I'm the idiot. The loser.' His hand dropped into the mud and he found the strap of the nylon bag beneath his fingers. Kevin grasped it and out of nowhere, a woozy bubble of laughter rose up and he let it go. 'But I fucked up your night good and proper, didn't I?'

Gripping the bag strap, he struggled up to one knee as the wind blew hard against his back, ripping the words from his mouth and past Oleg's scowling face.

Standing against the purple-pink aura of the dawn, the old soldier was a shape made out of shadows. Kevin saw weak daylight glitter off the barrel of the silver pistol in his fist, and the bright pinpricks of colour moving in the sky behind the other man.

Oleg lurched forward, striding into the hard wind across the runway, and once again he spun the pistol around and hit Kevin across the head with the butt of the weapon.

Fire and agony exploded inside Kevin's skull and he staggered backwards, barely able to stop himself from crashing back into the ditch. The wounds on his arms had reopened, and his head rang like a bell. *Everything* hurt.

'I want my money, thief,' Oleg rumbled. 'I don't give a shit if you are with that whoreson politician or not, you stole from me! I am owed it!'

'You don't deserve anything,' Kevin retorted. 'I'm a thief? You're a murderer! People like you are a fucking cancer!' He shouted at the other man, unable to stop the words spilling out into the chilly air. 'You want this?' Kevin wrenched the bag up from the mud and shook it in front of him, stumbling back to the edge of the runway asphalt. 'That's all you care about!'

'You took it,' Oleg retorted, moving to flank him. 'Don't pretend you don't understand.' He jerked his chin at the bag. 'Money is power. Power is everything.' Then Oleg pulled back the pistol's hammer with his thumb. 'Give it to me.'

'Fucking have it then, wanker!' Kevin pitched up his voice as loud as he could, to keep Oleg's attention solely focused on him. The old soldier didn't see what was coming.

Oleg reached out and snatched at the other end of the bag, and for a moment the two men were caught in a violent tug of war, the cheap nylon carry-on shaking back and forth. Overladen as it was, the material split under the strain, the bag's zipper snapping as it stressed past breaking point.

Then the wind abruptly changed direction, and brought with it the howling roar of two Rolls-Royce Trent jet engines. Barsbeker's first arrival of the new day was an Airbus A330 cargo freighter, diverted there because of a mechanical fault requiring an immediate landing.

The aircraft thundered out of the dawn sky, passing scant metres over their heads as it dropped towards the runway. Kevin yelled, but his voice was lost in the deafening noise. The hot backwash of the engines slammed into him, a churning wall of invisible force reeking of Jet A-1 fuel. It threw both men off their feet and finished the business of tearing open the carry-on.

Blasted by the aircraft exhaust and the headwinds, the contents of the bag exploded into a wild blizzard of fluttering, spinning paper. Thousands of euro notes swirled away in all directions, curling into sharp vortices, rolling like waves across the tarmac, spilling over the wet grass.

A wordless scream of frustration cut through the wet air and Oleg lurched up, grabbing madly at bunches of notes as they whirled around him, missing far more the he could get his hands on. His face turned crimson with anger and exertion, briefly rendering him as comical as he was murderous.

Pressing one hand to his brow to hold back the blood oozing from a cut, Kevin snorted loudly and gave a grim, hollow laugh. Oleg whipped around with the gun and swore violently in a language Kevin didn't understand.

'You're a joke,' he managed. 'You are nothing . . . You *got* nothing!'

'You mock me?' Oleg bit out the words and pulled the pistol's trigger, but the gun gave a hollow click and didn't fire. Swearing again, the old soldier pulled at the semi-automatic's slide, trying to dislodge the stoppage there. 'I'll kill you.'

'You still lose,' Kevin retorted. He threw a glance over his shoulder, at the distant hangars. He could see people coming this way, but whomever they were, they were still minutes away.

He tried to stall for time, 'Shit, look at me? I let myself think like you, obsessing over money, look what happened!'

'Like me? You could not be a soldier,' said Oleg. 'Too weak. Too sentimental. You are a sheep dreaming of being a wolf.'

'What a load of bollocks!' Kevin shook his head. 'A wolf? Nah, you're a mad old rabid dog, mate. A fucking *animal*, not a man!' He stood up, finding a fatalistic measure of resolve. If this was going to be how it ended, he would bloody well *not* meet it on his knees. 'I'm not like you. I remembered what matters, and it's not this shit.' He kicked at a mess of banknotes on the asphalt.

Oleg grinned at him, showing bloodstained teeth. 'Good for you. Go to your grave believing that. And know I will find your bitch of a daughter, and sell her to men who will use her until she dies of it.' He raised the gun again.

'No.' Hobbling on one injured leg, as pale as a corpse, the woman Sasha approached them from the wrecked BMW. She had a short-frame shotgun in her hands, wedged against her body, and it pointed at Oleg. 'No more,' she gasped. 'I see their faces in my sleep ... The ones in the container. In the brothels. No more.'

'Sasha.' Oleg saw the pain in her eyes as Kevin did, but he spread his hands, almost offering her an embrace. 'I knew you were strong. You make me proud. You are not like those others.' He nodded to himself. 'They were fragile. Pathetic. You prove you are better.' Then a thought occurred to the man, and he nodded in Kevin's direction. 'The police are coming. Kill the Englishman, and we will go.'

Sasha shook her head. 'I will not hurt people for you any more.'

'Do not disappoint me again.' Oleg's tone became a warning. 'Do not disobey your commander's orders!' His gun swung in her direction.

'*I will not!*' Sasha screamed the denial and pulled the trigger. The shotgun thundered and Oleg took a bellyful of shot at close range. He had barely hit the ground before the woman pumped another round into the gun and fired again. Oleg twitched and fell still.

Kevin shrank back, terrified that the next blast would be for him, but Sasha sank to her haunches and tipped the gun back to press the muzzle against the bottom of her chin.

'No, no! Don't do it!' He scrambled towards her. 'Please, don't!'

Sasha's ruined and tearful gaze met his. 'Why?' She poured pure, raw agony into that single utterance, so much that it took his breath away.

'Because he would win, wouldn't he?' Kevin said, at length.

The patrol cars were closing in, lights flashing and sirens keening, and gently, as if the thing was made out of spun glass, Kevin took the shotgun out of her hands and laid it on the ground.

Apparently unaware of the tears streaming down her face, running lines through the patches of dried blood on her cheeks, Sasha leaned forward over Oleg's body and pulled something from around his neck – the tiny black memory card on the chain Kevin had seen earlier in the hangar. She tore it free and held it tightly in her fist.

'What's that?' he asked.

'Absolution,' whispered Sasha.

A repeating tone reached Kevin's ears, and with a jolt he realised it was the stolen phone, still there in his pocket. He raised it to his ear. 'Hello?'

'*Hey, Pop.*' The voice on the other end of the line was the one he wanted to hear more than anything in the world.

His daughter was alive and whole, and no matter what happened next, the most important part of Kevin Tyler's life was safe. That was all that mattered.

'Hey, Mads,' he smiled, and for a moment, it was like the sun had come out.

# THIRTY

The taxi dropped off Kevin on 5<sup>th</sup> Avenue, past the huge, elegant frontage of the Metropolitan Museum of Art. Checking the tour guide app on his phone to make sure he was in the right spot, he followed a footpath heading west into Central Park. He led with the metal walking stick his doctor had suggest he use, at least until his injuries had healed and he was back to something approaching 'normal'.

Presently, he reached the spot where they were supposed to meet, a bronze sculpture surrounded by benches that depicted three bears atop a rock, one on its hind legs, the two flanking it on all fours. It was, obviously, called *Group of Bears*, or so the guide app said.

The day was hot and sunny, the air packed with sounds of life, and the area around the bears filled with children running and playing, laughing as they took turns to clamber over the sculptures. Kevin watched the kids having fun and a pang of bittersweet emotion unfolded inside him. He remembered Maddie at that age, fearless and carefree, and it made him smile.

At once, he felt joyful and terrified. It was a parent's dilemma, to be happy to have a child you loved, to be afraid for them out in a wide world full of unknowns. But it was impossible to have one without the other.

And then he saw Maddie sitting on a bench among a group of other young people, laughing at a joke, her face animated and alive. She caught sight of him and he managed a wave before she was racing over to embrace him.

His daughter squeezed him so tightly he made a quiet sound of distress and she pulled back. 'What? Too much?'

'Still healing up,' he said. 'But worth it.' Kevin sighed. 'Hey, Mads. I'm so happy to see you.'

'Same.' She looked him up and down. 'You look good.'

'Fibber.' He chuckled. Months had passed since the never-ending night at Barsbeker, but he was still feeling the after-effects of it. 'I'll pretend it's true, though.'

Maddie hugged him again, a little more carefully this time, and Kevin let himself enjoy the moment before she walked him over to her friends.

Andrea stood up and offered her hand. 'Kevin,' she said, with an incline of the head and a smile.

He accepted the woman's handshake, and Andrea's long fingers immediately clasped his in a bone-crusher grip. Kevin smiled fixedly through the moment, and mercifully, Andrea let go without breaking anything. He thought about the men who had been on the wrong end of her ire and counted his blessings that he wasn't one of them. *Not any more, I hope.*

'It's good to meet you, Andrea,' he said, starting as he meant to go on, with honesty.

Andrea nodded and a silent communication passed between them.

The tall young black man standing nearby gave a stage cough. 'We, uh, we're happy to know you too.' He indicated Maddie's other friends, a wiry Asian guy and a shorter black woman with dyed-blue cornrows.

'I'm Isaac,' said the Asian guy, with a welcoming smile. 'That's Deon and that's LaShawn.'

'Pleasure,' said LaShawn, cocking her head.

'Well, hello to you,' Kevin replied. 'You don't know how much it means to me to see that Maddie has good friends looking out for her.'

'It's what you do for the people you care about, right?' Andrea's hand touched Maddie's and they clasped together. In that moment, Kevin saw what he had heard on that fateful night down the phone line. He saw Andrea's tough, uncompromising shell briefly slip away and reveal the person beneath.

Kevin wanted to say something more, but the words turned to dry ash in his mouth and he frowned. On the flight over, he had gone around and around trying to find the best way to articulate his feelings, but as always, nothing was *right*.

'Dad, are you OK to walk?' Maddie indicated the stick at his side.

'Yeah, no problem,' he said, grateful for the distraction. Together, the group set off deeper into the park, passing joggers, dog walkers and dozens of other New Yorkers out to take advantage of a beautiful day.

Kevin couldn't stop himself from looking around, acting the tourist as he peered at the iconic skyline rising up beyond the wall of trees.

'Yo, Mister Tyler,' began Deon, picking up on an opportunity, 'like, if you want a tour of the city, my cousin Jay's a driver. I can get you a special deal . . .'

Kevin blinked. 'OK.'

'Don't let him take you for a ride,' countered LaShawn. 'Jay drives a school bus, not a tour bus.'

'A bus is a bus.' Deon shrugged.

'He just got here,' added Isaac. 'Give the man a chance before you hustle him.' Off Deon's smirk, the other man nodded at Kevin. 'Good flight?'

'First class,' said Kevin. 'Figuratively and literally.' He explained how the management at KnightSky Air had been falling over themselves to look after him, in the wake of the negative publicity that had connected their airline to the events at Barsbeker. Giving Kevin a complimentary Platinum Status frequent-flyer card and a first-class flight to New York City was good PR he was more than happy to take advantage of.

In truth, Kevin was surprised that the German police had let him go home after the initial investigations in the aftermath of the shootings and the fire at the airport. But with the assistance of Officer Berend Alfons – who had turned out to be a nicer bloke than first impressions suggested – Kevin's part in the events of those desperate hours soon become background noise to a series of bigger and more scandalous discoveries. The news grew from criminal arrests and the discovery of murder victims, to the uncovering of a silent conspiracy hiding human trafficking, smuggling and worse.

The woman who had hurt Kevin and then turned around and saved his life brought with her the contents of that mysterious memory card when she surrendered to the police. Sasha's confession went hand in hand with the files on the card, a treasure trove of blackmail material and documented evidence of malfeasance going back years. In return for giving the authorities a complete accounting, Sasha had disappeared into the Federal Police's version of witness protection, and despite what she had done to him, Kevin hoped she would get the help she needed, and maybe even a chance at a better life.

Top of the list of people implicated by the files was Lars Von Kassel, who was currently experiencing a whole new way of life in a German low security prison, while he awaited trial on charges of corruption and manslaughter. Von Kassel's political party had ejected him the moment the evidence of his illicit dealings could no longer be dismissed, and that in turn saw the assets of his private company frozen by the authorities. With Zett Holdings no longer able to carry out their part of the land deal, the Montag family had come back to Kevin and Luna Designs with cap in hand.

Kevin was still debating what to do about that particular detail. A renewed version of the Montag deal would save his bottle-making company and everyone who worked in it from losing their jobs, and the fickle investors who had fled before were now coming back around. Without his former partner

Colin Fish in the mix to take advantage – the man was *in the wind*, as they said in the movies – Kevin hoped there would be a real chance to actually make something of this opportunity.

He would have to do it on his own, of course. In the past, that was something Kevin would not have thought himself capable of. But that night in at the airport, and everything he had seen and endured, had made Kevin Tyler think differently about what he could do, if he put his mind to it.

As he reached the end of his rambling account, they emerged at the bottom of the Great Lawn, a huge oval of grass seeded with a half-dozen softball fields. Isaac and LaShawn had brought picnic fixings, and blankets which they spread out so everyone could sit.

Kevin parked himself where he could look south, towards a lake that Andrea told him was the 'Turtle Pond', overlooked by its own gothic mini-castle. He grinned without realising it, taking in the airy, warm sense of the sprawling park. It felt like another world, compared to the memory of the panic and terror of the desperate hours he had spent trapped beneath a storm.

As Maddie and the others sorted out the contents of the bags, Andrea sat next to Kevin and leaned in to speak quietly. 'You don't need to worry about her,' she told him. 'Those *pendejos* who took Maddie? They won't be on the street again for a long time.'

Andrea explained that the police responding to the anonymous tip leading to the building where Madeline had been taken found not only some trussed-up criminals with dozens of outstanding warrants, but also a large stockpile of unrefined cocaine. It turned out that Oleg Gorod's cousin had been running a key link in a smuggling chain up from Florida, and the cops had resolved their unexpected windfall into a major drug bust that was splashed across the media.

'Maddie's real strong,' Andrea concluded. 'And she has me. I'll keep her safe.'

'Thank you. I'm grateful. More than I can say.' He smiled. 'You really do love her.'

'As much as you.' Then a frown passed over the young woman's face. 'Can I tell you something?'

Kevin nodded immediately.

Andrea sighed, getting her thoughts in order. 'Like, when I'm out there . . . ' She raised her fists, as if shadow-boxing, as if in an imaginary ring. 'I used to overthink it, y'know? And I was knocked down, over and over. So I learned to go on instinct, not to get so caught up in my own head. And it was right. It made me better.' She nodded at Maddie. 'You and her, you're alike. You both overthink. You get caught . . . You get stuck in your corners and you don't . . . connect.'

'I know.' Kevin sighed. 'I'm just afraid. I'm afraid I'll do it wrong again.'

Andrea stood up. 'Maybe you will. That's the risk. But if you don't connect, one day you'll look up and you'll both be miles apart.' She shook her head. 'Won't be just an ocean between you.'

Before Kevin could respond, Andrea marched away, grabbing Deon and the others and herding them in the direction of the nearest softball field. Drawn by something neither of them could articulate, Maddie came and settled on the blanket next to her father, giving him a questioning look.

'Pop,' she began, 'is something wrong?'

*No*, he thought, taking a breath, *everything is right.*

'Hey, Mads,' said Kevin. 'Let's talk.'

# Acknowledgements

My eternal gratitude to Pauline Swallow, Mandy Mills, Ben Aaronovitch and all my friends for their enduring support; my thanks to Robert Kirby, Kate Walsh and the team at United Agents; to Mark Smith, Jon Elek, James Horobin, Alexandra Allden and everyone at Welbeck Books; and to Andrew Crompton, Misha Glenny, Biggin Hill Airport, Birmingham International Airport, East Midlands Airport, El Matorral Airport, Gatwick Airport, Kiel Airport, London City Airport, RAF Cosford, *Core77*, *Terminal Cornucopia*, *Just Like Oma* and the *Until We Travel* project from *Cities and Memory* for information, resources and research materials.

While I based much of Barsbeker Airport on actual places, it is a fictional creation and is not meant to reflect any real world location.

*Airside* was conceived in economy-class cabins and aircraft hangars, in first-class lounges and customs halls, in departure terminals and on airfields, and was written on location in London and the Canary Islands.

# About the Author

James Swallow is a *New York Times*, *Sunday Times* and Amazon bestselling author of over fifty-five novels, and a BAFTA-nominated screenwriter. The creator of the critically acclaimed Marc Dane action thriller series, he has written for franchises such as 24, Tom Clancy, Star Trek and many more, along with scripts for radio, television and interactive media. Find him online at his website *www.jswallow.com*, or on Twitter at *@jmswallow*.